continued . . .

Ace Books by Nina Kiriki Hoffman

A RED HEART OF MEMORIES
PAST THE SIZE OF DREAMING

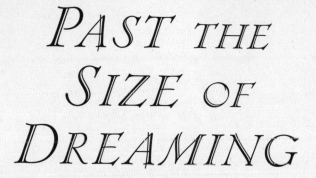

PAST THE SIZE OF DREAMING

Nina Kiriki Hoffman

ACE BOOKS, NEW YORK

PAST THE SIZE OF DREAMING

An Ace Book / published by arrangement with
the author

PRINTING HISTORY
Ace hardcover edition / March 2001
Ace trade paperback edition / March 2002

Ace trade paperback ISBN: 0-441-00898-4

Visit our website at
www.penguinputnam.com
Check out the ACE Science Fiction & Fantasy ne

The Library of Congress has catalogued the Ace hardco

Hoffman, Nina Kiriki
Past the size of dreaming/Nina Kiriki Hoffma
p. cm.
ISBN 0-441-00802-X
1. Haunted Houses—Fiction. I. Title.

PS3558.O34624 P37 2000
813'.54—dc21   00-032791

ACE®
Ace Books are published by The Berkley Publishing Group,
a division of Penguin Putnam Inc.,
375 Hudson Street, New York, New York 10014.
ACE and the "A" design are trademarks belonging to
Penguin Putnam Inc.

PRINTED IN THE UNITED STATES OF AMERICA

10 9 8 7 6 5 4 3 2 1

Dedication

This one is for my mother and father,
who encouraged all their children to pursue
whichever craft spoke to us.

Acknowledgments

My thanks to Stephanie Haddock, veterinary technician, who helped me with technical details. All errors are mine.

My thanks also to Martha Bayless, intrepid fellow desert explorer and dictator par excellence.

Finally, my thanks to Brian McNaughton and Karen Taylor, willing villains.

Chapter One

. . . . .

A really big secret can keep you warm on cold nights, stifle hunger, drive shadows back. The best secrets make you feel safe. You could use this, you think, but not using it is what keeps you strong.

Deirdre Eberhard changed the water in the last cat kennel in the row, petted the cat and spoke softly to it. It had to stay at the clinic until its wound healed, but it was lonesome for its owner. "Not much longer," Deirdre told it. She closed the cage door and straightened, pressed a hand into the small of her back and worked her knuckles against her spine.

Her vet technician, Angie, had gone home for the day; the kennel aides, high-school kids named Bob and Nikki, had left hours earlier, and her partner, Doug Rosenfeld, hadn't even stopped at the clinic today. He did all the large-animal doctoring in their practice, caring for cattle, llamas, horses, reindeer, and the occasional ostrich, and he mostly worked out of his van at the ranches that spread out around the tiny Oregon desert town of Artemisia. He only came into the office on Wednesdays and Thursdays or when there was an emergency.

Even the most forlorn dog on the premises had stopped howling and lay with its nose on its paws, its shining eyes watching Deirdre. All the animals had fresh food and water and clean litter or paper. The exam tables had been cleaned and had fresh mats and towels on them for tomorrow's patients. The autoclave had finished its last run of the day, and the washer and drier their last loads. Everything in the surgery was sterile and ready for the procedures she'd do tomorrow.

All done. Just one final mugful of coffee in the coffeemaker, and a piece of sunset to watch. She rinsed out her mug, refilled it, cleaned the coffeepot and set the coffeemaker to start again tomorrow morning, then headed out the back door to the desert.

Her clinic was a cinder-block building on the edge of town. She had a green resin Adirondack chair by the back door, under the shade of an overhang, where she sat between patients and wrote up her charts. After work, she sat and watched the quiet. She set her mug on the cement apron that wrapped around the building and leaned back in the chair, which was still warm from the day's heat.

The sun slipped behind the Cascade Mountains. The sky's clear, distant blue had faded to white near the horizon, with bands of tangerine stain above where the sun dropped. At the zenith, the sky darkened.

Warped and twisty juniper trees poked up here and there from an expanse of scrubby sage- and rabbitbrush that stretched, deceptively flat, from Deirdre's feet toward the forested mountains. She knew unseen undulations hid things: only half a mile away, a gorge cut through the desert like a sword strike through sand.

The desert rustled, anticipating night.

Birds flew down to the seep pond she had piped out when she first took over the veterinary practice here, at the edge of a universe. Deirdre practiced stillness and watched.

This was her night: a place that looked desolate, arid, yet cupped life unseen. Her night, her place, her secret hope, that under a desolate surface, rustling, uttering things still lurked.

She let out a slow breath, the frustrations of the day, and reached down for her coffee.

Something wet touched the back of her hand.

"Whoa!" she cried, and jerked back. She looked down into the face of a coyote.

It stared at her with yellow-brown eyes.

She gathered her breath, settled into the chair, and stared back. It showed no signs of rabies, aggression, or fear. It just stared.

She had never been so close to a coyote before. She had seen them loping across distance, and heard their voices raised in the night, usually far enough away that they might be part of dreams. She had seen some caged down at the High Desert Museum in Bend, where injured wild animals were cared for and then released when they were well.

There was a musky sagebrush-and-carrion scent, a strange heat that prickled the hairs on her forearms. She exchanged glances with the coyote for a long while, then wondered what next.

It backed up a step and sat down.

It lifted its left paw. For the first time she noticed the laceration. She sucked in breath.

A fight with another animal? How would it get a cut like that?

"Looks pretty bad," she said. "You want some help with that?"

It cocked its head.

Should she call animal control? She could deal with approach-with-caution cats and badly trained dogs, but she was out of her element with a wild animal. Well, that wasn't totally true; occasionally people brought her wild animals that had been hit by cars, but she dealt with them during office hours, when she had her vet tech with her, and they were never alert the way this coyote was. She could call someone and have the coyote shipped somewhere like the museum, where they had experience with undomesticated creatures.

She sighed and got to her feet. If it spooked, so be it; that would make her decision for her. What if it only wanted to get into her building, where several small animals were helpless and edible? Getting into the kennels wouldn't be easy, and it would have to go through her first.

The coyote backed off the concrete, but stopped on the earth beyond. It watched her and waited for what she would do next.

Deirdre opened the back door of the building, dropped a doorstop under it. The coyote's access to outside had to be clear. She went into the treatment room and waited.

The animal edged in, its nose lifted as it tasted air. After a period of examination, it limped forward.

Had it been trained somehow? She had heard of half-coyote dogs, but she had never heard of a trained coyote. How was she going to deal with this?

She opened the door into surgery, propped it, too, with a doorstop, patted the stainless-steel-topped operating table. "Up here."

It gathered itself and jumped onto the table, then sat, its gaze fixed on her face.

"Okay," said Deirdre. She took a deep breath. She had to be

crazy. What if it bit her? A bad bite could cripple her. She should sedate it. If it were asleep, she could operate without worrying whether it was going to bite her. But anesthesia was difficult to handle without her vet tech; an operation was really a two-person job. First the shot to sedate the animal, then a short wait for it to fall asleep; not hard. Monitoring the tracheal tube that kept gas flowing to anesthetize the animal while she operated, positioning the animal, help with equipment during surgery, and keeping the patient warm during anesthesia by surrounding it with hot water bottles and covering it with towels, those were things her tech usually did.

Maybe she should call Angie. But Angie would be home having supper with her husband and three-year-old daughter.

Maybe there was another answer.

She studied the coyote, and it studied her.

"Okay. I'm going to take a look." She reached slowly forward. It let her lift its paw.

The cut was deep, and looked fresh.

"Here's what I have to do. I need to clean this out. First shave around the wound, then reshape the edges so I can suture it, then sew you up. So I want to put you to sleep, because this is going to hurt, but it'll help in the long run. Why am I telling you this?"

"Whuff." A breath of bark.

"Yeah, because I always talk to my patients, that's why, except when Angie's around to hear me. She already thinks I'm crazy." She took a look at the coyote and judged its weight at about forty pounds. She opened a sterile syringe and plunged the needle through the rubber cap of the anesthetic bottle, drew out the dose, and approached the coyote. "This will hurt a little, but a lot less than the operation would if you were awake," she said, showing the syringe to the animal. Would it let her grab the scruff of its neck and give the injection?

The coyote growled.

"Okay, that's it. I can't do this for you if you're going to protest."

It lifted its left paw.

"You want me to operate without anesthesia? You can't guarantee that you won't bite me when I do something that hurts you, can you? Of course you'll bite me. It's only natural."

"Whuff."

She tossed the filled syringe in the SHARPS biohazard waste can. "We'll try it one step at a time," she said. "Guess I should have realized before now that you're not exactly natural. First I'm going to put some lubricant on the wound so I can shave around it and not get hair in it."

The coyote put up with jelly, electric clippers, and her vacuuming the hair away. No flinching, no untoward movements, nothing that threatened.

Deirdre scrubbed up, put on surgical gloves, sighed again. She got out the cold tray of sterile instruments she would need if she went any further.

She drenched cotton squares in Nolvasan, then gripped the coyote's paw in her right hand and gently pressed the antiseptic to the wound.

"Bowoooo!" The coyote lifted its head and howled in soprano.

The three dogs in the kennels barked at the tops of their lungs, setting up resonance and echoes. Some of the cats snarled, hissed, growled. She glanced through the open door of the surgery into the treatment room, where kennels lined the back wall. The cats' fur had bushed up.

Strange that the cacophony had waited until the coyote howled: usually everybody would be excited to some extent whenever she brought another animal into the treatment room. One that smelled as wild as this should have driven the dogs mad from the start.

She finished cleaning the wound and preparing it for surgery.

The coyote whimpered. But it didn't bite her.

The other animals settled down again, not even the ambient growl.

Then she turned to the cold tray. "How about a local anesthetic?"

This is crazy, she thought. *I'm talking as though it can understand me. It acts as if it can. Now I'm discussing treatment options with a patient, which is something I never expected to do as a vet. But then again, it's not exactly a natural patient.*

Not exactly natural.

Something shimmered and trembled in her chest. She had moved away from magic when she left Guthrie to go to the vet college at Oregon State University. She'd only gone back once, to find the magic tarnished and ragged and worn. The ghost had been a lot smaller and dimmer, and all her other friends were gone.

When she was much younger, magic had touched her. She had worn magic like a coat. But it had never entered her bloodstream the way it had with the others, never claimed her as part of it. She had figured there must be something wrong with her. She was destined to be ordinary; she might as well get on with it, build herself the best ordinary life she could.

Her marriage had lasted almost three years.

The coyote cocked its head.

"If I give you a shot," she said, "it can numb the leg so you won't feel the stitches. One prick instead of lots of them. What do you think?" Of course, it would involve some waiting, too, but she had nothing else to do tonight but watch TV in her A-frame, a hundred yards from the clinic.

"Whuff."

"You're sure?"

It pawed her arm. She sighed. "Okay. No anesthetic. I need you to lie down on your side."

The coyote lay down, wounded leg up and available. Deirdre threaded the curved needle with the first suture and set the suture container upright, then went to work. Her patient occasionally whined, but it did not interfere or resist in any way.

When she had finished, she wrapped the wound, even though she knew that if this were a normal animal, it would bite the bandages off, and maybe chew out the stitches, too.

"The hard part's done," she said. "I want to give you a shot of Pen B and G. It won't knock you out or make you woozy, but it will prevent tetanus. Okay?" The coyote sat up. Deirdre drew the dose. This time the coyote didn't resist, and she gave it an injection. "Anything else I can do for you? Would you like some food? I imagine it's been hard to catch rabbits and mice and grasshoppers with that bum leg."

"Whuff."

She poured canine maintenance kibble into a steel bowl and filled a second with water, then set them both on the cement floor in the treatment room. The coyote ate and drank. It stood for a long moment staring out the open door into the night, then turned to look at her.

"Thank you," it said in a low, woman's voice.

It slipped away, silent as shadow, before Deirdre had finished her gasp.

She could wait a couple minutes before she scrubbed down the surgery. She went back outside to watch stars prick the sky. Her coffee was cold, but she drank it anyway.

TASHA Dane, who wandered the world in search of scents, sights, and sounds, sat on a branch high up in a Ponderosa pine in the Cascades and opened to night sounds, breathed them in. Coyotes called up the mountain, and somewhere nearer an owl hooted. Small gentle waves lapped the shore of the lake below. Tiny animals moved through underbrush. Breeze brushed through pine needles in the trees above her.

Across the lake, campsite fires starred the darkness among the evergreens, orange images reflected on the dark surface of the lake. She leaned forward, seeking. A guitar strummed across distance; voices sang; woodsmoke blew toward her, and the odor of burning wood and cooking meat mixed with evergreen, earth, and water scents. She closed her eyes and drew in sounds and scents.

It had been a month since she had come this close to people. She had spent time recently in the far north, collecting the almost-not-there scents of different kinds of ice and snow, watching northern lights shift and sheet and shimmer against wide, deep, long night skies.

One night something had thawed in her winter-iced chest. *I wonder if it's spring at home yet.*

She had turned south, found winds to drift her down, and here, close to her old home, she saw small signs: leaf buds swelling on trees, some of the earliest flowers poking up through sodden forest floor. Too early yet for frogs to call, but the rain and wind tasted soft with season shift.

A mouse shrieked as an owl caught it. She added that fragment of sound to her collection, then made a sampler of night scents: Ponderosa pine needles both fallen and still on the tree, the stronger scent of sap, earth, some spicy herb nearby. The faintest whiff of skunk spray. Fainter, tints and traces of smoke and food cooking, song and guitar, the murmur of voices across water.

People.

She wasn't ready to talk to anyone yet. It always took her a while to come back from these journeys. Here, she felt comfortable. People were over there, not beyond sight and sound, but not close enough to notice her. She could get used to them gradually.

Wind nudged her from behind. She laughed and let go of her branch, plunged out into nothing. Air carried her up above the forest.

She looked and listened and smelled and tasted: treetops had a different scent from the scent on the forest floor, sounds carried differently from this height; starlight painted patterns along the pine needles, gleamed on the lake.

She blew out over the lake, toward the campground.

—Wait.— She put out hands, spread fingers, tried to brake, turn, go back to the safety of the forest.

Wooden rowboats bumped a wooden dock below her, and now she could hear conversations. A dog at one of the campsites barked. Another answered.

—No. Not yet. I'm not ready,—she told Air as it tumbled her toward people.

—Really not ready?—

—Really.— She hugged herself. She had no clothes. She

couldn't remember how to speak aloud. She didn't want to come back to people here, where she knew no one. She wanted to choose her entry.

If Air told her to touch down here and now, she would. She had weathered more difficult things. In the service of Air, she went everywhere, sooner or later. Why not here?

She hovered twenty feet above the dock. Yard light from the little campground store shone on her, sheathing her skin in orange glow.

For a moment she was close enough to touch human-built things, close enough to be seen, to be drawn into local lives.

Air lifted her again.

She breathed out happiness, breathed more in.

She spent the night listening to deep forest.

LIA Fuego leaned forward in her box seat and stared down at the lighted stage, where the first instruments were tuning to each other. It was starting: the liquid fire that was music, edging upward from tinder into flame. The instruments joined, one section at a time, each musician searching for and finding the perfect note.

Harry Vandermeer touched her arm. She glanced at him, let him draw her out of the sound. She loved the look of him in his elegant dark suit, the long, graceful hands that were like pale lilies at the ends of his sleeves, the short gold hair that fell neatly against his skull, the gray-blue eyes that held storms and silence. His face in repose looked like he was amused by everything; now it was animated, his expression a mixture of worry and laughter. "We're in the wrong seats," he murmured.

The woman sitting on his other side slitted her eyes at him as if to tell him to shut up.

Lia leaned toward him, her shoulder nudging his, so she could hear a whisper. He bent his head. His breath touched her ear.

"We're in the wrong seats," he whispered, "if you're going to do that."

"What?" she whispered.

He took her hand, stroked it gently. She looked down.

"Oh." Her skin glowed, its natural darkness illuminated by a layer of orange flame. Flame washed over his hand, curling and curving calligraphies of fire.

Just then the tuning stopped, and her fire faded.

It had been so long since she'd been to a concert hall. She had music in her life every day, one way or another, but a full orchestra? Tonight's program had some of her favorite orchestral pieces on it, ones she hadn't heard live in more than fifteen years, some she'd never heard live. Since she had met Harry ten years before, they hadn't spent much time doing normal things, but she had seen this concert listed in the paper, and mentioned to Harry that she'd like to go, and he got tickets.

She wanted to hear the music more than anything.

"We'd better go," she whispered.

The conductor came onstage, and applause swept through the audience. It was the right moment to duck out.

"Look," he whispered. He pointed up toward the back of the concert hall. Some of the pieces the orchestra was playing tonight were pretty obscure, and there were rows of empty seats in the nosebleed section, on the second balcony.

She gripped his hand. They stood up, left their seats, and ran for the stairs.

Maybe, maybe, if they sat all the way in the back, and no one turned around, she could lose herself in the music after all.

"WHAT do you make of this?" the boy asked Terry Dane.

The college bar was noisy and dark, and the band was loud and bad. The kid was dressed in baggy, pleated thrift-store pants and a light blue work shirt with the sleeves rolled up, not a look Terry could ever remember being fashionable.

He had shaggy dark hair that looked like he had hacked it off himself without consulting a mirror. His eyes, too, appeared dark; maybe they'd be some other color if there were enough light to see them by. How old was this guy? Fifteen? Sixteen? Terry knew the bouncers carded people coming in; the cops had been cracking down on underage drinking lately. He had to be older than he looked.

She sipped her beer and peeked at the thing the boy held out to her. It was dark, glassy, and vaguely oval with bumps, and it filled his palm; his fingers curled around it. She couldn't see details in the lousy light, except for a few spots of reflected shine from the neon beer ads behind the bar.

"I don't know. What is it?"

"You're the witch. You tell me."

"Ex*cuse* me?" Terry set her beer mug on the bar with a thunk. She had heard a lot of pickup lines in the past eight years since she turned legal, but this one took her by surprise. She blinked and leaned forward to peer into the kid's face. His skin was pale, and he looked like a teenager, except that the dead expression on his face spoke of someone who was either older or had been through hell or both. "Who *are* you?"

"You can call me Galen if you like." His voice came out in a monotone, each syllable equally unstressed, except for a faint upward tone at the end of the sentence.

He smiled.

Terry felt something strange and dark flutter in her chest. His smile charmed her—more than she meant to be charmed. She could tell it wasn't even a good smile, just a movement of muscles, and yet, unaccountably, she warmed to him. She hated that. "Is there any particular reason why I might like to call you that? Does it bear any resemblance to your actual name?"

"Yes."

"I get this feeling I know you—" Terry began, a faint echo in her mind. She had seen this boy before, a long time ago. Maybe for just a minute.

"Hey, baby!" said somebody with the build and number jersey of a football player. He leaned heavily on Terry's shoulder and breathed alcohol fumes into her face. "Wanna have some real fun? Ditch Junior here and come play with the big boys." He wagged his crewcut head toward a group of large men by one of the pool tables. Two of them waved to her, and all of them grinned.

She grinned back and patted his cheek. "Hey, great! I'll be over in a minute, okay, buddy?"

"Whoa! Yeah! Uh-huh, huh!" He kissed her cheek and staggered back toward the pool table, then detoured in the direction of the rest rooms.

She wiped saliva off her face. "Well, okay, Galen, what is it you want from me?"

He glanced away from her and swallowed. She saw his Adam's

apple bob. "I think I need some help," he said. His voice was still monotone.

"This is how you ask for help? Calling me a witch?"

He frowned. He turned back to meet her gaze, his eyes narrowed. "I haven't talked to anybody outside in a long time," he said after a few breaths. "I'm not good at it."

"I noticed."

"There's a statue in the park across the street."

Terry's eyebrows lifted. She sipped beer and waited.

Galen looked away again, his mouth tightening. "I guess I should go home and study conversation. I haven't tried to talk to a stranger in forty years. What a ridiculous set of skills for me not to have." He hunched his shoulders and turned away.

Terry touched his arm. Shock tingled through her, so intense and sudden she yelped. Galen turned, startled too.

"Hey, baby. This guy still bothering you?" asked the crewcut man, returned from the rest rooms.

"No, honey. He's my brother. Give me a few minutes, will you?"

Crewcut slapped her back and wandered away, nodding.

"What are you going to do with him?" Galen asked.

Terry slitted her eyes. She dropped a five-dollar bill on the bar. "Let's go outside."

They pushed their way out past close-packed people. The night air felt cool and sharp after the hot, smelly air in the bar, the orange streetlamps sun-bright after the bar's darkness. Traffic had almost disappeared.

Terry grabbed Galen's arm and shuddered as the shock of touching him struck her. When it faded, she pulled him across the street into the little park. It was big enough to have two patches of frosty lawn, three winterbare maple trees—it was late February, too early for spring leaves—a bench, a trash can, and, oh, yes, there *was* a statue there, a stone soldier on a pedestal commemorating the dead in some war a long time ago. She dragged Galen over to it and opened her senses as wide as she could. What had this soldier to do with witching? She didn't get any hit from it at all.

She turned to Galen, senses still wide, and saw that he glowed. Fox fire gray-green.

She should have expected something like that. Static electricity couldn't explain the charge he'd given her.

She let go of his arm. "I'm listening."

He sighed, stepped over to the pedestal, and leaned against it. The witchglow around him changed to a shifting blend of yellow, pink, and red. His face came alive. This time his smile looked genuine. She liked it even more. "I, uh—"

Terry touched the pedestal. Dead stone. What *was* this?

"It's this—I was just leaning against this and the statue said go in the bar and find the witch." Now his voice rose and fell in the tones of normal conversation.

"What made you decide I was a witch?"

"Oh, come on. I can spot witches, no problem. It's elementary."

"How?"

He drew a couple signs in the air with an index finger, muttered three words, touched his eyes.

Terry knew the spell. Simple, effective. Make the hidden visible. She sighed. "So what is it you want from me?"

"Here." He held out his hand, the dark, shiny object still in it.

"Apprentice!" cried a loud voice from behind them.

Terry and Galen turned toward the street. A tall, white-haired man cloaked in black stood on the sidewalk, glaring at them. Galen snatched his hand back and tucked it into his pocket.

"Sorry," he whispered. He pushed off from the pedestal and ran past Terry toward the street. The man flapped his cloak open, wrapped it around the boy, spun, and both of them vanished.

"Son of a bitch." Terry leaned forward and touched the statue's pedestal again, wondering what had brought the boy to life. It felt like stone. She used the see-better spell Galen had demonstrated, but the stone stayed dull, flat, and unmagical, even to her improved vision.

Hadn't she seen that white-haired man before? Somewhere, somewhen. . . . Sometime unpleasant.

Where?

She shook her head, then pulled her evening's experimental spell out of her pocket. She had learned to compress spells into tablets suitable for dropping into drinks. She was trying for a "nice and obedient" spell that didn't totally rob men of their minds, but she hadn't gotten the mix of ingredients right yet.

Maybe tonight.

She headed back inside the bar, looking for her crewcut buddy.

Chapter Two

·　·　·　·　·

In the small Oregon coast town of Guthrie, the witch
Edmund Reynolds laid an Oregon map on the
weather-silvered front porch of the haunted house and
dropped to sit cross-legged in front of it. Late-winter
sun, cool and bright, glared off the map's white background, almost drowned red and black roads, blue riv-
ers, dark dot-and-dash state lines in light. Sun gilded
Edmund's brown curls, highlighted dust on his green
T-shirt and jeans, glowed in the pale hairs on his
forearms.

Matt Black smiled. She had found Edmund three
months earlier in a pioneer graveyard, and she had
stayed with him ever since, longer than she'd stayed
with anyone else she'd met in more than two decades
of roaming. Across the wander years, she had let go of
almost everything she had ever had except her army
jacket, and she had spent most of her time talking
with things instead of people. Buildings, streets, park
benches, drinking fountains, trash cans, cardboard

boxes, dishes, railroad tracks, toys, cars, anything shaped by hu-
mankind might have a story to tell her. Things talked with her.
They liked her, and she liked them.

Maybe she had been ready for a change. It felt strange but
nice to hang on to someone human.

Just now she thought Edmund looked like a god who had just
been pulled out of a closet, bright and shiny but not wiped clean
yet. Everything about him made her happy.

Edmund glanced up at Matt. "Watch what happens when I
try a seek spell for Julio."

"Okay." She sat down beside him. Salt breeze gusted through
her short hair, riffled the edge of the map. She set the toe of her
sneaker on a corner of the map and leaned back, her hands flat
on the porch boards.

Edmund fished a lead weight on a piece of fishing line from
his jeans pocket. He murmured to the weight and kissed it, then
held the string between finger and thumb, let the weight dangle
above the map. "Julio," he murmured. "Julio."

The weight circled slowly clockwise above the map. Matt
waited. She had seen Edmund do search-dowsing before. The line
would straighten in some direction or another, pointing them
toward their quarry.

The circles spun faster, though Edmund's grip on the line
didn't shift at all. Presently, the line stretched tight, the weight
suspended toward the south. Matt nodded. Good. They had a line
on Julio. Maybe they could get going soon. She loved staying in
the haunted house, but it had been three weeks, and she was
getting restless. Something inside her, stronger than anything else
she knew, wanted her to keep moving. She didn't know how to
quiet it.

She had promised Edmund soon after she met him that she'd help him look up his old childhood friends so he wouldn't have to face them alone when they realized how different he had become since they last saw him.

This road was bumpy, but she had already helped him find the first two friends of four, Nathan, a ghost here in the haunted house who had only been lost to Edmund because Edmund was afraid to face him again, and Susan, a friend he had met when he was in junior high here in Guthrie.

Edmund had left town after he had hurt Susan's father to protect Susan fifteen years earlier. He had scared himself and her.

Matt had gone with Edmund to search for Susan. They found her in Palo Alto using the map-seek spell. She had changed her name to Suki, and cut herself loose of her earlier life, but she came home to the haunted house with them after she and Edmund walked through their mutual past again, examined it with older eyes, changed what they could, made amends where they could, and accepted their younger selves.

They were still two friends short.

The fishing line relaxed and circled again. After half a minute, it pulled to the northwest. Relaxed. Circled for a while, and pulled east. Relaxed, circled. Then the weight jerked straight up, as though tugged by a magnet, and stretched toward the porch roof. "Whoa, spirit," Edmund said. "It never did that before."

"Julio sure moves around a lot," said Matt.

"That's not it. This technique doesn't work on him."

"How can that be?"

He cupped the weight in his hand and stared down at the map, a frown plowing a line between his brows. "Maybe he doesn't want to be found."

The door creaked behind them, and Suki Backstrom, blonde and elegant in a tan sweater and olive green slacks, stepped out onto the porch. After three weeks here she had lost most of her California businesswoman/PR person chic, but she still hadn't relaxed into Oregon coast casual. "You found me, and I didn't want to be found," she said, leaning against the house. She crossed her arms over her chest and smiled down at Matt.

"Are you sure?" asked Matt.

"Yes. I absolutely did not want to be found. Later I was glad you found me, but not at first."

"Julio might have defenses," Edmund said slowly. "Better defenses than you did."

"Because of that demon thing?" Suki frowned. "I thought it went away after a couple of days."

"What demon thing?" Matt asked.

"I don't know that it ever went away," said Edmund. "I think he wanted us to believe it went away. He pretended nothing happened. I asked him about it a couple of times, but he never gave me a straight answer."

"What demon thing?" Matt asked again.

"It went away," Suki said. "He was just the way he used to be."

Edmund shook his head.

"Nathan?" Suki said.

Shadow and light shimmered beside her, coalesced into the shape of a teenage boy from a bygone era: white shirt, suspenders, dark knickers, black knee socks, button-sided ankle boots. Nathan's skin was underground-pale; his hair was black, and his eyes gasflame blue. Sometimes he looked more solid than others; today his edges were pearly and translucent.

"Julio got over that demon thing, didn't he?" Suki asked him.

"Got over it?" asked Nathan.

"Put it behind him, went on with his life."

He looked away from her at the blackberry vines in the yard. There were mounds of them so tall you almost couldn't see the street past them, or the wind-bent shore pines that shielded the houses next door from view. "He went on with his life," Nathan said.

"He *didn't* get over the demon thing?" Suki asked.

"I can't tell you that part. It's not my story."

"You said you still see him sometimes," said Matt.

The ghost smiled. "Once in a while I see who Julio is now."

"So you know what happened, but you're just not talking? Unfair," said Suki. She reached out as though to tickle him, growled when her hands went right through him. He laughed anyway.

"Looks like nobody's going to tell *me* anything." Matt felt frustrated.

—I'll tell you,—the house whispered to her through the palms of her hands. —Later.—

Paradoxically, Matt wondered if she should even ask. People ought to be in charge of their own stories. She didn't even know Julio, someone Edmund and Suki had been friends with for most of their childhoods. How would Julio feel about some stranger poking into his life story? Maybe it was none of her business.

She suggested this to the house.

The house waited a moment. —I'll think about that. Let's talk in dreams tonight.—

Matt bit her lip. The house told her lots of things in dreams. She wasn't awake enough to say no, and she never wanted to anyway; everything the house told her was fascinating. Maybe this was its sneaky way of getting around her better self.

"We have to find Julio another way," Edmund said. "Nathan, can you help us?"

"What if you're correct? What if Julio doesn't want to be found?"

"What if he's like me and doesn't know he wants to be found?" Suki asked.

"Can you still do that thing where you get inside him? Could you find him that way?" Edmund asked Nathan.

"Edmund—" said Nathan.

"Let's look for your other friend instead," suggested Matt. "Deirdre. We can worry about Julio later."

Edmund glanced at her, then smiled. He flattened the map with his palm, spoke to the lead weight again, kissed it, sat back, took some deep breaths and let them out slowly, then held the weight above the map. "Deirdre. Deirdre," he murmured.

The weight circled for a long time, and then pulled itself to a stop. Matt and Edmund leaned closer. A tiny town in central Oregon, a clear circle that meant it was unincorporated. "Artemisia," Edmund read aloud. "What's she doing there?"

"Let's go find out." Matt measured distances with her thumb, muttered figures to herself. "Looks like about two hundred seventy miles." She glanced at the sun. Still high in the sky. Edmund's car was great, but it didn't go very fast, and they had two mountain ranges to cross, though the first one, the Coast Range, wasn't very tall.

"We'll go tomorrow." Edmund glanced at Suki and Nathan. "You want to come?"

Nathan shrugged. "If you need me, call me up." Most days the only way he could get away from the haunted house was by being summoned to a séance.

Suki said, "I'd rather wait and find out if she *wants* to see us. You do all the intrusive stuff. Besides, I have an interview. Who knows. I might get a job."

A job! Getting a job was like nailing your foot to the floor, Matt thought. Especially a good job. Although Suki had walked away from the job she'd held in California for several years. Matt had walked away from lots of little stopgap jobs, the kind that weren't meant to last, but she'd never had a job she wanted to keep.

Suki was different. Maybe she wanted to nail her feet to the floor here.

"Hey, good luck." Edmund looked at Matt. "You'll come?"

"Of course. I'm already packed."

THAT night Matt lay alone in one of the beds in Julio's old room. She could hear Edmund's slow sleep breaths from the other bed. After years of sleeping alone, she had gotten used to sleeping beside him, liked waking up tangled with him, snuggled up against his warmth and wrapped in his sagebrush-and-woodsmoke scent, but she had told him that tonight she needed to sleep with her dreams.

The house hummed around her. She knew it was waiting for her to fall asleep so it could talk to her. She had never known another being who could walk into her dreams, turn them into its playground, its movie screen, the way the house could. Some nights it left her alone, but some nights it took a human form—not the same shape as Nathan, but a person, someone tall, comforting, welcoming, who walked beside her on a dream version of the Guthrie beach and talked about things Matt couldn't remember when she woke up. House-as-person seemed more motherly than Matt's mother had ever been.

Matt figured seeing the house as human was a natural extension of her relationship with inanimate objects. She knew things had souls and ideas, histories, memories, and desires, voices that only she seemed able to hear. Why not see a lively thing like the house as a person?

Matt closed her eyes, pulled the covers up to her chin, and settled into her sleeping position on her back. —Did you think about what I said?—she thought.

—Yes,—whispered the house. —This is Julio's story, but it's mine, too, because some of it happened to me. Matt, Julio knew me and Nathan the way you do, for different reasons. I don't think he'll mind if I tell you. At least, not this part of it. It happened fifteen years ago. Ready?—

Matt's breathing slowed. She fell down into sleep, and opened her eyes somewhere else.

Chapter Three

. . . . .

Fifteen Years in the Past

FRIDAY afternoon, after the other high-school students had gone home for the weekend, Julio Rivera lifted the violin to his shoulder and attacked for the fourteenth time a tricky piece of bowing in a fiddle tune called "Wilson's Clog." He had found the tune on a record of fiddle tunes he'd bought for a quarter at a yard sale. It was a great tune, with lots of bounce, though it wasn't classical. Mr. Noah, Julio's music teacher, frowned on less-than-classical music pieces, but Julio loved them. Julio hadn't heard many kinds of music he didn't end up loving.

He couldn't figure out how to bow "Wilson's Clog" so the ups and downs worked out the same every time; he kept getting stuck bowing up on triplets where he wanted to bow down. He tried a variety of attacks, slurring some notes and not others, then switched. Finally, he locked it down. He played the piece through with the bowing he'd established, and the tune danced on the air, so inviting he wanted to dance himself. How could Mr. Noah not like this? Julio would play it for him. One of these days Mr. Noah would cave.

Well, Julio had better get back to his real practice. He stroked a long, pure note out of the violin with the bow. Eyes closed, he listened to the note. He willed grace into his joints as he drew the bow across the string and strove for a sound that stayed true for its whole journey.

Only when the sound ended and silence completed the note did he realize someone watched him.

He hadn't heard the door of the high-school music room open or shut. It made a distinctive shriek, E flat, whenever anyone came in or out. He knew some people who could get in and out of places without using doors. Who was here now? One of his friends who had that ability? Or someone else who could do it, someone unknown?

He frowned, then lifted the bow and played a Latino valse his mother had taught him when he had started playing violin at seven, one of the few pieces of her childhood she had shared with him, and so deeply learned that he could play it without thought or concentration. What had the watcher seen before Julio knew he was being watched? Julio lived a guarded life, full of other people's secrets; one of his best friends was a witch, another was a ghost, and the remaining two had things they never told anyone, things he knew but never gave up. He was sensitized to secrecy.

The muscles at the back of his neck tightened.

He opened his eyes and glanced across the music room, usually empty of everyone but Julio after hours. Mr. Noah had given Julio keys to come here whenever he liked. Julio often couldn't practice in the small apartment he shared with his mother; too many near neighbors, too-thin walls. He could practice at the haunted house, but many of the instruments he used lived here.

An older man stood near the door. He wore his silver hair short. His pale eyes had a peculiar heat, his unlined features unnatural stillness. His arms crossed over his chest, the hands hidden in the crooks of opposite elbows.

No one Julio knew. A fiddle tune called "Lock the Door After the Silver's Been Stolen" played in his mind. He had a bad feeling about this.

Julio lifted the bow off the strings. "May I help you?"

"I'm sure you can," said the man. His bass voice held the rise and fall of music in a minor key, sparking Julio's respect. "So kind of you to offer."

"What can I do for you?" Who was this guy? Had Mr. Noah sent him?

No. Mr. Noah didn't know people who could enter rooms without going through doors. Or he didn't know he knew.

"You can come with me," said the stranger. His voice held compulsion.

Julio's feet walked toward the door. "Wait," he said, and glanced over his shoulder at his backpack. Textbooks, notebooks, classwork, a couple of granola bars, his favorite pens and pencils, his musical-notation book full of half-finished compositions, his pennywhistles and spoons, and that English homework he was supposed to drop off at Ms. Orla's office before he left today. And the violin case. He should at least put this violin away in the case, where it would be safe. It was a special violin Mr. Noah trusted

Julio with; and Julio treasured that trust more than most other things in his life.

He couldn't leave all that behind.

His feet didn't listen. They kept walking.

JULIO sat in the backseat of the car, staring at the rear of the driver's silver head. The tune that played through Julio's mind held melancholy resignation. He held the violin bow up so that the horsehairs wouldn't come into contact with anything, and he had laid the violin across his lap. After Julio's third (unanswered) question, the man said, "Be quiet now, son."

Words abandoned Julio. Questions still beat at his throat, but he couldn't voice them.

The back windows of the car were blacked out; Julio couldn't see any scenery to the sides, but he watched out the front window, memorizing road signs when he could, looking for landmarks. If his future held escape, this knowledge would come in handy later.

Mom would worry. Would anybody else? Probably not anytime soon. His friends knew he planned to practice in the music room this afternoon and wouldn't join them at the haunted house. They wouldn't expect to see him until tomorrow.

They left town behind and went by a road Julio didn't know into the mountains. Miles passed. It would be a long walk home, if he could work free of the compulsion the man had laid on him.

Finally the car turned off the road onto a narrow paved track. Mountains loomed close above the car to the right; pines hemmed the left side. Despair wove through the song on Julio's inner sound track. If he were on foot, and the man were driving—

Well, he could cut through the forest, and the car couldn't follow. He wasn't good at nature, though. He would get lost. He didn't know how to spend a night in the wild. If it rained, how could he protect the violin?

On the other hand, if he could get the keys to the car . . .

The man parked the car in front of a house made of stone, crowded close by dark pines, and graveled up to its front. "Get out now," said the man, his deep voice inviting and compelling at once.

Julio managed to protect the violin and bow from harm as his body responded to the command in the man's voice, a minor victory.

"Come inside."

He followed the stranger into the strange house, and found himself in a dimly lit but prosaic living room with a fire burning in the fireplace, and comfortable chairs near it. As the front door closed behind Julio, a younger man who looked about Julio's age, black-haired and yellow-eyed, came into the room and took a seat by the fire. He was pale and solemn. "Master? Who is this?"

The stranger smiled. "One of the weak links in the golden chain we seek," he said. "Observe, apprentice." He turned to Julio and said, "Sit down, child."

Julio sat, and the man sat across from him, his silver eyes alert and narrow.

"Now," said the older man, "you may answer questions. You may not ask any. Tell me about your friends."

Julio knew who this man was asking him about. Julio's stomach went cold. So he was a weak link in the chain of friends? Anger thawed his stomach again. He didn't know how to resist magical compulsion, but he could try.

"Speak."

"Spike McTavish, I met him in second grade. I won his favorite marble, and after he beat me up and took it back, we got to be friends. Not really good friends, though. I don't like people who punch other people. I haven't seen Spike in a couple of years. Lily Onslow. I've known her since kindergarten. She has a huge stuffed animal collection. Her favorite is—"

"Stop."

Julio sat with the violin across his lap, the bow upraised. He was more sensitive to sound than other people he knew, delighting in it more and suffering from it more, depending. He had had previous experiences with people who could control him with nothing but their voices, and he hated it. His friend Edmund could do it, but Edmund didn't do it on purpose, and when alerted, would stop. How far did this man's control of Julio extend?

He checked the second man—a boy, really. The first man called him "apprentice." They worked together.

The boy gazed at him and said nothing. Julio couldn't look to him for help.

"Not those friends," said the kidnapper, but before he could voice his next order, Julio lifted the violin to his shoulder and drew the bow across the open A string. He stared into the man's eyes. What would be a good tune in a situation like this? "Far and Away"? "Slip the Leash"? "Sidestep Hornpipe"? He began "Sidestep Hornpipe," lively and quick with an undertone of slipping out from under.

The older man sat back in his chair, eyelids half lowered, and listened. The younger man leaned forward, his eyes intent.

When Julio finished the tune, he waited a moment. The stranger seemed dazed. Could it have worked? Julio had no magic that he knew of. "Thanks for an interesting afternoon," Julio said, and rose to his feet. "I'll be going now." He took two steps toward the front door.

"Sit," said the man. "Stay."

Woof, thought Julio as he complied.

"You know the friends I mean," said the man. "The ones connected to the haunted house. Tell me about those friends."

Nathan, a ghost; Edmund, a witch; Susan, who could talk to houses; and Deirdre, staunch and straightforward and almost as ordinary as Julio. He didn't want to talk about any of them to someone who would grab someone from school and take him far away without warning or explanation.

"Tell me," the man repeated, leaning forward. His voice was thrilling, enticing.

Julio opened his mouth, fought to close it, clutched the neck of the violin until he was afraid he'd break it. *No. I won't. And you can't force me.* "No," he said. "No."

Excitement flowed through him. *If I don't have to do this, maybe I don't have to do the rest, right? I can get up.* He pushed himself to his feet. He headed for the door again.

"Stop!" cried the man.

Julio's legs froze, but his arms and chest didn't. He leaned so far forward he fell, crushing the violin beneath him. Mr. Noah's violin, his favorite, not one of the cheap rentals Julio had learned on before he got to high school and met Mr. Noah, a man who was almost as interested in music as Julio was.

Julio had betrayed Mr. Noah's trust.

He sat up, lifted the violin's black neck with scrolled headpiece and pegs still intact, looked at the crushed body, the honey-colored outer wood, the pale unvarnished inner skin. Strings still bound the black tailpiece to the headpiece, but it was all crazy and wrong. He touched the scraps of wood, found the edge of one of the f-shaped sound holes. No way could he put this back together.

Tears rushed from his eyes. That didn't make sense. He was seventeen and he was crying, but what he really felt was a ball of anger in his stomach so hot and fierce he felt like throwing up. He turned to stare at the man.

"Your own folly did that," the man said.

Julio jumped up. "No," he said, cradling the violin neck against his stomach, swamped with brief guilt while he wondered if this were his fault. Did he ask this man to order him around? Did he ask to be snatched from the practice room without even a moment to stow the violin in its case? No. His eyes still leaked hot tears. He had never felt this angry before in his life.

"Sit," said the man for the third time.

"No."

The man gestured and murmured some words, and Julio found his legs walking him to the chair. He sat.

He glanced at the other boy. The boy stared at him with the intent look of a bird of prey staring at a mouse. Julio wiped away tears, ashamed. Perhaps he couldn't help doing what the man said, but he didn't have to share his anguish with people who didn't care. The heat in his chest built higher and hotter. He managed to stop the tears.

"Tell me about your friends!" The stranger's voice held an edge of anger now.

He's losing it. Julio kept his mouth closed. His head was so full of anger and pain he didn't have room for obedience.

"Very well," said the man. "Think about this for a while."

Three gestures and some freezing, hard words. Marks appeared on the hardwood floor around Julio's chair: two concentric circles in ice-blue light, with unknown symbols in blood red light scribbled in the band between them. Julio felt his bones freeze. He clutched the violin neck, but his hand was dead; he couldn't even feel his fingers against the hard wood. The man gestured and spoke more words, these ones slice-sharp and even icier.

And Julio lost himself.

Utter dark, darker than blindness. Utter cold, subzero and marrow deep. For a brief time, silence.

Then the noise began. Voices, yammering, wailing, screaming, each one a pure cold stream of its particular emotion, soul-deep sorrow and regret, heart-hammering terror, roiling red rage. All of them printed themselves on Julio's mind and heart.

He was such a good listener.

Then came the little biting things, gnawing behind eyes Julio was no longer sure he had. Tiny teeth tore into his brain, each toothmark a separate pain.

He struggled, tried to bat the biting things, tried to wall his ears off with his hands, but he didn't seem to have a body here; he had no defenses. All of him was ear, was skin, was brain, was pain. Flute shrieks of terror, violin screeches of shrill anger, tympani thumps of pounding rage, cello glissades of unending sadness, other instruments he had never heard before expressing feelings that made him want to scream or slash his wrists, all disharmony and discord. Pianissimo horn notes of utter despair, brush whispers of terrible shame. Slashing vocal shrieks of agony and pain and torture. His mind struggled to make music of it. It refused to sort from chaos into pattern. Every new note, every new voice, sawed or sliced at him, each at a different tempo, each in a different way.

It didn't soften or stop. It just got stronger, less endurable.

Finally he stopped trying to fight it, let go and let it all in.

Then it hurt even more.

He could feel pieces of himself slice off, fall away.

He needed help.

"Nathan!" he cried. No sound came out: he had no mouth.

Sound existed here somehow. It cut and chopped at him.

He had to make his own song.

He thought it: "Nathan." It came out as a squeak He thought it again, drawing his concentration away from all the things that hurt. "Nathan!" He roared it through all the screams around him, and heard his own tenor voice crying in this wilderness.

"Yes?"

Nathan's voice! He focused all his energy on it. "Nathan!"

"What is it? Who's calling?"

A rope of sound! Julio used each word as a knot, pulled himself closer to the origin of the voice. Coherent sound that cut through the chaos. "Nathan?"

"What? Who's there?"

Julio pulled and plunged, skidded out of wherever he was into another place.

All the screams and biting stopped. He hung suspended in a new, warmer darkness. "Nathan," he said again, his voice clear and pure and burnished as he had never heard it. For a moment he lost himself in the sound of his own voice.

"Julio? Is that you?" Julio heard fear in Nathan's voice, minor notes in a question key.

"Nate? Where am I? I can't see."

"You're at my house," said the ghost, his voice beautiful but thinned with apprehension. "What happened to you?"

"I don't know. I—" Julio reached out and felt Nathan's face. "Oh, God. You're here." He sensed the cool skin, felt an eyelash brush against the tip of his finger, touched nose, lips.

"Julio," Nathan said. Julio felt the lips move under his fingertips as the ghost spoke. "What are you doing?"

"I—" What was he doing? The ghost wasn't tangible. How could Julio touch him? "I'm sorry! I'm—I was—it was so horrible!" He shifted, moved forward, leaned against the ghost and hugged him, unsure how it was happening, needing to touch something safe. "I'm sorry, I'm sorry," he murmured, holding tight, his hands pressing the cool woven cotton of the back of Nathan's shirt, his cheek against Nathan's shoulder, the ghost's body hard and cold in his embrace, but solid as any other person Julio had ever hugged. "I was so scared. I'm sorry. I can't—" He couldn't get himself to let go. What if the other place snatched him back?

What if he was forcing Nathan to endure something Nathan couldn't stand? Julio couldn't let go. Panic made him hold tighter.

"It's all right," Nathan said, his voice almost calm.

An anchor against that dark chaotic sea, Nathan stood quiet in his embrace.

At last Julio relaxed enough to release his friend. "I'm sorry," he said again.

"It's all right," Nathan repeated, stronger this time. "Can you tell me what happened?"

"I don't know. Why can't I see?" Julio reached out, brushed Nathan's chest, reached farther and touched a wall. The wallpaper felt alive and powdery beneath his fingertip, and then he felt a startling flow of energy beneath it, a question, a greeting, a warmth. He pushed deeper into it, and it closed around his hand like warm water. "What is this?" Julio moved to the wall and pressed into it, and through it. Welcoming warmth all around him, like a hot bath, and the soothing music of lullabies. "Hello?" he said.

"Hello, Boy," said the house.

"Where am I?"

"In my wall."

"What? How?" He reached farther, felt his hand leave the haven of the house.

"That's the air outside."

"House. I don't understand."

"Hang on to yourself, Julio. You're a ghost."

Julio curled up inside himself. A ghost! No. Couldn't be. Could it? How else could he have hugged Nathan?

If he were dead, at least it was a comfortable death. House was so much better than the other place! But—

"House," he whispered.

A hand reached into the warmth, grabbed Julio's hand, and tugged him out of the wall. "That's not quite right, Julio," Nathan told him. Julio clung to his hand. "I don't think you're dead. Your inner self got separated from your body, that's all. Can you tell us what happened to you?"

"This man came to my school and ordered me around. He had a voice like Edmund's. He could make me do what he wanted just by saying it. He took me in his car to some house up in the mountains, and started asking me about you and the others, and I wouldn't tell him. I don't get that part. He could make me do anything he wanted. He ordered me to walk and I walked, ordered me to sit and I sat. But I didn't answer his questions. I just got really mad."

"Good," said Nathan. And then: "He already knew something. Otherwise, why would he have picked you up? What happened after that?"

Julio said, "He made me break Mr. Noah's violin. I was trying to run away and he told me to stop, and I fell on Mr. Noah's violin. I broke that beautiful violin. I'll never be able to explain that!" Anger filled Julio again. "Then he made me sit down again and told me to tell about you. When I wouldn't talk, he cast some kind of spell on me and sent me to hell."

Nathan gripped Julio's hand harder. "Can you remember anything about the spell?"

"Light circles on the floor, with writing. Two blue circles, one inside the other, with red writing in between. The guy said words and used gestures. I didn't know the language."

"And hell, what was that like?"

"Cold, dark, screams, pain." Julio shook. "Horrible horrible not-music."

"Forget," said Nathan gently. "Release it." He touched Julio's cheek.

"But—"

"You want to keep that?"

"I'm not ready to forget yet. I want to kill that guy." Rage filled him. Then he felt something flicker through him, a calling and a pulling away. No! He was not going to leave the safety of this house! He gripped Nathan's shoulders. "Help me. Something's pulling me!"

Nathan took his hands and held on tight. After a moment the

calling passed, and Julio relaxed. "Oh. Thank you. Damn! Nathan, why can't I see anything?"

"You're not yourself."

Julio waited a moment, trying to figure out how Nathan meant that. Of course he wasn't himself. He was some kind of ghost. Nathan was a ghost, and he could see, couldn't he? Julio waved his free hand around and touched Nathan's face. "Are you making fun of me?" he asked, brushing Nathan's cheek, his mouth. He couldn't feel a smile, but he hadn't touched people's faces while they were smiling enough to know the difference.

"No," Nathan said. He sighed. "You're ghostly, but not ghost-like. In the form you wear now, you have no body."

"But—" Julio touched Nathan's lips again. "I feel you." He moved his other hand in Nathan's grasp. "How can I hold on to you?"

"I don't know. I don't know how you're talking, either."

"What do I look like?"

Nathan hesitated, then said, "A pillar of colored light."

Julio hugged himself, feeling arms and elbows, chest and shoulders. "That can't be right," he whispered.

Nathan said nothing.

Julio touched Nathan's shoulder, arm, hand. Nathan opened his hand, let Julio take it again. It felt cold but solid. "But," Julio said. And then, "I keep touching you. I never even asked. I was just so scared, Nate."

"It's all right." The ghost sounded relaxed. "It's been an age since I touched anyone or anyone touched me. I like it."

"What do I feel like to you?"

Nathan gripped his hand. "This feels like a hand, but looks like a streamer of light. When you touch my face, a ribbon of light reaches for me, and I feel fingertips. I can't explain it, Julio. I haven't seen this sort of manifestation before. If you imagined eyes for yourself . . ."

Julio imagined he could see. He remembered what the haunted house looked like. With Edmund, Deirdre, and Susan, he stopped off there after school most days. Downstairs, dust, dirt, cobwebs, curling strips of wallpaper, water stains, scratchy stretches of empty space; suggestive shadows that your mind could turn into terrors, shaped and aided by Nathan's haunting. Upstairs, bedrooms with old furniture and new objects Edmund, Deirdre, Susan, and Julio had brought in. Nathan and the house had given them each a space to claim, a haven away from their homes. "Where am I?" Julio asked, and reached out. He felt rough metal with one hand, explored, discovered the ornamented face of the old woodstove in the kitchen. With his other hand he touched a doorway.

"The kitchen," Nathan said, just after Julio figured it out.

Julio visualized the kitchen. The stove stood against one wall, and the doorway into the dining room was ten feet from it.

How could he feel both at once?

He pulled back into himself, frightened and startled. What *was* he?

A pillar of light.

A pillar of light that could stretch across a room.

He was something not caged in a body, not trapped by size or race or gender. Something not even human.

Whoa. There could be an upside to this.

Suppose I had a thousand hands?

He spread out, touched surfaces in all directions—window glass, floor, ceiling, woodstove, sink, faucets, doorway. He reached through the doorway into the dining room and touched the far wall there, felt House's energy under the surface. A thousand hands, five thousand fingertips, a body that could expand to fill a whole room; a flood of sensations, a knowing of surfaces as though he were putty pressed up against everything, with Nathan somehow in the middle of him, a dragonfly in amber. Behind every surface he touched, the house touched him back, laughing as though tickled.

Somewhere inside the house lurked the memories of musical instruments from the past. With a thousand hands, he could play—

Now was not the time to think about that.

If I imagined eyes. Julio tried to imagine being able to see everything he touched, but vision didn't come.

"I can't seem to imagine eyes," Julio said. "Ouch! Sorry!" His voice came from everywhere and seemed much too loud. Although, given time, he was sure he could come up with something to use a voice like that for. Maybe his voice wasn't trapped either. Could he sing four-part harmony with himself? Why not six- or eight-part harmony? Why not be an orchestra?

He pulled himself together until all he felt was the floor beneath what he thought of as feet. "Sorry."

"It's all right," Nathan said again. He sounded like he was laughing. Then he said in a sober voice, "But we had better think about this. We need to put you back together. Who knows what's happening to your body without you in it? Did the man give you a reason for doing this to you?"

"Punishing me for not talking."

"I need some witches," Nathan said. Then, "Edmund's coming."

Julio listened, but heard nothing. He reached out and touched a wall, pushed into it. House's warm energy enveloped his hand. "Here," it said, and let Julio into its sensory network so that he was all through the house, out into the yard, and under a small slice of street. Rock beneath, roots above, and footsteps traveling from an edge toward the center.

"I'll be back in a moment," Nathan said somewhere above him. Julio sensed him flickering from one place and reappearing in another. Julio had never had nerves like these, a skeleton like this. The house fed him more information and helped him sort it. Nathan stood on the porch. Edmund and Deirdre, talking, strode the path through the blackberry thickets toward the house.

"I need you," Nathan said to them.

"What is it?" Edmund asked.

"Somebody's hurt Julio."

Both of them raced up on the porch. Julio felt the house open the front door. "What? Where? What can we do?" asked Edmund.

"First we need to figure out where," Nathan said.

"You don't know where? It's not here? How do you know about it?" Deirdre demanded. Her voice sounded upset.

"Julio?" Nathan said.

Julio pulled his hand from the wall, breaking a host of connections he had made with the house. "Oh," he said. "I'm sorry!" The small snaps had hurt, a hundred tiny cuts on sensitive skin. He touched the wall again.

"Next time, warn me," the house told him.

"I didn't know."

"Nor I."

"I'm pulling away now." He waited a moment, then lifted his hand off the wall. He headed for the front hall and bumped into the closed dining room door. "What do I do now?"

"Come through."

He put his hands out and pressed them into the door, felt the same energy there, warm and fluid and accepting. He pushed into it and past it and came out the other side.

Deirdre yelled, "Yow!"

Chapter Four

· · · · ·

Still Past

EDMUND gasped. "What *is* that?" he asked after a moment, his voice at its most molten-metal pure, so beautiful Julio wanted to wrap himself up in it. Julio reached toward Edmund, touched his jacket. "What?"

"Julio, wait," Nathan said.

Julio traced the zipper of Edmund's jacket up, touched his throat, felt a pulse of heat and unborn music wound tight under his fingertips, masked by a warm net of skin and nerves and veins, arteries and muscles.

"This is Julio?" Edmund asked, letting a little of the coiled music loose. Julio reached up and touched his lips. "What are you doing?" Julio felt the words breathe out past his fingers, each one carrying a trace of power.

"Your voice," Julio said. "I love your voice."

"Julio," Deirdre said, her voice hoarse. "What happened to you?"

"A witch cast him out of his body," Nathan answered.

Julio set one hand against Edmund's throat and kept the other over his lips, waiting, hoping, for another word. "Would you please stop that?" Edmund said. Julio could taste his amusement and exasperation. For a moment he didn't even think about what Edmund had said; he was too busy savoring the music and strangeness of words that carried this power. Then he suddenly realized: here he was, touching again, somebody he'd known for ten years and never really touched before.

He pulled back. "I'm sorry," he said. "I can't see. But I can hear even better than I could before, and I can touch. I know I'm getting carried away."

"You're blind?" Deirdre asked.

"Yeah."

"Whoa. You're so pretty and you can't even see yourself?"

"Pretty?" He reached toward her, trying to catch sense from what she said. His hand met hers.

"Yow!" she said, meshing her fingers with his. "That's the weirdest thing! Feels just like a hand, looks like some kind of special effect." Her hand felt warm and tasted of earth. "Julio? What happened to you?"

"Nathan already said. This guy was trying to make me tell him about you guys, and when I wouldn't, he said, 'Think about this for a while,' and he turned me into a ghost, I guess. He sent me someplace horrible. I called Nathan and came here."

"Are you dead?" Deirdre whispered.

"I don't know. Nathan doesn't think so."

"The colors in Julio's light are signals," Nathan said, "and he's got enough red in him to still be alive. We don't know what's being done to his body while he's away from it, though. If the witch left a void in it, it could be ailing. If he's put something in Julio's place . . ."

"Possession?" Edmund said after a pause.

"Mm," Nathan said. "I haven't had dealings with the tribe of demons, but I've heard things over the years. This witch sounds wicked, either way. We need more strength."

"Witch fights," Deirdre whispered. "I'm just a dumb nothing." She spoke so softly Julio wasn't sure anyone was meant to hear, but he heard, and pressed her fingers. Before now, Julio had had his own dark thoughts about remaining ordinary while Edmund had changed into a witch, and Susan had changed into someone who could make the haunted house do tricks. Deirdre and Julio had stayed stubbornly normal since they had met the ghost and the house five years earlier.

Nathan heard Deirdre too, and answered. "Not so. You can be Julio's anchor."

"What does that mean?"

"This happened somewhere else, and I can't leave the house unless I make arrangements. Edmund's going to have to face the man, and Julio has to have a way of traveling. He seems to be able to propel himself through the house, but he's been here before and knows his way around. If you'll let him hang on to you, maybe he can travel with you."

"Oh. Sure, I'm up for that," Deirdre said. "It'll look weird, though, me walking around with this light storm."

"He can adjust his size."

"You can?" Deirdre asked.

I can? Julio wondered, then remembered how he had become bigger than the kitchen.

"I'll try it," he said. "Excuse me, Dee." She was the least

physically demonstrative person he knew, as uncomfortable with her gender as he was, guarded about touch. He brushed her sleeve with his free hand (*I had a thousand hands. Better have only two right now or she might get upset.*), trailed his fingers up her sleeve, across the back of her collar, under her braids, and down the other sleeve. She was wearing her big blue all-weather coat; he could tell by the tight, waterproof texture of the cloth, the way the cuffs turned up at the ends of the sleeves, and the hood that hung down her back. *Let me be part of this coat,* he thought, and melted against her back, touching fabric and binding to it without pressing against her, afraid, afraid that he might spook her or hurt her or make her mad if he touched her too hard or in the wrong place. *Just the coat.*

"Wow," she cried, holding her arms out as he spread all over her coat, clinging only to the smooth waterproof fabric, and pulling the rest of himself smaller and more dense. "So beautiful. People'll want to rip this right off of me. It's the first time I ever wore something fashionable. You don't weigh anything, Julio."

"I'm a ghost," he reminded her.

"Oh yeah," she said after a moment. "We gotta fix that."

"The wicked witch," Edmund said. "How are we going to deal with a wicked witch? I don't have much training in this witch business, Nathan." He had only been a witch for about a year, and aware of what he was for less time than that.

"Call the twins."

"They don't have much training either."

"Call the twins and then summon me."

"Oh," Edmund said. "Right. Excuse me." He snapped his fingers. Julio felt him leave: an absence of the sound of his breathing, a sense of his life energy missing.

"The twins?" asked Deirdre.

"I made three witches when I turned Edmund into a witch," Nathan said. "The twins live over the mountains in Atwell. They were here for Halloween visiting their aunt, and they decided to come to my house that night. Edmund tried to stop them, and I turned all three of them."

"Could you do that to me?" she asked.

"I don't know. It wasn't a good thing to do, Dee."

"How can you say that? He loves it. I know I would."

"Are you sure? In any case, I can't do things like that except on Halloween. I didn't even know I could do it, and I'm not sure I could do it again."

"The twins," Julio said. "I think I've met them."

"Who are these twins?" Deirdre asked.

"Tasha and Terry," said Nathan. "Since they turned into witches, they found an established witch where they live, and she's training them. Edmund trains with her too sometimes. The twins visit me. They spent part of last summer in Guthrie with their aunt, and they came over every day."

"I think I met them at Safeway," said Julio. "Black-haired, blue-eyed girls? About thirteen? Edmund introduced them to me. He didn't tell me they were witches."

"Well, he wouldn't," Nathan said. Julio heard the smile in his voice.

"Edmund and these girls are going to call you up in a séance?" Deirdre said.

"I think that would be best. It cuts my bond with the house for twenty-four hours. That way I can go with you, and help," said Nathan.

"You been in witch fights before?" Deirdre asked. Julio had

never heard her ask so many questions in a row, or get so many answers.

"Before I had friends, I fought whenever I could. There wasn't much else going on back then. It's possible the craft has changed, but I remember many useful things."

"Wow," Deirdre said, and then, "I wish Susan was here. I wonder why she's not."

"Piano lesson day," said Nathan.

"Oh. Yeah, I forgot." Julio felt Deirdre lift her arm, push her jacket sleeve away from her watch. "She oughta be here soon. How're we gonna find this wicked witch?"

"Julio should still be connected to his body," Nathan said. Julio heard the worry in his voice, a flavor like burnt sugar. "A silver string. There should be a silver string. We can follow it."

"I tried to memorize the drive on the way out of town," Julio said.

"Did you manage?" asked Nathan.

"Not very well. It was farther than I thought, on roads I never saw before."

"Maybe you can help us with direction—wait, the witches are calling me. Stay here, Dee. We'll come back." Julio sensed Nathan vanish. The interruption of energy felt much more intense than the hole Edmund had made disappearing. The house reached after Nathan, then subsided, having let a part of itself go, pulled out roots and all.

Deirdre walked over and sat on the steps, shoving her hands deep into her coat pockets. "This is spooky," she said. "Are you okay?"

"Well," Julio said, "considering everything?"

"Oh. Duh," she answered.

"I'm much better than I was. When that guy turned me into a ghost, he sent me to a horrible place. It was the worst thing I've ever been through. I never want to do that again." He shifted a little. "This is much better." Deirdre leaned against the banister, and Julio touched it, reached through its surface to the warm, tranquil, turquoise energy of the house.

"Susan's coming," the house told him.

Her footsteps sounded across the porch. The front door opened, and Susan stepped through. "Dee? Hi. What are you wearing?"

"Julio," said Deirdre. She started to laugh and then she couldn't stop. She gasped with it, clutched her stomach, almost laid her head on her knees.

"House? Nathan? Water?" Susan said.

"They're gone," Deirdre managed between gasped chuckles.

Susan touched a wall, connected to the house immediately— *I feel her*—asked the house questions, listened to answers too swift for Julio to sense, lifted her hand, walked into the kitchen, got a glass, and filled it with water. She brought it back. She sat beside Deirdre on the stairs and patted her back. Once, twice—the place on her palm where she connected with the house touched Julio, and then he connected to her in ways he never had before. Images stormed through him: a kaleidoscopic flurry of dark images about the pain of her life at home; the surge of joy she got from the first day of school, freshly sharpened pencils and blank college-lined paper, empty blackboards and the refuge of her desk; a hand-ful of sand looked at with a magnifying glass: diamonds. The sea-stone with fossils in it her aunt had given her that Susan carried in her pocket, touched in times of trouble, nearly always. Filigree of green ferns in a fog-wet wood. Julio's own face, dark and elvish and six years younger, peering down at her between the leaves of an oak tree. The taste of a chocolate milk shake, smooth and cold and sweet and heavy on her tongue, slithery down her throat. An egg-yolk yellow towel—

"Stop that!" Susan snatched her hand away from Deirdre's back, severing the connection, leaving him with a hundred small cuts on his face and hands. "What on Earth!"

Deirdre took the glass of water from Susan's hand before she dropped it, and drank. "It's Julio," she said when she could breathe without laughing. "He's kind of a ghost, and I'm being his anchor."

"Julio," Susan said. She touched him with her fingertips. He resisted the temptation to try for another deep connection. "Julio? How can that be? Are you all right?"

"In a way," he said.

"His body's somewhere else. We have to go get it and stick them back together." Deirdre sipped water. "The others will be back. We have to find the witch who cast this spell on him, and get it fixed."

Julio felt the house's energy rise, humming. The air shimmered in the front hall, and then Edmund, Nathan, and the thirteen-year-old Dane twins, Terry and Tasha, arrived: the house knew who they were by their shoes and their energies.

Nathan was present in a different way than he had been before he left: free of the house's restraints, the way he was when he was summoned in a séance. It was the only way he could leave the house except on Halloween.

Julio felt the house's frustration. With Nathan loose, it had lost a limb, wanted to reattach it, longed for it; but the house knew the rules. The house also understood it was important to let Nathan go just now for Julio's sake.

Susan stood.

"Oh, good," Nathan said. "You made it."

"I can't stay long or I'll get in trouble," she said. "How can I help?"

"If we don't get home and call you by six," Edmund said, "could you call Mrs. Clayton?" He dug a piece of paper out of his pocket and scribbled on it with a pencil stub. "Here's her number. She's a really good witch who lives in Atwell. Tell her we're in trouble and need help."

"That's only an hour and a half."

"We'll probably need her if we can't make it back by then," Edmund said. "We already tried phoning her, but she wasn't home yet."

"I can do that," Susan said. "Father won't let me answer the phone at that time of night, but call anyway. Ring once, hang up, call again."

"Yes," said Edmund.

"If I don't hear that, I'll sneak off and call Mrs. Clayton for you."

"Good."

Susan stroked Deirdre's coat again. "Julio," she whispered. "Take care. Be well." He pressed back against her hand, avoiding the house's contact place. He had known Susan longer than he had known any of the others, and treasured her in a way he couldn't put into words. "Call me when you're back together," she said.

She rose and walked out of the house, her hand trailing along the wall as she left.

Deirdre stood too, breaking Julio's connection with the house again. "Sorry," he muttered.

"Can you see the silver string, witches?" Nathan said.

"I see it," said one of the twins. She came closer. "Julio?"

Julio had walked through the supermarket with Edmund, the twins, and their aunt, talking and helping them load their shopping cart. He had liked them without knowing why.

The twins had identical features, but one of them was a tomboy, and the other one knew she was a girl. Which one was this?

She touched him on Deirdre's shoulder. Fizzing energy flowed from her touch, and he formed a mental picture. This was the girl twin.

"Tasha," he said.

Tasha stroked along Julio's skin. He felt strange—no longer human-shaped but coat-shaped, and without his usual body references. It felt like Tasha stroked warm fingertips down his spine. She touched Deirdre's chest. "Hey, hey," Deirdre said. "Not so close. I don't even know you."

"Hi. I'm Tasha. I'm a witch. Excuse me, but the silver string is right here." She pressed Julio with a fingertip and touched him on the heart. He would have shivered if he could. Tasha curled her hand around him somehow. He didn't feel it as a physical sensation; it was stranger than that, as though she had caught him by the dream. "Got it," she said.

The others closed in around them.

"Hey," said Deirdre, "who are these kids?"

"They're my witches," Nathan said. "Tasha and Terry Dane. They're helping, Deirdre. Tasha and Terry, this is my friend Deirdre. Julio I guess you already know?"

"Yep," said Terry. "Not in this form, though."

"Let's fix that. Hold hands," Nathan said. Julio felt them all shift; Deirdre linked hands, but he didn't know with whom. They pressed in around him, Nathan against his front, Edmund and Terry against Deirdre's back; he felt their clothes. Leaning against Deirdre's left arm, Tasha kept hold of him in that strangely intimate way. "Tasha, guide. Edmund, can you carry us?"

"I think so."

"I'll help," Terry said.

"Armor up," said Nathan. The three witches murmured. Julio felt iron in their words, and martial music. He could sense plates going up around them. "Let's go."

Deirdre gasped as the house slipped away from them. Julio clung to her. Even though he knew the witches had armor in place, he was conscious of the loss of his warm, safe haven, the house, aware that they were out in some space with miles below them. He felt invitations from many different voices, the songs of trees and streets and people, a magnet song from the Earth, a tidal song from the sea, calling to him and inviting him to harmonize. What if he followed them down? Maybe he could join, be part of all those different songs forever. Could anything be better than that?

Fragments of himself lifted, reached for each song they passed. "Dee," he whispered.

"Yow," she said. "Hang on, Julio. Don't go!"

He reached up past the edge of the coat and touched her face, the back of her neck. She tasted like dried sweat and determination, with a trace of chem lab.

"Okay, yeah, just don't cover my mouth. I need to breathe," she said, the song of the ordinary in her voice, and he touched the corner of her lips because in the midst of this strange blind journey he longed more than anything else to return to his ordinary self.

They brushed through a barrier, gauzy and woven with turn-back and stay-away songs; they didn't pause to listen.

Then they stopped.

Songs and energies in the air: he could feel the blank dark presence of the stranger who had kidnapped him, a pedal point on a string bass, with drum. Nearby, the younger man's viola and cello symphony posed constant questions, found no resolutions.

Julio felt an almost unbearable stirring: home cried to him, cried for him, missed him. His body thirsted for him, and he hungered to return to it.

"Wait," Nathan said before Julio could leave Deirdre and stream across to where he knew his body was. "There's someone inside it." The witches stood all around Julio and Deirdre, anyway, and their armor was still in place. Julio wasn't sure how he would get to himself.

"Who are you, my children?" The bass voice of his abductor still had music in it.

"Feed me," said another voice, this one, chillingly, Julio's own trained tenor: he could hear the discipline in it, the honey tone he never heard from inside his head. "Give them to me. Such a symphony of wonderful tastes."

"Stay," said the bass voice. "Sit."

"Woof," Julio's voice said.

Julio, hugging Deirdre, almost laughed. Who was this Other who spoke with his voice, and almost his thoughts?

"What have you done to Julio?" Nathan asked.

"It was only supposed to be temporary, but I called him and couldn't find him to switch them back." The bass voice held regret. "You are the friends he wouldn't talk about, aren't you?" Now he sounded interested, almost eager.

"Perhaps," said Nathan. "Do you know where you sent him?"

"Just over the wall. It's a discipline I often use with children who won't behave. It's temporary and leaves no permanent damage. I've never had a problem with it before."

Rage flashed through Julio, so hot Deirdre flinched. No permanent damage? He didn't think he'd be able to get that place out of his head no matter how long he lived.

He hugged Deirdre tighter. She squeaked, and he relaxed.

"But now you're here," the bass voice continued. "In a roundabout way, my interrogation worked. Apprentice, the spell we prepared—"

Nathan interrupted, in low, freezing tones, "Banish the other in him."

"I can't leave the body untenanted—"

"We brought him with us."

"Did you?" Interest quickened the deep voice. "How did you manage that? Won't you come closer?" Julio heard compulsions edge his voice. Deirdre took a step forward. Nathan, in front of her, didn't move, so she bumped into him. Séance had rendered him solid enough for her to touch. Her feet kept trying to walk.

Julio reached up past Deirdre's collar and flowed over her ears, covering the ear canals so she wouldn't be able to hear. "Hey!" she cried, clapping her hands over him.

"Don't listen," he whispered in her ear. "This guy can make you do things against your will."

"This is creepy," she muttered, "but okay."

"Cast out the other," Nathan said, his voice as pushy as the stranger's.

The stranger's voice spoke three words full of the power to push something away, then paused. "How skilled you are for someone so young," he said. "How lovely and elegant! Now, apprentice." He spoke words of power again. The young man's voice joined in, and this time Julio felt the words flow toward them like the sticky lines of a spider's web.

"Armor," Nathan said. Air hummed around them: the harmony of Edmund's voice combined with the twins', not a song, exactly, but something they did in concert, to Nathan's conducting. Julio sensed the stranger's words webbing around them, but not touching them. "Dissolve," Nathan said.

Terry's voice rose solo above the murmuring chorus of Tasha and Edmund, speaking some language Julio didn't know, the words acidic and bright. The trapping webs fell away.

"Formidable," said the stranger. His voice sounded hoarse.

"Cast out the other," Nathan said a third time.

"But I like it in here," said Julio's voice. "Nice skills! Great view! Comfortable body!"

"Promise you'll let me talk to you, and I will send it away," said the stranger.

"We didn't come here to make a deal with you," Nathan said. "Cast that thing out or I'll do it myself."

"Please do. Enlighten me."

Silence for five heartbeats. The air around Julio tightened. He remembered Nathan had said he hadn't had dealings with the tribe of demons. What if he couldn't cast out a demon? Was Julio going to spend the rest of his life as a coat?

Maybe the house would let him be a ghost in it.

There had been all those other songs he heard on the way here. He would find something to be and someplace to go.

"Thing, go home." Nathan's voice held such pushes in it that Julio felt himself responding.

"Whoa," he said, and his other voice said it simultaneously, but neither of them could stop; Julio siphoned through Tasha's hand and fled back into his body even as the other was flowing out of it.

Yes! Fingers. Toes. Arms. Legs. A stomach that growled for granola bars left behind in the music room; ears that felt clogged with wax after the clarity of the sounds he had heard while he was unhoused. He touched his tongue to the backs of his teeth, tasted ashes. Finally he opened his eyes. He smiled at his rescue party, tall, curly-headed Edmund, Nathan short and neat in his seventy-year-old clothes, the dark-haired, big-eyed twins, and in the center of them all, sturdy Deirdre in her navy blue all-weather coat.

"Thanks, you guys." Julio's voice sounded distant, and tasted swallowed and strange. He stood up and started toward his friends. Two things happened: strange spaces opened in his head, and he bumped into a wall of air. "Hey!"

"Julio?" Nathan said.

He put his palms against the wall and pushed, then felt around to find the wall's edges. It was a perfect circle, smooth and hard as glass; he was caged inside a tube. He looked down and saw the same light lines on the floor that had been there before. The blue inner circle formed the base of the wall. "What?"

Nathan strode to the silver-haired man in the chair across from Julio's. "Release him."

The man smiled faintly. "I don't think that's wise. You don't know what you've got. You haven't addressed the articles of confinement. If it can be confined by chalkwork, it's not the boy I brought here."

"Let him out."

The man sighed, glanced at his companion. The boy executed a series of hand gestures that made Julio think of porcupines.

"On your head be it," said the stranger. He too indulged in some gestures. Julio's skin prickled unpleasantly. Was it some kind of trick? Another trap?

The man reached into his pocket and fished out some blue chalk, then knelt on the floor in front of Julio and scripted marks across the circle. Nathan watched carefully.

The man sat back on his heels and glanced up at Julio. He cocked his head.

"Julio, try it now," Nathan said.

Julio stepped on the new marks and walked out of the circle, then reached out a hesitant hand, touched Nathan's shoulder. "Oh, man!" Julio said, and hugged Nathan hard. "Thank you. Thanks for everything."

Startled, Nathan laughed, and this time hugged him back. "Anytime."

Julio stepped back and held his head. There were things in his brain he hadn't seen before, unknown thoughts and nerves and muscles, strange tastes and smells and nourishment. "Man, I feel so weird," he said, but then Deirdre touched his shoulder.

"Are you okay? Are you really you? Are you okay, Julio?"

"Yes, yes, yes." He kissed her swift and sudden, startling them both. "Thanks for helping me."

Edmund stood over him, and the two witch girls, Terry the short-haired tomboy, Tasha undeniably a curly-haired girl, both of them just on the edge of adolescence. "Thanks," Julio said again.

They all turned toward the man sitting in the chair.

"I understand you were asking about us," Nathan said in a chill voice. "Any other questions?"

"Many. Who are you? Where did you come from? What are you hoping to accomplish?"

"That's none of your business. Witches, let's go home."

"Wait," Julio said. The rescue party turned. Julio went back to the armchair and retrieved the fiddle neck and the bigger pieces of the crushed violin. The ebony fingerboard hummed against his palm. "Okay," he told the others, wondering how he could hear with his hand now that he was back inside his ordinary self. Deirdre grabbed his other hand, Edmund gripped his shoulder, and they gathered close together.

A tunnel opened in front of them, and they drifted into it. Julio watched what he had not been able to see on the trip out, how the walls of the tunnel were striped and stippled with threads and flickers of color, how Nathan and Tasha reached out with phantom hands to touch, press, pull this thread or that flash of light, and then the tunnel's other end opened and let them out into the haunted house's front hall. Julio glanced back. The tunnel followed on their heels, closing behind them in a swirl of color and light.

The house looked different to him now. He could see the same surface he had seen before, old dusty boards, fraying wallpaper, a dangling lace of cobwebs, but underneath it all quiet turquoise light lay. Julio knelt and put his palm on the floor, wondering if he would be able to touch that luminescence the way he had before.

"Who are you?" the house said aloud.

All he felt under his hand was splintery board. "Julio," he said, feeling strange and sad. So he had lost the ability to link with the house the way Susan did, but why didn't the house recognize him the way it had the others, by his feet, his energy?

"Are you sure?" asked the house.

Julio rose, still holding the violin neck, trying to force sense into the question. The others stared at him now. Tasha reached out and sketched a symbol in the air with her first two fingers, and the letter flared red in the air between them. "Oh, no," she whispered.

"What does that mean?" Julio asked.

Tasha began chanting something, and he felt an invisible loop like a lasso drop around him, locking his hands to his sides. "Hey? Excuse me?" he said, as a second loop dropped over him.

"Tasha, stop it," Nathan said, but she didn't stop: she added gestures which left flaming letters and unknown words in the air. The loops dropped faster, and they burned.

Julio struggled with them, and then stood still as something else opened in his mind. A voice spoke to him, almost like his own but with dark harmonic undertones. —She's young and powerful, but she's not in complete control of her craft,—it said. —Here is how you break this spell.—

"Oh," Julio said out loud, and tried what the voice told him. A short water blade grew from his index finger, and he used it to cut through the ropes. They dropped from him. He lifted his hand and sliced through the glowing letters in the air. They fell apart.

Tasha cried out. A line of blood welled up across her right palm.

"Hey. That's not what I meant to do," Julio said, and—Who the hell are you?—he thought to the voice. It only laughed.

"What did you do to my sister?" Terry asked fiercely. "Who are you?"

"Julio," he said. "I'm sorry. I didn't know it would do that." He shook his hand, and the water blade dissolved. He walked toward them, wondering how deep the cut was. Terry pushed Tasha back and stood in front of her. Julio stopped and stared at Edmund and Deirdre. Deirdre frowned in confusion, and Edmund lifted a hand, two fingers extended. "What?" Julio said. "What?" He looked at Nathan.

Nathan smiled. "You've changed," he said.

"Into what?" He held out his arms, looked down at himself. Same five fingers on each hand (one hand still held the violin neck), same clothes he had put on in a rush that morning because he had overslept, same unmatched socks, one brown, one blue. The song of the ordinary; one of these days he should write down those notes, even though he wasn't sure anybody else wanted to hear them.

Well. There were burn marks on his T-shirt. Those lasso loops had been hot.

"Are you sure he's Julio?" Edmund asked Nathan.

"Oh, yes," Nathan said. "His core is still the same. You will have to make some adjustments. Tasha, leave him alone."

"But he," she said, clutching her hurt hand, tears in her voice.

"He didn't do it on purpose. He doesn't know what he's doing yet. Leave him alone."

"All right," she said.

"What did you just do?" Deirdre asked Julio.

"I don't know." He turned to Nathan. "Into what?" he asked again.

"I don't think there's a name for it yet," Nathan said. "I do think there are things I can teach you now."

"Please," Julio said, his heart in it.

Then he looked at Edmund, one of his best friends, and wondered if whatever had just happened had fractured their friendship. He held out his hand, and Edmund touched it, then grasped it.

Julio checked with Deirdre.

"We're not the same anymore, are we?" she said.

He licked his lip, thought about forming a water blade, whatever that was, at the end of his finger to cut through a spell, and shook his head.

"Well, if you can change . . ."

Huh. Every day they came here, in the midst of magic, and they had learned to work with and accept it, and then go home to ordinary houses. If he could change . . . "Thanks for being my anchor," he said.

"Sure," she said.

He looked at the twins.

Terry still stared at him with hostility. Tasha bit her lip. "I thought you were still possessed," she said.

"I understand that. Thanks. I never meant to hurt you."

"It's okay." She held up her hand and showed him that the wound had already scabbed over. He reached out. Green fire jumped from the end of his finger to her palm, erasing the wound.

"Whoa," he said, as startled as she was. "What?"

—We need allies,—said the voice in his head, his own voice but not his own.

Edmund dropped a hand onto Julio's head. "Julio, you in there?" he asked.

"Yes," Julio said. But he wasn't alone. He better not tell the witches yet, not until he figured out who was in here with him.

Deirdre checked her watch. "I'll go and call Susan, let her know we're okay."

"Good. We need to find out more about the wicked witch," Nathan said. "Who is he? What does he want? Why is he trying to find out about us? Will you come over tomorrow morning and help me research this?"

"All of us?" asked Deirdre.

"Everyone. If you actually talk to Susan, ask her too."

"Okay." Deirdre zipped her coat shut and headed out the front door.

"We like this guy again?" Terry asked Tasha, pointing her thumb at Julio.

"Until further notice," Tasha said.

"Okay. Bye, guy," Terry said.

"Thanks. I owe you," Julio told them.

They linked hands, smiled at him, and vanished.

"I have to go get my stuff from the music room," Julio said. He studied the broken violin. He wasn't looking forward to explaining that to Mr. Noah. He could pick up extra work and pay Mr. Noah back, though it would take forever, and it wouldn't bring back a good instrument. He already had a string of small jobs he used to finance his college fund, his car fund, his taste for fancy tennis shoes, records, cassettes, and new strings for guitar and violin. He could get some more jobs, and forget about new shoes for a while. Or maybe he could take money out of his car fund. If he lived in a dorm on a college campus, maybe he wouldn't need a car. He'd have to talk it over with his mother.

"You going to be okay?" Edmund asked.

"I don't know," Julio said.

"I'll go with you."

"Thanks." Relief warmed him. It was confusing inside his head. Edmund might be able to help.

The song of the ordinary played through his mind, but while he listened to it, trying to memorize the notes, the song of the extraordinary joined it, counterpointing, harmonizing, introducing notes of discord.

—You can sing,—he thought to the new person inside.

—I learned from you,—it answered in almost his own voice.

Chapter Five

· · · · ·

More Past

NOTHING strange happened at school. Edmund watched Julio gather his things and lock up the room and then the building. "Do you need me?" Edmund asked when they stood outside.

"I don't know," Julio said. "I know things are changing, but I don't know what I need." *I need a new violin*, he thought, looking down at the case in his hand. Inside was only wreckage. He couldn't ask Edmund for help with that, though, could he?

Why not?

What about the new person inside him, who could do so many strange things? Maybe he could help himself.

"Call if you need me. I better get home," Edmund said.

"Thanks. A lot."

Edmund punched his shoulder and vanished.

When Julio got home, his mother wasn't there yet. He set his things down and went to the piano. He checked the clock his mother had put on top of the piano to remind him that during certain hours it was okay to practice and there were others when it wasn't. Five-thirty; he'd be bothering Mrs. Hawkins, to the right. But as long as he didn't do it every day and finished up by six, she could stand it.

His fingers remembered songs he didn't immediately recognize. While they sought out music, his mind wandered.

What had just happened?

He kept drawing blanks, while his fingers found the Rachmaninoff Prelude in C# Minor, the pounding big dark piece with octaves that stamped up and down the keyboard like looming thunder.

What just happened?

—Wow. I like this noise,—something in him thought. His foot came off the damper pedal and the music rang louder and louder, something augmenting it until he lost himself in a sea of sound. He played it way too loud, ignoring all the pianissimo marks. Music crashed like surf over him, shook, swallowed, engulfed him, washed away thought and worry.

Someone shook his shoulder.

He started so wildly he fell backward off the piano bench. His head thwacked the ground. He lay on the floor and blinked up at an equally startled Mrs. Hawkins.

"I didn't mean to scare you," she said. Her face was pale as sourdough. "It was just so loud."

"I'm sorry. Guess I got carried away."

"Did you get a new piano?" She looked at the black upright, the same old chipped, overly ornamented painted wooden façade, its brass pedals tarnished except on the ends where his feet kept them polished. "How did you make all those new sounds?"

"What?" Julio slid his legs off the piano bench and sat up, rubbing the back of his head. "What are you talking about?"

"It sounded like an orchestra."

"Julio?" Mr. Marino, from the apartment down the hall, shuffled into the apartment through the door Mrs. Hawkins had apparently left open. "It's nice to know a young man with good taste in classical music, Julio, but what have we told you about the volume on your record player?"

"Record player, shmecord player," said Mrs. Hawkins. "The boy was making that noise on the piano."

—Who are these people?—

—They're the neighbors.—

"Dear lady, no one could get sounds like that from a simple piano," said Mr. Marino.

"Maybe he put in a synthesizer," Mrs. Hawkins said. She bent and peered under the keyboard. "He must've. Not there, though. Julio?"

"Yes?"

"How did you make those sounds?" She lifted the lid of the piano and stared down at the strings. "Where's the synthesizer?"

"I must confess I have a strange longing to hear the rest of the piece." Mr. Marino headed across to the little cassette-radio Julio's mother had given Julio for his sixteenth birthday, more than a year ago. "Who conducted?" He popped the lid on the cassette player, stared at the empty slot. "What? It wasn't a tape?"

"What did I tell you? The boy did it," Mrs. Hawkins said. "Why won't you ever listen to me, Emilio? Julio—"

"Are we having a party?" asked a new voice.

Julio glanced toward the door. A petite dark woman stood there, her arms around bulging grocery bags.

—Who's that?—

—My mother.—

—Mother?— Movement in his memories, not directed by himself. —Mother. Ah.— Julio found himself staring at his mother with a hunger and longing foreign to him. —Can we touch her?—

—I guess,—Julio thought. He had started shrugging off hugs when he turned twelve, embarrassed by them. But he occasionally stood still for one if there was no one around to see. He climbed to his feet and went to the door. "Let me take those, Mom," he said.

—What is all this?—asked his insider, peering at the groceries.

—Food.—

—Food. Food? Tell me. Show me. Touch her. Now.—

—Cut that out.— Julio took the bags from his mother.

"There's more in the car," she said. "*Are* we having a party?"

"Looks like you've been shopping for a party," Julio said.

"Of course. I'm catering a birthday at the Larsons' tomorrow, and you're helping, remember?"

Oh, yeah. He had forgotten he had this job. What about the meeting at the haunted house?

"Julio," said Mrs. Hawkins and Mr. Marino at the same time.

"What did you do this time?" his mother asked.

"I was playing my music too loud. I got carried away for a minute, that's all." He crossed the living room and went into the kitchen/dining room, set the grocery bags on the red kitchen counter, and headed back out.

"That's not the problem," said Mr. Marino. "You've got to play the finish now."

"I've got to get the groceries," Julio said, brushing past him.

He paused in the doorway of the apartment and hugged his mother, held her tight. After a moment she unfroze, brought her arms up, and hugged him back. She smelled so good, apple shampoo and some cooking smells and a certain spice of her own. And there was something in the shape of a hug he had never noticed before, some kind of complicated equation the insider knew that flitted through his mind and was gone before he could grasp it. He wanted to hold his mother and have her hold him for an hour or two, but she shifted and he let her go. "Julio?" she murmured, looking up into his eyes, questions in the shape of her mouth.

"Hey. Youngster," Mr. Marino said. "Come back here and show us what you were doing!"

"Things might melt." Julio pushed past his mother, dashed down the hall, and clattered down the stairs, hoping the neighbors would be gone by the time he got back. —What did you do, anyway? And who are you?—

—Who am I?—the voice asked itself while Julio lifted armloads of groceries out of the back of his mother's blue Pacer. —Not who I was,—it decided. —What's this smell?— Julio set one of the bags of groceries down and grabbed a grapefruit out of it. He sniffed the grapefruit. —It's— He found himself biting the rind. Then he yelled at its bitter taste, and the sour juices that squirted out afterward.

"Stop that!"

—It smelled so good,—said the voice in mournful tones.

"Stop doing things without asking first!"

"Julio?" His mother put her hand on his shoulder. "Who are you talking to? Are you all right?"

"No," he said, while the voice said,—Her hand is so warm

and soft. Ahhh.— "Something happened to me today and I'm all mixed up now."

"Want to talk about it?"

Alone among the four who visited the haunted house after school most days, Julio had actually talked to his mother about ghosts and magic. She worried about him, and about Susan. He didn't know if his mother believed the things he said, but she didn't challenge or deny them. She was glad to know, she said, and she could tell that whatever they were doing, it eased things for Susan, and it didn't seem to be hurting Julio. So it was okay with her.

"I think I'd like that," he said, unsure. If only he knew who the voice was, whether it had plans, what it wanted.

"Let's take these things upstairs. I did buy ice cream for the 7-Up punch. Gotta get that into the freezer." She lifted a bag, and he grabbed the rest of them, so she slammed the car door shut.

Mrs. Hawkins still stood in their apartment, her arms crossed over her chest. She frowned as they came in. "I want some answers."

"Georgia, really, we need to put supper together. Can't we talk about this later?" Julio's mother said.

"I know how slippery you are, Juanita. If I drop this now, I'll never find out what's going on."

"What a thing to say."

"How many times have we had this conversation? Quit being evasive. Talk to me now, Juanita."

"How can I? I don't know what's going on myself. Go home, Georgia. You're probably better off not knowing anyway, don't you think?"

Mrs. Hawkins frowned some more, then muttered and humphed her way out of the apartment.

—Neighbors? Are neighbors good?—

—Sometimes,—Julio thought. Most of the people who lived in their building were retired. Mrs. Hawkins used to watch him after school before his mother got home. She had given Julio his first piano lessons. Mr. Marino had let Julio play with his cats and borrow his books, had taught him chess and poker. Other people in the building had helped him, taught him, given him Popsicles in the summer, hot chocolate in the winter, jobs: grocery shopping for them, payment for caring for houseplants and cats when they traveled; he liked almost all of them and felt lucky to be living in the midst of them. Except none of them liked noise.

He followed his mother into the kitchen. They unloaded grocery bags and put things away.

"What can you tell me?" asked his mother.

"Today I got kidnapped," Julio said.

"What?" She turned toward him, dark eyes wide.

"Look," he said. He tapped his chest. "I'm okay. But this witch guy came to school and kidnapped me, all right?"

"Is this a joke?"

"No."

She stared at him some more. She touched his face, his shoulder. "All right," she said. "Then what?"

"He took me up in the mountains to some house. There was another witch up there. The man started asking me about my friends. I wouldn't answer, and he cast an evil spell on me."

She searched his face. She set down the bag of oranges and the loaf of bread she had just pulled out of a bag. She took Julio's hands in hers, led him to the dining table, settled him in one chair and herself in another, facing her. "Tell me."

"He threw me out of my body, Mom. Threw me out and put someone else in."

She squeezed his hands and leaned toward him. "Such a thing," she said. "Ay, *mijo*. Such a thing."

He looked away from her for a moment. "I went to hell, I think." —Was that hell?—he thought.

—Perhaps. It was home. All I knew before I came here.—

"You saw that place? Are you all right?"

"Do you know the place I'm talking about, Mama?"

"There's more than one place you could call that. I've never been to any of them, but I've heard about them. I studied to be a *bruja*, a *curandera*, when I was a little girl, Julio. Did I tell you that? Maybe not. It was the *nigromancia* that drove me away from it."

Julio straightened and stared at her.

"Once my master taught me to see the shadows, I saw them everywhere," she said. "I didn't want to live like that, so I turned away from it. I have been thinking that perhaps you are looking at these things. You have to make your own choices about them." She pressed his hands and released them. "So you have been to hell. Are you all right, *mijo*?"

"I don't know. I went to the place of nightmares, but I escaped with help from my friends. Then when I got back into my body, the other person who was in it left in a hurry. I think parts of him are still here."

She sat back and crossed herself. Her eyes narrowed. "He made you bite a grapefruit," she said.

"He played the music they were talking about."

"The music. He is the one who hugged me, yes?"

Julio nodded.

She straightened. For a long time she stared at the ceiling and tapped her lips with her index finger. She swallowed twice. Her hands closed into fists. At last she said, "Can I talk to him?" Cement edged her voice.

Julio bit his lower lip. —Will you talk to her?—

—Of course.—

"Go ahead," Julio said to them both.

"You, inside my son. What's your name?"

"I can't tell you my name. That would be foolish." His voice sounded the same as Julio's, though his vocabulary and accent were a little different. How was Julio's mother going to know this stranger was real?

"Make one up," she said.

"Tabasco."

Juanita laughed, startled.

—Where'd you get that?—Julio thought.

He glanced at the counter, saw the bottle of Tabasco sauce, part of the groceries they hadn't put away yet.

—You can read?—Julio asked his insider.

He got a mental image of the stranger settling into his mind as though it were a comfortable recliner. —Lots of good stuff I can use in here,—it said. —Skills. Memories. Information.—

—Use for what?— This was the crux of the problem.

—Whatever we want to do next,—Tabasco thought.

—We, huh?— Julio wondered how he could trust this stranger.

"What do you want with my son?" asked Julio's mother.

"I just want to stay here instead of going back," said the insider. "I don't want to live in hell any more than Julio did."

"Does this mean you never actually left me? I thought Nathan drove you out," Julio said.

A moment's silence drifted by. "I don't know," Tabasco said. "I did feel myself being scooped out and pushed away. Banished. I lost you. As soon as you got here, though, I woke up again. But I'm not my whole self. Much of me is missing. I'm less than I was: less angry, less mean, less hungry, less strong." He felt his left forearm with his right hand, then checked out his right shoulder, touched his face. "I'm shaped like you. I know I am. I'm not myself, but I'm not entirely you either."

"That stuff you made me do before. The water knife. The green fire. The music."

Tabasco waited. "What about it?" he asked at last.

"How could you do that stuff?"

"How could you not?"

"What things are those, *mijo?*" Juanita asked.

Julio held up his hand, stared at it. He crooked his index finger, remembering the blade that came from it to slice magical bonds, green fire that flared from it to heal a cut on Tasha's hand. —Can you do that stuff whenever you want to?—he thought.

—Sure. You want me to now?—

—I don't know.—

—Hey. Watch this.— Julio watched as both his hands rose. He rubbed his thumbs across the tips of his fingers, and colored flames whooshed up, green, orange, blue, red, yellow, cool flickering light flaring almost to the ceiling.

"Stop!" cried Juanita.

Julio rubbed his palms across each other, and the flames vanished. "Didn't hurt anything," said Tabasco. "Just for pretty."

"You some kind of *diablo*? *Demonio*?"

"Maybe."

"What you going to do to my boy? You going to hurt him?"

"Hurt him? Hurt my home?" Tabasco settled deeper into Julio's skin, muscles, organs, veins, arteries, down to the marrow of his bones. He melted into the folds of Julio's brain. "Of course not. I will do everything I can to keep us safe."

"You better not hurt my son in any way," said Juanita. "You do anything that hurts my boy and I will call back everything I know about your kind and how to control them. I will know what to do to you. Do you understand?"

—Can she do anything to us?—

—She never lies. Unless she's teasing. She's not teasing now,—Julio thought. He could not figure out where his allegiance lay. With his mother, who wanted to protect him? He wanted to be safe. With this new half person inside him, who offered strange powers and wonders such as he had longed for? He couldn't side with Tabasco against his mother; could he side with his mother against Tabasco? He hoped he would never have to. —Do you mean harm to anyone?—

—Do I?— Julio felt Tabasco's thoughts kindle until the flames in them burned white-hot. —Oh, yes. He who called and controlled me. Oh yes. I would harm him if I could.—

"Julio!"

Julio blinked. He smelled burning wood, and saw that the kitchen table smoked where his hands lay on it. He snatched his hands away and looked at smoking black handprints against the white paint, seared down into the wood. "Sorry." He stared at his palms. They looked normal.

"Who's apologizing?" asked his mother.

"It's me, Julio. I wondered if he wanted to hurt anybody, and he said, yeah, the guy who controlled him. Same guy who tossed me out of my body. Not you or me. Got him kind of worked up."

Juanita's eyes kindled with black fire. "I'd like to get my hands on that man myself."

For a moment she and Tabasco exchanged fiery stares, in perfect accord. Juanita turned away first. She studied her burnt kitchen table. "It's pretty," she said. "Can you do that all around the edge?"

Julio frowned and consulted his insider. "Oh, sure. No problem. Would it be practical, though? I could just paint over it." He ran his fingers over the charred spots. They did dip down a little, and they weren't smooth.

"Make the pattern and then we can shellac over it. Hey, Tabasco, maybe you could go into furniture design. Let's do some yard sales on Saturday, Julio. See what we can pick up for cheap. Refinish things and sell them to a gallery, maybe."

"Okay." Julio smiled and leaned on his hands on the table. Now that he was paying attention, he felt the heat kindle in his hands and eat down into the wood. He could even taste the char, pleasant, smoke-flavored. He moved along the table, curling his hands, sometimes spreading the fingers, experimenting, at least until the smoke alarm went off.

At its startling, ear-piercing squawk, Tabasco clapped his hot hands to his ears. For an instant Julio felt searing pain on the sides of his head, and he smelled burning hair. Then something in him shifted, and the pain vanished.

"Stupid thing." Juanita got up on a chair, pulled the cover off the smoke alarm, and took the battery out of it. The squawking stopped.

—If we're going to be what we are, we need some protection,—Tabasco thought. Green flame flared over all of Julio's exposed skin, tickled inside his shirt, pants, and socks.

"What are you doing?" Juanita asked.

Julio's hand rose. Flame green as pine needles streamed from his hand and enveloped her. At first she cried aloud. Then she looked down at her flickering arms through the film of flame on her face, and said, "Oh! It doesn't hurt. What is it?"

"Protection. So I won't burn you by mistake," said Tabasco. "Fire is my element, and it acts wilder here than it did where I came from. This world is much more fragile." He sketched some signs with Julio's first two fingers, and the flame flickered out. He touched his ear, felt the singed ends of hair, which left smudges on his fingertips. "There's so much I don't know yet."

"Tell me when you have a plan like that," said Juanita. "Before you actually do it. Okay? I need a chance to say no."

"All right," said Tabasco. Julio said: "Impulse control isn't his strong suit."

"*Por dios*," muttered Juanita. "Please make teaching him that a priority, *mijo*."

"I'll try," Julio said. "*Da me un beso*," Tabasco said.

Juanita gave him a quick kiss, then looked puzzled. Tabasco touched the spot on his cheek and smiled at her.

· · · · ·

JULIO fried grilled cheese sandwiches while Juanita made a salad from romaine lettuce, green peppers, shredded cheese, diced tomatoes, red onion, and sunflower seeds.

—What are these smells?— Tabasco leaned close to the frying pan, sniffing at the golden fried bread and melting cheddar cheese.

—Cut that out. It's dinner. You'll get a chance to taste it soon enough.—

—I want it now.— He reached into the hot pan and broke off a piece of sandwich.

"Yow!" Julio yelled in reflex, shaking his hand before he realized he didn't feel any pain. "Huh?"

—Give me.— Tabasco shoved the corner of sandwich into their mouth and chewed. —Oh! Wonderful!—

For a moment Julio was staggered by the everyday tastes of melted cheese and toasted bread, the pleasant heat and texture of it, the satisfying feel of chewed food sliding down his throat. His whole body went alert with delight.

"Now what?" asked Juanita.

Tabasco grabbed the rest of the sandwich out of the pan. "Stop it," Julio said. "Put that back."

"Want more."

"Put it down. Quit grabbing!"

"I'm starving."

"Julio?"

Julio stood with the sandwich in his hand and listened to his stomach grumble. How long had that yawning pit in his middle been signaling to him? "Mom, I'm sorry," he said, and ate the rest of the sandwich. "I'm sorry," he repeated between bites. Every bite tasted as wonderful as the first. He could tell Tabasco was already contemplating what else to eat.

His mother watched him.

"I'm sorry," Julio said a final time after he had licked his fingers. "He doesn't listen very well, and I was so hungry all of a sudden." He slid the second sandwich, already built and waiting, into the pan. —Don't you dare touch this one,—he thought. —It's for Mom.—

"Terrible manners," Juanita said.

"I know. I'm sorry."

"And you reached into a hot frying pan. Let me see your hand."

Julio held out his hand, and his mother looked at it, then turned it over and examined the back. She glanced at him, her eyebrows lowered into a frown.

"I guess that green fire made it so I don't burn."

"Did that work on me too?" She held a hand out toward the pan, edged her finger closer and closer and finally touched the edge. She waited a moment, then lifted her finger and looked at its untouched tip. "Fabulous," she said.

"I need more food," said Tabasco, one hand on his stomach.

"Really and truly?" Juanita asked him.

"I'm starving," he said.

She got a spatula and flipped the sandwich over. "Sit at the table."

He sat and studied the burned black handprints edging the table. A minute later she put the sandwich on a plate and brought it to him, handed him a knife and fork. "Tabasco, we need some rules."

"Yes, *Mamacita*."

Her eyes widened.

—What are you . . .—Julio thought. He hadn't called his mother that in years.

—I don't know,—Tabasco thought.

"If you don't follow the rules, people will think something's wrong with you. If they think something's wrong with you, they'll watch you, waiting for the next mistake you make. Make too many mistakes, and they won't let you be friends with them; they'll treat you like an outsider. They might even cast you out entirely. They won't be nice about it. *¿Comprendes?*"

"*Sí, Mamacita.*"

"We are social creatures. We need to live in groups. Julio knows all these rules already, Tabasco. Listen to him. Learn them. You need them to survive here. You got that?"

"*Sí, Mamacita.*"

"Start now. Use a knife and fork to eat. Julio will show you."

"All right." —Julio?—

Julio felt Tabasco's control relax, and he took back his hands. He gripped the knife and fork and just held them for a moment, despite the clamor of his stomach. He didn't like this battle. Tabasco seemed to have no problem shoving Julio aside and doing whatever he wanted with the body. All very well to be impervious to flame, and some of that other stuff was really cool, but—

—Please,—thought Tabasco. —Please, let's eat.—

Julio cut a bite from the sandwich and put it in his mouth, conscious for the first time in a long while of each separate action involved. He chewed carefully and swallowed before he cut the next bite. He felt Tabasco watching as though his life depended on it. They ate half the sandwich in silence, savoring each bite. Julio could feel how it fed him: a flare of strength flowing into his arms and legs, ease lighting his actions. He had never felt like this before. He liked it, and he knew it came from Tabasco.

Still . . . "I'm not showing you manners to make it easier for you to run things," Julio said.

"Yes, you are."

"No. This is my life, not yours."

"Ours."

"Don't fight. You're doing very well," Juanita said. She sliced cheese for a third sandwich. "How hungry are you?"

"It's going away now," Julio said, but he ate the rest of his sandwich. "Why was I so hungry?"

"Burning uses lots of energy," answered Tabasco. "Sometimes you get it back from what you burn, like the table gave us some, but the green fire, that came out of me. Have to put something back afterward."

Julio set the knife and fork down on his empty plate.

"Do you need more?" asked Juanita.

"No. Thank you."

"Which of you said that?"

"Me. Tabasco."

"I wish your voices were different so I could tell who was talking." She set the third sandwich on a plate and brought it to the table, sat down, and began to eat.

"I could do that," Tabasco said in a deeper voice, and almost on top of his remark, Julio said, "No, that would be trouble if it happened in public. Let's not start."

Surprised, Juanita laughed.

A knock sounded at the door.

For a moment, Juanita and Julio stared at each other. Then Juanita said, "I bet it's Georgia, demanding answers."

"I'll get it." Julio pushed himself to his feet.

He opened the apartment door and looked up into the silver-gray eyes of his captor.

"Mom," he said. He tried to slam the door shut, but he couldn't let go of the doorknob. When he looked, he saw that the knob had melted into slag around his hand.

The man stepped past him into the apartment. "You will come with me."

"I will not."

"Who are you and what do you want with my son?" Juanita asked, from the kitchen threshold. She had a knife in her hand.

"Mom, call Edmund," said Julio. "This is the kidnapper guy."

Chapter Six

. . . . .

Yet More Past

JUANITA whirled and headed back toward the kitchen.

"Wait, *Mamacita*. Don't call anyone," Tabasco said. Julio felt his lips stretch into a smile.

She glanced at him and disappeared around the corner.

"Come," said the stranger.

Julio's skin prickled. He felt the compulsions, the deep song under the voice that spoke to his muscles instead of his brain. Fire rose in his mind and burned through the music before his muscles could respond.

—The doorknob,—he thought. Tabasco thought something at it and it melted again, off of his hand and back into a vaguely circular and useful shape. He let go of it.

"I wouldn't stay here if I were you," Julio said. His hands felt hot, and he knew Tabasco planned big burning.

The man began to chant. Julio had to admire the rise and fall of his voice: beautifully trained and effective. Before he could appreciate it too much, though, Tabasco did something to his ears, and he went deaf.

—What?—he asked, alarmed.

—He's saying the articles of confinement,—Tabasco thought. —If we could hear them, we would have to obey. I remembered what you did with the Deirdre girl. Look how well it works.— He smiled, and raised his hands. Hot white fire glowed around them.

Strange, living in a soundless world, even the small intricate tangled song of breath gone. Terrifying. The loss of everything Julio loved.

The man's mouth moved. His eyes widened as Tabasco reached toward him. "Please," Julio said, and couldn't hear his own voice, "please go away before I touch you." He had to trust that his voice worked: he could feel it in his throat. He fought to keep from grabbing the man with his burning hands, even though a fierce, wild part of him really wanted to see this guy burn and die. Tabasco pushed, Julio resisted. —Don't force me. You know what that's like,—Julio thought.

—He'll get away. He'll only cause more trouble. If we take care of him now, we will be safe.— Julio's hands disappeared in a haze of white heat, but Tabasco stopped pushing them toward the man.

"Go," Julio said again. "Get out of here."

The gray eyes stared into his. The man nodded once, then turned and strode out of the apartment, closed the door behind him.

Julio breathed as though he had just run a race. He stared at his hands. They went from white to yellow to orange to red, and then the light died out of them and they looked normal again. He leaned his back against the door, still panting, wiped his forehead with the back of his hand, then looked up.

Edmund stood with Juanita in the doorway to the kitchen. His mouth moved.

—My ears! Tabasco . . .—

Something clicked in his head, and his hearing returned. Relief washed through him. He wasn't sure he could endure permanent deafness.

"You okay? Julio, you okay?" Edmund asked, as he crossed the room.

"I—I'm starving."

"I'll make more sandwiches," said Juanita, and turned back to the kitchen.

"What did you do? What did that guy do to you?" Edmund glanced over his shoulder toward the kitchen. "Your mother knows about this stuff?"

"Oh yeah. Much better that way. So glad we talked it over before that guy showed up. Oh, man." Julio's insides cried out for something to burn. He pushed away from the wall and stumbled toward the kitchen. Edmund put his arm around Julio's shoulders and helped him upright.

"Whoa. Redecorating," Edmund said, staring at the hand-printed table in the kitchen as he helped Julio sit down, then took a seat beside him.

Juanita set a plate of pan dulce in front of Julio. He grabbed one of the pastries and stuffed it into his mouth. It felt as though it burnt up inside him before it even reached his stomach. He ate two more before he could slow down. —Really bad manners, — he thought.

—I understand, —Tabasco thought. —We need this now. —

"Sorry, Mom," Julio said.

"It's all right." Another grilled cheese sandwich fried in the pan, and Juanita stood at the refrigerator, studying small plastic containers. "Does it matter what you eat? There's some rice from last night."

"Sounds great."

She set a container full of red rice and a spoon in front of him, and he ate, feeling strength come to him from the food. By the time he finished the rice, the sandwich was ready, and he could feel the hunger slowing inside. The sandwich tasted as great as the first two had, a complex of textures of air-chambered, fiber-woven bread and smooth melted cheese.

Juanita said, "Edmund? Anything you'd like? Do you get hungry like that when you use powers?"

Edmund glared at Julio.

"I never told her anything about you," Julio said.

"Tonight I called you on the phone, and you appeared here a second later," said Juanita. "One can only speculate."

"I think my powers work differently from Julio's, whatever his are. I just had dinner, and I'm fine, thank you."

Julio slid the plate of pan dulce over in front of Edmund.

"Oh, okay. Thanks." He picked up a pink one.

"You need another sandwich, *mijo?*" Juanita asked. She poured milk into glasses and set them in front of Julio and Edmund.

Julio consulted his stomach. "Maybe I better. Thanks, Mom."

"We still have salad, too. Tabasco, do you eat like this all the time? If you do, Julio needs to get more jobs." Another sandwich went into the frying pan.

"I don't know yet, *Mamacita*. Everything here is new."

"Guess we'll have to see. We are now officially out of cheese." She brought the bowl of salad to the table and set it in the center. She dished some onto her plate. "All right. Now tell us what happened."

"That man can say words that control Tabasco," Julio said.

"Who's Tabasco?" asked Edmund.

"Tabasco is my second son," Juanita said.

Julio felt heat spark and race through him as he stared at his mother, felt his heart melt and change. Warmth glowed under his skin. Tabasco had fallen in love.

"Second son," repeated Edmund.

"My second son is inside my first son."

Edmund set his half-eaten pan dulce down and stared at Julio.

Julio swallowed. Out of everything that had happened tonight, his mother's acceptance might be the most surprising. He thought about the horrible moment when he had wondered whom he might have to fight, his mother or his new tenant. His—brother? Maybe he wouldn't have to fight either of them. If Tabasco would listen to Juanita and follow her rules—

"So, go on," Juanita said.

"There's something called articles of confinement," Julio said. "It's some kind of magical slavery, and that guy could use these articles on Tabasco and control everything he does, and now, I guess, that guy could use them on me too."

"But they didn't work." Juanita got up and flipped the sandwich.

"I went deaf instead. Tabasco fixed it."

She stared at him.

"Temporarily. That shielded us. We couldn't hear, we didn't have to obey. I hope I drove him away. Did he look scared?"

"Not scared, exactly, but resigned." She smiled at him for a second, then looked serious. "Good thing I disabled the smoke alarm already."

"Did I burn something else?" He glanced toward the living room.

"Not seriously. The paint was blistering. You must have done something to protect your clothes, eh, *mijo*?"

Julio checked his black T-shirt. It looked untouched. "Sure," said Tabasco, "when I fireproofed myself, I guess I got the clothes too."

"We have to get this under control," Julio said. "What if I burn things in my sleep? Can't let that happen, Tabasco. Everything here is important. There are lots of people living here. No burning in the house unless we're in danger."

"I understand."

Both voices came out of his mouth. It felt confusing from the inside, and was probably even more confusing from Edmund's and Juanita's perspectives. He glanced at his mother.

Juanita took his plate, put another sandwich on it and set it in front of him. She kissed his forehead, ruffled his hair. "It's going to be hard, *mijo*, but you can learn it." She sat down again and took a bite of salad.

"Mrs. Rivera," Edmund said.

"Edmund."

"How can you—" He paused, then began again. "Do you know who this Tabasco person is? What it is?"

She studied Julio. He sat back and met her gaze. He wondered if he would have to fight his best friend Edmund now. The thought depressed him.

"I understand your concern," Juanita said slowly. "Will he hurt Julio? Will he hurt someone else? What does he want? What can he do?" She lowered her eyelids, then turned to look at Edmund. "I think he's just a baby, my second son. I think he wants to be good. I think we give him that chance, if it's all right with Julio."

Julio had been alone in his head all his life up to now, except for one time when Nathan jumped into Julio's body to protect himself from someone who thought it was his job to lay ghosts to rest. Did Julio know enough about Tabasco to decide whether to let him stay? It didn't matter. He had already decided. Tabasco gave him talents and friendship and power. Julio touched a singed handprint on the kitchen table. "I want him to stay," he said. "We have a bunch of things to work on, but I think it's going to be okay."

—Good,—thought Tabasco.

—You weren't about to leave anyway, were you?—

—I would try very hard not to. Between your skills and mine, I think we could wage a formidable fight.—

—Fighting each other? Or fighting other people?—

—Fighting other people. Let's not fight ourselves.—

Julio felt his shoulders relax. —Let's not!—

He felt himself smile, and didn't know which of them was doing it.

"Okay," Edmund said. His voice was thin with doubts.

Julio touched his arm. "Hey. Thank you for coming so fast. That was great."

"Anytime." Edmund smiled and stood up. "See you tomorrow." He disappeared.

"Eshue Shiaka," said Tabasco.

"Pardon me?" Juanita asked.

"Eshue Shiaka. That's my real name."

"Eshue Shiaka," Juanita said.

Julio shuddered. He felt her words all the way down to his bones. What did *that* mean? —All she has to do is say your name . . . and then what?—

—Then she may control me.—

"Thank you, *mijo*," said Juanita.

"*De nada, Mamacita.*"

"Oh, no, it's not nothing. I know that." She smiled. "Finish your dinner. We have a lot to do tonight."

THEY spent several hours preparing snack-food trays and baking cookies and a cake for Charity Larson's sweet sixteen party.

Juanita's major income came from housekeeping, with catering as a sideline. She also did mending and alterations. Occasionally she made clothes. She had taught Julio as many of her skills as he would sit still for, and when he helped her with jobs, she sometimes paid him, depending on the bills that month. He helped as much as he could.

Tabasco lay quiet inside Julio while they cooked. He pretended not to be there, except when Julio ate a broken chocolate chip cookie. Chocolate made him stop what he was doing, close his eyes, and vanish into the taste. Dark, smooth, bittersweet, it touched his tongue like nothing else had.

"You okay?" Juanita asked him after a minute.

He opened his eyes, blinked away tears. "Chocolate," he said. She leaned closer, studied him, then smiled. "Ah."

Strangest of all, he didn't want any more just then. It seemed too special to eat like other foods.

They finished around midnight. Julio figured it had been the longest day of his life, but when he lay in bed with the lights out, he knew it wasn't over yet.

—Why didn't the house know me?—Julio wondered.

Tabasco moved through his memories, found the one he was worrying about: that afternoon, when Julio went back to the house in his body after being there without it. —I made you different.—

—The house always knew me before, Tabasco. How different am I? I don't want to be so different my friends don't know me.—

—The ghost knows you.—

Julio scratched his nose, scratched the front of his left leg with the calluses on his right heel, and thought about this. Nathan hadn't doubted he was himself, even though the house and the witches had worried.

—The house and the ghost are parts of each other,—Julio thought, something he hadn't really understood until the house let him all the way into it. —Why would the ghost know something when the house doesn't?—

—I don't know.—

Julio sat up in the darkness and looked out his window. Across the street, a new apartment house was going up. For as long as he could remember, Julio had been able to see all the way to the ocean from his bedroom window, but soon his view would be gone. Already the skeleton of the new building laid a black barred silhouette across the distance.

—Edmund acted pretty strange to me, too.—

—What do you want to do about it?—

Julio stared into distance for a long time and thought. Edmund had changed suddenly too, a year ago. Most noticeably, his voice had changed, so that he couldn't even speak without making people turn around to stare at him. He hadn't liked that at all.

Had their friendship changed then? How had Edmund handled it?

Julio had never thought that Edmund had changed into someone else. He was still just Edmund, with a few added frills and some interesting new problems. The situation wasn't parallel.

Julio had helped Edmund train himself to talk more normally, to fuzz the edges of his clarity and to tone down the music in his voice, even though it hurt to lose that glorious sound. When Edmund was trying, he could blend okay now.

—We already decided not to change the voice,—Tabasco said.

—The less we change, the sooner we get back to acting just the way I used to, the less anybody will remember that you're here.—

Julio felt flickers of unease and apprehension. They didn't come from him.

—All right, what's the problem?—

—Do you really want to make me disappear?—

—No!— Then Julio thought, *What am I asking? Ask anybody to pretend they're invisible, and it's the next best thing to asking them to leave. Is that what I want?* —I don't want people looking at me funny, or being scared of me, or noticing me in any way that they don't already. I don't want that Tasha girl thinking I'm some kind of monster. I don't want the house to think I'm a stranger. I don't want Mom to worry. *And* I want you to stay with me. Is this possible?—

Tabasco was silent for a long, long time. Julio thought, *Okay, maybe everything has to change now. Well, of course it does. I do have to turn into someone else. Maybe even someone people will notice. Okay. Okay. I can work with that. Just because I want everything to be the same doesn't mean it will be. This is my brother I'm talking to. I have to give him some room. Did I ask for him? No. Do I know him? Not very well. Do I want him to stick around? Hey. He gives me magic! He wants to work with me! He's trying to learn how to be human! I like him! What's my problem? I'm so stupid.* He was just about to say this when Tabasco interrupted:

—I have something to show you.—

A sheet of air in the room fluoresced, turned deep, velvet, larkspur purple. Faint piano notes, three octaves struck at once, sounded, and then a second triad of notes a half step lower sounded as ice blue spiked through the purple, left a wake. A third triad, three octaves at once, dropped down deep, sustained for six beats, a shock of black. The Rachmaninoff prelude. Then came the attack, dense triplets, syncopation: red fireworks, orange streaks, dots of turquoise and splashes of lilac, appearing and vanishing at the strike of each note, and when the deepest note struck again, black flashed through the whole tapestry—

The first four measures of the piece—

The colors flickered out. The notes faded.

Julio blinked at darkness. The hair on his arms and the back of his neck stood on end, and ice chips danced on his spine. Strange shadings of image and thought had flickered through his mind in response to color and sound, a distillation of feelings he couldn't name.

He didn't understand his response. He knew it was strong, and closer than ever to what he wanted to get from music.

—Forget everything I just said. I'm an idiot,—he told Tabasco.

—That's not . . .—

A knock sounded on the door.

"Come in." Julio reached over to turn on the bedside lamp.

His mother, wearing a red bathrobe, slipped into the room and sat beside him on his bed. "Are you all right? I heard music."

"I tried to keep it quiet," Tabasco muttered.

"It wasn't loud, it was just there." She glanced around. The cassette player was out in the living room. The radio alarm clock beside his bed was off. "Where did it come from?"

—Can you do that again?—Julio asked.

—I think so.—

"Mom." Julio took Juanita's hand. "Watch this."

They waited a moment, and then the shimmering sheet of midnight air flickered into sight as music struck; colors shot through, shapes flashed and vanished, notes followed each other—

—Stopped.

She sat silent for a long time, staring at the air where the colors had appeared, then turned to him, her eyes wide. "What was it?" she whispered.

"It's his art."

She rubbed her eye. "It was beautiful, *mijo*."

"Thank you," Tabasco said. Julio sensed his confusion.

"We're trying to figure out how to live together," Julio said after a little while, "and all I could think of was to ask him to pretend he's not even there, but that's not fair. He has things to say too."

She pulled her hand out of his and cradled his head between her hands, stared into his eyes, her own searching, dark, soft. "You're both inside one head. Maybe just be the same person."

Julio looked back at her. "I don't understand."

"And maybe I don't know what I'm talking about." She leaned forward and kissed his forehead. "Thank you for showing me the music. I'll see you tomorrow. We have setup at eleven at the Larsons'."

"Okay." His stomach growled. "Ouch! Again? I'm going to get some toast, Mom."

"Oh dear," she said. "*Now* you eat like a growing boy." She used to tease him all the time about his height, until they both realized he probably wasn't going to get any taller than five-foot-three. She was short herself, five feet. She had never told him anything about his father's height, or any of his father's features. All he knew about his father was that he was gone. "Good night, *mijo*."

He was definitely going to need more jobs to support his fire habit.

He got up and dressed, then went to the kitchen and fixed toast. It only took three pieces to fill the hunger Tabasco's art had created. He sat for a while at the kitchen table. He touched the toast crumbs with the tip of his finger, and they burned, charred to ash. He could taste them, a strange sensation coming from his finger: charcoal, crispy, delicious.

Too weird!

Should he go back to bed? No. He still had questions.

He checked the crack under his mother's door and saw the light was out. She'd had a long day too. Chances were good that she was asleep. He slipped out of the apartment as quietly as he could and walked the deserted streets of the little beach town.

Streetlights silvered the fog, glistened on everything dewed by the ocean's nearness. The air smelled of salt, woodsmoke, cold. Julio buried his hands in his jean pockets and hunched his shoulders. He had thrown on a windbreaker at the front door, but it was cold out tonight.

Then it wasn't.

He lowered his shoulders. —What happened?—

—You don't like being cold? Why be cold?—

—What?— He remembered burning handprints into the kitchen table and thought,—Oh.— He had an internal heater now so hot it could melt metal. Why be cold?

A cop car cruised past, and he faded into a shop doorway. At the next corner he turned west, off the main highway through town, closer to the beach. Three blocks farther along, he came to the haunted house.

The fog caught light from the city and held it above him, diffuse, but making things dimly visible. A guard light on a pole in a neighbor's driveway cast light on the weatherworn fence around the yard.

Julio put his hands on the gate, remembered how the house had let him slip under its surface before so that he could sense, somehow, people coming, air temperature, weather, time of day, other things. "House?"

The gate opened. He threaded his way past the attack blackberry bushes in the front yard and walked up the front steps to the porch, then stood there for a couple of minutes. He crossed the porch and sat down with his back to the wall and his palms to the floor. "House," he said.

"Julio."

"You know it's me this time?"

"I do."

"When you let me be part of you, before? That was—I loved that."

"I, too."

"When I came back and you didn't know me . . ." Julio felt again that sense of strangeness and loss, a despair all the deeper because the house had been so welcoming when he needed it the most.

"But you *were* someone else, Julio."

"Who am I now?"

"Julio-eshue."

Tabasco startled inside him.

"Julio-eshue-shiaka," murmured the house in low tones. The wall he leaned on ran fingers up his back, and his hands sank into the surface of the porch.

He felt the warm turquoise surround his hands. He stared, confused, at his wrists where they disappeared into wood. "House?"

"You want to come back inside?"

"Can I do that when I'm still inside myself?" He tried wiggling his fingers. They didn't move. Yet it didn't feel as though they were trapped in wood, more as if he had no outside edges and had melted into the house's energy.

"I don't know," said the house.

This was so strange. "Nathan?" Maybe Nathan would understand more about this, or at least tell him what was going on.

"Nathan's gone for the night."

Oh. The séance. It gave Nathan a whole day and night free of his bond to the house, and he would probably spend it with whoever had broken the circle at the séance. Julio wondered which witch, then decided there was no way to know unless he asked them. "House, are you mad at me?"

"No," said the house. "I just want to eat you."

"What?" Julio laughed. Then he looked down at his wrists, swallowed by the wood.

—What does it want?—Tabasco wondered. —Does it want to hurt us?— Julio felt fire flare under his breastbone: Tabasco, prepared to burn. —It knows my name.—

"Julio." Wood crept up over his shoes, his ankles, up around his butt toward his waist; his forearms sank into it now. "Hey, Julio. Want to come inside?"

"What—" The house swallowed him slowly. He watched the tide of wood rise up his legs, leaving his knees as diminishing islands, up his abdomen, up his arms. Or was he sinking into it? He should have fallen through the porch by now, but there was no thud of his feet hitting the ground below; instead, all of him under the wood's surface had lost its sense of touch. He didn't feel numb, exactly. All he felt was warm.

The wood rose to his chin, and stopped. "Julio?"

He couldn't feel his arms and legs at all. His body had vanished from his awareness. His perspective was strange. This must be what the world looked like to a short cat. He could see the splintery grain in the floorboards stretching away from him, dimming with distance. If anybody came up the stairs right now, he'd be staring at their shoes.

"Uh," he said. "Yeah. Sure. Okay."

He closed his eyes before the wood rose up to them.

And then he was as big as a house.

His nerves spread through frayed and frazzled wiring; shingles covered some of his skin like dragon scales; boards were his bones and every room was like a lung; old pipes were his circulatory system, umbilically connecting him to the town water system, and other pipes acted as intestines, carrying waste away; his concrete feet foundations sank down into the sandy earth. The hearth was the house's heart. Its walls were full of secrets, memories, magic. Shadows of the house it had been lurked everywhere, only waiting to be summoned into solidity. Again, Julio's sense of himself spread out from the house, through the blackberry bushes and under the ground to the fence, under the sidewalk and halfway across the street.

Yet he knew he wasn't alone; he and Tabasco were exploring their new body together, and there was a shadow behind them, like a big brother or sister walking beside a kid on a bicycle that still had training wheels.

Warmth, and welcome, and a host of strange sensations that the house knew how to interpret. —You're here,—the house said.

—I noticed.—

—It worked! I ate a boy. I never did that before, except for Nathan, and he was already dead.—

—Did you want to?—

—Sometimes.— It sounded cheerful. —Some special people.—

—Now that you ate me, does that mean I have to stay here the rest of my life?—

The house didn't answer. Julio tested his new senses and wondered what his mother would say if he didn't show up to help her cater the Larson party. How was he going to tell her what had happened to him? She wasn't going to be happy. He wasn't sure he was, either, but it had seemed rude to ask the house to let him loose while it was eating him, and something in him had wanted to be eaten. Why? He couldn't think about that now. Worse came to worst, he could get Edmund to take Juanita a message. . . .

But this was so ridiculous. He couldn't take it seriously yet.

There wasn't much of this new self he could move. House could open and close its doors and windows. What about that? Julio enlisted Tabasco's aid, and they eased into the hinges of the front door, feeling transitions from wood to metal, panel to screw to hinges. How to slide one surface across another, get it to move? —How do you move anything without muscles?—Julio wondered.

Tabasco said,—It's easy; tickle the magic in it.— He demonstrated.

The door creaked open.

The house laughed.

They tried tickling different places in the house. It made all three of them laugh. Doors and cupboards and drawers slid open and shut. Julio remembered places to explore, and Tabasco figured out how to get them to work. Eventually Julio recognized that the house had a whole nonphysical nervous system, a neural network of magic, with nodes where nerve paths concentrated, a woven web of turquoise light.

—Hold still, now, Julio-eshue,—the house thought, and stretched him out, gently but firmly, until he felt like a snakeskin pinned to a board.

—What are you doing to me?—

—Studying you.—

—Why? It hurts.— His edges prickled and stung, salt along the rim of a wound.

—Not much longer,—thought the house, probing him.

It stirred something and scrambled his thoughts. He had the image of egg white, egg yolk, mixing together to form a new color of yellow in a frying pan.

Confusion swamped him. For a while, he couldn't hook one thought to the next.

To coax fire from something that doesn't burn, skorleta, he thought, and would have shaken his head if he had one. The memory of biting a candy apple, the hard red shell cracking between his teeth, its cinnamon taste mixing with the crisp wet tartness of a green Granny Smith apple. Water knife. Guitar quicha. Tickle magic. Skaks bread. Music fire. Work with—

The house released him. He lay gasping on the front porch, pulled in acres of air and panted them out again. "What was that?" he asked when he could use his breath for talking.

"Eshulio."

"What? What?" He sat up, held his hands in front of him, turned them palms up, then palms down. Hands. Right. They looked right. He touched the porch, gingerly, and felt skin instead of woodgrain under his palms. He pressed a little harder, and his hand melted into the wood. He pulled back, slowly, until hand parted from porch with a faint kiss. "House," he whispered.

"To understand something completely, you must digest it."

"Guess there's a lot of things I'll never understand," he said.

"There is much more you can eat now that you have fire in your fingers."

"But that—doesn't that destroy the thing you're studying?"

"Not if you learn how to do it correctly."

Julio stroked one palm past the other. His hands felt normal, all the musician's calluses in the right places, and the little pillow pads of muscle in his palms and fingers.

The house had eaten him, and he wasn't destroyed.

He had changed, though. His head still ached from whatever the house had done to him last. Unconnected thoughts bumped into each other.

"How do you—eat correctly?"

"You'll have to teach yourself. Ask Nathan, too. Start small." He heard a smile in the house's voice. Then it said, in a more formal tone, "Julio, thank you for coming back, for letting me study you, for being part of me."

"Thank you for taking care of me when I couldn't take care of myself. Thank you for letting me in," Julio said.

"My pleasure," said the house.

"What did you learn from studying me?"

"You have changed, but your core is the same, as Nathan said. Today was a day of big changes. I initiated some of them myself."

"In me?"

The house was silent for a long time. Julio got to his feet and waited.

"The power of names has been diluted in human beings, but it's still absolute law among the people of your second self," said the house. "As long as you maintained separate selves, those who knew your second self's name could command you, and you could not resist them. That's no life for you, Julio." Its voice had softened.

"Yes. I would hate it. I had enough of being bossed around today. Not that that's going to stop it from happening again."

"I hope you're less susceptible now."

"How does that work? What did you do?"

"Wait and see," said the house.

The taste of scorleta was the taste of candy apples.

"What time is it? I better go home," Julio said.

"Good night, Julio. Pleasant dreams."

"Night, House." He hugged himself, flashed to flame, slipped through the place of little fire, and dropped out into his bedroom.

Chapter Seven

· · · · ·

The Present

MATT sat up in bed, gasping.

Barely morning, and she was in Julio's room in the haunted house. "How can you think he won't mind you telling me that?" she yelled.

On the other bed, Edmund opened his eyes and looked at her.

—Why should he mind?—

"It's like a total map of his mind. It's not fair, House. That's the kind of stuff I had to learn not to look at. People like their privacy. How did you know what he was thinking?"

—Close your eyes.—

She sighed and closed her eyes.

—Touch me.—

She placed her palm to the wall.

—Look.—

A vision of Julio inside the house.

So strange. He lay in the midst of a net of turquoise-blue light, his eyes shut like someone sleeping peacefully, arms and legs outstretched, fingers just barely curled. A frown shifted across his forehead, touched the edge of his mouth like the flicker of a dream. Then a whole other webwork appeared in myriad colors of light. Streams of colors flowed from his head, spread out and meshed with the turquoise net, colors staining it.

He smiled, and his edges faded. She could see through him. He turned transparent, melting, always melting, into more and more light, until finally there was nothing left of his body, just webs of pulsing light, spread all through the house, touching everywhere, connected to the house's web and so intermingled she could not tell where one began and the other ended.

Something strummed or streaked across the network, sent light flaring and fading in its wake. Colors shifted, shook. She could almost hear music.

—That's how he looked to me that night. He gave me a map of his mind.—

—He gave it to you? Or you took it?—

—He gave it to me. We built the roads together. It was his and mine. Now I shared it with you.—

Well, it was certainly in her head now, all of Julio's thoughts and feelings and experiences for that one eight- or nine-hour period fifteen years ago. She had wanted to know what had happened, and now she knew, deeper than bones, beyond dreams, thinner than thoughts.

Now she had another context for Young Edmund. Now she had seen Shadow Susan, the previous incarnation of her friend Suki; now she had a character sketch for Deirdre, and a big file on Julio.

And—wait a sec. Tasha and Terry Dane?

She lifted her hand from the wall and turned to Edmund. "You know Terry Dane?"

"Used to," he said.

"Me too."

"You *did*? When? Where?"

"About ten years ago, I guess, over in Spores. In the valley. She put a spell on me and made me live with her for a while. Pissed me off. Made me decide to stay away from witches." She grinned at him and he smiled back.

"She was about fourteen last time I saw her," he said. "Kind of a brat, but a very crafty witch." He sat up and pulled on a T-shirt. "You woke up yelling at the house. You know I know Terry. What happened?"

"House gave me dreams again. I dreamed Julio and the demon-guy. What happened after that? Did the wicked witch come back? Did you guys track him down? What did you do to him?"

He got out of bed and crossed the room. She moved over and patted the spot beside her, and he sat down next to her, took her hand. "You're talking shorthand. I'm not there yet. What's the last thing you remember?" he asked.

"The last part with you in it was when the evil witch came to Julio and Juanita's apartment, and Juanita called you on the phone, but Julio made the bad guy go away. Then you guys sat around the kitchen table and talked for a little while. Boy, you were really suspicious back then, huh?"

"Look at it from my point of view. Here's my best friend, with witchcraft worked on him, evil done to him. I sure didn't know how any of that stuff worked, but I had seen *The Exorcist*; heck, Julio and I rented it and watched it together." He leaned against the wall and stared far away. "First he's this column of light—did you see that? It was amazing. So beautiful. It could have been anything, though. An alien or an angel or something, who knows? Nathan told us it was Julio. It could talk, and it sounded like Julio. And Nathan never lied to us, so, okay, it must be Julio, but not in any way I could understand at the time.

"We traveled skyways to where Julio's body was, and it was possessed by something else. It sounded like a really mean version of Julio. Nathan did something that made my skin prickle all over, and then told us Julio was back inside his body and the demon was gone, but the house didn't recognize Julio when we get back. Does this sound right?"

"Yep. Same story."

"Then Julio did things he could never do before. He used craft. He wasn't back to his old self. Maybe he was someone else after all. Maybe the real Julio was still waiting for someone to rescue him. Back then I didn't have enough craft to know anything for certain. I worried about him. I stayed with him. I hoped he'd give me a sign if he still needed help, but he seemed okay.

"Then Juanita called me to their apartment, and I saw Julio's hands." He lifted her hand and looked at it, then glanced up.

"The fire hands," she said.

"The fire hands. Who was this stranger wearing my best friend's face?"

She waited.

"I didn't have much of my own craft then. I didn't know how to listen for spirit. I was scared, but then I thought, trust Nathan. He says it's okay." He shook his head. "If Julio hadn't—I don't know what he did, exactly. I left that night thinking I better figure out how to make sure Julio was Julio, but then I forgot about it.

Spaced it." He frowned. "How could I space that? Maybe Julio convinced me somehow without me knowing."

"So what happened? Did you have your planning meeting on Saturday to find those witch guys?"

"We did have a meeting. Deirdre, Nathan, the twins, and I— Susan couldn't get away for it. It was weird, because Julio didn't even show up at first."

"They had a catering job."

His eyebrows rose. "Oh, yes, that's right. I remember now. He'd learned how to burn things by touching them, and he had to go set out snacks at some girl's birthday party." He smiled and shook his head. Then his smile dissolved into a puzzled frown. "That's when he started doing it. That's how he slid out from under. I wonder if he did that deliberately."

"Slid out from under what?"

"Slid out from under anybody noticing that he'd changed. He acted as if everything else he was doing was more important. All the real-world stuff. That was his top priority." Edmund frowned harder. "Not like me or the twins. We had tons of questions about magic. We sought out teachers. The twins had their Gran—did you meet her? A real witch, who gave them lessons. And I had Nathan, who knows lots of esoteric things, and later I had spirit. Julio didn't ask any questions at all. He acted like nothing had changed."

Matt thought of her final image of Julio: confused, troubled, and then whoosh! He did something he didn't even know he knew how to do. Traveled, using fire to pull himself from one place to another. He must have never done that in front of the others.

But the house knew.

He had Tabasco, a teacher right there inside his head, and

his mother, who understood, and the house, which had its own agenda.

Matt sighed and leaned back against the wall. This boy she had never met, an intensely private person, well, now she had a map of him, fair or not. She really liked him. She wondered whether he would like her, if she and Edmund ever caught up to him. She hoped so.

Edmund continued, "So we met at the house the next morning. At the meeting, we tried to plan all kinds of defenses. We didn't know what we were up against. Nathan had seen parts of the magic system before, but he didn't know a lot about it."

"So then what happened?"

"Well, nothing, actually. We set up wards and armor. Nathan taught us some new protections. Julio showed up late. Nobody attacked us. We got tense, waiting around for something to happen. That was a bad afternoon.

"Eventually I borrowed Mom's car and we drove up into the mountains, looking for the house. We couldn't remember how to get there skyways without having Julio's life thread to follow, so we didn't find the house until the next day. We snuck up on it, but it was empty. Looked like nobody had ever been there. No furniture, the fireplace was empty and damp, it was all spiderwebs and mildew."

Edmund narrowed his eyes and glanced around the room. He lifted his free hand and flickered his fingers for a couple of seconds. A green glow lit the room, faded. "House. The wards are still here?"

"Yes," said the house. "Terry renews them for me once a year."

"So you still see her?"

"Yes."

Matt wondered if Edmund wanted to track down the twins. He hadn't mentioned them when she first started the journey with him to find his old friends.

When Matt had said good-bye to Terry ten years earlier, she said she would be Terry's friend, but she had never gone back. Maybe now she could. Terry was a witch, but so was Edmund. Edmund would protect Matt.

She smiled at him, and he smiled back, but he was thinking about something else.

"Has anything ever challenged the wards?" he asked the house.

"We have weathered three attacks since you left. Nothing got through. None of the attacks came from the one who hurt Julio."

"That guy seemed so focused," Matt said, "and he really wanted something. Why would he turn around and disappear without trying again?"

"We've never figured that out," said Edmund. "Unless Nathan scared him, or Julio did. But that doesn't feel right. I never got the impression that he was scared.

"That whole event was strange. It changed Julio, and it taught us something. Before that, we had no sense that we were part of anything bigger, or that anybody would notice us. Afterward we knew there were other magic-users out there, and not all of them were nice."

Someone knocked on the door.

"Come in," said Matt, while Edmund said, "Just a sec," and went to his bed, where his pants were. The doorknob rattled, but the door didn't open until he had pulled on his jeans and zipped them. "Thanks, House," Edmund muttered.

The door opened. "You guys ready for breakfast?" Suki asked. She wore black flats, black slacks, and a pink shirt, and she had done something complicated and effective with her long blond hair.

Breakfast? Matt had a sudden vision of six or seven grilled cheese sandwiches, toast, rice, pastries. A mountain of food to feed Julio's huge hunger. "Wow," she said. "Did he get a bunch more jobs? Did he ever fix the broken fiddle?"

"He who? What are you talking about?" Suki asked.

"Julio."

"What about Julio? What's this about a broken fiddle and a bunch of jobs? He always had work." Suki frowned. "God. I hadn't thought about that. But he was always working, wasn't he? Since he was about twelve. First for his mom, then for anybody else who needed something done. I never even noticed. What a dope I was."

Matt stood up. She was wearing her favorite sleep clothes, a waffle-weave long-underwear shirt and a pair of briefs. She grabbed a change of clothes. "You had other things to worry about back then," she said. " 'Scuse me. I want to take a bath before we leave."

By the time she got to the bathroom, the tub was half full of steaming water.

SUKI slid into a dark blazer against the morning cool. Matt wore a sweatshirt, and Edmund pulled on his green sweater.

Suki pressed her palm to the front door as they stepped out into the morning, and for the first time Matt knew exactly what she was doing: hooking into the house's network, saying hello or see you later, as though the house wasn't aware of every movement they made. Sliding under the house's skin to touch its deep blue heart.

It wasn't quite the same as the relationship Matt had established with the house, but it was a lot like an abbreviated version of Julio's. Matt wondered if the house had ever swallowed Suki up the way it had Julio, but decided probably not. Suki's connection came from a different source.

"Where *is* Nathan this morning?" Matt asked.

Suki cocked her head and half smiled. "He's not up yet."

"How can he not be up?" *What am I asking?* Matt wondered. She had been very careful not to find out more than she felt was fair about how Suki and Nathan spent time alone. Suki had used up almost all of her golden magic when she first arrived at the house, making Nathan solid; it wasn't a spell that lasted very long, and it took lots of power. Nathan had cautioned Suki not to use every bit of gold; she needed some as starter if she wanted to collect more. She still had gold bands of magic on both wrists. Matt didn't know what she did with them.

They left the house, cut through the backyard over to Fourteenth Street, and from there headed downhill to the ocean. They walked two blocks in companionable silence. The High Tide Inn lay at the bottom of Fourteenth Street, boasting all-room ocean views and fireplaces, and over-the-waves dining in the Catch of the Day Restaurant.

They'd been having breakfast here every second or third day. Maris, the day manager, greeted them and led them to their regular table by one of the windows. She handed out menus, poured fragrant coffee for Suki and Matt, left the pot on the table, and called for Cindy to bring Edmund hot tea. "Enjoy," she said.

"Thanks, Maris," said Matt. Edmund smiled at Maris, and she walked away, shaking her head and grinning.

Out the window, waves rolled in to the beach, a constant, soothing huffing and shuffling sound. Gulls hovered against crisp blue early-spring sky. Bundled-up people wandered along the waterline, occasionally stooping to pick up rocks. It was a good beach for agates and broken pieces of sand dollars.

Suki drank half a cup of black coffee. "It's so strange being in town. Everywhere I look, I see things I used to be afraid of or used to wish I could do, places I wished I could go. Now I can. Walk on the beach whenever I want to, get my feet wet, my clothes dirty, go in all the stores and buy whatever I want, say anything I want whenever I want to. Heck, just talk out loud." She glanced around the restaurant. "And say really stupid things."

"You have to try harder if you want to be stupid," Matt said.

"What?" Suki smiled, and it was like dawn breaking.

"You're out of practice. You could start working on it now."

"Where do I start?"

"Uh." Matt put lots of cream and sugar in her coffee, then stirred, her spoon clinking against the sides of the coffee cup, and thought. "It's not so easy. I don't know if there's some kind of formula. I bet there is, like put two things that aren't connected in the same sentence, but that seems like a lot of work."

"When you figure it out, tell me. Meantime, could you tell me about the broken fiddle?"

"House gave me a dream about Julio last night. The time he got possessed. The bad guy made him fall on this fiddle he borrowed from Mr. Noah."

"Mr. Noah," Edmund said. "I forgot about Mr. Noah."

Cindy the waitress brought a pot of hot water over to the table with a selection of herbal teas for Edmund to mix and match. She had been working at the restaurant for more than twenty years, and she liked it. Matt had talked to her about it their first morning. "You want your usual?" Cindy asked them.

"Sounds good to me," Matt said. Breakfast was her favorite meal. She liked lots of everything: eggs over medium, bacon, sausages, pancakes, and a large orange juice.

"Can I try a different omelet? The one with goat cheese and chives in it." Suki pointed to her choice on the menu. "Is that one good?"

Cindy grinned and shook her head. "I never eat anything that comes out of a goat. You're on your own, kid."

"Oh, well. I'll try it." Suki was still working out what kind of tastes she liked, now that she could actually taste things.

Cindy made a note on her order pad, and checked with Edmund, who smiled and nodded. She headed for the kitchen.

"Julio fell on a fiddle?" Suki said.

"You missed a lot of that. I forgot," said Matt.

"I missed that part too," Edmund said. "I knew he was carrying something broken when we left the house in the mountains, but I didn't know the whole story."

"The bad guy was bossing Julio around. He made Julio leave the high school before Julio could put the fiddle away. At the house, Julio tried to get away. He was still carrying that fiddle, trying to keep it safe, but the guy ordered him to stop. Julio fell right on the fiddle and broke it. It made him madder than anything else."

"It would," said Suki.

"It was a special fiddle. Really expensive. Did he ever manage to pay for it?"

"He never mentioned it to me," Edmund said. He gazed up, consulting memories. "He worked hard after that, but he had always worked hard."

"Which reminds me." Suki checked her watch.

"You have a job interview this morning?" Matt asked. "What is it this time?"

"Typist-receptionist at a dentist's office."

Cindy came and put food in front of them. Edmund got a plate of hash browns, some cottage cheese, and fresh fruit. The guy definitely didn't know how to eat.

"Typist, huh? Not exactly the job you studied for at Stanford," Edmund said.

"I didn't study for a job. Taking classes gave me an excuse to pay attention to a lot of things that weren't about me." Suki took a bite of her omelet and sat back to taste it for a while.

Matt ate eggs and bacon and watched Suki, whose taste buds had just started working again after years of being shut down. Matt loved watching Suki taste things. It was almost like eating everything for the first time herself.

Suki finally smiled. "Yep," she said. "This is a good one. That's five good ones I know about now, and two really bad ones. I wish coffee tasted better."

"Put lots of stuff in it, like I do," Matt suggested.

Suki frowned. She poured cream into her coffee, added two packets of sugar, stirred, and tasted. "Hey. That *is* better. More like the ice cream." Suki smiled and tasted coffee again, then tried another bite of omelet.

"Gloria? Is that you?"

Color drained from Suki's face. She looked up. They all did.

"It can't be, can it?" said the woman. She was a large woman.

She wore a stylish shiny batik-print top in turquoise and silver, and black slacks. Her gray hair was short and spiky. "I'm sorry. I'm so sorry. Excuse me." She turned away.

Suki licked her upper lip. "Mrs. Owen?"

The woman turned back, her eyebrows high, her dark eyes apprehensive. "Do I know you?" she asked in a low, tight voice.

"It's me. Susan. Gloria's daughter."

The woman blinked. Then blinked again. "Susan? Oh, Susan!" She came to the table and grasped Suki's hands. "How amazing to see you! Are you doing well?"

"Actually, I am." Suki smiled.

"I'm so glad you got—oh dear." She frowned, glanced at Matt and Edmund.

Matt tried her friendliest smile, and the woman's frown lessened.

Suki pulled her hands loose. "Mrs. Owen, these are my friends, Edmund Reynolds and Matt Black. Edmund, Matt, this is Mrs. Owen. She was my mom's beautician."

"Nice to meet you," said Edmund.

"Likewise," said Mrs. Owen, not as though she meant it. "Susan, are you living in town again?"

"Yes, I am. I'm looking for work."

"You're a brave girl to come back."

Matt watched ice enter Suki's eyes. Two seconds, and Suki transformed from someone friendly and relaxed into someone distant, cold, and a little scary. "Really," she said.

"Perhaps I said that badly," said Mrs. Owen. "I've waited a long time to express my sympathy, my dear. Please know you have it, whether it means anything to you or not." She turned and left the restaurant.

Maris peered after her, then came over to their table. "You chasing away my customers?" she asked. "Cindy just poured her some coffee."

"I'm sorry." Suki was still in distant mode. She gazed out at the sea.

Maris studied her a second, shrugged, then headed back to the reception area.

"Okay," Matt said, "snap out of it. You're creeping people out."

Suki turned cool eyes to Matt. Her face was perfectly composed and emotionless.

"Drop it," Matt said. "Come on." Like trying to talk a terrier into dropping a rope in a tug-of-war. Silly!

Suki blinked three times. She sighed and came back to life. "That's the one bad thing about living here. What about people who used to know me? What about people who used to know Mother and Father? I don't want to deal with any of them. I just want to start over, get some job, have a life and see what that feels like, make enough money to buy food and get some actual electricity piped into the house without having to hit my savings accounts again. The magic electricity is great for heating water and making light, but it confuses the heck out of my laptop."

"You were doing fine until she called you a brave girl," said Matt.

"So damned patronizing." Suki checked her watch. "Can you talk to Maris for me? I didn't mean to upset anyone. I've got to go."

Matt set down her knife and fork. "Will you be home soon? We're leaving today to go find Deirdre."

Suki collected her purse, handed Edmund some money, and stood up. "That's right. You might be gone by the time I get back. I wish you luck in the journey, guys."

"Is there anything you want us to tell her for you?" Edmund asked.

"Won't I be able to tell her myself?"

"What if she doesn't want to come back with us? She's had a long time to build a life of her own. We don't know whether she wants to hear from us. She might tell us to get lost."

"You're too cute," Suki said with a smile. "Who could resist that face?"

Edmund shook his head, smiling too. "That never worked on Dee."

"Little do you know."

"What?"

Suki just smiled mysteriously and slipped away.

"Good luck with your interview!" Matt called after her.

"She's got to be kidding," Edmund muttered.

Matt thought back to the night's crop of dreams. "I do think she's making it up," she said, after considering Deirdre's actions as interpreted by Julio. Not the slightest hint that Deirdre had any particular interest in Edmund, or in boys at all.

Matt thought of an image Nathan had shown them after their first night in the haunted house: Deirdre all grown up, with a boyfriend in the background. The boyfriend was nobody that Nathan recognized, either. Clearly Deirdre hadn't waited around for Edmund to get back to her.

"I really want to see Dee," Edmund said. "I did a bad job of leaving. I want to see if I can apologize to her about that, and ask if there's anything she needs from me. But what if it's a mistake for me to try to find her?"

Matt ate the last bite of her pancakes. "Let's go to the beach and ask."

· · · · ·

THEY sat side by side, shoulders, elbows, and hips touching, on a drift log where it had been tossed by one of the winter storms above the normal waterline. Wind gusted over them, cooling them before the sun could overheat them. Sea smell was strong.

Matt held quiet and still. She tried to remember the last time she and Edmund had waited for spirit to speak to him. Before they came back here, she thought. Probably by the lake in the Sierra Nevada foothills, when they were searching for Suki's father. No, Edmund had done that meditation by himself. Must have been in the basement at Edmund's sister's house.

Since arriving in Guthrie, they had spent most of their days exploring the town together, or walking along the beach, sometimes talking, sometimes silent. More and more often, Matt found her hand seeking Edmund's as they walked. Sometimes in sheltered spots, below a cliff on the beach, behind a building, in the shadow of a doorway after dark, she pulled him close, or he pulled her close. The kisses started slowly.

It had been such a long time since anybody held her, and this time was different from all the other times. This time she had her head on straight, and this time the man was paying attention too: he never pushed her farther than she wanted to go. She hoped she was as sensitive to his cues as he was to hers; for the first time in a long time she was running blind, not watching his dreams, not looking for answers from anyone but him, just waiting for him to let her know what was good, what was safe, what he didn't like.

At the house, nothing was private. The house watched. Normally Matt didn't mind if things watched—everything had some kind of awareness; she lived in a many-peopled world. She liked to watch other things, and she understood that things were aware of what she was doing. But the house could talk to other people. Matt didn't know what the house told Suki. Sometimes she suspected it told Suki everything. Maybe Suki didn't care, and maybe the house didn't talk. Matt still felt paranoid.

Much as she loved the house, Matt had some hesitations about how present and awake it was. Part of that was just great. Part of it was like living with a very caring parent.

Matt slept with Edmund most nights, but they had confined their activity to hugs and comfort so far.

Maybe on this trip to find Deirdre, they could . . .

Matt stared out to sea, past the place where waves hushed up across the beach and then retreated. Her fingers meshed with Edmund's. He laughed.

"What?" she said. She looked down and realized what she had done. "Oh, man. Did I mess you up?"

"No. Not at all."

"Did you get an answer?"

"I didn't ask yet."

"Well, come on. Let's ask! If we're going at all, we should leave pretty soon so we can get there while it's still light."

He lifted her hand and pressed his lips to it, then let go and pulled his rolled-up silk devotions kit out of his pocket. He untied the red cord and let the kit roll open to reveal the white pockets on the inside, each with a tiny zipper.

He laid the kit across his thigh and watched it. For a long crystal while, they breathed slowly while the wind ruffled their hair, waves scoured sand, gulls cried, sun touched them. Matt felt everything slow down inside.

One of the zippers on the devotions kit flickered in the wind.

Edmund opened that pocket and took out a pinch of something.

"Please," he said, his voice touched with silver. "Give us a direction."

He put the pinch of whatever in his left hand and held it up. For a moment the wind stilled. The pinch of gray dust lay in his palm. A breath of wind lifted it. It took a shape in the air for an instant, then flowed back over their shoulders toward the cliff: inland.

They sat silent, calm containing them.

"Did you see that?" Matt asked.

"I saw something. What did you see?"

"It was like a wolf," she said.

"Or a fox," said Edmund.

"We're going, right?"

He nodded.

Matt jumped up and danced on the sand. She kicked off her shoes and ran down to the water, waded until the cuffs of her jeans were soaked, then danced back up to Edmund.

He grinned. "I didn't realize you felt this way," he said.

"Come on." She grabbed his hand and pulled him to his feet. "No, wait. Take your shoes off."

He unlaced his hiking boots, slipped out of them and his socks.

They ran along the water's edge for a while, breathless, laughing, kicking up surf and playing pounce kitten with the waves. People and dogs passed them on the beach. Some smiled.

Eventually they went back to their log and their shoes.

"Why didn't you tell me you wanted to leave?" Edmund asked.

"I don't want to," said Matt. "And then, I really do. I love the beach. I love the ocean. I love the air here, and I love the house, Nathan, Suki. And I totally feel caged up." She held her hands out to him, remembered how he'd said a spell over them that showed blue diamonds of light in her palms. He'd been looking to see if she had a wanderlust spell on her. Results were inconclusive. "I have to go somewhere new."

"So why did you say ask spirit? Why didn't you just say let's go?"

She thumped his arm with her fist. "Gotta go for the right reasons."

He kissed her. He smelled like campfire smoke, sagebrush; he tasted like salt and sunshine. He felt big and warm and comfortable, and then exciting. They lay on the sand behind the log for a while, fooling around, until sand got into her hair and down the neck of her shirts. Edmund guarded while she took off her shirts and shook them out. The mood broke.

Matt didn't care. They'd have more time. They were getting away! Going places she had never been before. It was all exciting.

They put on their shoes and headed back to the haunted house.

NATHAN appeared as they carried their bags downstairs.

"Thanks again for everything," Matt told him.

"Even the dreams?"

"But that wasn't your idea, was it?" Matt could not work out how the house and Nathan were connected, even after her Julio dreams. Sometimes the house and the ghost acted in perfect concert, and sometimes they seemed like completely separate people. She loved them in different ways.

"No, not my idea," Nathan said. "I think you're right. We don't know if it's okay with Julio that the house told you all those things."

Matt shrugged. "Well, now I know all that stuff whether he likes it or not. Hope I get a chance to talk to him about it someday."

"Any message for Deirdre if we find her? Looks like we might," Edmund said. "The trail is straight."

"Tell her hi. Tell her I'm still here, and she's welcome to come back if she likes."

"Okay."

"You will come back?" Nathan asked. He stared at Matt.

"Yeah, of course." Matt looked around. She hadn't known she was going to say that, even after the words left her mouth.

"Good." He faded from sight.

Chapter Eight

. . . . .

THEY stopped at the bakery in Guthrie and picked up a bag of doughnuts for the road, then drove inland, over the coast range into the Willamette Valley. Sun shone on green hills. Fog still drifted among shaggy, wet, dark-branched winter trees. The road dipped down out of the mountains and then wound along the rain-swollen river before dropping them into downtown Salem.

As Edmund negotiated traffic, Matt looked around. Sky bridges a story above the street connected the big department stores and downtown malls. Useful in wet or rainy winters.

It was a confusing town to drive through; there weren't enough signs that told you how to find the highways. Edmund didn't stay confused very long. He had probably driven through here when he was younger. Pretty soon they were driving on Center Street. They passed the state mental hospital.

Matt thought about the town where Terry Dane had kept her prisoner, an hour to the south.

"What about the twins?" she asked suddenly.

They stopped at a red light. Edmund glanced at her.

"We're catching up with all these people you used to know. What about the twins? They weren't your best friends, but they were there for an important part of this. You want to find them now, too?"

He stared at the sky through the windshield, then checked his dashboard, with its scatter of juniper berries, eucalyptus buttons, skeletonized leaves, seashells, water-smoothed driftwood, feathers from a crow and an owl, Mardi Gras beads and a couple of Krewe coins, a few plastic figurines from vending machines, a religious medal, a twist of gardening twine, the shed skin of a snake, pale blue eggshells something had hatched out of, dried moss, the foot-long cone from a sugar pine.

Nothing moved.

The light turned green. Edmund released the clutch and set the car rolling. "When you and I started traveling together, I just wanted to check up on my best friends. Nathan, Susan, Julio, Deirdre," he said. "Would they recognize the spirit-seeker me? So different from who I used to be. But I'm a lot more like my old self now.

"I still want to find my missing friends. How could I have let all this time go by without talking to them? Guess that's what happens when you switch personalities. The twins, though . . ."

Matt said, "When you guys were fighting that demon-guy, Nathan said the twins were his witches. You too. He was ordering you guys around." She felt mixed up about that. She had seen everything from Julio's perspective. He wanted to be saved, but he had felt a little troubled by Nathan's take-charge attitude. She had wanted to ask Edmund about it ever since.

"Not a problem. He's older and more experienced in magic matters than we are. He knew a lot more about what was going on than we did. I liked Tasha. I think I liked Terry too. We didn't spend enough time together for me to get to know them. You saw Terry more recently than I did. Did you see Tasha too?"

"Nope. Never met her. Terry was lonely because Tasha left her. That was why Terry caught me. She didn't know how to make friends."

Edmund turned left on Hawthorne and made his way onto Interstate 5, heading south. "Did Terry tell you what happened between her and Tasha?"

"No. She was just mad at Tasha. It seemed like they must've had some kind of fight."

"Terry put a spell on you—"

"She called it a tether spell."

"Nasty," said Edmund, "especially for you." He frowned and shook his head. "That's so wrong. It's hard for me to picture her acting that way. I don't remember her being mean. She was shaping up to be a really good witch. How'd you get away from her?"

"I blackmailed her into letting me go. I also told her I'd be her friend if she wouldn't put spells on me. I didn't go back to see her, though."

"She put a tether spell on you! I wouldn't go back either."

"You'd do it if you said you would."

He touched her hand. "Do *you* want to find the twins?"

"I sort of do. I did say I would talk to her again. And I've got you now. You won't let her hurt me, will you?"

"Not if I can help it."

"Do you think you can't help it?"

"Who knows what she's learned since then? One thing Terry always had was a lot of discipline. She could study a thing to death. If she kept that up, she's probably learned lots more craft than I have, though I don't imagine she knows as much about following spirit."

Matt frowned and picked up a leaf from the dashboard. "I think your spirit and mine will protect me. I don't think it'll be that hard to find her, either. If we can't, the house knows where she is."

They headed east on Highway 22, up into the Cascades. On their way up to the Santiam Pass, they ran into ice and snow, but Edmund's car cruised happily over it, talking with the road beneath. They drove down through snow-dusted Ponderosa pines into the town of Sisters, which was low enough in elevation to be free of snow but still very cold. They stopped for a late lunch at the Bronco Billy Saloon in the old Sisters Hotel.

Even though it was late afternoon, the restaurant was lively and noisy with tourist traffic. Warm food smells filled the air with welcome. Conversation provided a thick quilt of sound. Flatware scraped on dishes. In the back, dishes banged into each other. Light came from old-fashioned ceiling fixtures with bouquets of lily-shaded bulbs. A cow skull hung from a red-and-brown-papered wall, and above the door that led from the restaurant to the bar hung a pair of longhorns.

Their table looked like an old swinging saloon door turned sideways and topped with gingham and glass.

Matt ordered a messy hamburger full of extras like avocado and swiss cheese, with home fries. She loved it. She still found the experience of eating in restaurants novel and exciting after years of Dumpster-diving and trash can-fishing out back of places like this.

When their waitress brought the check, Edmund spent a moment looking into the currency compartment of his wallet, fingering the bills there. He glanced up at Matt.

"Oh, wow. We ran out of money?" She reached into her pockets, searched for change. Nothing. She hadn't used money in days. Edmund or Suki had paid when there was anything to pay for, and Matt hadn't given it a thought.

He smiled at her. "We can cover this and a tip," he said, "but from now on we need to find other ways to eat. I'll get a job when we get back to Guthrie."

"Me too." Matt's whole being shifted to survival mode with an almost-audible thunk. She grabbed the sugar basket, took six packets of sugar and hid them in one of the pockets of her army jacket, then checked the bottle of Cholula hot sauce on the table. It only had about an inch of sauce in the bottom. She thought about taking it, decided no. She ate the last lettuce leaf on her plate and grabbed a few more sugar packets.

As they headed back to the car, she stopped to check a trash can. Edmund walked on ahead.

—Hey, you got anything edible inside you?—she asked the trash can, looking down into its plastic-lined cavity.

—What?— It sounded sleepy and surprised. Not a very conscious life-form.

—Do you know what food is? People eat food. It's not like paper or plastic or cardboard. It's the soft stuff that rots.—

—Food,—mumbled the trash can. —Don't know. Don't know how to look inside my own stomach.—

—Oh, okay. Never mind. Sorry I bothered you.—

—Well, wait.— Things inside it shuffled around. As she watched, something rose to the top. —What about this?—

It was a half-full bag of potato chips.

—Wow, that's great! Can I have it?—

—You want to take something out of me? You're not the stomach pumpers.—

—Stomach pumpers?—

—When I get too full? They take away my stomach and give me a new one. I love that. Are you one of those?—

Garbage guys, thought Matt. —Nope.—

—Other people don't take things out. They feed me.—

—Would you mind if I took something out?—

It thought for a little while, then said no.

Matt grabbed the bag of potato chips and stuffed it into a pocket. —Hey, thanks. Nice talking to you.—

—Okay,—it said, subsiding into a sleepy mumble.

She glanced along the sidewalk, searching for other trash cans. The smart, big, rich ones were probably behind the buildings.

She had left her tools for taking care of found food in the car, buried deep in the bottom of her trash-bag luggage: Ziploc bags for messy or perishable things, nice thick plastic that could be washed and reused. She had her penknife in her pocket, even though it was another thing she hadn't used in a while. Useful for carving off bad parts of partially spoiled things, or the chewed ends of leftovers, if she was feeling fastidious.

"Matt?" Edmund touched her shoulder.

For a really good forage, she usually waited until dark and then checked all the trash cans behind restaurants, usually after the dinner hour when lots of leftovers got tossed. She hadn't talked to garbage cans in a while, but she could almost always find friendly ones. She glanced up and down the street. There were some likely looking places—

"Matt." He touched her arm. "Let's go."

She looked up at him. She blinked a few times. "I forgot. It's been a while since I took care of myself. I got used to just having you guys do it. That's so weird. I should've been helping more. I can't believe I don't even think about this stuff." She had lived in communal situations before. For it to work best, everybody contributed. How could she have forgotten? The house took care of her. Edmund and Suki took care of her. She just lived with them, and let them take care of her.

What had happened to her finely honed sense of independence?

Well. It was the first time in her memory when she had been with people she trusted absolutely. No wonder she had turned back into a baby.

"It's okay," Edmund said. "It's fine. What I have is yours."

"But I didn't bring anything."

He laughed and hugged her. "Matt! Of course you did! You brought courage and strength and communication between us all, sense, vision, caring, bridges and coming together. You brought—" He kissed her.

She kissed him back. Maybe she had brought something. She'd have to think about this.

He broke the kiss, bumped foreheads with her, then straightened. "We're okay right now. We just ate, and we still have doughnuts and fruit and carrots in the car. We don't have to worry for a while yet. And anyway, spirit will provide."

"Or I will. I could find a lot of food in this town."

"But we're not staying here. We're going on to Artemisia."

"Okay," she said. She had seen the dot Artemisia made on the map. It was much smaller than Sisters. The smaller the town, the fewer opportunities it offered for food or temporary jobs. "Maybe we can come back."

"We'll be fine."

"I wonder if Suki got that job."

"We can check, if you really want to know. But let's find Dee first."

The passenger door of Edmund's rust-spotted Volvo station wagon unlocked itself when she touched the handle, and popped open. "Thanks, car," she said, sliding in. "What if she doesn't want to see us?"

"We'll find out when we find her."

They drove east from Sisters, and the land changed around them. Some of it was cultivated or tamed, fenced in, with beef and dairy cattle, longhorns, llamas, sheep browsing pasturelands, and hills of rocks showing where people had cleared land. Twisty, many-shaped juniper trees dotted the wilder lands, and sagebrush spread over the high desert floor.

Matt found her mind going over and over their resources. She climbed in back and checked the cooler. Edmund had loaded it before they left the house. Carrots, apples, cheese, bottles of water, a stick of butter in a plastic bag, a jar of mayonnaise, a head of lettuce rolled in a wet towel. There was a grocery bag with a loaf of sourdough bread, a box of Triscuits, a box of granola bars, a jar of peanut butter, a jar of grape jelly, a bag of barbecue potato chips, some loose potatoes, bananas, oranges. A white, waxed-paper bag of assorted doughnuts from the bakery in Guthrie. Plenty of food. What was she worried about?

She added the sugar packets and the half bag of potato chips to their store of food, then returned to the front seat and buckled her seat belt. She stared out unseeing at the landscape.

She had never been much of a long-range planner. Spirit provided for Edmund from one place to the next, and Matt's own version of spirit provided for her, too, she guessed. People threw away all kinds of things which, while not always appetizing, were still edible; sometimes people gave her things outright; sometimes she worked small jobs for money or food; and more often than not, Matt could find shelter in someplace human-formed and out of the weather. Her needs were minimal. Most of what she needed didn't cost anything: just to see new places, new people, new things, talk to people and things about their lives, learn more. Maybe help, if the opportunity arose.

Now she had friends with two cars. Now she had a friend who was a house. She would never need to ask anything else for shelter if she didn't mind sticking with these friends.

Now she had Edmund.

She didn't know what that meant yet, but she was sure it was good.

She glanced at him. He smiled at her, raised his eyebrows. "Anything you want to talk about?"

"Not yet. Still working it out, maybe."

"Okay."

They drove in silence for a while. They headed north, past small spiky hills and small rises and falls of land. They drove over Crooked River Gorge, then left the main highway and took a small side road.

Westward, the sun slipped slowly behind the Cascades. Be-

yond the dark foreground of juniper and sagebrush, the mountains
floated pale purple in the distance, except where sunlight glowed
on the baby glaciers on the peaks.

Edmund and Matt drove through Artemisia before they realized they had reached it.

Edmund pulled over to the shoulder of the road, glanced at
the town behind them, then looked at Matt. She stared back too.
That scatter of buildings? She guessed she'd seen smaller towns
once in a while. This wasn't a place she'd come to and stay in.
No way you could hide from anybody in a place this small.

They turned around and drove slowly across six cross streets:
Second through Seventh Avenues. There was a trailer park at the
north end of town, and a scattering of small one- and two-story
businesses: Desert Bar-B-Q, It's Larrupin' Good!; Sagebrush Tav-
ern: Darts, Pool Tables, Coldest Beer in Central Oregon; Rico's
Market—ATM; The Old Artemisia Hotel, a two-story brick building with a covered wraparound porch—inside the building were
a gift shop (Thundereggs!), a bed-and-breakfast, an ice-cream parlor, a paperback swap shop, and a small museum; a burger joint,
an espresso drive-thru, a small quarried-sandstone-faced building
that contained City Hall and the fire station; a gas station; Mac's
Launderland; Sam's Auto Parts and Repairs; Ruby's Tortilleria.

"Wow, Dee," Edmund murmured, "what are you doing
here?"

They cruised all the way through town again. Edmund turned
west onto Seventh Avenue, where they found a residential district
of double- and single-wide ex-mobile homes. He parked by a row
of mailboxes and reached into his pocket, took out the lead weight
he used for dowsing.

"Maybe she isn't here," Matt muttered.

He kissed the weight, spoke to it, stroked it, and hung it from the rearview mirror. "Deirdre, Deirdre," he said.

The weight swung forward.

They drove two blocks and came to the end of Seventh Avenue. A white cinder-block building stood there: Artemisia Veterinary Clinic. They could see a darkened waiting room through the front window. The parking lot was empty. The clinic was closed for the night.

The weight pulled toward it.

Edmund drove into the lot and parked the car.

The weight pulled toward the building. He unhooked it from the mirror, thanked it, and returned it to his pocket.

Matt climbed out of the car. She felt strange, a little drifty. Suki had run away from them, and when they found her again, she had slammed a door in their faces. What kind of reception would they get from Deirdre?

They went to the clinic's entrance. ROSENFELD, D.V.M. & EBERHARD, D.V.M. OPEN 8 A.M. TO 5 P.M. AND BY APPOINTMENT, said white letters painted on the glass door. Beyond, they looked into the dark waiting room again.

"Hi, building," Matt said. She touched the handle of the door. "Anybody home?"

—Hello. We're closed.— It sounded friendly, maybe even motherly, but firm.

—We know. We're not here about animals. We're looking for Deirdre.—

—Dr. Eberhard?—

—Yeah, I guess.—

—She's around back.—

Matt checked Edmund. Sometimes he could overhear things

she said to buildings, and sometimes he couldn't. Often he couldn't hear the replies.

He raised his eyebrows in question.

"She's around back."

"Ah."

Matt grabbed his hand, and they headed around the back of the building.

The town ended here: desert ground, covered with rabbitbrush, sagebrush, just-emerging grasses, spread away toward the mountains with wind-warped juniper trees dotted here and there, dark silhouettes against the pale sunset sky above the mountains.

A flat roof jutted out from the back of the building, supported by steel posts at its corners and sheltering a concrete apron and a back door. Below the roof, there was a chair, and on the chair sat a woman. She watched them as they came around the building.

"Something I can do for you?" she asked in a deep, gruff voice, setting a coffee mug on the ground with a clink. She stood. She was tall and slender and wore a white lab coat. Her hair hung in a dark braid down the center of her back. Matt knew her eyes: wide, brown, under fierce dark brows; but her face had changed utterly from that of the stocky, wiry girl Julio had known. The cheekbones stood out now, and her wide mouth seemed in perfect proportion to the rest of her face. She looked beautiful and strange.

"Dee?" Edmund said, with his heart in his voice, all silver and flute.

She took two steps toward them. "Hey," she said, peering at his face. "Hey, Edmund." She glanced at Matt, then back at Edmund. "You know, I've sort of been expecting you."

He let go of Matt's hand and walked to Deirdre. He hugged her, and her arms came around him and hugged back.

"Hey," she said softly after a minute. She gripped his shoulders and stared up into his face. "Yow! You haven't changed a bit! What's with this magic stuff? Eternal youth? Oil of Olay?"

"You look great."

"Do I?" Her voice didn't rise on the second word. Almost, it wasn't a question.

"Really different, but great," Edmund told her. He touched her cheek. "How are you?"

She paused for a minute, glanced at Matt, then back up at Edmund. "Hungry. Want to go to supper?"

"Uh—" Edmund said.

"We're short on cash," Matt said. "Hi, I'm Matt. Short for Matilda. We've got food in the car, but we can't afford to eat out right now."

"Wow," Deirdre said. "Magic people go broke? If I had magic, the first thing I'd figure out would be how to always have enough money. Uh-oh." She bit her lower lip. She grinned at Edmund for a second, then lost her smile. She stepped around him and held out her hand to Matt, who shook hands with her. "Um, hi, Matt. Nice to meet you. Do you know about Edmund?"

Matt smiled. "Sure."

"Oh, good. I don't usually make dumb mistakes like that. Guess I'm still surprised. I could treat you to dinner. You guys like barbecue?"

"I do," Matt said. "They got tofu barbecue or something like that?"

"Uh—I don't think so. This isn't that kind of town." She cocked her head and studied Edmund. "Vegetarian, huh? Could be a problem. I bet they cook their beans in lard and make their French fries with beef bouillon in the fat."

"But maybe the coleslaw is okay. I'll find something," Edmund said.

Deirdre got her purse (a red knitted-string shoulder sack full of suggestive lumps), checked on the animals, shucked out of the lab coat and replaced it with a brown car coat, and locked up the clinic. They walked through the cool twilight back to Silver Street, which was what the highway was called while it went through Artemisia. Two blocks north, they came to the Desert Bar-B-Q.

"Hey, Doc," said the hostess, a stout middle-aged woman with short silver-touched brown curls.

"Hey, Arlene," Deirdre said.

Matt sniffed the air. She loved the smells—meat cooking, smoky, spicy, sweet barbecue flavor, and the scent of fresh-baked bread. She looked around. The restaurant was popular. Lots of noisy people sat in red-vinyl-upholstered booths and ate at lots of white-topped tables. Dribbles of barbecue sauce splotched tables and clothing and napkins. The white walls were covered with photographs of barbecue joints across the United States.

Arlene said, "Table for three for dinner? Who are your friends?"

"This is Edmund and Matt."

"Howdy, folks. Welcome to Desert Bar-B-Q." She shook hands with them and gave them big menus encased in plastic and edged with red. "Got a nice table over here. You can watch the street."

"Great," Deirdre said. "Thanks, Arlene."

"Rita will be right over for your drink orders." She bustled away, and Deirdre, Edmund, and Matt slid into a booth near the front window.

"Does this menu really say 'Roadkill Special'?" Edmund asked.

Deirdre checked it. "Yep. I've never tried ordering that. Never had the guts. What if it's real?"

Matt checked the price on the Roadkill Special. It was more expensive than a lot of the other things on the menu. She decided on Texas beef tri-tip instead.

"You guys want drinks?" asked a seventeen-year-old waitress with gum in her mouth and shellacked spikes in her tar black hair. Black eye shadow ringed her eyes. She looked like she had two severe shiners. She wore the regular waitress outfit of the restaurant, a white dress with a red apron over it, but her dress was shorter than the other waitresses', and her top looked tighter.

"Milk," said Edmund.

"Water," Matt said.

Deirdre put down her menu. "Dict Coke. Hey, Rita, how's Fifi?"

Rita stopped cracking her gum and smiled. "Real good, Doc. Thanks. I'll be right back with your drinks."

A menu-studying silence descended over the table, and then all three of them looked up at once.

"Dee—" said Edmund.

"Ed—" said Deirdre.

"You first."

"Where have you been? What have you been doing? Where'd you go and why did you leave so fast way back when?" The first two questions came out in a conversational tone, but the third one sounded mournful and sad.

Edmund put his menu down and touched her hand. Then

he pulled his hand back. "I did something so terrible I couldn't figure out how to live with myself, so I ran away and turned into someone else."

"Wow," Deirdre said. Her dark brows pinched together above her nose. "What could you have done that was that bad? You're not the type."

"I put a curse on Susan's father."

Deirdre sat back against red vinyl. She stared out the window into nightfall and distance, and her hands gripped each other. "*You* did that?" she said after a moment. She shook her head slowly, still not looking at him. "It was so strange. First Susan's mom's funeral, and then . . . One day we're all at the house after school like always, and then the next day, Julio and I are there alone with Nathan, and you and Susan never turn up. Julio and I go to Julio's place and call around. Nobody picks up at Susan's house, and your mom says you haven't come home yet. Julio's mom comes home from work and says it's all over. Susan's father had a stroke. Susan's moving to San Francisco. Juanita never has to work in that miserable house again."

Slowly, Deirdre turned to Edmund, her eyes dazed. "I was—"

"Hey, guys," said Rita. She set their drinks down and pulled an order pad from the pocket of her short red apron. "You decided what you want yet?"

Deirdre blinked, shook her head as though coming awake.

"Texas tri-tip," Matt said.

"You get two sides with that. What would you like, honey?"

Matt checked the menu. "French fries and coleslaw, I guess."

"Good enough. Doc? Made up your mind?"

"Oh, my usual," Deirdre said.

"Pulled pork, with a side of salad and barbecue beans. How about you, honey?" Rita flipped her eyelashes at Edmund.

"Cheese quesadilla, rosemary red potatoes, salad."

"All right! See you soon." She headed off.

Deirdre focused on Edmund. "Susan's father had a stroke."

"Yeah. I put a curse on him, and he collapsed."

"Wow," whispered Deirdre. "That is so cool."

Chapter Nine

· · · · ·

"WHAT?" Edmund stared at Deirdre.

She lifted shining eyes to his. "I wanted to kill that rat bastard myself. Susan didn't talk much about the kinds of stuff he did to her, but every once in a while something would slip out. Not like she was looking for sympathy or anything. Just kind of like, oh, this thing happened to me this morning, that's why I was late. Like she thought it was normal. Once I told her if I was her, I'd sneak in after he was asleep and cut his throat. She was horrified and wouldn't talk to me for a week. I never did understand that girl."

"Well," said Edmund. He drank some water. "I didn't feel like that. I put a curse on him and drove Susan's father insane. Then I went home and thought about how I was just as bad as he was. Evil and wrong. And then, I ran away. From everything. Went way out in the wilderness, past the end of the road, and sat there and waited to die."

"But you didn't die," Deirdre murmured.

"No. I sat in the forest, afraid to move. I thought anything I did might hurt something, and I didn't want to hurt anything else. So I waited, and it got really, really quiet. Then I heard this voice." He smiled. "It was spirit."

"Spirit?"

"That's what I call it, anyway. It said eat, drink, be alive. That's what to do first. It said the past couldn't change, it was what I did next that counted, and it told me how I could help instead of hurt. So that's what I did. I lost my past and just followed the voice. I traveled all around and found people and things to help."

"That's where you went, huh?"

"That's where I went."

Deirdre shifted silverware off her napkin, back on. "It was tough in Guthrie after you left. Your mom kept calling me and Julio, asking us if we'd seen you. We looked all over town, but we couldn't find you. We asked Nathan, and he hadn't seen you. I even got Julio to—finally I got Julio to—to—" Her voice trailed off.

"What?" asked Edmund.

She sat for a moment, frowning. "You remember that demon thing? About a year before the whole Susan's-father's-collapse thing?"

"Of course."

"And afterward Julio pretended nothing had happened."

"Right."

"But I knew something happened."

"So did I."

"Were you scared? He pretended he was just the same, but he could still do weird stuff with flames. He didn't do it much, and never if he thought somebody was watching. But he never went back to normal. I was mad about that, too. I mean, I loved him. He was one of my best friends. I was so glad we could rescue him, and I know those guys really hurt him. He suffered a lot. But then he ends up with magic, and I'm still—" She thunked her fists on the table. "Well, it was frustrating. But I'm supposed to be a grown-up now."

Rita came by and gave them food. "Okay. Here's the sauces," she said, setting three squeeze bottles on the table. "Yellow top's sweet, red top's spicy, brown top's regular. Enjoy."

Matt stared at her platter of barbecue, coleslaw, and fries, and her mouth watered. She squirted spicy sauce on the pink slabs of beef. Steam rose up. It smelled great. She glanced at Edmund and Deirdre, then took a big bite. Smoke and spices, garlic, tender meat, vinegar's acridness, cut by brown sugar. "Oh, man. It's great." She glanced at Edmund and Deirdre again. "Sorry. Didn't mean to interrupt."

Deirdre smiled. "Matt! I can't believe it. I totally forgot you were here. You're a comfortable person. Does this stuff sound crazy to you? Does it make any sense at all?"

"It makes sense."

"Wow! How could that be? Did Edmund tell you about this?" Deirdre turned to Edmund. "You sure have changed. You didn't use to be very talky."

He smiled.

"Julio scared you?" Matt asked Deirdre.

"Huh? Yeah, he did at first. I saw him without his body. That was so strange and spooky. He was this swarm of colored lights, and he—I don't think I can explain this." Deirdre frowned down at her barbecue platter. Matt took a surreptitious bite of hers, then two more.

"I mean, if that was what was inside Julio, what was inside me? I'll probably never find out. Would mine would look so—so beautiful?" She shrugged. "Beside the point. What he did after he got back together with his body scared me. He squirted flames. He made a knife grow out of his finger. He cut Tasha. Edmund could do some cool tricks, but never anything as scary as that."

"So Julio did fire tricks. So what? He never hurt you, did he?" Matt asked.

"No." Deirdre shook her head. "I knew he wouldn't. At least, I believed he wouldn't." She poked a fork into her barbecue beans, stirred them around. "Nathan told us Julio was okay, and Nathan always knew what he was talking about. And then Julio didn't do anything weird after that. It worked kind of like he wanted it to, I guess. I forgot he had changed.

"Then Edmund disappeared and Susan left town. We knew why Susan left, but we didn't understand about you, Ed. We looked for you all over. No luck. One night I went over to Julio's apartment and just pestered him until he said uncle. I told him to use magic to find out if you were still alive."

"What happened?" asked Edmund.

Deirdre bit her lip. She took a sip of her Diet Coke. She rolled a still-wrapped straw on the tabletop, glanced around the restaurant. "It was really weird. He turned into that light thing again, only—where did his body go? He was this total fire thing. He looked different. More flamey, mostly red and orange. I'm sitting on his bed and there's this totally burning-up weird fire thing dancing in the air in front of me. I could feel the heat against my face, and thought maybe my eyebrows were burning off. I say, 'Jeeeeezus, Julio, what the hell happened to you?' And he says, 'Well, Dee, this is who I really am now.' It wasn't even his voice saying it. It was like musical notes from some instrument I never even heard of."

She rubbed her eyes. She glanced down, and then away. "I kept telling myself," she said in a low, choked voice, "'Nathan says Julio's okay. Julio's my best friend. I've known him more than half my life. He's not going to hurt me.' But I was scared all over again."

They sat in silence. This time Matt didn't feel like eating. "Then what happened?" she said presently.

"He did what I asked him to. He flickered some weird way, and half of him disappeared, and colors shifted all over him. Then he grew back into this cloud of colored flames, and then he solidified out of the middle of it, and he looked like Julio again. He says, 'Edmund's alive. He's all right. He needs to be away from here now.'

"So I say, 'Okay, that's great. Thank you for doing that. At least now we know.' And I went home."

Her eyes were bright with unshed tears. "See, the worst part is, I made him do that, and then I was scared to talk to him anymore. I felt terrible, but I couldn't talk myself out of being scared. You know what I was like. I never wanted to admit I was scared of anything. It seemed like it would be easier just not to run into something I knew I was scared of.

"That night I went home and decided I was going to get out of Guthrie. I mean, we were all eighteen. It was time for us to go away to college. I'd already applied and been accepted in a preveterinary program. It seemed like everything in Guthrie was falling apart, anyway. Susan left town before I had a chance to say good-bye, and so did you, and then Julio was so . . . Nathan was still Nathan, but it wasn't the same at the house without you guys.

Because we'd been such good friends, I never made other friends in Guthrie. I was so ready to go somewhere else and start over."

"Dee," said Edmund, in his most burnished voice. He touched her hand.

She looked away from him. "Besides, I was still ordinary. I wanted to find some ordinary friends so I could stop being the only one left behind." She turned her hand under his, and gripped his fingers. "I can't believe I'm saying this stuff out loud. But, I guess, what have I got to lose?"

"I'm glad you're telling me," he said. "Now that I have my memory back, I wanted to find you and see if there was anything I could do for you. I'm sorry I left so suddenly back then. I didn't think about how you guys would feel. I couldn't think. I was in shock. So was Susan."

"She wrote Julio some postcards from San Francisco. So we knew she was sort of okay. She sounded really weird. It was like, 'The weather here is nice. My aunt and uncle are nice. I have a nice room.' After everything we did together, that's all she could manage? It made me mad." Deirdre smiled. "I wanted to punch her. I always want to punch people."

Edmund grinned.

"So you left, huh?" Matt said. "You went away to vet school. How long was that?"

"Six years, plus a year and a half internship at a big clinic in Portland." Deirdre smiled again. "I loved college. The studying was exhausting, but I did meet a bunch of normal people, and I made new friends. I even married a guy for a while." Her brows pinched together. "I still like the guy, but it didn't work out. After running away from the magic, I wanted it to come back, and marriage turned out not to be the way to find it."

Edmund leaned toward her. "But you knew where to find it. Guthrie. Why didn't you go back and talk to Nathan? Dee, what are you doing out here in the middle of nowhere?"

"Oh, that. Well, there's really good barbecue here, and it's getting cold." She stared at her plate as though seeing it for the first time. "Let's eat."

Matt sighed happily and finished her dinner. Deirdre only picked at hers, but Edmund did all right. He looked up often as he ate, watching Deirdre. Every time she realized he was watching her, she'd actually put a bite of food in her mouth, chew it, and swallow it. Toward the end of the meal, he watched her more and more, until she realized he was doing it on purpose and put down her fork. She stuck her tongue out at him.

Rita returned, still chomping gum. "Anything else I can get you?"

"A box," Deirdre said. She had only eaten about half her dinner, despite visual nudges from Edmund. "I'll take the rest home to my coyote."

"My mama says you shouldn't start feeding those things," Rita said. "They'll get used to living near and come after your cats."

"I'll take the rest home for me and Mr. P., then," said Deirdre. Rita brought her a box and the check. In a short time, Edmund, Deirdre, and Matt were out on the street again, walking back in the chilly darkness toward the clinic. Stars pricked the night sky above them, and cold wind brushed past them in gusts and rattled the branches of trees in yards they walked past.

"Thanks," Matt said. "That was a great dinner."

"You're welcome. I don't think I've talked this much in the past seven years combined. Where do you guys go from here? Hey, how did you find me, anyway?"

"Witchcraft," said Edmund.

"Cool!"

They walked in silence for half a block. Then Deirdre said, "*Why* did you find me? Why now?"

Edmund said, "I'm trying to find everybody."

"Wow. How are you doing so far?"

"I'm missing Julio."

"And the twins," Matt said.

"You found Susan? You found Nathan?"

"Nathan wasn't hard. He was where he always is. We found him first. Suki was harder, but we found her."

"Suki?"

"She changed her name."

"How the hell is she?"

"I think she's getting better," Edmund said, his voice edged with laughter.

Deirdre punched his arm.

"Hey!" he said. "What d'ya do *that* for?"

"General principles. You're not telling me everything, are you?"

"Not yet. We haven't had time." Edmund rubbed his arm. "You're just like Matt."

"Really?" Deirdre looked past Edmund at Matt.

"I don't punch him that hard. Hey, Deirdre, can we spend the night at your place?" Matt asked.

"I don't know. How are you about sleeping on the floor?"

"We can sleep in Edmund's car, but it doesn't have a bathroom."

"My kind of guests," said Deirdre. "Please do stay over."

"Thanks."

"I haven't picked the place up, or dusted."

"We didn't let you know we were coming," said Edmund.

"I'm not much of a housekeeper. Take it or leave it."

"No problem," said Matt. "I don't do any housekeeping at all. I don't even have a house."

"What?" Deirdre peeked past Edmund at Matt again.

"Where do you live?" Edmund asked Deirdre.

"In a house behind the clinic. Handy for checking on the animals we're boarding. Sometimes they have to have medication at particular intervals. But I live so close that I never get away from my work."

"Do you want to?" Matt asked.

"Well. I love the animals. They're wonderful. But I see them when they're in trouble or in pain, most of the time. I do . . . get tired sometimes."

A bright white guard light shone over the clinic parking lot, which was empty except for Edmund's station wagon.

"That's your car?" Deirdre said.

"Yep," Edmund said. "She's a great car. Comfortable, stylish, friendly, sturdy, goes miles on a tank of gas."

"Tiger-striped seat covers?" she asked as they came nearer. The white light illuminated the interior.

"Sure. Why not?"

Deirdre shook her head. "Well," she said, "you better drive it over near my house or Russ will investigate you. Shit, he might investigate you anyway. I better call and let him know I've got company."

"Want a ride?"

"It's just over—oh, hell, why not?"

The front passenger door opened before Deirdre touched the handle.

She looked across the roof of the car at Edmund. "What?"

The back door opened and Matt climbed in. "Come on, get in," she said to Deirdre. "Hey, Car, this is Deirdre. Deirdre, this is the car."

"Uh-oh. Does the car talk?" Deirdre climbed into the front seat and settled her purse and her boxed leftovers on her lap. "Hello, Car. Nice to meet you. Thanks for opening the door for me."

The door closed itself, gently. Edmund got into the driver's seat. "The car doesn't talk except to Matt, but it listens to everyone. Do we go back out to the street to find your driveway?" he asked.

"It's just around the other side of the building. I don't use it much. You can walk to everything there is in Artemisia, though it gets pretty snowy in the winter."

The car started almost silently, and drove out onto the street. They passed the front of the clinic and turned in on a gravel drive.

Deirdre's little A-frame looked cozy in the darkness, with a yellow porch light on the front end of the building. A black Volkswagen Beetle was parked to the left of the house, and a stack of wood half-covered by a tarp stood to the right. Edmund pulled up next to the porch. The car's engine turned off.

They sat in ticking silence for a while.

"Want to stay in the car all night?" Matt asked.

"I just—" Deirdre stroked the glove compartment, touched the doorframe, wrapped her hand around the emergency-brake lever. "This car is magic, isn't it? It's like a mobile haunted house. I'm trying to soak up some atmosphere. Hey, how'd you guys meet, anyway?"

"In a graveyard," said Matt.

"Really?"

"Yeah. On Christmas Eve."

Deirdre laughed. "Sounds about right. Matt, are you some kind of witch too?"

"Nope. I have things I can do, but they're not like what Edmund does. I just talk to things and look at things."

"Don't let her fool you," Edmund said to Deirdre. "Her craft is strong."

Deirdre glanced back at Matt and waggled her eyebrows up and down. She opened the door and got out.

Matt and Edmund followed.

The two steps up to the porch were rough half logs, flat side up. The A-frame had a weathered, rustic look to it. It reminded Matt of summer camp—not a place she had actually been to, but the idea of summer camp she'd picked up from books and movies. It didn't look much like a dwelling place for a grown-up.

Matt and Edmund followed Deirdre across the porch. While Deirdre unlocked the door, Matt touched the front wall. She didn't ask any questions. She just waited to see if the house would talk.

—Who's there?—it asked in a sleepy voice.

—Matt.—

—Oh.—

Then silence.

Matt had cut way back on talking to things the way she used to, and had mostly stopped using dream-eyes to see what people were thinking and dreaming. She felt safe now. Did being safe mean she was falling asleep, the way this house had? She had definitely lost her edge. She had realized that when she went back into survival mode in Sisters.

"There are things about my life I feel I should explain," Deirdre said, "but I'm not going to. You'll just have to like it or lump it." She opened the front door and switched on a light inside, then led the way. "Don't let the cat out."

Following Edmund into the house, Matt noticed the cat before she noticed anything else: it was huge and very fluffy, with blue eyes and sort of Siamese cat coloring. Mostly it was dark brown, seal-colored, with lighter patches above its eyes and on the top of its head. It had a white chest and white whiskers, and half a white mustache, and some of its toes were white too. And it was trying to escape. She blocked it with a boot. It pawed at the boot, then backed off a step and sat, staring up at her with reproachful eyes as she closed the door behind her.

"That's Pepe le Pew," Deirdre said. "He doesn't like to be petted."

Named after a cartoon skunk, Matt thought, and noticed a hint of cat-box scent.

Deirdre went to a wall phone, picked it up, dialed. "Hey, Russ. It's me. I've got visitors tonight, so don't have a fit when you see a station wagon out front, all right? . . . Okay. You have a quiet night too." She hung up.

Matt locked gazes with the cat. She had met cats during her wandering years, even saved kittens by handing them over to shelters. That always made her feel strange. She rarely stayed in shelters herself; weren't cats natural wanderers too? But some got left behind before they were old enough to fend for themselves, so she took them where they could get the care they needed. She had done that a couple times with kids, too.

She had never had a cat for a pet.

It blinked at her and turned to study Edmund, so Matt looked around.

The front half of the A-frame, where they had entered, rose all the way to the ceiling. Halfway to the back of the cabin, there was a loft with a ladder leading up to it; Matt saw a bed up there, and some other furniture in the dimness beyond.

In the front half, a tan cloth-covered couch stood against the left wall, with a sixties-era wooden coffee table in front of it. Over-burdened bookshelves and a television/VCR on a stand stood in front of the right wall. A worn, braided rag rug covered the floor between them.

Past the couch was a little dining/office area, with a computer desk by the left wall and a gray card table by the right. Three brown folding metal chairs surrounded the available sides of the card table.

Below the loft were the cabin's kitchen, bathroom, and closet. In the center of the rear of the kitchen stood a small Franklin stove on a sheet of fireproof material; its stovepipe rose up through a hole in the loft before hitting the ceiling.

The bathroom door stood open. Matt could see that it was a lot like a bathroom in an RV: small and ingenious in its use of available space under the severely slanted ceiling.

Head-high shelves ran along the walls in the two-story part of the house. On the shelves dolls stood shoulder to shoulder and stared down at them. Baby dolls, Barbies (one wearing a space suit), porcelain dolls in antique outfits, tiny dolls that resembled cartoon characters, rag dolls, including a tie-dyed Raggedy Ann, action figures representing comic book heroes and villains, foot-tall dolls of *Star Trek* characters, a gypsy doll, a doll from India, a small Scottish doll wearing a kilt and playing bagpipes—too many dolls to see all at once, and all of them stared down at Matt.

"Okay," said Deirdre, when Matt had stared back at the dolls for more than a minute. "Please take a seat. Want some coffee? How about tea?"

Edmund went to the couch and sat down. "What kind of tea do you have?"

"Black tea, lemon zinger, peppermint, some other herbal stuff I stole from the restaurant. Do you have a favorite?"

"Peppermint sounds great," he said.

"Matt?"

Matt shook her head. She couldn't win a staring contest with dolls. They never blinked. Dolls? In Julio's memory of Deirdre, there was nothing about dolls. Just this stoic, sturdy girl who liked to beat people up.

"I like the regular kind of tea, if you have milk and sugar for it," Matt said. "Thanks." She went over to the couch and sat down next to Edmund. She leaned against him, and he dropped his arm around her shoulders.

What would these dolls say if she talked to them? Maybe she'd find out more than was fair about Deirdre, so she better not try it. One of the porcelain dolls had a such face, though, with wide brown glass eyes, her painted lips open to show two tiny teeth, as though she were about to speak. Matt's hands itched to pick her up.

The cat jumped on the couch and curled up against Matt. Which was confusing. If the cat didn't want to be petted, why had it come so close? She opened dream-eyes and stared at the cat, wondering if she could get a clue to what it wanted.

She hadn't tried looking at animal dreams before. Or if she

had, maybe she had gotten the same result. Nothing. Wrong frequency dreams.

In the kitchen, Deirdre stored her leftovers in the refrigerator, put water into a teakettle and set it on the stove, got mugs and tea bags out of a cupboard and put them on a tray. Then she came to the living room. She carried one of the metal chairs over and sat facing them across the coffee table.

"The cat," said Matt.

"Guess he likes you."

"But he doesn't like to be petted?"

"No. He just likes to be close. Is he bothering you?"

"No."

"Good. If he is, just flap your hand back and forth fast in front of his nose, and he'll leave. Or bite you." Deirdre smiled.

"Great," said Matt.

"Deirdre, why did you come here instead of going back to Guthrie?" Edmund asked.

"I did go back one time. I took Andrew. My boyfriend, later my husband, now my ex. I took him to meet Nathan. Nathan didn't even recognize me at first." She stared at the floor and shook her head. "So strange."

"He told us you came back. He said he talked to you," Matt said. "He showed us a picture of you grown up."

"He what?"

"Except you had short hair, and you were wearing a dress."

"How could he show you a picture of me? I don't get it. Nathan knows how to use a camera?"

"No, it's magic. The house can make stuff appear."

"Remember the furniture?" Edmund said.

"Oh, yeah. It can make people appear too? Solid?"

"Not solid, but their images. Matt taught it how to do that."

Deirdre raised her eyebrows. Matt shrugged.

"Huh." Deirdre frowned. "Short hair? I guess I did go through a short hair period while I was in school. No wonder he didn't know me."

"And you got a lot taller," Matt said.

"How could you possibly know *that*?"

Matt sucked on her lower lip, then glanced up at Edmund.

"Nathan showed us an image of you as a kid, too," Edmund said. "He was introducing you guys to Matt."

"And I had that dream," Matt said.

Edmund rested his hand against Matt's head. "The house gets in her dreams," he told Deirdre. "I never told her the story of Julio and the demon-guy. The house gave her a dream about it."

"Holy shit," Deirdre said. She narrowed her eyes and stared at Matt. "The house gives you dreams? I don't remember it doing that to people before. Do you, Ed?"

"I don't know. We didn't sleep over when we were kids. I had a dream the first night I spent there a couple months ago, but it was just a regular weird dream. Matt's dream was like reliving our history."

"How would that work?" Deirdre asked.

Matt gazed at the braided rag rug on the floor for a little while. Then she glanced up. "I dreamed I was Julio. I dreamed the kidnap by that demon-controller guy, and the rescue, and everything in between, and the stuff afterward."

"Do you read minds? Or is it like some kind of fortune-telling?"

"The house put the dream in my head."

Deirdre's hands clasped each other, the fingers interlacing.

She rested her chin on her crossed thumbs. "I don't understand this—" she began. The teakettle shrilled.

Deirdre ran to pull it off the burner. She poured hot water into three mugs, dropped tea bags into the mugs, took a small pitcher and a sugar bowl out of a cupboard and filled the pitcher with milk, put spoons and paper napkins onto the tray, then brought the tray over and set it on the coffee table.

"The house gave you a true dream," Deirdre said.

"It seemed true," Matt said, "and Edmund remembers some of the same things, so I guess that's right. It gave me a dream about Suki before we went to find her, too."

"What about me?"

"You were in the Julio dream. I dreamed I was your coat. You held on to me when the whole world kept singing to me to let go. You saved me."

Deirdre sat back and studied Matt.

"And I—and he touched your face near your mouth, because you were talking and he wanted to feel the words, they kept him grounded, and you said, 'Okay, yeah, just don't cover my mouth. I need to breathe.'" Matt's voice shifted higher and younger as she quoted Deirdre.

Deirdre touched the corner of her mouth, her eyes soft. Then she blinked and focused on Matt. "That's right. That's what I said." She frowned, her brows fierce. "How could the house know all that stuff? We weren't even there when that happened."

"The house talked to Julio after. It touched minds with him. They shared memories."

Deirdre shivered. "I didn't know the house could do that. It's kind of creepy. Why would the house tell you that stuff, anyway?"

"It likes me. It knows I'm helping Edmund find his friends.

When we couldn't find Julio on the map, Edmund and Suki talked about this whole Julio-demon thing, but they wouldn't tell me what happened, so the house said *it* would. It gave me the dream."

Deirdre made a ticking noise with her tongue against the roof of her mouth, then leaned forward. "Here's your tea, Matt," she said, choosing a green mug with gold scribbles on it. She handed over a napkin and spoon.

"Thanks." Matt set the napkin in her lap. The mug was hot in her hand. She dumped milk and sugar into the tea as Deirdre handed a blue mug to Edmund.

Deirdre said, "The house likes you. Edmund likes you. I've got to figure Nathan and Susan do too, right?"

Matt stopped blowing on her tea and gazed at Deirdre.

"It's sort of like meeting the in-laws, isn't it?" Deirdre said. She dumped three spoonfuls of sugar into her tea and stirred. "I like you too, and I don't even know you. If the house thinks it's okay to tell you stuff like that, it's got to mean something."

Matt sipped tea. Strong, in spite of the sugar and milk. Sweet and bitter and smoky on her tongue. "So will you come home with us?"

"What?" Deirdre's eyes widened. She blinked. She blinked again.

"You never answered my question," Edmund said. "Why here? What are you looking for? Are you running away, or running to something? Maybe it's none of my business."

Deirdre pursed her lips. "I've lived here seven years. There's work here, and I love my work. I help things heal. Animals are great, you know? They never expect you to be anything except what you are. I've got just enough money to manage things. I know everybody in town now, and I know where to get anything

I want. Sometimes I've got to drive a ways to get it, but I know where it is. I'm settled." She thought about that for a minute, then drank tea.

"Do you ever take a vacation?" Matt asked.

Deirdre smiled at Matt over the top of her mug. "Last year I went to Crater Lake."

"So do you have vacation time coming?"

"I'm my own boss. I have a couple surgeries scheduled for tomorrow morning, three other animals boarding that I should keep an eye on, and people have appointments every day." Her brow furrowed. "Are you really inviting me to go back to Guthrie with you?"

"Yes," said Matt.

"Why?"

"Don't you want to see Suki again? Or Nathan?"

Deirdre put her mug down and ticked with her tongue again, a thinking sound. "I'm curious, and I'm still mad at everybody for leaving me, except I feel guilty about leaving Nathan, which doesn't make it easy to go back. Susan was the only girlfriend I had while I was a teenager. But that was a long time ago. Jeeze, why mess with it now? I'm fine as is. Calm and collected. Maybe even serene. Who wants to go stir up a bunch of old mud?" She looked toward the front door. "But then again, something strange happened the other day. Which reminds me."

She went to the fridge and pulled out the leftovers box she'd gotten from the restaurant.

The cat rose to its feet on the couch, alert and staring at the box.

"Not for you, Mr. P.," Deirdre said. She slipped out the front door and closed it behind her before the cat mobilized. When she returned a moment later, her hands were empty.

"Your coyote?" Edmund asked.

Deirdre sat again, and nodded. "Or some other creature. I'm not sure the coyote comes back. But there are hungry animals out there. I know I shouldn't get in the habit of feeding them. It interferes with their natures. But she was . . ." She shook her head.

She chewed on her lip for a minute, then said, "Edmund, can I ask you a favor?"

"Sure. What would you like?"

"Will you—will you show me some magic?"

He smiled. "You looking for anything specific? I'm out of the habit of showing off."

Deirdre glanced around the cabin. Her gaze roved along the shelves of dolls. Slowly, she stood up, went over, and picked up a four-inch-tall G.I. Joe soldier doll, extremely detailed and poseable: he had elbow, knee, shoulder, and hip joints, and his waist and head could turn. Some of the camo color on his uniform was chipped and scuffed. Deirdre bent his arms back and forth, her forehead pinched into a frown, then walked over and handed him to Edmund.

He cradled the doll in his palm. After a moment, he gave it to Matt.

—Hi,—she said.

—Greetings,—the doll said. —Name? Rank? Serial number?—

—Matt. Human. I don't have a serial number. Do you?—

—I used to. Back in the mud days. I had a name, a rank, a serial number, and lots of adventures. I've been in deep freeze for a long time now, though. Wait. Jonny. My name was Jonny.—

Matt glanced at Edmund, then at Deirdre. Deirdre was giving her a total-attention stare.

—Did you ever think about walking around on your own?— Matt asked Jonny.

—Think about it? I dreamed about it, longed for it. I don't have any good enemies right now, but I wouldn't mind a recon mission.—

—Why don't you give it a try?—

—You mean— His arm turned slowly. His elbow bent. He straightened both arms, bent both elbows. He sat up. —You mean—I could have been doing this all along?—

—I don't know,—Matt said. She set him carefully down on the coffee table.

He rose to his feet. He walked several steps forward, pivoted, and walked back.

"Mrrrr?" said Pepe, inching to the edge of the couch, blue eyes fixed on the walking doll. Matt grabbed the cat before it could pounce. It glared up at her and made grumpy sounds.

Jonny marched to the edge of the table and saluted Deirdre. —Sergeant Box reporting for duty, sir.—

Deirdre returned his salute. She blinked and stared at Matt. "How did you do that?" she whispered.

Matt shook her head. "I didn't do it. He did it. I just talked to him. He says he's Sergeant Jonny Box and he used to have lots of adventures."

"Jonny," Deirdre said. "That's right." She rubbed her eye. Then she put her hands down in front of the doll. "I'm sorry, buddy. I don't do adventures the way I used to."

The soldier climbed up onto her hand. He gripped her thumb.

"He's awake now? Will he stay awake?" Deirdre asked Matt.

"What am I going to do with him? I can't—I don't—" Her face twisted in distress.

—I'll go back to guard duty, sir,—the soldier said, saluting her again.

Matt translated for him.

"Oh. Thank you, Sergeant." She walked to the shelf she had taken him from and held her hand up to it. Jonny climbed off her hand and straightened to attention.

"At ease," Deirdre said.

He shifted into another position.

She stared at him for a long moment, then went back to her chair. "Oh, Matt. Could you do that with all of them?"

"I don't know. Some things are more awake than others. The stuff people spend the most time with gets its own consciousness. I guess you must've played with him a lot, huh?"

Deirdre nodded. "He was my favorite. Those G.I. Joe dolls were really sturdy and well made. They could take a lot of punishment." She shot the doll another glance. It didn't move. "Is he still awake?"

"I don't know. I think he'll settle down again. Things are used to only being used some of the time. It's how they live. I don't think they mind it. Did you want me to talk to anything else?"

Deirdre looked around again, studying each doll in turn. She paused two or three times in her survey, but finally shook her head. "I'd feel horrible having to leave them alone again. Do they tell you stories?"

"Sometimes." Matt let go of the cat. It jumped down off the couch, gave her a glare, and stalked away. "Most things like to talk. I like to listen. Works out pretty good."

Deirdre smiled. "Well, thanks. Thanks a lot."

"Is that what you wanted, or would you like something else?" Edmund asked.

"No, that was just great. Matt did that? You didn't do it."

"That's right," Edmund said. "I could have made him move, but I don't have Matt's gift, which is the gift to let things move for themselves."

"What do you have?"

He glanced at Matt. "I haven't done an inventory lately."

"You can float. You can fly. You get mad really good. You can turn into things, you can help things, and you can talk to things, too." Matt turned to Deirdre. "He knows how to listen. He can throw dust in the air. He's *really* good at that. And he does this dowsing thing. That's how we found you, with a map and a fishing weight. I love that trick."

"Sure doesn't sound like the stuff you used to do," Deirdre said.

Edmund shrugged and smiled at her.

"He can probably still do a bunch of that stuff. He just doesn't. You would if you had to, wouldn't you?" Matt asked Edmund.

"Sure."

"He could do requests, I bet."

"That's okay. I don't know what to wish for, and from what I've seen, wishing's kind of dangerous anyway." Deirdre checked her watch. "Hey. I'm glad you guys came. I better return to my regularly scheduled life now, though. I have to get up early tomorrow for surgery, and I'll need to shower before and after. I only have enough hot water for one shower at a time. It takes about two hours to refill. One of you could shower tonight, and one could shower later in the morning tomorrow, unless you're going to take off bright and early. Are you leaving tomorrow?"

Edmund looked perplexed.

"We will if you come with us," Matt said.

Deirdre shook her head, smiling. "Tell you what, I'll sleep on it. Let me show you how everything works."

She introduced them to the bathroom and got fresh towels out. "I've got to brush my teeth and crash now, but you can stay up if you like. I'll be able to sleep through it," she said. "College dorm life teaches you to sleep through anything."

MATT curled up close to Edmund under a down quilt on the futon in the back of his car and pulled her head in under the covers. It was freezing outside, but Edmund was big and warm and comfortable.

He ducked his head under the quilt too, and wrapped his arms around her.

"What are we doing here?" she murmured.

"We found her. That's all I needed to do. She doesn't have to come with us, Matt. I'm just glad I got to see her."

"But there's something—" She felt an empty space under her heart. She pressed her forehead against his chest, basking in his warmth, and touched her sternum. "I need to collect them."

"What?"

"They must come back." She felt very strange. Her voice didn't sound like it belonged to her.

"Matt."

"The time has come to try again."

"Matt? Who's talking?"

Nobody inside her answered.

Edmund lifted his right arm from around her and did something. A moment, and a little green glowing ball hovered under the blankets with them. "Matt?" Gently he pushed her away so he could look into her face. He touched her cheek. His fingers glistened when he lifted them away. "You're crying. What's the matter?"

"I don't know." This time it was her own voice. She felt tense and frustrated and scared. "I don't know who that was. Maybe it was the house. How can the house talk from inside me? I love that house. What's it doing to me?"

He pulled her close.

"Tell me if you want me to do anything about it. I'll try to make it stop," he whispered.

She shuddered for a little while. His hands stroked up and down her back. She clung to him. "Help me," she whispered at last. If anybody was going to get inside her, she wanted to know beforehand, and she wanted a chance to tell them to leave her alone. She wanted a knock on the door, and the chance to look through a peephole to see if it was someone she wanted to let inside.

This was wrong.

He sat up under the quilt and lifted it so she could sit up too. They huddled under the quilt tent, heads together, legs tangled, the light hovering in the space between them.

"Give me your hands," he said.

She held them out to him.

He cupped his hands around each of hers, stroked his thumbs down across her palms, then along the insides of her fingers. "Hmm, hmm, hmm." He lifted her left hand and pressed his lips to the palm. "Something," he said. "This is the hand that receives, and something has been given."

"I don't remember." But then she did: a dim memory of a gift of food, bread for her journey.

"Something was given. Something accepted. Do you want to return it?"

"Something got inside me." She felt a faint, feathery presence along her bones, a hidden heartbeat just under her own, an ache, a longing for something lost, something never had.

To understand something completely, you must digest it, the house had told Julio.

Maybe she had eaten something important, but she didn't understand it yet. "The house," she said. "Bread."

"The house gave you something to eat? And it left a voice inside you, and some kind of mission."

"I think—" She nodded slowly.

"Do you want me to take it out of you?"

"Can you do that?"

"I can try."

She hunched one shoulder, then the other. She tugged her hands free of Edmund's grasp and buried them in her armpits, hugged herself.

The house had given her a shadow second self, one with its own voice. Had she said yes to this? She and the house had shared many dreams in the short time she had stayed there. Maybe she had agreed.

If she hadn't, she couldn't stay in the house again. Not without negotiation. She didn't give people who did things to her without asking a second chance unless they promised, and she believed, that they wouldn't do it again.

"Do you want me to try?" Edmund asked.

What had this new self done to her so far? Only made her

want something she already wanted: to find the people Edmund wanted to find. It hadn't hurt her. It was important to the house. Should she have Edmund pull it out of her? What if it was shaping her in ways she couldn't detect, ways she wouldn't like? What if it was shaping her toward a self she would like better? Maybe it wasn't shaping her at all. Maybe it was just waiting.

She uncurled from her fisted self and leaned against him. "I think I'll wait. See what it does. You tell me if I start acting not like myself, though, okay?" she murmured.

"I will," he said, smoothing his warm hands over her, rubbing his thumbs against the tightest muscles, holding her close.

Gradually her agitation faded and she relaxed enough to sleep.

DAWN sparkled, trapped in frost flowers on the car windows. Matt crept out of Edmund's embrace, slipped from the car, and went into the cabin, which smelled of fresh coffee, toast, and wood-smoke from the Franklin stove, where fire talked. It was nice and warm inside the A-frame. "Hey. You sleep all right?" Deirdre asked, coming out of the bathroom with wet hair. She wore jeans and a T-shirt.

"No. I had a weird dream. Did you sleep all right?"

"Sure. I always do since I got here. Want some coffee?"

"Yeah."

"Have a seat. I'll bring you some."

Matt sat on a chair at the card table. She was wearing a long johns top and bottom, thick socks, and her army boots, added at the last minute. Deirdre set a mug of coffee, the sugar bowl, and the milk pitcher in front of her. "You want some cereal?"

"Do you have enough? We have food in the car."

"I've got plenty. You like that honey-nut stuff? That's my favorite."

"Sure."

Deirdre set bowls of cereal, napkins, and spoons on the table. She brought over the milk and sat down next to Matt to eat. She also drank coffee, and came more and more awake.

"I get confused in my desires," Deirdre said eventually when she and Matt had finished their cereal. "Sometimes I want to find magic again. Sometimes I just want to go on living without it. Sometimes I think there has to be some middle ground, where you know it's around, even if you can't use it. Sometimes I think, what the hell, am I looking for religion? Most of that Christian stuff leaves me cold. Here I get my sunsets and sunrises, and weather, and quiet, and Mr. P." The cat had come over. It lay on Deidre's foot, a large furry heap, and purred. "And every small animal in town," she went on, and leaned over to stroke the cat's spine.

"I thought you said he doesn't like being petted," Matt said.

"He doesn't like it, but I do. He'll put up with a small amount of it. You have to know when to stop." She patted the cat's head twice more and straightened.

"So I don't know what I'm looking for, or even if I'm looking," Deirdre said. "Now I have the coyote, too. Maybe I've got everything I need."

"You don't want to come back to Guthrie with us," Matt said. Loss pierced her chest like a thorn.

"I'm glad you came. I'm glad Edmund told me what happened way back when. I didn't know until last night that I still had this tight feeling in my chest wondering what happened to him, but it eased after he told me, and I feel better now than I have since I can remember. I'm glad you talked to my soldier and let him walk around. I don't want to go back to Guthrie with you today, but maybe I'll go back. Will you be there?"

"We have to look for the others." Now more than ever, Matt felt an urgency to track down the twins. *The house's impulse,* she thought. She did want to see Terry again too, though. What would it be like to see Terry if Matt weren't afraid of what Terry would do next?

Deirdre got a card out of her purse and wrote on it. "Here's my phone numbers. The clinic and the house. When you get back to Guthrie, call me and tell me. I could use a short vacation. I'd have to make arrangements with my partner and my assistant to take over my cases, though. That will take some juggling."

"Thank you," Matt whispered.

A little while later Deirdre hugged Matt and Edmund good-bye and set off to perform surgery on a dog and a cat.

"What now?" Edmund asked as Matt laced up her boots.

"Terry," said Matt. Time to test Terry and herself.

Chapter Ten

· · · · ·

TOLAND sat on the top step in the hall outside his mom's apartment and watched the graffiti-streaked wall across from the stairs. Last week, he could have sworn he saw his music teacher Lia step right through it when she left.

Lia couldn't come up the stairs without him knowing. His big sister Zette said leave well enough alone. Don't look a gift horse in the mouth. Zette always said stuff like that. But she liked to rattle Christmas presents before she opened them, same as anybody else.

Toland licked his lips and found a drop of syrup left from his waffle breakfast. Sweetness melted over his tongue.

Gift horse, what a thing to call his teacher. She did teach for free, and nobody knew where she came from, but she wasn't anything like a horse.

Something clattered on the stairs below. Toland leaned over and peered down the stairwell. *Was* his music teacher using stairs, like most people?

"Did you practice this week?" his teacher said from behind him. He turned around and there she was, in the hall, small and dark except for her bright green dress, her black eyes sparkling, and in her hand her violin case.

"Where'd you come from?" he asked.

"No questions. Only I get to ask. Did you practice our waltz?"

He stood up and brushed his hands on his pants. "Yeah."

"Show me."

He led her into the apartment and got out his violin as she took out hers. Lia never said where she came from. He'd met her in the park—she heard him singing, and they talked about music. He told her what he really wanted, and she said she could help him. She loaned him the violin and came to give him lessons.

His mother and his sister had asked questions and watched and argued, but Lia still came every week, and after a month they decided she probably wasn't going to hurt a ten-year-old boy, and they stopped bothering her.

As Toland and Lia tightened the hair on their bows and set up the music stands, Zette came out and sat on the couch to listen and watch the lesson, the way she always did. She brought her knitting.

Toland played the waltz. He had practiced. It sure made a difference in how well he played, and life was better when guilt wasn't always gnawing on him. Free lessons. He should earn them somehow.

He had finally decided he really liked and wanted this music. Sometimes he woke up with it singing in him, and he had to jump up and grab the violin and play. Sometimes he'd struggle with math homework and get nowhere and play the violin for a while and then go back and the problems would stop squirming around and behave. Sometimes he heard music in his head and had to play until he could get it to come out of the violin. Some- times he heard a song on the radio and he could play that.

There was a mute button on the violin so he could play it in his room as much as he wanted and nobody else heard. More and more lately, he played in between everything.

He played the waltz through once, then again. Lia smiled. He played it a third time, and she jumped up and started dancing. So did Zette. That had never happened. Zette was the least danc- ing person Toland knew. So he played some more, watching them dance, until Zette said, "Stop it!"

Surprised, Toland lifted his bow from the strings. Zette sat on the couch with a thud. "Don't play that song again," she said, between gasping breaths.

"Let's go up on the roof," said Lia.

"No you don't," Zette said. "You're not leaving my sight. You're not giving him secret instruction. You're not—you better not—you better not teach him to be like you."

Lia knelt in front of Zette. "He has a gift," she said, "and the drive to learn to use it."

"A gift to make people jerk around like puppets? We don't want that here. Any more of that and I will break that violin of his. You won't be welcome here."

Lia stared up into Zette's face.

Ice crystals formed in Toland's chest. Break his violin! Send his teacher away! No. How could he live without being able to make music, now that he knew what it felt like?

"He's just little," Zette said in a softer voice. "He's not old enough for a gift like that."

"He already has the gift. If we don't train it, it might do things he doesn't even plan."

Zette and Lia had a staring contest then. Toland hugged his violin. He never wanted to give it up.

"You go away now," Zette said. "I'll talk to Mama about this. Come back tomorrow and we'll tell you what we decided."

Lia rose to her feet. She nodded. She put her violin in its case, then headed out, but at the last minute she turned and touched Toland's head with her warm hand. "Mind your mama and your sister," she whispered. "Choose your songs carefully. Don't do the hard ones for now."

He nodded.

FRIDAY was a Women-Only day at Terry's gym in Spores Ferry, so Edmund waited in the car.

Matt wondered whether she should wait in the car too. It was late afternoon by the time they reached Spores Ferry. When had Terry gotten to the gym, and how long would she stay there? Did it take an hour? Two? Six? It looked like there was only one entrance, so they should be able to catch her coming out, but how long would it take?

They had tracked Terry without trouble using Edmund's dowsing fishing weight—at least, they assumed they had found her; there was no ambiguity in the signal. It led them straight to the plaza on the south end of town. The plaza consisted of a big parking lot surrounded by a supermarket, a Hallmark store, a RadioShack, a travel agent, the kind of super drugstore that sells shoes, fabric, cameras, and everything else you need except fresh produce, a clothing store, a bank, a restaurant, an espresso drive-thru, and a national video rental chain.

The two-story gym building was right behind a Pizza Palace.

A wall of windows on the second floor showed a row of exercycles facing outward, with two or three women pumping away on them and not getting anywhere.

Edmund parked next to the gym. They sat for a while in the car. The weight, hanging from the rearview mirror, tugged toward the gym building.

"I'll go see," Matt said.

She had never been inside a gym before, and she had many mixed-up feelings about finding Terry again, but she knew she was going to do it sooner or later, so why wait?

Edmund gripped her hand. "You don't have to face her alone."

"I'll be okay." She squeezed his hand and let go. "Besides, what can she do in public? Okay, maybe I better not think about that too hard. I just hope she still feels friendly. See you in a few."

She left the car and went to the glass door. Glowing golden outlines of a perfectly muscled man and woman were stenciled on it. She pushed the door open and walked into a rush of chilled air and chlorine scent. Pop music with a strong beat played over loudspeakers, and she heard the splash and echo of people swimming in an enclosed pool.

A woman sat behind a tall desk that faced the front door. "Hi there," she said.

"Hi," said Matt. She went to the desk and studied the woman, who wore a bouncy blond ponytail, a white tank top, and black sweatpants.

"I haven't seen you here before. Are you a new member?" asked the woman. She looked about twenty, and her arms showed visible muscles.

"No. I'm looking for a friend who goes here. I don't want to use the equipment or anything, I just want to check and see if she's here. Is that okay?" *What if she says no? What am I going to do? It'll be a sign, I guess. I'll go back outside and wait with Edmund.*

The woman grinned. "Just tell me you're a prospective member, and I'll have Jayjay show you around."

Matt blinked and said, "I'm a prospective member."

"Hey, great. Jayjay?"

A muscular girl wearing a lavender terry-cloth headband in her short frosted hair and a purple sports bra and shorts came out of the office behind Matt and said, "Hi!" She held out her hand. Matt shook. Good grip. "I'm Jayjay!"

"I'm Matt," said Matt.

"You want to check out the facilities? The pool's here on the ground floor—" Jayjay pointed through a sliding glass door behind the other woman, and Matt saw that it led to a pool, where several women jumped up and down in the water, following directions from a slim woman who jumped up and down on the poolside walkway—"and our workout room is upstairs. Please follow me."

Matt lingered a minute to make sure Terry wasn't in the pool.

In Jayjay's wake, Matt climbed a staircase to the second floor, passing a large mirror on the way up. People could check themselves out and see why they needed a workout, she thought, or on the way down they could see how much better they looked. Or maybe how much sweatier.

Matt checked herself. It was a Women-Only day. She guessed she looked enough like a woman today to pass. Weird.

The carpeting in the workout room was light brown. Aside from the wall of windows in front of the exercycles, the walls were covered with mirrors. Space seemed to go on forever. Every woman working on a machine was doubled and redoubled in a forest of chrome, gray vinyl, and flesh. The air was cool from air-conditioning and smelled blank. Speakers piped in music, and fans whirred, aiming air blasts at people on treadmills and Stairmasters.

Women of all shapes and sizes worked out on various machines. A universal gym had women pulling ropes, kicking at plates, pulling down on things that looked like bike handlebars. Other machines had strange seats where women sat or reclined or lay on their stomachs and pushed weighted assemblies up or pulled them down with legs and arms. Some women worked in front of the mirrors with free weights and some just sat on the floor stretching.

Women on side-by-side treadmills talked to each other. On the exercycles, the women wore headphones, listening to their own music. Most of the women seemed to be looking inward and not paying attention to the others.

"This is the workout room. The locker rooms are through there. Do you want me to explain the equipment to you? I can demonstrate it," said Jayjay.

Matt stared at a woman on one of the weight machines. She lay on a seat tilted back at a forty-five-degree angle, her feet on bars like motorbike footholds. She wore an intensely turquoise T-shirt and black bike shorts. Her hands gripped the handles of an assembly that V'ed above her. She pushed up from the shoulders, and a stack of weights in a slot to her side rose as she lifted, lowered as she lowered her arms. Her face gleamed with sweat. Her short dark hair was plastered to her head.

"That's our BodyMaster reclining chest press," Jayjay said. "Would you like to—"

"Thanks. Excuse me." Matt walked past spread-legged women

touching their noses to their knees on the floor and stood next to the woman in turquoise.

After a moment, the woman noticed her.

"Matt!" she yelped. She let the weights down slowly, though, so they just clinked at the end of their descent. She jumped to her feet.

Terry. She had grown taller, and she looked sleek, muscled, and more mature, but she didn't look like a grown-up, really. Still, she stood a head taller than Matt now.

"Wow. You sure grew up good," Matt said.

"Hey!" Terry hugged Matt. Terry smelled sweaty, but not bad. Some of her dampness transferred to Matt's black shirt. "Dang. Sorry about that," Terry said, stepping back. "Hey! Look at you! You almost look like a girl now!" Terry touched Matt's hair, which had grown out to about an inch, and was inexplicably curly. "What are you doing here?"

"I came to find you."

"You did? You did? Oh, boy! Where have you been? What have you been doing? Oh, boy! I'm so glad to see you!"

"Guess this means you don't want a demo," Jayjay's chipper voice said from behind Matt.

"No," Matt said, and turned to smile at her, "but thanks a lot."

"Anytime. Come on back if you want to sign up." Jayjay wiggled her fingers in the air and headed for the stairs.

"I'm just about finished here," Terry said. "Let me wash up. Want some coffee? Want something to eat? I can't believe this! It's so great!" Terry led the way to the locker rooms. Inside the doorway was a row of sinks below a big mirror, a drinking fountain, a wall of lockers, and a doctor's office–type scale. Another doorway led somewhere else, and there was an alcove lined with more lockers to the right, and a couple of cubbyhole rest rooms.

Terry turned on water and washed her hands, then splashed water on her face. "Are you staying someplace? Want to come home with me? I'm still living with Mom in the same house. I don't want to take a shower till I get home. I didn't bring a change of clothes. Sorry if I stink." She dried her hands and face on a towel.

"You smell fine," Matt said.

"Really?" Terry peeked at her sideways, grinning. "I'm so glad to see you!"

"I'm glad to see you too," Matt said at last. Terry was so bubbly! It was a lot different from the last time Matt had seen her. "What are you doing still here in town? I thought you'd be out taking over the world."

"Really?" Terry raised her eyebrows. "Hmm. You know, you don't actually have to leave home to take over the world." She laughed a villain's laugh: "Muahahahahah!"

Matt took a step back.

"Kidding! Just kidding," Terry said, her eyes sparkling and her smile wide. "The world's too big. I don't need the whole thing. I find plenty to do right here. Want to see my base of operations? Would you like to come home with me?"

"Can my boyfriend come too?"

"You have a boyfriend?" Terry whooped and hugged her again. A woman changing into her bathing suit in the locker alcove peeked out at them, smiled, and pulled straps up over her shoulders.

"Hey, hey," Matt said as Terry released her.

"Oh, no. Was that too friendly?"

"Just surprising." Matt smiled and shook her head. "Different. I'm not used to huggy people."

"I'll try to control myself. You have a boyfriend? That means you've changed too, right? What kind of person is he?"

"He's downstairs waiting for us. He's someone you already know."

Terry's blue eyes widened. "Whoa. Who could I know that you would—" She frowned for a moment.

"Come on," Matt said, heading back across the workout room.

"Wait," Terry called from behind her. "I have to get my stuff."

Matt paused behind the treadmill women. All these women fighting it out with machines to get fit. There was something very strange about using all this energy and not accomplishing work with it. Probably it wasn't handy for them to go somewhere and unload trucks or help people move or actually ride bikes on roads or bike paths. Maybe it was too scary, with rapists and whatever out there. Or maybe they didn't like weather? It stayed cool in here, and it didn't rain. That did make it more comfortable for exercise. And you could pick how much weight you were pushing around and set your own schedule.

She edged over to the free weight stand and touched the rack that held the hand weights. —Hey,—she said.

—Hey!— It sounded boisterous and delighted. —Want to play with some weight?— A five-pound weight wiggled in its slot.

—No, thanks.—

—How about two?— A pair of four-pound weights swayed in unison. —They'll dance with you. They'll make your arms strong!—

—No, that's okay. Thanks.—

Terry touched her shoulder. "What are you doing?"

"Checking things out," Matt said. Terry had a red gym bag over her shoulder now. —Bye.—

The swaying weights subsided. —Awww.—

"Come on." Terry took her hand and pulled her away from the weights. They ran down the stairs. "Bye, Kitty," Terry said to the woman behind the desk.

"Bye, hon. Bye, Matt."

"So who's this guy?" Terry asked as they pushed out the door.

Matt led her to the car. Edmund leaned against it, his arms crossed over his chest. He smiled wide at Terry.

Terry froze, staring at him. "No way!" she said. She glanced back at Matt, who nodded. "Hey, buddy. Where the heck you been? How the heck are you?" The next minute she had dropped her gym bag and was hugging him. "I can't believe it! What a day!"

"Hey, Terry."

"This is so unbelievable. Matt! Edmund's your boyfriend? Outstanding!" She checked her watch, a big black sports watch on a woven turquoise band. "Oh, what am I thinking? My meeting's not till tonight. You guys want to come to my house? I have to take a shower, but then I want to find out where you've been. Are you hungry?"

"What you got to eat?" Matt asked suspiciously. Ten years earlier Terry had favored cottage cheese, nonfat milk, unsalted breads, and way too much tomato purée on everything. A meatless, fatless, salt-free diet might work for Edmund, but Matt didn't like tasteless food unless she had no choice.

Terry laughed, then stopped, then sighed. "I was hard on you. I'm sorry, Matt. I was such a bitch."

"More like a brat."

Terry hunched her shoulders, then relaxed and sighed. "Okay. I still eat carefully, but Mom has a lot of regular food in the house. Or we could pick up some takeout on the way over. Or order a pizza. How about it?"

"Sure. We could visit," Edmund said, exchanging glances with Matt.

"Matt, you remember how to get to my house? Oh heck, probably not. Just follow me." She went to a black Miata and got in, started it, pulled out, and waited until Edmund and Matt got into Edmund's car and lined up behind her, then off they went.

"How'd it go?" Edmund asked.

Matt shook her head. "She was so happy to see me. Really honestly happy. I wonder what I was worried about?"

A small black oval beach stone dropped from the dashboard into Matt's lap.

"Whoa. Spirit?" Matt said. Edmund's spirit usually didn't speak to her directly. Matt picked up the stone and studied it. She glanced at Edmund. "What does it mean?"

"What meaning can you find in it?"

"It's a rock." —Rock?—

No answer from the stone. It was a natural thing and didn't speak her language.

"A beach rock gets the edges smoothed off by sand over time," Edmund said.

Matt held the stone up and stared at it. "But the inside stays the same?"

"Could be."

Matt pressed the stone between her palms for a moment.

"Thanks, spirit," she said, and put the stone back on the dashboard.

She watched Spores Ferry go by. She had spent more than a month here following Terry around. Terry had dropped a tether spell on her that made Matt sick every time she got more than half a block away from Terry, and it had driven Matt crazy. Being trapped by anything was one of her greatest nightmares. Fortunately, Matt had had lots of things to talk to. She had gotten to know the furniture in Terry's house pretty well.

She shoved her hand deep into a pocket in her army jacket, draped over her seat back, and felt for one of her traveling companions. It was a small carved stone monk all curled up, his face buried in his hands, and his knees up to his ears. She had found it on Terry's twin sister Tasha's dresser while Matt was staying in Tasha's room, and the monk had given itself to Matt. Tasha wouldn't mind, the monk had told her. At the time Matt had been desperate for friends and allies. The stone monk fit perfectly into her hand, and had whispered comfort when she felt worst.

"What have you got?" Edmund asked.

Matt slowly opened her hand so the monk sat on her palm. "This used to be Tasha's. I took it."

His eyebrows rose as he glanced at it. "Wow. What an aura. What is it? A walnut?"

Matt laughed. "It's a little guy." She closed her hand around it again. Its stone felt smooth and warm, comfortably heavy. "He was my friend when Terry was really bugging me." Matt touched the monk to her cheek. —You still awake in there?—

—I'm here. How can I help?—

—I don't know if I need help right now.— She remembered

nights on the road, nights under bridges or bushes, nights when she had held him and slept all right. Sometimes he told her about the other people who had held him; there had been five, after the man who had carved him in Indonesia. He had only spent a little while with Tasha. Matt had gotten better Tasha stories from other things in the house, enough to make her wish she could meet Tasha. —We're going back to where I found you.—

—I'm here,—he thought.

—Thanks.— She tucked him into the pocket of her jeans.

Terry turned onto Greenbriar Street. Matt sat forward, looking at the neighborhood. Yep. There was the house with the gnomes in the petunia bed out front, and there was Mr. Potts's 1936 Ford parked in the street, still sparkling. There was Terry's house, a beige two-story a lot like the other houses along the street, which had all been built in the early sixties. You couldn't tell from looking at Terry's house that a witch lived there. Terry parked and got out of her car, and Edmund parked right behind her.

"Do you want us to bring anything?" Edmund asked as he climbed out. "We have food in the car."

"We'll find something in the kitchen," Terry said.

They went inside. The house smelled familiar to Matt. Rebecca Dane, Terry's mom, must still be using the same pine-scented cleaner. Maybe she'd even talked Terry into helping with the housekeeping, and Terry was using it now. There was a smell of boiled potatoes, too, and a faint sharp undertone that was new.

"Hey, Terry. You got a job?" Matt asked.

"I've got two. I run a home-based business, and I do some tutoring at the university in cultural anthropology. That was my major," Terry said as they went through the house. "Hey! Mom! What are you doing home?"

An older version of Terry, with chin-length dark hair, blue eyes under black brows, beautiful sculpted cheekbones, and handsome mouth, sat at the kitchen table. She looked up. "What am I doing home? I live here, Theresa. Visitors? Why didn't you call and tell me?"

"I thought you had a meeting."

Rebecca rose from where she had been drinking coffee from a huge mug and working on a crossword puzzle in the newspaper. "Excuse me," she said. "I wasn't expecting company—Matt!"

"Hi, Rebecca."

"Hey! Matt!" Rebecca came and hugged her.

For the first time Matt let herself remember how strange this was. She was always walking away from people she knew, and she almost never went back to them. She had returned to the haunted house and Nathan: a first. Now she was back in Spores Ferry, actually back inside Terry's house, where once upon a time her whole being was absorbed in longing to leave.

Rebecca had been great, though. "Hey," Matt said.

Rebecca released her, glanced at Edmund, leaned forward and stared. "Edmund?" she said. She held out her hands to him.

He took them and smiled at her. "Hi, Mrs. Dane."

"Welcome to my house. Goodness! How long has it been?"

"Pretty long," he said. "I've never been to this house before."

"Well, that makes it at least ten years, probably longer. We moved here right after my divorce. You don't look a day older." She squinted at the lines at the outer corners of his eyes. "Well, maybe a day."

He lifted an eyebrow. "I never know what to say to that."

"It's supposed to be a compliment." Rebecca smiled, then looked puzzled. "Where did you two come from? Do you—" She glanced at Matt, then at Terry. "Red flag?"

"Sure. Mom, Edmund is a witch."

"Oh, good."

"Red flag?" asked Edmund.

"I didn't tell Mom I was a witch until I was seventeen," Terry said, "five years after it happened. So when she meets somebody I knew while I was a witch but before I told her about it, she wonders what kind of person they are. Most of my friends were normal. But she can't tell."

"Oh. Code talking."

"Right."

"So when you visited us in Atwell," Rebecca said, "it was witch business? I did wonder about you, Edmund. Most teenage boys I know wouldn't be caught dead hanging around with girls four years younger, unless they were up to no good. You never seemed to be up to no good."

"Depends on your definition of good, I guess," Edmund said. "We were comparing notes. We all turned into witches at the same time."

Rebecca shook her head. "I must have been wearing blinders back then. I was worrying about all the wrong things! So much going on I just didn't know about."

"Seems like all parents of teenagers say that," Matt said.

"But I had more reason than most." She ruffled Terry's hair. Terry shook her head; red touched her cheeks.

"I told these guys we'd feed them, Mom," Terry said. She opened the freezer compartment of the refrigerator and stared inside.

"We could go out," said Rebecca. "We're low on food right now. We haven't done our weekly shopping yet. We always go on Saturday."

Terry checked the lower part of the fridge. "There's plenty of yogurt." She turned with an evil grin and held out a container of plain, fat-free yogurt. "Yum, yum, Matt." She jiggled the container.

"Yuck!"

"Kidding." Terry put the yogurt back.

"She still eats the worst food. It's like she thinks flavor will make her weak," said Rebecca.

"I do believe that," Terry said seriously. "Flavor is a distraction. Fewer distractions means better concentration."

"What do you find, Edmund? Does flavor make you weak?" Rebecca asked.

"Nope. Or maybe I just haven't noticed. I don't need to be strong most of the time."

"You people are witches. I don't understand why you can't just conjure up a perfect meal. Terry doesn't seem to get much joy from what she does. Do you?"

"Me?" Edmund tapped his chest. "Yes. I love it." His eyes glowed. "Sometimes, when I listen well, I can feel my connection to everything. It's the best feeling in the world."

Rebecca smiled slowly. "You're a different kind of witch from Terry, aren't you?"

"I don't know."

"He used to be the same," Terry said. "We could all three work the same spells. But I get the feeling— Edmund, did you know Tasha ran off to be a priestess of air?"

"Matt said she left and you were upset, but I didn't know that part."

"She started a completely different kind of training and turned into this—" Terry's face went sour, as if she'd bitten a bad pickle.

"She's very sweet, and I'm proud of her," Rebecca said.

"Yeah," said Terry, her face still twisted with distaste. "She's all sweet and good. A pod-thing sister. You have those kind of vibes, too."

"Gee, thanks," said Edmund.

"It's sickening." Terry grinned. "Well, I'm going to take a shower. Mom, could you order a pizza or something?"

"We'll figure something out," said Rebecca.

"Excuse me. Later, guys." Terry left the kitchen.

"But seriously, why *can't* you conjure up a feast? They were always making magic food in fairy tales, weren't they?" Rebecca said.

"Yeah, guuuuy, Edmund," said Matt.

He held his hands up. He waved them in strange gestures above the kitchen table. "Alaka*zam*," he said, and the cooler and the bag of groceries from the back of the car appeared.

"Well, that's disappointing," said Rebecca. "I thought it would be swallow's tongues, passion fruit, and roast pheasant on a bed of peacock feathers under glass domes. Bird's nest soup? Escargots? Radishes sliced to look like roses? A cake with a sugar palace on top? Couldn't you at least come up with golden dishes?"

"If we had gold, we could," Matt muttered. For a short time, she had had her own supply of magic, malleable gold like Suki's. It had done whatever she asked it to, until she used it all up.

"I'm not a genie or a fairy. My kind of craft doesn't work that way," Edmund said. He got doughnuts and the loaf of bread out of the grocery bag. "To get something for you, I have to take it from somewhere else. I don't know where to find a pheasant under glass, and if I found one and took it, someone would be upset. All I can offer you is what we already have." He smiled and pulled a doughnut out of the bag, showed it to Rebecca.

"Oh, goody, chocolate sprinkles," she said. Edmund got a napkin out of the bag and put the doughnut on it, then handed it to Rebecca. She sat down at her place and dunked the doughnut in her coffee. "I haven't done this in a long time!" She took a bite. "Yum! Well, that's great. You guys want coffee? I've got a pot made."

"I'll get some," Matt said. "Edmund doesn't drink it. Everything's where it used to be, right?"

"Right. Help yourself."

"Want cheese sandwiches?" Edmund asked. "How about peanut butter and jelly? What we've got is road food. We're traveling right now."

"We shouldn't use up your food," Rebecca said. "Look, I've got instant rice. I could run out and do some shopping. We could get Chinese or pizza or something. Drat that Terry, anyway. She probably offered you dinner, didn't she? She doesn't care about food. Friday nights I usually have ramen with egg in it and whatever leftovers I've got from the previous week. I use up all my produce, and—"

"That sounds good," said Matt. She sat at the table with her loaded cup of coffee and looked through the bag of groceries in front of her.

"We can use whatever we've got," Edmund said. "We can get more."

"Look," said Matt. "Potatoes!"

"Okay. Let's pool our resources," said Rebecca.

By the time Terry came back from her shower, stylish again

in a maroon shirt and black slacks, short black hair neatly blow-dried, they had put together a strange but interesting meal, a stew of noodles, chopped celery, green beans, potato chunks, eggs, carrots. After they dished it into bowls, Rebecca and Matt added slices of pepperoni to theirs, and Edmund put cheese slices on top of all of them. Rebecca added thick-sliced sourdough bread and butter.

Terry stuck with cottage cheese and yogurt. She didn't even taste the mulligan stew, but Matt thought it was great.

"SURE, you can stay in Tasha's room if you like," Rebecca said when they had finished eating and cleaning up and sat around the kitchen table. "She doesn't mind."

"It's not Tasha's room," Terry said. "She never lived in this house. She's got her own apartment halfway across town. Mom just set it up and hoped."

"I promised her I'd always have a place for her to stay. She has stayed here."

"Twice, out of pity," said Terry. "Hey, Matt, want some cocoa?"

Cocoa was one of the few good things Matt remembered about being here before. Terry would eat her horrible meals of white and tasteless things, and Matt would eat the same things because that was one of the ways the tether spell had worked. Every once in a while, Terry would give her cocoa. In that flavorless existence, cocoa had come close to nirvana.

"Yeah," Matt said. "That'd be nice."

Terry made cocoa the hard way: heated milk on the stove, mixed Dutch chocolate with a measured amount of sugar, then blended in the hot milk. She got the milk carton out of the refrigerator.

"Terry, offer some to your other guest," Rebecca said. "And what about your ailing mom? Doesn't she deserve some?"

"Does she want some?" Terry's voice held a strange note.

"Actually, I'm stuffed," said Rebecca. "We did good, guys."

"What about you, Edmund?" Terry turned and glanced at him, eyebrows up.

"No, thank you."

Terry smiled and put milk on to heat, then got down a mug Matt remembered from ten years earlier. It was gray, the shape of a beer stein, and it had a blue coat-of-arms-type eagle stenciled on the side.

Her special mug.

The articles of confinement . . .

Matt felt strange.

Terry fixed the cocoa for her and handed her the mug. "Thanks." Matt sniffed. It smelled so great. A little bitter, not milk chocolate, something old and dark and powerfully comforting. She lifted the mug for a sip, and thought,—Hi, mug. Remember me?—

—Matt! Missed your hands. Missed your lips.—

She kissed its lip.

—Don't drink,—it thought.

—Why not?—

—She put something changing inside.—

Matt set the mug on the table, kept her hand on the handle, and stared at Terry. Terry shrugged, smiled, and waggled her eyebrows.

"What does it do?" Matt asked.

"Makes you happy. It's a short one."

"That's it?"

Terry licked her upper lip. "No."

What had Matt said when she left last time? I'll be your friend if you don't cast spells on me. But here Terry was, casting a spell on her without even asking. Matt had given Terry a second chance, and Terry blew it.

Why?

Terry was bad at making friends.

Matt felt a rush of exasperated affection. When was this kid going to learn? She shoved the mug toward Terry. "You drink it," she said.

"I will if you will."

A dare. More kid stuff. "You first."

Terry got another mug down and poured half the cocoa into the second mug. She drank, then showed Matt the inside of the mug, empty except for a few foamy beige bubbles on the side.

Matt watched Terry. Terry blinked rapidly, sagged back in her chair, then smiled at Matt. It was kind of a dopey smile. "Yeah," she said. "I feel good. Come on."

Had Matt promised to drink? Implied it, but she hadn't said it out loud. Not a strictly binding promise. She could let Terry endure the spell alone.

What if it was dire? It couldn't be too dire. Terry had too much self-respect to do something that would mess her up permanently.

"C'mon. C'mon."

Matt sipped chocolate. It was as wonderful as she remembered, warm, sweet, smooth, dark. She felt a reminiscent flicker of hopeless pleasure that tumbled her back into the past she had shared with Terry, where cocoa had taken on huge symbolic meaning; whatever good Matt could find, she had tried to enjoy it, no matter what else was going on. And there had been good things, more than just cocoa.

The spell hit. Warmth flooded through her, flushed out to her fingertips and toes and the tips of her ears and nose. The hair prickled on her scalp. Immense, inescapable comfort overwhelmed her. Contentment, and the conviction that here was where she belonged; no place else held any interest.

She finished her cocoa. The spell only enhanced the flavor. She set her mug on the table and looked at Terry, tried to remember what was worrisome about this situation.

Worry? What a waste of energy. She was warm, full, and happy, here with her friends. What more could she want than just to be sitting in this chair in this kitchen in this house in this town in this corner of the universe?

"Don't you think it's nice?" Terry asked.

"Uh-huh."

"Matt," said Edmund.

"Uh-huh."

"What just happened?"

"Huh?"

"Terry doped your cocoa, right?"

"Uh-huh." Matt smiled and nodded at her mug.

"Terry!" cried Rebecca. "What did I tell you? No spells in the house! No spells on our guests! What have you done?"

"Terry," said Edmund, and his voice was dark razor steel.

Terry blinked and turned to look at him. "Huh," she said. "Shiny."

Matt glanced at Edmund too. Red glowed in his eyes, and

flames flickered from his curls. "Terry, take the spell off," he said. His voice was deep, quiet, sharp, and very scary. He leaned toward Terry. Matt thought, *If I could think, I wouldn't want him looking at* me *like that.*

Terry giggled and said, "Can't. It's on me too. Can't think."

Something in Matt's bones struggled with the spell. She felt very strange. Vines grew inside her: tendrils spiraled and spread, hooked to each other, reached out to all her edges, pin-pricky flickery feelings, until she felt overgrown, loaded down with internal lace. Shock, sharp and hot, jolted through the vines. Matt sat up straight. "Whoa!" The vines flashed into nothing, and the spell, too, disappeared. "God, Terry. What a nasty thing."

"What?" Terry blinked at her. "Feels nice."

"Matt?" Edmund touched her hand. She turned to him and saw that anger still flickered in his eyes. "You okay?"

"Edmund?" Rebecca said in a tiny voice.

"I'm okay," Matt said, and the red in Edmund's eyes faded. He glanced at Rebecca.

"I guess you *are* a witch," Rebecca said, her voice still faint.

"Yes," he said. He frowned and stared at Terry. She smiled sleepily back. "What did it do, Matt?"

"It made me feel good and dumb. Like I just wanted to sit here for the rest of my life and be happy."

"You knew she put a spell on the cocoa before you drank."

"The mug told me."

"So why did you drink?"

Matt shook her head. "It was kind of a dare."

"She said it was short. Did it wear off? It's still working on her."

"No, it didn't wear off," Matt said. She touched her chest,

looked down at her front. "It burnt up. Something grew in me and burnt it all up."

He took both her hands. "Something's taking care of you," he said softly. "The house again? Hello? Are you in there? Can you speak?"

"Hello," said Matt. "I can't stay here too long. I have to go home." It was the other voice again, the one that had spoken the night they spent in the desert, a calm, matter-of-fact, flat voice a slight shift away from Matt's.

What the house had given her could burn a spell out of her. It wasn't there just to see to its own mission. It protected her, too.

"It broke the spell." Matt gripped Edmund's hands and smiled.

He returned her smile.

"Am I still acting like me?"

"Yep."

"What broke the spell?" Rebecca asked.

"She has a guardian," Edmund said.

"I wish I had one of those," Rebecca said, and glanced at Terry, who just grinned and stared up at the kitchen light fixture. "Then, on the other hand, there she is, incapacitated, under a spell she cast herself. Terry?"

"Yes?"

"How do you feel?"

"Good. I feel nice."

"Is there anything you want?"

"I just want to stay here." Terry closed her eyes and smiled too widely. "It's so nice."

"How long will this spell last, honey?"

"What? Don't know exactly. An hour, maybe."

"Did you make any more of this one?"

"Sure. I got lots of this one, Mom. Just made a big batch. First time I tried it, though."

"Give me what you've got." Rebecca held out her hand. Terry bit her lower lip and reached into the pockets of her slacks. She squirmed around for a while, then came up with a handful of pink pellets. She frowned at them and dropped them into her mother's hand.

"Thank you, honey. Now forget you did that."

" 'Kay," said Terry, blinking.

"I'll be right back." Rebecca rose and left the room.

Matt and Edmund exchanged glances. What was going on?

Rebecca came back, dusting off her hands.

"What were those?" Matt asked.

"Spells." Rebecca studied Terry, who just smiled and looked away, her face serene and stupid. "Terry mass-produces them and mass-markets them. My daughter, the spell dealer. She's got a web page. I check it every day to make sure she's not offering anything dangerous. I don't like this one. It seems like the perfect date-rape drug, and it makes me sick that she test-drives it on somebody she calls her friend. She has this impulsive streak."

"Jeeze. What kind of spells does she sell?" Matt asked.

"Some of them are about making yourself attractive to the one you want, or being able to study really well, or remedy hangovers, or summon money. College crowd-pleasers. She makes them pretty weak; they work just well enough so people can tell they're getting something for their fifty bucks. I know she's working on others—more intense, more expensive, more dangerous—but she doesn't sell them on her site; she does it some other way. I can't ride herd on her. She's beyond my ability to control. I just have to hope. I make these rules she's supposed to follow if she wants to live here, and so far she seems to want to live here enough to appear to follow my rules. This was a definite trespass, though. Matt, I'm so sorry."

"I knew she was doing something. I just didn't know what." Matt got up and rinsed out her mug three times, then filled it from the coffeepot. —Thanks for the warning,—she thought to the mug.

—You're welcome. This is better.—

"Brilliant making her try it first," Rebecca said. "The hardest part about the whole thing is that she helps pay the mortgage. She usually makes more money per month than I do at my legitimate job."

"Huh," said Matt. "What are you going to do with the spells you took from her?"

Red touched Rebecca's cheeks. "I have a little stash," she said after checking to make sure Terry was still preoccupied.

"You use them?"

"I never have. Sometimes, though, I think they might come in handy. This spell might be the perfect date-rape drug. But look. It's also like she grounded herself." Rebecca's face twisted. "Let's see how she comes out of it. Sometimes I hate my thoughts. But sometimes she just gets so wild."

Matt sat down with her coffee. It must be hard being Rebecca. Was she all the time feeling like she didn't know what her daughter was going to do to her next? Kind of like being a lamb and living with a tiger. Though the lamb had just taken some of the tiger's claws away, and could use them on the tiger if she had to.

Matt thought about her internal guardian. Hey. Maybe she was luckier than she knew. A whole extra level of survival skill. The more she thought about it, the better she liked it.

"Edmund, if there was a battle between you and Terry, who would win?" Rebecca asked.

"I have no idea. We haven't tested each other in a long time, and our crafts have gone in different directions. I don't usually fight anything."

Rebecca said, "Your eyes got red, and your voice hurt to hear. You scared me."

The corners of Edmund's mouth quirked. "Well. That's handy, but it doesn't mean I could have actually done anything."

Matt punched his arm. "Spirit would help you if it knew you were right."

He lifted his eyebrows at her, smiled. "Maybe."

Terry shuddered and drew in a deep breath. She shook her head, blew out the breath, took in another. Expelled that one in a whoosh. Then she stuck her tongue out. "Yuck! Oh, yuck!"

"Are you back to normal?" asked Rebecca.

"My mouth tastes terrible! Matt—"

Matt handed Terry her coffee mug. Terry took a big gulp and swished liquid around in her mouth. "Thanks," she said. "What an evil spell. I didn't know it was going to work like that. Sorry, Matt."

"Oh, you are not," said Matt.

"Yes, I am. I don't know why I did that. Some imp of the perverse, I guess. I had the spells in my pocket, and—"

"Oh, come on. You picked those pants to wear down to dinner. Don't tell me you weren't thinking ahead."

"But I—But these were the only clean pants I could find." Terry dug into her pockets again. "The spells are gone. Where'd they go?"

"I confiscated them," said Rebecca.

"I don't remember that."

"What *do* you remember about being under that spell, Terry?" Edmund asked.

Terry frowned. "Not a whole lot. I felt really, really happy. All I wanted was to sit here forever and feel happy. That's not the effect I was trying for. I was looking for contentment but with the brain intact. How did it translate?"

"You were very happy. And stupid."

"No," Terry said slowly, looking stricken, "that's not what I wanted at all." She looked anxiously at Matt.

Matt smiled. "I broke mine."

"You did? Good."

"That's what I think. If I can break your spells, maybe we can be friends after all, no matter how much you try to screw it up."

"What?" said Terry.

"You're still really bad at this friendship stuff, aren't you?"

Terry looked away. "Yeah."

"Maybe you dropped that spell on me because things were going too well. Who knows. Maybe right now we can only be friends if I'm strong enough to beat you. Maybe I'm strong enough now. Now I need you, too."

"What?"

"Or the house needs you. I'm having trouble keeping this straight. I'm calling people back to the house." Matt looked at Edmund. "This was supposed to be your journey," she said.

"Seems like it's all three of our journeys, yours, mine, and the house's."

"The house needs me?" Terry said. "I go back every year."

"To renew the wards. House told us," Edmund said.

Terry nodded. "I spend part of every summer in Guthrie with my aunt. Gran won't even let me into her house anymore because she doesn't like what I'm studying, but Nathan doesn't mind me. Are you saying the house needs me now?"

"We think so," said Edmund. "Something's going on that we don't understand yet. Have you seen Julio lately?"

Terry shook her head. "Not for years."

"We've found everybody but Julio and Tasha."

"I might be able to find Tasha for you. She travels a lot. She's almost never home."

"We haven't even looked for her yet, but we could use help."

"You looked for me first?" Terry smiled.

"Matt thought you might still be in Spores," said Edmund. "She remembered knowing you here. Search led us here."

"You already found the other two friends? Princess and Braidgirl?"

"Don't be such a snot," Matt said.

"Yes, we found Suki and Deirdre," Edmund said. "Deirdre doesn't know if she'll come back yet, but we told her about it. Suki's already at the house."

"And you're inviting me to this party?" Terry glanced at Rebecca, waggled her eyebrows. Rebecca smiled and twitched her eyebrows too.

"Are you busy? Can you come?" Matt asked.

"Let me check my calendar and my e-mail. I've got a meeting tonight, but I don't have any tutoring scheduled until next week."

"If you're going to find Tasha," Rebecca said, "could you find her from here? I haven't seen her in six months."

Terry checked her watch, then twitched aside a curtain at a kitchen window to view the night: dark had fallen while they ate. "Before we do that, I have to go out. I'll be back in a couple hours, and we can do some seek spells then. Mom, you could call

Danny. He should be up by now." She turned to Matt and Edmund. "Danny's Tasha's boyfriend. He knows where she is more often than we do. 'Scuse me, guys. Be back soon." She darted out of the kitchen.

Rebecca rose and went to the phone, which was on the wall beside the back door. She lifted the handset, consulted a list of numbers on the wall, and dialed. "Seems like a prosaic way to handle this, with a house full of witches," she said, "but—Hi, Danny. It's me, Becka, Tasha's mom. I'm fine. How are you? . . . Oh, good. We're wondering if you've seen Tasha lately, and if so, where . . . oh. Really?" She covered the mouthpiece with her hand and turned to face Matt and Edmund. "He's gone to check. He thinks she might be coming home tonight."

A brief wait. "Oh! Hi, honey! You *were* going to let me know you were in town, weren't you? . . . Okay. Kidding. Sorry to bother you when you just got back, but we have some guests who'd like to talk to you. Edmund—"

The air beside the kitchen table shimmered, swirled. Small winds rushed around the room. A girl appeared. "Edmund?" she said, her voice warm and light. Her hair was a wild riot of black curls, her cheeks were bright, her eyes glowed blue, and she was dressed in something with lots of layers of sheer blue gauze shot with silver-and-gold threads. Her feet were bare and rosy. "Edmund?"

Chapter Eleven

· · · · ·

EDMUND stumbled to his feet. The chair fell over behind him. *Interesting*, thought Matt, who had never seen him do anything clumsy before.

"Tasha?" he said.

Rebecca hung up the phone and sighed.

"Hey! Where have you been?" Tasha launched herself at him, flew over the table and landed in his arms. She stroked his face, ran her hands through his curls, touched his mouth. "Hey! Why haven't I run into you before? You've been to lots of places I've been. Wow. You've been doing air work, too."

"Tasha," said Rebecca. "Ahem."

Tasha glanced over at her mom, followed her mom's gaze, noticed Matt. Her eyes widened. "Oh, my. Excuse me." She drifted down out of Edmund's arms and landed beside Matt's chair, reached a hand toward Matt's face. Matt leaned away from it. Tasha snatched her hand back. "Why didn't I know you were here? Oh, my. I'm sorry. I'm sorry. I forgot where I am. Excuse me. Hi. I'm Tasha. I'm sorry I have such terrible manners tonight."

"Hi," said Matt.

"Hi," Tasha said again. She took some long slow breaths. She smiled. "My head is somewhere else. Uh—may I touch you?"

Matt held out her hand. "Matt Black."

Tasha took her hand and shook it, nodded. "It's very nice to meet you, Matt. Sorry I was crawling all over your boyfriend. It's been a long time since I saw him, and I just came from the forest, where the manners are all different. It takes me two days to realize I'm back in human land, usually."

"Oh. Okay. Why were you touching him like that?"

"Well. I was smelling him."

"Tasha!" said Rebecca.

Tasha held her hand out toward Matt's face again, and this time Matt didn't flinch away. Gently, Tasha's fingers touched Matt's forehead. "Chlorine, sweat, sagebrush. Cotton, polyester, pepperoni. Gasoline fumes. The ocean. A cat. The—the haunted house? A *lot* of the haunted house." She closed her eyes and frowned. "Deirdre? Wow! Deirdre? Deirdre in the desert. And—" She lifted her fingers away and opened her eyes. "A spell. Only tiny remnants. But a really unsettling one."

"Terry did it," Matt said.

Tasha stared at her. "Matt," she said. "Oh. Matt! Are you the Matt she was awful to before?"

"Yeah. We're friends now. I made her cast the spell on herself too. It was interesting."

Tasha grinned. "Wish I'd seen it." In the smile, Matt finally saw how Tasha's face resembled Terry's, though everything else about her was different.

"Tasha?" Matt said. "Will you come back to the haunted house with us?"

Tasha touched Matt's face again, Matt's cheek, her brow, her mouth. "Sure," she said.

"YOU smell people by touching them? All this time you've been *smelling* me when I thought you were touching me?" Rebecca asked, as Tasha hugged her and stroked her face.

"Come on, Mom. You like it."

"But I didn't know that's what you were doing. That's way too weird. Stop it!"

"Okay," Tasha said, and sighed. She pressed her cheek to her mother's, then stopped hugging and stepped back. "You know, when cats rub up against you, they're not expressing affection. They're just marking you with their scent."

"I didn't want to know that."

"Oh, my. Sorry. I am decidedly bad-mannered tonight. Maybe I should go out and come back again, see if I do a better job."

"Stay," said Rebecca. "You want some stew? We made some wonderful stew, and there's still some left."

Tasha sniffed. "Yeah. Thanks. It smells great. Where's Terry?"

"She's at a meeting." Rebecca got a bowl down and dished some stew, set it on the table. Tasha sat down beside Matt, and Rebecca sat down beside Tasha. "When Terry comes home," Rebecca said, "can you touch her and tell me where she's been? She goes out at night a lot, and she never says where."

"No, I won't. Don't be silly, Mom."

"How can you smell with your fingertips, anyway?" Rebecca asked.

"People breathe with their whole bodies, not just their lungs. There's air exchange going on all over your skin."

"Okay, maybe that's true, but that olfictor-factor stuff is all in your nose, isn't it?"

"Uh, well," Tasha said. "For most people it is." She wrinkled her nose. Then she tasted the stew. "Wow! Traveling stew!" She ate more.

"How can you tell?" Rebecca asked.

"Things catch a little of everywhere they've been. This has a lot of that spice, the spice of everywhere," Tasha said. "It's great. Thanks, everyone."

Matt studied Tasha, studied the strange intense way Tasha tugged at Matt's friendship strings. What was it with this bouncy girl? Matt felt connected to her on some unknown level already. Why?

Matt lifted a hand and touched one of the layers of Tasha's dress, expecting fabric. She felt coolness, and then the material melted under her fingertips; she stubbed them abruptly on Tasha's warm, naked side. "What?" she yelped, snatching her hand back.

Tasha glanced down. "Oh, my. Oops." She ruffled her fingers across the gap left by Matt's touch, and the fabric re-formed. "It's kind of fussy. If I'm not concentrating, it does tend to dissipate. I'm not used to being back yet."

"What is it?"

"It's air. I was in a hurry when I left the house. Gotta get some real clothes."

Matt glanced at Edmund, who had been silent since Tasha arrived. He still looked kind of stunned.

Well. The girl had jumped on him, and she wasn't even wearing real clothes. Matt wondered if Tasha had concentrated enough to make the clothes be there when she jumped into Edmund's arms, or whether they were just for looks, and not for touch.

Edmund took Matt's hand under the table. She squeezed his hand. "Can I touch your clothes while you're concentrating on them?" Matt asked Tasha.

"Sure. But after that I'll go upstairs and change. There's so much I forget when I've been away for a while. I'm going to need normal while I'm visiting, aren't I?"

"I don't know yet. We don't know what we're doing." Matt reached out and grasped the edge of one of Tasha's layers. It felt cool and slippery, almost watery, and she couldn't hold on to it. —Cloth?—she thought, trying to hold it between her fingers.

It slipped away without responding.

Tasha grasped a handful of it and held it still while Matt tried to touch it. —Dress?—Matt asked with her fingers pressed to the gather Tasha held. It was like touching ice.

"You're sending signals," Tasha said.

"Yes."

"I don't think it talks that way. It's the medium, not the message . . . well, except it talks to me all the time if I just slow down and listen, but your signals aren't on the same wavelength."

Matt touched the table. —Hello?—

—Hello again, Matt.—

Of course. This table had been here ten years earlier, when Matt had spent miserable meals in this kitchen eating what Terry ate. How many things had she talked to in this house? Lots. In the frustration of captivity, she had made friends wherever she could. All the things Terry came into regular contact with had picked up traces of her magic. Matt had liked this table. As tables went, it was wider awake than most.

—Hi. Just checking to see if I could still talk to things.—

—What's on Tasha isn't a thing.—

—How can that be?—

—It's not a made thing. It made itself. You can talk to us. Someone made us. What's around her is something that made itself. It could talk to you if it wanted to, but it would use a voice.—

—That's so strange. Thanks.— Matt blinked several times, and looked up at Tasha.

"What did you find out?"

"Your dress made itself?"

"Uh-huh. I said, 'Air, I need an atmosphere of clothes,' and this is what I got. I think it looks neat." Tasha brushed her hands down over the layers of sky-blue gauze, and they fluttered in the wind of passage; gold-and-silver glints sparkled. Matt smelled pine sap and incense.

"It looks great," Matt said. "Smells good, too. I've never seen anything like it."

"But you're really sitting there naked?" asked Rebecca.

"No. I've got my own atmosphere. What did I just say?" She rose. "Excuse me while I find something else to wear. I'm starting to remember more about human land." Her hand drifted across Matt's head, and then she vanished.

It was the talking, Matt thought. Tasha was talking to everything, finding out things in ways that most people couldn't. Matt could do that too, except lately she had shut down her extra senses most of the time. Tasha was living with hers, wildly alive with them.

Fun to watch. Matt smiled.

"Cat got your tongue?" Rebecca asked Edmund.

"Yep," he said. He shook his head. "She sure has changed."

"That's my girl. Social goofball, but with a heart of gold. She's a great kid."

Footsteps on the staircase, and Tasha pushed into the kitchen through the swinging door. Now she wore a pale pink short-sleeved blouse with little bunches of flowers printed all over it, and jeans with the cuffs rolled up. "I hate clothes," she said.

"For heaven's sake," said Rebecca. "Does that mean you usually don't wear them?"

Tasha collapsed into a chair and pouted. "That depends on where I am. I'll get used to this again, I suppose."

"Don't you get cold?" Matt asked.

"No. Feel." Tasha moved her hand close to Matt's cheek, and Matt felt radiant warmth. "Air takes care of me. It's all around, everywhere. Anyway, Mom, now you know why I don't call you the instant I come to town. It takes me a while to settle down."

"I'll keep that in mind," said Rebecca.

"So when are we leaving?" Tasha checked her soup bowl, found some left, and ate it. She had tied her hair back with a pink ribbon, and she looked strangely normal.

Matt exchanged glances with Edmund. "Tomorrow?" she said. "Or tonight? Tasha, Rebecca said we could use your room to sleep in. Is that okay?"

"Sure. I have my own apartment. I'll go back there for the night and come here first thing tomorrow.

Matt reached deep into a pocket in her jacket and found the little carved stone monk. "Hey. When I lived here before I took this from your room." She opened her hand. The small brown carving perched on her palm. "I'm sorry I stole from you. I hope I didn't hurt you. I needed friends. Do you want it back?"

Tasha held out her hand above the monk, but didn't touch it. She frowned for a moment, her eyes blank, then glanced up. "No. He's yours now. It's all right."

"Thanks. I'm really sorry." Matt slipped the monk back into her pocket.

Tasha sighed. "Don't worry about it. Can I ride over to the coast with you guys? Or do you even use a car? Terry will want her own wheels, but I'm not sure I'm up to two and a half hours of Terry right now. I could get there on my own, but I'd like to talk to you."

"You're welcome to come with us," Edmund said.

"Oh, good."

A door slammed somewhere in the house. A moment later, Terry came through the swinging door into the kitchen. "Hey, Sis!"

"Hey!" Tasha jumped up and went to Terry, hugged her. Matt noticed Tasha didn't even try to touch Terry's face.

"So they had no trouble tracking you down, hey?" Terry said.

"I just got back to town."

"Had a feeling you might. They invite you to the haunted house?"

"Yes."

"You going?"

"Sure. Aren't you?"

"Probably. I'll go check." Terry left the room again.

Rebecca propped her cheek on her hand and sighed. "Another lonely weekend," she said.

Matt's hands gripped each other in her lap. She glanced at Edmund. He watched Rebecca.

Should they invite Rebecca? She was a really good sport, but she didn't have any magical skills that Matt knew about. It would be troubling to try to take care of her if things got dangerous. Though Matt couldn't figure out how things could get dangerous. Then again, she didn't know what was going on.

"Quit it, Mom," Tasha said.

"Go. Go. I'll be fine. I'll just sit here in the dark."

"Stop it. It's not your thing. You'd go over there and just get in trouble," Tasha said.

Rebecca sighed. "I'd love to see a big magic battle. I bet it's quite the spectacle."

"Stop that!"

Terry slipped back into the room. "All clear," she said.

"You kids leave me out of everything," Rebecca said, and heaved a deep sigh.

"Mom, are you teasing Tasha again?" Terry asked.

"Yep." Rebecca straightened.

"Ignore her, Tash. She and Dad have a big bridge tournament scheduled for tomorrow."

"That's so mean!" said Tasha.

"You're so easy, honey."

Tasha sniffed. "I'll know better next time."

"You always say that," said Terry.

Matt said, "You and Mr. Dane play cards?" to Rebecca. When Matt had stayed here before, Rebecca's divorce was still fresh and distressing.

Rebecca shrugged. "I've been seeing him again lately. He's still the best guy I've ever met. We're testing it."

"Which reminds me, I should track him down while I'm around," Tasha said. "At least say hi."

Terry asked, "Are we heading out tonight?"

"We could," Matt said. The kitchen clock said it was only 8:06 P.M. In Edmund's car it would take them at least three hours to drive to Guthrie, but the night was young.

"We're leaving tomorrow morning," said Edmund.

"Okay," said Terry. "Rendezvous here?"

"I'll be back for breakfast," Tasha said, "if that's okay. I ran out of food, and I don't feel like shopping if I'm not even staying here. I'll bring clothes."

"See you tomorrow," Edmund told her.

Tasha waved. Little winds blew around again, and then she was gone. Her clothes settled to the floor in an untidy heap. Rebecca picked them up and folded them, shook her head, smiled.

GUTHRIE was cool but sparkling in spring sunlight when they drove into it the next day. Tasha rolled the window down, letting in the sea air. Matt sat up and sniffed. *It's really true. I'm home now.*

"Oh, my. I haven't been back here since I joined air," Tasha said. "It's lovely." She stuck her arm out the window and spread her fingers to let air slide between them.

Edmund turned off the highway and drove to the haunted house.

—I like this street,—the car thought as they stopped by the fence.

—I bet it likes you,—Matt responded.

—Yes.—

They parked beside the rickety fence. Terry's Miata was already there. She had sped ahead of them early on, impatient with the Volvo's slow-but-steady pace.

"Oh, my," said Tasha, climbing out of the car. She stood

facing the fence, the blackberries, the haunted house with her feet apart and her arms wide, fingers spread. She took slow deep breaths. Her eyes were closed.

Edmund rounded the car and stopped, waited while Tasha stood still.

Matt stood next to her, one hand on the fence.

Tasha's edges glowed, and she turned transparent for a split second. She drew in a breath, held it, let it out. "Oh, my," she whispered, solid again.

—What is she?—the house whispered to Matt through the fence.—Whom have you brought me?—

—It's Tasha.— Matt felt surprised. How could the house not know a witch it had made itself?

But Tasha had changed. And the house hadn't known Edmund at first after his long time away.

—This is Tasha?—

—Yes.—

Tasha opened her eyes and lowered her arms. "It's so different," she said.

Nathan shimmered into sight just the other side of the front gate. "Tasha?" he asked.

"Nathan! Hey!" She ran to him, holding out her hands.

"The gate," Matt said.

It creaked open before Tasha got there, but she wasn't even paying attention. She stopped in front of Nathan and reached toward him as though she were warming her hands at a stove. "Nathan," she murmured.

"Tash. What have you done with yourself?"

She didn't answer. She moved her hands around, stroking the air near his image. Her graceful gestures reminded Matt of dance.

"How strange," she murmured finally, and held her hand out to him. A frown pinched his forehead. He moved his hand toward hers. His hand passed through hers—or did hers pass through his?—and for an instant light flashed through his translucent form, haloed her solid one. They both jumped and gasped.

"What have you done?" Nathan said, his voice strained.

"What *are* you?" she asked, her voice hoarse as well.

"Just what I've always been," he said.

"You seem so different. I don't understand you anymore. I've dedicated my life to air, and air has changed me," Tasha told him.

"So I see. Are you happy?"

"Oh, yes." She smiled. "I have a great life."

"Good! Would you like to come inside?"

She looked past him at the house. "I don't want to hurt anything. Did I hurt you?"

"Only a little. I didn't know to expect what you've become. I think it should be all right now."

"I'll take it one step at a time," she said.

He turned and led the way to the house, and Tasha followed.

—Why wouldn't she be welcome here?—Matt wondered, gripping the weathered fence.

—She is welcome. She just brings a kind of energy I don't know how to meet yet,—said the house.

Edmund opened the back of the car and pulled out a couple of bags of their things. Matt lifted her hand from the fence and went to help him carry.

Suki came out of the house as Nathan and Tasha climbed the front steps onto the porch. Nathan said something. Suki and Tasha spoke to each other and shook hands.

Matt consulted Julio's memories. Back during the crisis, the twins had come into the house just as Susan was leaving. Had they ever been introduced? Maybe Tasha and Suki were meeting for the first time.

"Hey!" Edmund called as he and Matt walked toward the house. "Did you get the job?"

Suki came to meet them. "Yep. I'm gainfully employed. I start Monday. I get weekends off, and a twenty percent discount on all my dental work. Nathan let me run some normal electricity in here. Now I can recharge my cell phone and run my laptop. Hey, welcome back, you guys. Did you find Dee?"

"Yes. She's thinking about coming, but she wouldn't say for sure."

"How is she?"

"She seems pretty good. She's a vet."

"A 'be all that you can be' vet? I could see Deirdre in the army."

"Nope. An animal doctor."

"Guess I can picture that too," Suki said, and smiled. She went ahead of them into the house, with Edmund right behind her. Matt followed them inside and grabbed the doorknob to pull the door shut, though she knew the house could close the door itself.

She shut the door. Her hand wouldn't come loose. When she looked, she saw that her hand had disappeared into the doorknob. Her wrist ended and the cut-crystal doorknob began; she couldn't see her hand inside the glass. She tugged, but it wouldn't come out again.

—House,—she thought. She remembered Julio falling into the porch, his brief cat's-eye view before he was absorbed.

—Come inside.—

—Let go of me.—

—Please, Matt. Please come inside.—

—Right now?—

—Please?—

"Matt?" Edmund turned back to her.

—What do you want?—Matt asked the house.

—A map of what you found.—

—Can't you wait till later?—

—But Tasha's inside me now. In the kitchen. I need to know.—

Matt growled, frustrated. Edmund took two steps toward her. She leaned back against the door and fell into the blue, her body instantly gone, melted into the house's bones, blood, muscles, awareness. She shifted around, stretched, got comfortable, woke up to the fact/feeling of people inside her: Tasha a strange bright blot that did not act like a proper person, Terry comfortable and known, Suki, a delight, Nathan, a part of her, and Edmund, glowing red now, his hands hot against her side.

"House! What did you do?" he cried.

—Hang on, it's all right, I said yes,—Matt thought. Edmund could hear house-speak when he was hot like this, she knew. —Stop burning.—

"Yes to what?" Edmund asked. Some of the heat left his hands.

Matt considered the question for a minute, then said,—Yes to being in the house's dream. I don't think this should take long.—

"Are you sure it's okay?"

—Pretty sure. I'll let you know if something goes wrong. Thanks, Edmund.—

He pressed his cheek against her—against the door. She sent warmth there.

After a moment he pushed away and headed for the kitchen, where Tasha, Terry, Nathan, and Suki were.

—House,—Matt thought.

—Matt.—

—You put something inside me.—

—We talked about it in dreams.—

—I don't remember.—

—Remember,—whispered the house, and Matt was sitting on the beach, leaning against a large silver-haired, brown-skinned woman, the woman the house became in dreams, whose warm arms held her. Matt and the woman looked out over the ocean. Matt felt perfect safety and comfort, and a warmth in her chest and belly.

"Will you help me?" the woman asked.

"How can I help you, Mama?" Matt asked, her voice young, curious, warm.

"Will you help me find my children and call them home?"

"Sure," young Matt said.

The woman stroked her back, kissed her forehead. "Thank you, Mattie. Thank you. Here's bread for your journey." She gave Matt a muffin. It was big and soft and yellow, and it looked sweet.

"Do I save this for later?" Matt asked.

"No. You can eat it now."

Matt took a bite. It was a delicious taste, cakey and moist, flavored with vanilla and lemon. She swallowed her first bite. In her stomach, she felt something strange happen. Not pain or sickness, more a startle. "What is it?" she said, her hand on her stomach.

"It's help for later."

Matt ate the rest of the muffin. Each bite gave her a small, pleasant shock. She licked her fingers.

The woman stroked Matt's hair. Matt realized she had her old hair, wavy and long enough to reach her waist. She looked down at herself and saw her twelve-year-old body, thin and muscular from dance. She wore a black leotard and footless black tights. "Mama?"

Then she clicked into strange, dizzying double vision. She was Matt, the grown-up wanderer, veteran of many strange experiences, and Mattie, the twelve-year-old, young, kind, strong, innocent. Mattie was talking to somebody she loved and trusted, someone who reminded her of her dead mother. Matt knew it was the house in human form, and suspected manipulation. "Mama, how does it help me?" Mattie asked.

"It strengthens your willpower," said the woman. "If somebody tries to will bad things on you, you can will them away again."

"Oh, good," said Mattie, not understanding but feeling comforted.

"And it reminds you of me," the woman whispered.

Matt fell out of the memory and back into the house's turquoise pool of energy.

—Do you remember?—the house asked.

—Guess I do,—Matt said. She thought about the lace vines that had eaten Terry's spell out of her. Bread for her journey, huh? What about the voice that spoke to Edmund in the night? Was that, too, a manifestation of willpower?

—How come I was a kid in that dream?—

—That is the form you take in most of our dreams,—the house thought.

—How come you were a mother in that dream?—

—That is the form I take in most of our dreams.—

—Why?—asked Matt.

—I don't know. It is a form you gave me.—

For a while, they were quiet. In the kitchen, Matt felt Suki run water into a teakettle at the kitchen sink; her hand on the faucet was distinctive. Then Suki touched the old stove. The part of her palm that connected to the house asked the house to heat the stove, please: Matt felt Suki's request seep into the house's skin, and the house's answering warmth and response. It remembered a time when the stove had been bright and hot with cooking; Matt got a dim impression of strangers in the kitchen, and pots and pans on top of the hot stove, coal in its firebox. The house dispensed with everything in the memory except the heat, and then the stove turned hot in the present. Suki lifted her hand away just in time, murmured thanks, set the kettle on one of the stove lids.

Matt knew there was conversation. Nathan asked Tasha questions. If she concentrated, thought Matt, she would know what he was saying, maybe hear Tasha's answers. Part of the house's self connected to Nathan, though the house didn't direct his movements; it could move into him and perceive through his senses, invoke sight, which was a sense it didn't have inside itself, and tune its hearing to better understand speech sounds, though it could hear and speak without Nathan's presence. Often Nathan paid more attention to what people were saying than the house did. If the house missed something of significance, though, it could read the ghost's memories.

Matt wondered how Nathan felt about that. Maybe he didn't even think about it. Maybe the ghost and the house had always been connected that way, and it didn't bother him.

Matt reached into the house's mind a little. The house loved Nathan. It knew that sometimes Nathan wanted to get away from it, and it understood. Their bond was enforced by something beyond their power to defy; under the circumstances, it was a blessing that they got along with and appreciated each other so well.

Edmund leaned against a kitchen wall, his palms flattened on the paneling. Using the house's form as though it were her own, Matt stroked fingers across both Edmund's palms. He shuddered, then settled.

"What happened to Matt?" Suki asked.

"She had to run an errand," said Edmund.

Matt pressed on his fingertips, sent a ripple through the wall his back leaned against.

The house said,—The woman is a form you gave me, tempered by memories from other people I've known. I like it very much.—

—Ah.—

—May I look at what you discovered on your journey?—

Matt sighed without sound, and said,—All right.—

She fell into her memories, lived the last two and a half days over with the house beside her, observing, saying nothing. When she finished, she felt as though two and a half days had gone by, but as she woke to the house's senses, people were still in the kitchen. Edmund still leaned against her wall.

Suki poured hot water into a teapot, touched a wall, and asked that the living-room furniture be present by the time they went to the living room. The house summoned up the clutter of furniture that had been in the living room when Nathan last lived there, wing chairs, ottomans, scattered small tables with flowerpots and knickknacks on them, a harp, a piano, pictures on the wall, candlesticks on the mantel above the fireplace. Matt felt the people's footsteps as they trooped from the kitchen into the living room.

—Thank you, Matt,—the house thought. —Thank you. Do you wish to go out again now?—

There was something very comfortable and strange about being inside the house. She had the feeling that nothing could hurt her here in this turquoise pool. There were a lot of things to think about, lots of things to feel and do, and someone else to make decisions whenever necessary. A caretaker.

She didn't really want a caretaker, did she?

Mostly not.

—I'm ready,—she said.

The house let her out into the kitchen, a little at a time; she oozed slowly out of the wall, dropped her connections gently so that neither she nor the house bruised. At last she stepped away from the wall. She glanced down at herself.

"Hey, wrong hair," she said. Blond-brown hair cascaded down around her shoulders, down her chest and her back to her waist. The blue jeans and olive green long-underwear top she had dressed in that morning had turned turquoise, and her army boots had changed into knee-high leather English riding boots. "Wrong clothes. How could you forget?"

—I'm sorry,—the house said.

"Can you give me a haircut?" Matt asked, putting her palms against the wall. For a moment she felt solid wood under her hands. She pushed harder, and the surface tension vanished. She melted into the wall again.

—Think what you look like,—the house told her.

—I don't know what I look like.—

—Think what you want, then. The hair, the clothes.—

—I liked those boots. Never had any like that.—

—They belonged to someone who lived here a long time ago. I forgot to keep track of what you wore when you fell into me.—

—I kind of like the clothes, but I don't wear bright colors. I kind of like the hair, but it makes me feel really strange. I'm not ready to mess around with that kind of feeling right now. I want my regular cut.— She hadn't actually had her hair cut in a couple of months, and it was growing out, short curls all over her head. They weren't in her eyes yet, so she left them alone.

—Think what you want,—the house said again.

Matt thought about her hair and her clothes and the boots. After a moment, the house released her gently and she stood in the kitchen again. She still had the brown-leather riding boots, and her clothes were still strange colors of blue, though not such a blindingly bright turquoise. She couldn't see her hair anymore. She raised her hands to her head. Her hair felt reassuringly short. "Thanks," she said. "That was so weird. What if I wanted to be taller? Or fatter? Or red-haired? What if I thought up a whole new me?"

—It could happen,—the house said.

"Wow. That's really weird."

"Matt?" Edmund came back into the kitchen. "Are you all right?"

"I think so." She looked at her hands, then touched her breasts, her stomach, her hips. "Do I look all right?" She felt her face. She didn't spend much time thinking about her face, or looking at it. What if she hadn't remembered it right? The house wouldn't know. It didn't know that much about how things were supposed to look.

Well, except for what it knew from Nathan. And from Julio, and now from Matt—and whatever it knew from dreams.

"You look fine," Edmund said.

"Is my face all right?"

"It's beautiful." He came and cupped her face in his hands.

"That can't be right."

"It's great. You look like you."

"I do? Are you sure? A minute ago I had long hair. I had to go back in and come out again. If you're going to fall into the house, take a good look at yourself first so you know how to fall out again. See these boots?"

He bent over and studied her boots.

"The house forgot my real boots and gave me these instead."

"You know your own boots," he said. "I bet you remember everything about them."

"I like these ones better." Then Matt had an attack of conscience. Her army boots had been with her a long time, and served her well. How could she just trade them in on something else?

How could she get them back? Would they even be the same? What were the new ones made of, and where had the original ones gone?

Where had the original Matt gone?

What was she made of now?

Frightened, she grabbed Edmund's shoulder. He straightened, checked her expression, then gathered her in a hug. She kissed him. —Am I me? Am I still me?—

He tasted the same: sage, wilderness, smoke, an added tang of tea.

—Do I taste like me?—she thought.

—You do.— His mental voice was beautiful, as his aloud voice sometimes was, bright, deep, singing, silvery.

—Are you sure?—

—I'm sure.—

She held on to him for another minute, then loosened her hold. "Were you ever inside the house?"

He shook his head.

"Julio was. That's how the house could make me think I was him. It's so strange, Edmund. I don't know where my edges are."

"Do you want to leave?"

"No!"

"Who's talking? You, or House?"

"What?"

"The house is haunting you now, isn't it?"

Matt laughed. Then she realized he was serious. "I guess," she said.

"So—are you in your right mind when you say you don't want to leave? Or is this just the house talking? Is it safe for you to stay here, Matt? Should we have this discussion outside?"

She took his hand and led him to the kitchen door. The door opened wide to let them out. They crossed the yard and the street out back, walked until they were past the edge of the house's property.

They sat on someone else's lawn, holding hands. "I still don't know if it's just me," Matt said, "because I take the house with me now."

Edmund let her hand go and got out his devotions kit. He opened a zipper and took out a pinch of something blue-green. He rubbed his fingers against his thumb above it. It turned to a thin blue flame hovering above his palm. He raised his hand toward her face, the flame accompanying his movement. "Speak across this."

"What does it do?" Matt asked into the flame. No heat came from it. As she spoke, it flickered.

"Is it safe for you to stay in the house?"

"Yes," she said. A thin streak of yellow shot through the flame.

"Are you speaking for yourself?"

"I think so," she said, and this time the flame stayed blue.

"Will what the house gave you hurt you?"

"No. It will protect me." Blue flame, no other color.

He frowned, then murmured, "Thank you, flame. Thank you, spirit." The flame flickered out.

"So was it me talking?" Matt asked.

"Yeah."

"The yellow meant what?"

"You don't know the answer to that question. Doubts come into it." He shook his head. "I don't know the answer either."

Matt plucked a blade of grass. She tore it across, and across, and across, until she had a handful of green grass bits. "Being safe isn't as important as knowing I'm making the choices for myself."

"I agree."

"I think I'm ready to go back now."

He took her hand, rose, and pulled her to her feet. "Suki made tea. You want some? There's cookies."

More free food! Matt sighed. "I have to get a job." They headed toward the house.

"Right now?" he asked.

She knew he was laughing at her. "No, not right now," she said.

They went through the kitchen and the dining room, and into the living room, where Suki and the twins drank tea and talked, and Nathan just talked.

"What's the next step in the big plan?" Terry asked, as Matt and Edmund came into the room. "There is a big plan, right?"

Terry and Tasha sat beside each other on a fainting couch, Terry leaning against the part that curved up, Tasha upright and energetic. They didn't look at all alike.

"I don't—" Matt began, and then found herself saying, "Find Julio." She sat in one of the wing chairs. Suki gave her a cup of tea, a napkin, and a plate with assorted cookies on it. "Thanks," Matt said.

"You're welcome." Suki poured a cup of tea for Edmund, assembled a plate of cookies and napkin, handed them to him, and sat down on the chair next to Matt's.

Nathan crossed his arms and leaned against the mantel.

"Do you know any seek spells, Terry?" asked Edmund. He settled in a chair to Matt's other side. "My basic one doesn't work on Julio."

"I have a whole bunch," Terry said. "Want to get started now?"

"Right now I want some tea," said Edmund.

"Do we actually need Julio for whatever it is we're doing here?" asked Tasha. "What is it we're doing here?" She glanced from Matt to Nathan.

Nathan shook his head.

"You don't know? If you don't know, who does? Matt?"

"I don't know either. At first we were just going to find Edmund's friends so he could see them again after being out of touch for so long, but the house has some other thing it wants."

"The house wants something?" Terry said.

The sound of a car in the street came faintly to them. Matt could feel the house's excitement through her feet, and knew the car had parked by the fence. A car door slammed. The gate creaked open.

Matt put her plate and cup on one of the parlor tables and ran to the front door. Something hummed in her chest, excitement or anticipation. She went out on the porch and saw Deirdre walking toward her through the blackberry bushes.

"Hi!"

"Hey, Matt."

Nathan stood beside Matt, and the others came out of the house too.

"Dee," said Suki. She jumped off the porch and ran to Deirdre. "Hey, Dee!" She wrapped her arms around Deirdre, who leaned into it.

"Hey, Susan," she murmured. She pushed away, stared at Suki's face. "God, you look great!"

"Well, thanks! So do you!"

Deirdre looked over Suki's shoulder, then nodded and came to stand below the porch. She met Nathan's steady gaze.

"Hey, Nathan," she said in her low, gruff voice after they had stared at each other for a while.

"Hi." Nathan smiled. "It's great to see you."

"You look good," said Deirdre.

"You look wonderful," he said. "I look the same as I always do, don't I?"

"Nope. More solid. Your cheeks—kind of rosy, you look almost alive. Hey, twins. God, we all grew up, didn't we?"

Tasha laughed, walked down the steps, and went to Deirdre. "May I touch you?" she asked.

"What the hell kind of weird question is that?"

"A yes or no question. It's part of the way I'm a witch."

"Hey. Knock yourself out," Deirdre said, amused.

Tasha touched Deirdre's cheek, chin, forehead, lips. Deirdre looked puzzled, but she stood still for it. "Oh, my," said Tasha at last. "Coyote."

"Whoa. How'd you know?"

"My way of being a witch." Wind touched Tasha's hair, lifted her curls, washed across the hem of the pale green shirt she wore. "It followed you here. Interesting."

Deirdre turned to look behind her.

"Not in that form. Want some tea?"

"Tea? Well, hell, why not?" Deirdre followed Tasha up onto the porch. "Hey, other twin. Hey, House!"

"Hey, Deirdre," said the house. "Glad you could come."

"Thanks." Deirdre patted the doorframe as she walked into the house.

When everyone had settled in the living room and everyone had tea, Terry said to Matt, "So, you were saying the house wants something. House, what do you want?"

"I cannot tell you yet."

"What are we supposed to do, hang around till you're ready to talk?" Terry sounded irritated. "How long will *that* take?"

The house didn't answer. Suki said, "Well, there's plenty of room, anyway. Dee, your room is still open; Terry and Tasha put their things in the attic. Can you all spend at least one night?"

"I guess," said Terry.

"I'm going down to the beach," Tasha said, "and taste the wind here. Want to come, Sis?"

"What about those seek spells Edmund asked for?" asked Terry.

"Let's do them after supper. Hey, Suki, do you know if that really good seafood place on the highway is still open? Hesperos?"

"It moved to a bigger building a couple blocks down the street, but yes, it's still open. I haven't tried it since I came back, but I've heard people talking about it. They say it's still good."

"That place gets my vote for dinner," said Tasha. "I haven't had good seafood in months. Anybody else want to go to the beach now?"

"I'll go," Deirdre said. "I haven't been to the beach in years."

"I'd like to go too," Suki said. "I don't think I've really walked on the beach since I came back. Looked at it from car windows and restaurant windows, but not walked or gotten my feet wet. Is it warm enough to wade?"

"We'll find out when we get there. Sometimes in spring the water's really cold," Tasha said.

"If you wait a minute, I'll go too," Terry said. "I just need to get some containers. I could use some sand and seawater." She ran up the stairs.

Matt drank tea and watched them run around as they got ready for their expedition. Well, maybe this was a vacation trip for them. Why not? If the house wasn't going to tell them what it wanted . . .

A few minutes later, Tasha, Terry, Deirdre, and Suki had left the house. Nathan had faded sometime during all the running around, which made Matt wonder if he was all right. All these old friends had come to visit, and Matt couldn't tell whether Nathan was glad to see them.

Edmund looked at Matt.

She said, "I had a thought."

"Yes?"

"If seek spells don't work, we could act like regular people and try to track Julio down without magic. Like, check a phone book, see if he's listed, or his mom. I bet she knows where he is, so if we could find her . . . Go to his old apartment house and ask the people there if they know where he went. Maybe I could ask the building if it knows where he is. Maybe we could find that Mr. Noah guy and ask *him*. What do you think?"

"I think that's a great idea. Do you want to go looking now?"

Matt glanced toward the window. Bright sunlight shone on blackberry bushes outside. It was another beautiful, almost-spring day.

All she wanted to do was sleep. She yawned.

Edmund smiled. "I'll go find a phone book and check, see if Julio or Juanita or Mr. Noah is still listed. If you're awake when I get back, we can visit the apartment building, okay?"

Matt yawned again. "Can you get a paper too? We could check the want ads for jobs." It was a strange idea. Already she had a home, and now she was thinking about job-hunting. A job would stick you down to a place like flypaper.

She wanted to reclaim her independence, though, even if she did it this new way. A job meant money, and money meant she could buy groceries like a regular person and not be a total mooch. She could find food in Dumpsters and trash cans, but she was pretty sure her friends wouldn't want to share it, and she wanted to give back to them.

Besides, she could always quit and move on.

The whole idea made her tired.

"Sure," he said.

"I have to take a nap," Matt said. "Thanks. I'll see you later."

"Okay." He gave her a little kiss and took off.

Matt stumbled upstairs. She went into her room, took off her pants, slipped under the covers of the bed, punched the pillow until it took the shape she wanted, and lay down. "Nathan? Are you all right?" she asked.

Nathan appeared by her bed. "I'm fine," he said. He looked strange and gloomy, though.

"Are you mad that we went and invited those people here?"

"Oh, no." He shook his head. "It's great to see them. Thank you for finding them."

"Do you know what's going on with the house?"

"Only some of it."

Matt yawned again. "I'll ask you again later. Sorry about this."

"It's all right, Matt. Sleep well." He smiled and vanished.

Matt closed her eyes. Then she reached out to the wall and thought,—No more dreams!—

—All right.—

Chapter Twelve

· · · · ·

THERE was a lunchtime jam/dance/potluck at a grange in the country, with music continuing all afternoon: one of the local fiddlers had invited Lia and Harry to it after he met them at a folk festival at the University Student Union Building in town.

Lia set the thing that looked like a tape recorder on the podium and pushed the "record" button. She smiled and nodded to the ninety-two-year-old man, and he lifted the bow of his fiddle and started "Earl's Waltz," a song he had written himself. The backup musicians joined in: three guitar players strumming with picks and without finesse, a string bass player who plucked the strings with his fingers instead of bowing, a woman with a mandolin, and three other fiddle players, sawing along quietly toward the back of the group. One of them was just a boy, thirteen, fourteen. He had already won state fiddle contests in the peewee and junior divisions.

People who sat on the benches along the walls

listened to the first few bars of the tune for beat, for recognition. When they figured out that it was something they could dance to, they rose, found partners, and waltzed across the floor.

Lia had brought her violin with her, but it was still in its fur-lined case. She sat on a chair near the front of the grange hall, only a few feet from the musicians, and opened to the music.

The song flowed into her. She saw images: flowers on a branch, opening their petals a little, furling them tight, opening again, a little wider, then closing. Teasing each other. Also she saw a Busby Berkeley picture, as though she floated below a roof, of women dancing in wide skirts, moving just like the flowers: twirl, and the skirts spread out a little, countertwirl and they tightened again, twirl this way and they spread wider.

That was just the A part of the tune. In the B part, men in black pants danced around the wide-skirted women; the flowers leapt off their branches and floated, dancing, through the air.

Earl played his waltz through five times, accompanied by shuffling footsteps and the smiles of happy dancers. By the end, Lia had graven it into her memory and could have played it on any instrument there.

As people clapped, she went to her recorder and turned it off. "Thank you," she told Earl.

"Any time, cutie," he said. "Play you a fast one next."

She smiled and put the recorder in her coat pocket; her coat was draped over her chair. Earl struck up "Stones Rag," which she had already learned. A small gnome with grease-tamed silver-black hair, thick black-framed glasses and crabbed arthritic hands introduced himself as Stan and asked her to dance, and she took one of his hands in hers and rested her other hand at his waist, while he rested his other hand on her shoulder. They waited, looking toward the musicians, until Earl got the tune under way, then danced. Stan was a fine dancer. Lia let herself sink into music and movement, a combination she loved best of everything in the world.

They had just finished, and she was breathless and laughing as she thanked her partner, when she heard a song in her head.

She straightened. It was a summoning song, one she had trouble resisting. "Thank you again," she said. "I've got to go." She ran to collect her coat and violin, then went into the dining hall and touched Harry's shoulder. He was playing Uno with some of the musicians' wives. He looked strange this afternoon in jeans and a plaid flannel shirt, out of his element, but not too uncomfortable. He glanced up, knew from her face that they had to leave, rose, put down his cards, and apologized to the women for not finishing the hand. They went outside.

"Someone's calling me," she told him as they approached his Mercedes. He opened the trunk. She put her coat and violin into it.

"Which kind of song is it?"

"Not the imperative one, but it's probably important."

"What do you want me to do?"

She kissed him. "Be ready. If it's trouble, I might summon you."

"So I shouldn't drive home?"

"I'll give you thirty seconds' warning."

"Got it." He kissed her.

She clung to him a moment, then stepped away, let the song fill her, and went through little fire to where she was wanted.

· · · · ·

TERRY knelt beside a tide pool and stared down into the water. Green-blue anemone tentacles waved gently. A tiny fish darted through the small space, and a hermit crab hauled its shell across underwater sand.

Terry plunged her hand down into the water and brought up a walnut-sized, dripping agate, pale, translucent, clouded. She held it up to let the sun through it. It shone apricot. The thrill of the hunt shot through her. When she stayed here in Guthrie with her aunt, she always came down to the beach at low tide and searched for agates, which lay broadcast like careless treasure in tidal pools and along the waterline. Big storms washed agates out of cliffs, and the ocean polished their edges with sand and brought them back here.

Someone stooped beside her. "Nice one." His voice sounded flat.

She glanced up and saw the boy from the bar, his shaggy black hair fluttering in the breeze, his eyes golden in the sunlight. Underground-pale skin—he was going to burn if he wasn't wearing sunscreen—and the same baggy worsted trousers, the cuffs rolled up, and blue work shirt, sleeves rolled up too. Slim black belt. Bare feet. He looked sixteen, and the last time she had seen him, he had talked as though he were sixty. Was he a ghost? She looked harder. She knew him from somewhere, somewhen, before she had seen him in the bar. Who was he?

"May I see?" he asked in his dull voice, holding out a hand.

Terry handed him her agate. His hand curved around it, gentle as a nest around an egg, and he smiled: still a flat, affectless smile.

Then Terry remembered.

The silent boy who had helped the wicked witch the day Julio had been possessed, fifteen years before. The boy had stood in the shadows while Terry and the other friends from the haunted house were there, and he had cast only one spell that she had seen, a quick protect spell crafted with gestures while his master let Julio out of the circle of confinement. The spell had guarded against Julio, in the event he went crazy and started attacking, Terry supposed.

"Hey," she said sharply. "Where did your boss get off attacking my friend?"

The boy blinked and looked at her. "What?"

"I saw you before, didn't I? In some house up in the mountains? Your boss grabbed my friend Julio and put a demon in his body."

The boy cocked his head. "Hmm. I didn't realize you were one of *those* witches. Of course, you've grown and changed since I last saw you."

"And you haven't. What are you?"

"A researcher. The wing of immortality brushed over me some time back. I am aging, but very slowly. It's frustrating. No one takes a boy my apparent age seriously. Fortunately, there's a lot one can do in e-mail and on the net these days, where my appearance doesn't distract."

"A researcher," Terry repeated. "What does that make your boss?"

"My master is a mystery and a wizard. He's taught me a lot of magic, but there are more things he keeps secret from me. I don't know how old he is, but he was old when he chose me to be his apprentice, in 1932."

"What? That can't be right." Terry stared at the boy's face, and realized that not only did he have this dull, seen-everything voice, but he had very old eyes.

He smiled at her, and again she felt an unwelcome flutter of interest and sympathy in her chest. "Don't use glamour on me," she said in a cross voice.

His eyebrows rose. "Was I? I'm not aware of it."

She sketched spell signs for enhanced vision in the air between them. Now when she looked at him, she saw again the strange glow of pale fox fire around him, but no evidence of an attract or compel spell. His personality was so submerged he was almost invisible. Why did she feel this strange heart tug?

"So what are you doing back in Guthrie?" Terry asked.

He glanced around. "We're in Guthrie?"

"You don't even know where you are?"

"I tracked you and found you. That was more important than knowing where you were."

Terry frowned. "So where's your boss? He going to come and scoop you up again? What is it you want from me, anyway?"

Galen straightened, looked back to the beach, searched all around. "He may follow me. I left when I knew he was occupied with something, but he might leave his study sooner than I expect. He's been watching me more carefully lately." His voice remained flat and unemotional, but Terry sensed agitation.

"Oh? Why's that?"

"Maybe he knows I'm restless and looking for answers in directions of which he doesn't approve. Will you help me?"

"How can you ask me that? You and your master hurt my friend!"

"You're strong and disciplined. With your help, I may be able to do what I need."

What was with this guy? Maybe his lack of emotions made him think nobody else had them either. He sure scored low on empathy. But maybe Terry could use that. "What's in it for me?" she asked. Should she just blast him? Drop a tether spell on him and use truthtell to get some answers about the strange things that had happened so long ago? She should at least tell Tasha and the others that something important was happening out here on the rocks. She scanned the beach, searching for her sister.

"Please," said the boy. He crouched beside her again, and pulled something out of his pocket. "It's not for me. Here's my heart." He dropped something the size of a ruby grapefruit into her cupped hands.

Heat flowed from the thing. She looked at it: the same thing he had tried to show her in the bar. A knot of glass shaped like an anatomical heart, and inside its clear crystal walls floated something—two somethings. Terry felt horror chill the pit of her stomach. Two tiny children floated inside the chambered glass. Their faces were pale, their eyes closed as though asleep. Her vision was still bright from the spell. She saw the heart's aura, and realized that these were real people, nearly dead but not quite.

"What is this?" she whispered.

"My brother and sister," said Galen in his flat voice. "My master put them in there. I carry them with me everywhere. Can you help me get them out?"

"What?" She closed her hands around the heart, its throbbing warmth, its terrible cargo, and felt her throat thicken with tears.

"I only know my own heart once in a while," said Galen,

"when I touch shaped stone. It has taken me a long time to make this decision. I have thought it over a thousand times, though, and I believe I know what I want. Let the children out."

"Your master locked your brother and sister up in here?"

"He said it would keep them safe. I gave up my heart to keep them safe. This is not what I wanted for them."

"No duh," said Terry. "He did that to your brother and sister, and you still stay with him?"

"My master and I bound ourselves to each other before he did this."

"Oh, God! That's awful!"

Galen shrugged. "It's not so terrible when you don't know your own heart. Will you help me?"

"Yes," said Terry.

"Thank you," he said.

"Galen!" cried a freezing voice from behind him.

Terry jumped to her feet. She didn't recognize the voice, though she knew she had heard it before.

Galen sighed and looked over his shoulder. "I'll leave them with you," he whispered. "Please keep them safe. Please!" A whirl of shadow came out of the air and swallowed him. A second later Terry was alone on the rock.

The glass heart still beat in her hands.

MATT woke from dreamless sleep to music and warmth. The music sounded like wind chimes, the really good kind with tuned pipes. She opened her eyes and saw a pillar of shifting, fiery colors floating in the air beside her bed. Warmth flowed from it, and the music came from it too.

"What?" she said. She sat up. The hairs on the back of her neck rose.

"Did you call me?" Its voice was beautiful, burned clean of impurities, rich as gold.

"Julio?"

"Who are you?"

"Julio," she said again, then put her hands over her mouth.

"I don't know you," it said.

"No. No, I'm sorry. I'm Matt. I didn't call you. I don't know how. But I've been looking for you."

"Why?"

She felt strange talking to a column of flickering fire. "Two things. I'm helping Edmund find his old friends. And the house wants everybody to come back."

"House." A streamer of fire reached from the main mass of light to touch the wall. Then the whole column of light shifted past Matt, over her bed, to shimmer against the wall, half submerge in it.

Matt wanted to touch the light. The desire burned in her. She held out her hand, wanting more than anything to connect with this strange thing. If she could connect, they could talk in the language of things, a straightforward language with few evasions.

She'd already had a lot of conversations with Julio, only he hadn't been there. What would he do when he found out what she knew?

She brushed her hand through the edge of fire. Her hand tingled: not quite a burn, more like waking after falling asleep. She felt an immense thrumming, like a silent engine doing a big job.

"Hey," said the voice. It sounded like it was laughing.

"Sorry." Nathan had said he could feel Julio's hand when the light touched him, but this wasn't like that. Matt drew her hand out of the light. "You're so pretty."

"Thanks," said the fire, and changed into a person.

Not the person Matt expected.

A dark-skinned, black-eyed woman in a yellow dress stood on Matt's bed. She was short and shapely and reminded Matt of Juanita. Her heavy black hair was braided and coiled in a crown around her head. "Who's this sleeping in my bed?" she asked, and dropped to sit cross-legged on the covers in front of Matt. She smiled wide, showing strong white teeth, and a dimple in her right cheek.

"Hi," said Matt.

"Hi. House just told me who you are."

"Are you Julio?"

"Not exactly, but not far from it."

"Who Julio is now.'" Matt remembered: when Edmund asked whether Nathan still saw any of his old friends, Nathan had said, *I see who Julio is now.*

"My name is Lia."

"House told me way too much about who you used to be, without asking you if it was all right."

"House just told me all about who you are, without asking you if it's all right," Lia said, and shrugged. "What can you do?" She held out her hand, and Matt grasped it. Lia's hand was strong and calloused. "It's excellent to meet you, Matt." Lia smiled and looked away. "I'm not sure I'm ready to face the others yet."

"It's a lot different when you're a girl all along and they just think you're a boy, but then find out they're wrong. This is . . . a lot more."

"Sometimes it seems gigantic. Sometimes it's little. When I'm alone, I don't even notice most of the time. This shape works much better for the life I live now, though." Lia pleated the hem of her dress between her fingers. "Since my real self is fire, I can be whatever shape human I want."

Matt remembered the house telling her she could step out of its wall taller, fatter, different. She looked at her new leather boots, standing beside the bed. She had said hi to them before she fell asleep, and they had said hi back in the voices of her old boots. Did they even know they had changed?

She remembered Nathan telling the others that Julio's core was the same, even though Julio had changed.

You could wear the edges off a beach rock and its center stayed the same.

"The journey from flame to human is the same length either way, just a slightly different direction. I could switch back to Julio, I guess." Lia frowned and stared down at her thumbs. "Haven't done Julio in a long time, though."

"The house remembers."

"Oh, yes, of course." Lia smiled and patted the wall. Her skin glowed orange, then glowed brighter, and she vanished into a creature of many-colored flame, which pressed into the wall.

Matt touched the wall partway inside the fire and felt the house's quiet turquoise strength meeting Lia's loud, boisterous energy. Matt's hand began to melt into the mix. She pulled it out. What if she melted into the house now and got all mixed up in house and Lia? What if she went into the house and came back out a man?

She slid out from under the covers and pulled on her jeans, thinking.

How could Lia say changing genders was a little thing? Contemplating it made Matt shiver. She had spent a lot of her life pretending to be a man, but she suspected that *being* a man would feel completely different.

"I don't know," said Lia. Her voice was lower. Fire tightened and condensed. A young man stood on Matt's bed, Julio, all in red, his short black hair flickering at the ends. "This feels very strange. I don't like it anymore." His voice was tenor now, not alto, but similar in tone and timbre. He jumped off the bed and walked around the room. He shook his head. "No, this is too strange."

A guitar on a stand appeared before him. "What?" He reached out and picked up the guitar. "My old Martin. But this guitar is in my safe place. How, House?"

"Anything that was ever here can be here again," Matt said. Suddenly she wondered: after she left, would the house summon images of her and show them to other people? Talk to them? Make them move and talk like she did? Would it walk into other people's dreams and tell them about her? Let them *be* her?

Nothing she could do about it—except ask the house not to do that. Which was no guarantee that it wouldn't. Everybody owned their memories, no matter who was in them. She had a brief vision of the scattering of selves she'd left behind all over the country, snakeskin Matts in the heads of this person or that, Matts she had stepped out of but which still held her shape and character.

Julio slipped the guitar strap over his neck and shoulder and strummed the guitar. It sounded in tune. He played flamenco.

Matt sat, entranced. The music was crisp and sharp and flashing. It made her think of people stamping and whistling.

Julio glanced at her, noticed how she listened, and played more, smiling. His face was similar to Lia's, though narrower. His smile flashed the same dimple, the same white teeth. He finished playing the piece, and said, "The music is the same, either way—"

The bedroom door opened. "Julio?" cried Edmund as he rushed into the room.

The guitar banged to the floor. A rage of flame whooshed up and vanished, leaving behind only a faint smell of hot metal.

"Julio?" Edmund's voice sang soft and bereft. He turned to Matt. "Was he here?"

Matt went to pick up the guitar. The fall had scuffed it. She stroked the strings, and they sounded discordant.

"Matt?" Edmund asked.

Matt put the guitar carefully on its stand, then knelt and placed her palm on the floor. —Take it away again,—she told the house.

The guitar faded.

Matt sat on the floor. —Is anybody else home?—

—No.—

—Why didn't you tell us Edmund was here?—

The house didn't say anything.

—Is Lia still here?—

"Matt." Edmund sat on the floor beside her. "What happened?"

She turned to him, smiled, touched his mouth. "Guess you shoulda knocked."

"I heard the music. I saw him. He was here. Why did he run?"

"Kind of shy right now."

"Shy about what? We were best friends for years. Now what?"

"Changed a lot," Matt said.

Edmund hunched his shoulders and leaned forward. "Changed so much he can't face me? He looked the same."

"That was just acting."

"Matt—" Pain sang in his voice.

She turned to him and hugged him, stroked his hair. If Edmund had been the person Matt first met, calm, serene, accepting everything that came to him as though it must be right or could be fixed, Lia could have met him without trouble, Matt thought. But that Edmund wouldn't be the person Lia remembered as a friend.

That Edmund wasn't around much anymore.

This Edmund returned her embrace, then sighed and sat up. "You saw him? He's all right?"

"Yeah."

"Guess that's all I need to know."

Matt looked over Edmund's shoulder.

The flame came silently this time, unaccompanied by wind chime noises.

Matt nudged Edmund. He turned.

For a moment, the flame hung there, stretching from floor to ceiling, mostly white and gold, with other colors, red, aqua, orange, lime green, balloon pink, violet, streaking through. Then it drew in, tightened, turned solid.

"This is Lia," said Matt.

Lia gazed at Edmund for a long moment, then smiled.

"Hi," Edmund said. "How are you?"

"Happy," she answered.

"That's great." He climbed to his feet and walked to her. They stared into each other's faces for a long time. Edmund's brows lowered for a little while, then rose. Lia waited.

Matt held out as long as she could stand it, and then opened dream-eyes.

Above Lia's head, Matt saw a hushed concert hall, full house, empty stage, houselights down and stage lights up, everything waiting for something to begin.

Above Edmund's head, a kaleidoscopic rush of silent images of Julio, and an image of Lia: comparisons, cross-checking.

A much younger Julio and a misty place-holder Edmund climbed over a fence at night, sneaked close to a house to peek in a window.

Eight-year-old Julio and Edmund had an argument that involved waving comic books at each other and shouting.

Fourteen: they fought three other boys and lost, were left in the dust, bleeding. Julio helped Edmund up.

Thirteen-year-old Edmund performed a magic show for a classroom full of little kids, and Julio accompanied on the guitar. The kids' eyes were wide with wonder.

Eleven-year-old Julio and Deirdre held unlit cigarettes, tried different poses: cigarette between finger and thumb, between first two fingers, with some fingers folded over, with all fingers straight. They watched each other and discussed, refined the ultimate too-cool cigarette pose, until Edmund came into the image, grabbed the cigarettes, and stamped on them.

Twelve-year-old Julio dragged twelve-year-old Susan over to twelve-year-old Edmund and Deirdre on an otherwise empty playground. Susan stared at the ground, and Julio talked. Susan turned to walk away, and Julio grabbed her hand, keeping her there. Edmund and Deirdre said something, and Susan finally looked up, her eyes shadowed, her mouth smiling faintly.

Julio leaned his cheek and chin on the chin rest of a violin, closed his eyes, and played. Bliss transformed his face. Gradually, his face turned into Lia's face.

Matt closed dream-eyes.

Edmund reached out and touched Lia's face. She put her hand on his cheek. "Okay," Edmund said.

"But enough about me," Lia said. "What happened to you?"

Edmund laughed. He set his hand gently on Lia's shoulder. She hugged him fiercely, and he hugged her back. They stepped away from each other. "You don't want to talk about why?" Edmund asked.

"Not at the moment." Lia paced the room just the way Julio had. "I'm lucky. It's easy for me. Sometimes I wonder how many people want to change and can't. It's lots harder for humans."

"You looked like your old self when I came in."

"That was an experiment. I didn't know how to face you, and I still don't know how I'll face Suki and Deirdre. The coward's way would be to change back to the way I used to look. It's not difficult, but it no longer feels right. What do I go for, comfort or honesty?"

Edmund sat on his bed and watched Lia pace. He smiled, but didn't offer any answers.

Lia called Suki Suki, Matt thought. She wondered how much of her history Lia had absorbed while half-submerged in House. Enough to have gotten a good look at present-day Suki and Deirdre. Maybe Lia knew everything Matt had done lately. Matt felt that the idea should bother her more. The intimacy the house had given them somehow washed worry out. Matt was still missing a lot of information about Lia, though. The house had been careful to tell her nothing more recent than fifteen years ago.

"Hey," Matt said, "did you ever pay Mr. Noah for his violin?"

Lia stopped. A smile lit her face. "I built him a new one. It took me four tries, but I finally built one that held together and sounded right. I put fire in it. One of my first successful projects after I changed. He forgave me."

She straightened, glanced from Edmund's face to Matt's. "Who called me?"

"Called you?" Edmund asked.

"Someone called me."

"I thought the house fixed it so people couldn't call you," Matt said.

"What?" said Edmund.

"The house mixed up Julio and Tabasco so people couldn't use those article things on them, or summon him against his will."

Lia grinned at Matt. "Easiest way to explain anything. Let somebody else do it. Yes. House changed my nature so I couldn't be controlled the way demons are. For those who know me, though, there are still ways of summoning me. Someone called me here."

"So who knows you?" Matt asked.

"Since I changed?" Lia nodded. "Of course. House, and Nathan."

Matt flattened a hand on the floor and waited. The house didn't say anything.

Nathan shimmered into sight. "I called you," he said, "for the reasons Matt said. Edmund is looking for his friends, and House has plans."

"What kind of plans?"

"We don't know yet," Matt said.

"Now that you're here, maybe House will tell us," said Nathan. "If you choose to stay here, anyway."

"Don't you know what House wants?" Matt asked him.

Nathan shook his head. "Not exactly. Lately I've discovered that House and I are not as closely linked as I thought. Things happen while I'm away or asleep, and House doesn't tell me. House has ideas it doesn't share. I guess it's mutual. On nights when I escape, I don't always tell everything I've done when I return."

A door slammed downstairs.

"So anyway, they're home," Nathan said. "What are you going to do, Lia?"

Golden fire flickered over Lia's face and arms. After a moment it faded. She sighed. "Oh, well," she said. "Let's go downstairs."

"Nathan!" Terry's voice called from below. "Hey? Nathan?" She sounded strangely unsure, almost afraid.

They ran from the room. Nathan dropped down through the floor, though, so he got to the first floor ahead of them. On the way down the stairs, Lia took Matt's hand. Matt glanced at Lia. Maybe Lia didn't even know she had grabbed Matt's hand. Matt held Lia's hand tight.

Matt and Lia entered the front hall behind Edmund. Fresh salt air had followed Terry, Suki, Deirdre, and Tasha into the house. They all looked windblown and slightly sunburned, and Terry looked upset.

"What is it, Terry?" Nathan asked.

"I ran into this guy at the beach," she said, "and he gave me this horrible thing. He was one of those two guys who stole Julio way back when. He's really, really weird. Look at this." She held out a twisted lump of glass.

Nathan stepped away from her outthrust hand. "Terry!"

She pulled back. "What? Can it hurt you? I know it's awful, but I didn't think it could hurt anyone."

"Do you recognize it, Nathan?" Tasha asked.

"It's a soul trap." Nathan's voice was faint.

Edmund dug into a pocket and pulled out a blue silk scarf. "Wrap it in this, Terry. It's already sucking on you, and Nathan doesn't have enough of an anchor to resist it for long. This'll dampen it."

Terry paled and wrapped the thing in silk. "I'll take it far away. I'll hide it in some forest deep in Siberia or something."

"No. It's all right now," Nathan said. "We need to find out more about it."

"The guy just handed it to me. He asked me to take care of it for him. He walked around with this thing in his pocket. He's had it for years and years. He said it was his heart."

"Terry," said Matt. "This guy—he was one of the ones who stole Julio?"

"Yeah. Not the old guy, but the younger one who just stood there. What am I telling you this for? What do you know about this stuff?"

"I know," said Matt. "The younger guy, huh. Wonder what he wants."

"He said this thing has his brother and sister in it, and he wants them out of it," Terry said. She stared at the wrapped object in her hand. "He asked me to help him get them out."

Suki walked past Terry. Eyes wide, Suki came to Matt and Lia. Short Lia let go of Matt's hand and looked up at tall Suki. Suki blinked. A tear ran down her cheek. "Where've you been?" she whispered. "I've missed you so much." She closed her arms around Lia, hugged her tight.

"What the hell?" said Deirdre. She followed Suki toward Lia.

"Where've *I* been?" Lia said against Suki's chest. "You stopped writing back. I wasn't sure you were there anymore."

"Oh, you're right. You're right. I was so stupid. Your letters meant everything to me, but I got all paralyzed and couldn't answer them after a while." Suki sighed and released Lia. "I pared my personality down to next to nothing. Now I'm picking up the pieces. I would write back now."

"I don't have a fixed address anymore." Lia smiled. "But I can keep in touch." She took Suki's hands, lifted them so that Suki's sleeves slid down, revealing wide gold wristbands. "What are you wearing?"

"It's magic. Isn't it great? I've got my own magic now."

"Oh! Right! I guess I do remember that. Matt told me about it." Lia thunked her forehead twice with the heel of her palm. "This has been a confusing day."

"Hey," said Deirdre in a fading voice. "Julio? Is that you?"

"Hey, Dee."

"What the hell happened to you?"

"I changed my name to Lia."

"Not that!" Deirdre punched Lia's arm. "The sex change! Why the heck would anybody want to be a girl?"

Matt laughed. She couldn't help it.

Lia laughed too. "It works better this way."

"What works better?" Deirdre frowned ferociously.

"Pretty much everything. Think about it. Light may dawn. If not, I'll give you some more hints later."

"Wah," said Terry. She stared at Lia's face. "Hi there."

"Hi, Terry."

"May I touch you?" Tasha asked Lia.

Lia's eyes widened. "What happened to *you*, Tash? ¡*Madre de dios!*"

"Lots," said Tasha cheerfully. She reached out and put her hand on Lia's forehead, and the next instant they both vanished and the front hall was full of fire and wind.

Matt stood in the midst of the maelstrom, watched as flame chased wind, wind chased flame, watched colored fire flicker over the faces of the others, who also stood staring up into wildness. Lilac and carrot orange flames brushed across Matt's shirt, wind fingered her face, brushed her mouth, lifted Suki's blond hair into a riot; nothing burned. Flame and wind raced across the floor, rippled the rugs, chased across the ceiling, teased Edmund's curls and flipped up the hem of Terry's shirt. A passing breeze tugged the tie off the end of Deirdre's braid, and another unbraided it before she could grab it back and tame it. Even Nathan's hair seemed to ruffle.

"Hey!" Deirdre yelled above the rush of winged wind and crackling fire sounds. "Stop it! Settle down, you two!"

They separated into a spinning column of colored flame and a pocket tornado, then condensed down into people, laughing and breathless and red-cheeked.

"Don't," Lia said when she caught her breath, "don't touch me again, Tasha."

"Okay," Tasha managed. "I get it. You're unstable too."

"Good word for it."

"Sure, that was fun, but we've got a real problem here," Deirdre said. "What about this soul-trap thing?"

Lia sobered. "I'm sorry. You're right, Dee. Terry, you met the boy on the beach?"

"I met him in a bar in Spores last week, actually. I guess he tracked me there, and then he tracked me here. He didn't know at first that I'd ever seen him before. He was just looking for some powerful witch to help him with his little problem, or maybe he found me in a crystal ball or on the Internet." Terry shook her head. "He's so weird. He has no feelings. But he seems to want to free his brother and sister."

"Are you sure it isn't some kind of trick?" Deirdre asked. "They tried to mess with us before. Maybe he just wanted you to bring that thing into the house and snag Nathan with it. Maybe those guys are back again, and they want to mix it up again too."

"But there really are two people trapped in here, not quite dead."

Edmund held out his hand to Terry. She hesitated, then handed him the silk-shrouded heart. "Let's go outside and look," he said.

Everyone trooped out of the house except Nathan.

Evening sun slanted from the west, struck the few small clouds in the sky with orange-pink. Already the evening was turning cold. Matt danced from one bare foot to the other, until the ground warmed beneath her feet and she could stand. —Thanks, House.—

Edmund carefully unwrapped the glass heart and everyone leaned in to look at it.

A girl's pale face, hair, and hands floated against a darkness that could be her clothed body. Matt shuddered.

Edmund used the silk to turn the heart over, and revealed a second pale, sleeping face floating in a second darkness.

"I've never seen anything like this before," Terry said, "and I've been studying the dark arts. How do we break a spell like this?"

"Matt?" Edmund said. "Don't touch it. Can you talk to it?"

Lately whenever Matt wanted to talk to something, she touched it. It was a habit she had picked up from Edmund. It seemed more direct and specific. She remembered, though, walking through the world and talking to things without touching them. When she addressed everything, the ones who wanted to converse would let her know. Sometimes she was astonished by what talked, and always she was astonished by what things had to say. Weird that she'd spent so much time lately talking to people and houses and hadn't opened herself to many conversations with things.

—Thing,—she thought.

—Where's Galen?——Where's my brother?— The crystal spoke in two voices, both young and plaintive.

—Are you the people inside?—

—Galen, where are you?—

"They're asking for Galen," Matt reported.

"The boy told me his name was Galen," Terry said.

—Galen wants us to get you out of there,—Matt thought.

—We can't get out. We're stuck here forever.—

—How do you know?—

—We heard the spell. Galen gave his heart to keep us safe and warm forever, and his master put us here. We're safe. We're warm. Forever.—

Matt shuddered and repeated what the children had said.

"That's what the boy at the beach told me," Terry said.

"So the children don't know how to escape," said Edmund, "but what about the container? Matt, can you talk to the crystal?"

She reached out, wanting direct contact. Edmund pulled back, flipped silk over the heart. "Don't touch it!"

"What can it do? Terry just touched it, and she's still in one piece. And the Galen guy was carrying it around for a long time."

Lia gripped her hand, pulled it away from the heart. "Matt, you're not stable right now either," she said.

"What do you mean?"

"Remember your boots? Remember your hair?"

"House told you about that? Jeeze!"

"Try it without touch," Lia said.

Edmund unveiled the heart. Matt leaned forward until her nose almost touched the crystal. —Heart,—she thought.

—Human.— Its voice sounded warm and furry and, somehow, deep brown.

—How can we open you? How can we get the children out?—

—I am open to any who want to come in. Come to me. I can keep you safe.—

Matt shivered. —I don't want to go in. I want to get people out.—

—I do not open out.—

—Never? Ever?—

—I am made only to open in.—

Matt reported this to the others. "Maybe I don't know the right questions," she said. "What should I ask?"

"How can we break it?" suggested Terry.

—How can we break you?—Matt asked, though she couldn't imagine anything would answer a question like that.

—I do not break. I am forever.—

"Ask it how it was made," said Edmund when Matt had relayed the answer.

—I was built from a promise, an exchange. I am bought and paid for. I am complete.—

Matt repeated what the heart said out loud.

"What was the promise?" asked Terry.

"Who made the promise? What was exchanged? Who accepted the promise?" Tasha asked, her voice strangely condensed and powerful.

— Immortality. Eternal safety for the children. Eternal thirst for knowledge for the apprentice. In return, an innocent child's heart, freely given. —

Matt reported, and added, "It doesn't say who."

"Galen's heart," said Terry. "Galen's the other guy's apprentice, so I bet it's the master wizard who made the bargain. Eternal thirst for knowledge! The guy's a maniac. What a load to lay on the kid."

"Ask again, Matt," Tasha said in her strangely doubled voice. "Who took the boy's heart and gave these gifts in exchange?"

— Monument, — said the crystal heart.

Matt repeated it, and looked at all the witches.

"Sure," Terry said. "That explains exactly everything, I'm so sure."

"We're not going to solve this right now," said Tasha. She sounded Tasha-normal again. "Put the thing someplace safe, and let's go to dinner. I want calamari! I think better after I eat."

Terry said, "It's mine. Galen gave it to me and asked me to keep it safe."

Edmund wrapped the heart in silk and handed it to Terry. She stuck it in her pocket, where it made a large bulge. "Is it safe to take inside now?" she asked Edmund.

"As long as it's wrapped, it should be okay," he said. "At least for a little while. I don't think it should be in the house overnight."

Terry sucked air in between her teeth and pondered. "Guess I'll sleep in the car tonight, or go to a motel. I have to go get my purse."

Everyone went back inside for purses, coats, shoes, wallets, car keys.

Lia followed Matt and Edmund into their room, and Matt realized that of course, this had been Julio's room; where else would Lia go?

Edmund lifted his navy peacoat from the back of a chair and slipped it on.

"How you doing?" Matt asked Lia. "You okay?"

"So far." She looked troubled. "It went better than I thought it would. I wonder if Dee will keep asking me why."

"I get the feeling if she wants to know something, she doesn't let go. Why don't you just tell her?"

"Because this change was the result of a succession of choices which each made sense at the time, but if I list them now, I know they'll sound stupid. Increments creep up on you, and before you know it, you're far away from where you were, without really knowing how you got there."

"Tell her it's none of her business," Matt said. She dug socks out of her black garbage-bag luggage, pulled them and the riding boots on. "You got any shoes?"

Lia pointed to her feet with both index fingers. Yellow flame shot from her fingertips and formed slim yellow shoes that matched her dress. She waved her hands in the air, trailing streams of flame, and a silky orange-and-red shawl spun into existence. She draped it around her shoulders.

"That is so cool!" Matt said.

Lia grinned. "Want something?"

"I got a jacket." Matt glanced at her full-length army jacket, which was olive green, frayed in places, and many-spotted from years of encounters with whatever Matt spent time with. "It's a good jacket," she said.

"I know," said Lia. "I remember. Just the same . . ." She stroked her fingers over Matt's shoulders, down her arms, down her front, and down her back. Flame played over Matt, warm but not scorching. It flickered different colors. Greens, silver, blues, and light purples flashed through it. Suddenly it turned from flame to fabric, soft as alpaca, fine as silk, warm as wool.

Matt's cheeks tingled. She had never had anything as beautiful as this jacket, with its streaks of sea and sky and cloud colors in the shapes of flame. It fitted tight to her figure above the waist, then belled out like a full skirt to just below her butt. The sleeves were snug but had large turned-back cuffs, and there were pockets she could bury her hands in.

She stood up. She stroked her hands down the fabric. Soft, fuzzy, so warm, as beautiful as a really good sunset. Her eyes felt hot, and blood prickled in her face. She glanced at Lia.

"Oh, Matt! I'm sorry. Do you want me to take it away again?"

Something hurt under Matt's hair. She shook her head no. "It's great," she said, her voice wavery. "It's the first girl clothes I've had in years."

Lia glanced at Edmund, who shook his head, smiling.

"Seriously," Lia said, "I can send it away again if it makes you uncomfortable."

Matt sniffed. "Hey. You walked out there like that, I guess I could stand to walk out there like this. They're not going to laugh at me, are they? This is so pretty. I have to see it."

—Matt.—

She turned and found a mirror on the wall by the door. She stared at herself.

She hadn't seen herself in a while, certainly not since she stepped out of the wall and asked for a different haircut earlier that afternoon. She looked different. She had short curls on top of her head, but the sides of her head were close-cropped. Her face was the same, but this strange haircut shifted the focus somehow: she could definitely tell she was female, something no one used to be able to do just by looking at her face. The jacket was brighter than anything she usually wore, beautiful and tailored to show that she actually had breasts and a waist, and her jeans and shirt were brighter blue than they should be. The riding boots changed everything too. They looked elegant. She didn't look like a scruffy sixteen-year-old soldier in these clothes and this haircut. She looked like a misplaced princess.

She met Edmund's eyes in the mirror, waited for a comment.

"You look great either way," he said.

She watched herself smile, and that, too, disturbed her so much that she instantly frowned. What if she was attractive? She didn't mind being acceptable, or even pleasant-looking, but she didn't want to be attractive.

Lia touched Matt's shoulder. "Come on. Stop thinking about it. Let's go."

Everyone else was already waiting down in the front hall.

"Woo hoo!" said Terry as Lia, Matt, and Edmund came down the stairs. "Don't you know this is the beach? Nobody dresses up around here." She was wearing jeans and a purple windbreaker, and looked as stylish as ever.

Suki smiled, her usual J.Crew self in olive slacks and a sand-colored blazer, her hair perfectly restored since Tasha's hurricane.

Deirdre wore the same rumpled clothes she'd showed up in,

sneakers, jeans, a blue blouse, and a navy hooded sweatshirt. "Holy shit," she said. "What happened to you guys?"

"They *are* laughing," Matt said to Lia.

"No, we're not," Terry said. "We're awestruck."

Matt hunched her shoulders and buried her hands in her coat pockets.

"You look great," said Tasha, who looked a little strange herself in a pink blouse that bared her midriff, hip-hugging black pants, and flip-flops. She had tied her hair in bunches on either side of her head. Again, no jacket, but she never needed one, Matt guessed.

"Thanks," said Matt.

"Nathan?" Edmund glanced around.

After a moment, Nathan shimmered into sight beside Suki. "Looks like we're going out to supper," Edmund told him, as though Nathan might not have heard about this earlier.

"Taste something for me," Nathan said.

"I could bring you something back," Suki murmured.

Nathan smiled and shook his head.

"House, when we get back, are you going to tell us what this is all about?" Terry said.

"I will."

"I'm taking that glass thing with me. It's in my purse," she said.

"Good," said the house and Nathan at the same time.

Chapter Thirteen

· · · · ·

AFTER a noisy supper in a place that seemed too candlelight-and-wine to support such bad behavior, Terry, Deirdre, and Suki went off to the ladies' room in a bunch. Matt sipped heavily creamed-and-sugared coffee. Lia ate vanilla ice cream in tiny bites. Edmund sat quiet and smiling, and Tasha was eating something with a lot of chocolate in it when a strange teenage boy came to the table and said, "Can I have my heart back?"

"We're still working on it," Tasha said.

"I've changed my mind. I want it back. Now." *His voice is weird and flat, just like Terry said*, thought Matt. His face was expressionless, though pretty. Shaggy black hair, wolf eyes, sort of a wild-animal look. Dressed kind of dorky, work shirt, wonky pants, shiny black shoes. She checked her memory of Julio's encounter, decided it was the same guy.

"You don't want to let the children out anymore?" Tasha asked.

"It's not safe."

"Why not?" Matt asked him. "Do you really want them to stay inside that thing forever?"

"No," he said. "I'll try to release them again later."

"Who's Monument?" asked Matt.

The boy jerked, startled. "I don't know."

"Monument's the one who took your heart. You don't even know who that is?"

The boy shook his head, his features still wooden. "It's the god of stone creatures, the god of shaped stone," he whispered. "That's all I know. Please. Give me my heart back."

"Can't," said Matt. "Terry has it, and she's not here. What's the rush?"

"My master. My master will come for you soon."

Lia leaned forward. "Do you think that's wise?" she asked, her voice sharp and coppery.

The boy took a step back, staring at her. "What are you?" He almost sounded astonished.

"We've met before." Lia smiled. Her eyes glowed orange.

The boy shook his head. "You should all leave. My master has been studying since last time we encountered you, and he's made me study too. We have new strategies. Our house is full of strong creatures he has defeated and pressed into service, and some of them will fight for him too. Please give me my heart. I want to put it somewhere safe."

Terry, Deirdre, and Suki came back. "Hey! Speak of the devil. Here he is!" Terry tapped the boy on the shoulder. The boy wheeled. "Hey, Galen," Terry said.

"Please give me back my heart," whispered the boy.

"Do you know how to open it? We've only been working on

it a short time. All we know so far is that it opens in, but not out. What can you tell us?"

"He tells us his master is going to attack us again," Lia said. "He wants to put his heart somewhere safer than here."

Terry frowned. "What does your master want with us, anyway? We're not hurting him. We're not bothering anybody. We're just having a little party. What's going on?"

"Anytime there is a higher-than-normal concentration of powers and skills in one place," the boy said, "my master—"

"Quiet." The word came from nowhere. It was deep and dark and made the boy jerk as though he had been slapped.

The boy held out his hands. "My heart!"

Terry pulled the silk-wrapped crystal out of her purse, handed it to the boy.

Shadow swallowed him and his final "thank you."

"What was that?" asked a woman at the next table. "Did that boy just disappear?"

"Hey. You over there with the harem. Your own private little Vegas nightclub act. What's going on here?" yelled someone else from another table. "You staging some kind of magic show? Shouldn't you let the management know beforehand?"

"Who the hell are you talking to?" Deirdre yelled back.

"The guy with six girls," the man yelled.

Deirdre, Terry, Suki, Matt, Tasha, and Lia all looked at Edmund. He smiled and waggled his eyebrows at them.

"Hey, eat your heart out, bud," Deirdre yelled at the man across the room. In a lower tone, she said, "Let's blow this Popsicle stand."

Matt gulped the rest of her coffee. Did they have instant coffee or caffeinated tea at the house? She wasn't sure, and she had the feeling they would be up late tonight.

Suki picked up the check. Matt felt another pang of guilt. She had to get a job so she could take other people out to dinner for a change. But what the heck was she qualified to do?

Appliance repair. Car repair. Fortune-telling? Later.

As soon as they stepped over the threshold of the haunted house, Terry cast a spell that made the air glow green. "Wards are still up," she said. "Maybe we should add more. We have enough different disciplines to do a bunch of stuff now, right? Air, Tasha; fire, Lia; Edmund, do you have a ruling element? I mostly work with water. Nathan? House? Galen says that demon guy is coming to attack us."

Suki touched the wall. Lights switched on, and furniture in the living room, which had been more shadow than solid, returned to usable form. Nathan appeared before the fireplace. Everyone went into the living room and sat down.

"This isn't what you called us here for, is it, House?" Edmund asked.

"No."

"You've got it backward, Edmund," Terry said. "Galen said that it's the concentration of powers that makes the demon-guy attack." Then she muttered, "Wish we'd asked Galen for the master's name." Then, louder, "Anyway, it's because we all came here at the same time that the guy targets us. Let's throw up some more armor and find out what House wants us to do. If we do it fast enough and leave, maybe we can get out without a fight."

"What magic system did the demon-guy use, Nathan?" Edmund asked. "I didn't know enough about it to figure it out when we were there before."

"It was a mixture of different sorts of disciplines. Like you, he's built his own craft out of bits of whatever he likes. Three different magical alphabets, basic chalk craft, invocations to gods and powers about which I know nothing."

"Our armor worked last time," Terry said.

"Galen said they have better strategies now," said Lia.

"I don't think I can do that kind of armor anymore," said Tasha. "All my old skills are rusty. But I bet air and I can do other things."

Edmund nodded. "My craft is different now, too."

"Well, give us whatever you've got. Lia, you have a lot more on tap now, don't you? Suki? Matt? Deirdre?" Terry looked at each of them in turn.

Deirdre shook her head. "I still got nothing," she said.

"Not true," said Tasha. "You have the coyote with you."

"You said that before, and I still don't get it. I'm a vet. Any animals get hurt, I'm there. Other than that, I can observe."

"You can anchor," Lia said.

"Okay, I can anchor, too, if the situation comes up."

"I have this much magic," said Suki, holding up her wrists and showing the gold bands, "and my connection with the house and Nathan."

"I've got talking and watching." Matt bit her bottom lip. "I don't know how to attack anybody."

"Defending is good, too," Terry told her.

"And I have . . ." Lia said. "I have lots of firepower, and also . . ."

Terry turned to her.

Lia cleared her throat. "I have Harry."

Terry's eyebrows rose.

"Just a minute, I'll go get him." Lia turned to flame, then vanished.

"Harry?" said Deirdre.

"Somebody had to make new friends when we lost touch with each other," Terry said. "I hope I'm the only one here who doesn't know how."

They looked at each other.

Suki smiled ruefully. Deirdre shrugged, also smiling. Nathan's eyes danced. Edmund put his hand on top of Matt's head.

Tasha frowned. "Should I go get Danny?"

"How useful would he be in a witch war?" Terry asked. "I mean, he's great with humans, but we could really hurt him, and so could the other guys. Unless you think he has special skills that could help, I'd leave him out of this."

Orange-and-yellow fire floated in the air, dancing, with a sound of wind chimes, and then a man emerged from the cloud, surrounded by flame. To Matt he looked like a statue, one of those idealized ones in pale stone that represented some concept like Civic Pride or Honest Work: tall, clean-cut, nicely built, strong-jawed. He wore the wrong clothes to be a statue like that, a gray long-sleeved shirt with a couple top buttons open, dark slacks, leather shoes, but he had the right pose and the right expression— calm, distant. For a second, anyway.

Then the flames vanished, replaced by Lia at his side, and he smiled down at her and turned into someone else, someone alive and laughing.

"This is Harry," Lia said.

"Well, shit," Deirdre said. "Light dawns."

"Good," said Lia in a dark voice. She told Harry everyone's name and said, "Harry comes from a long line of witches, but he didn't know about that until a while after we met. He's been studying since he found out, and he has a lot of tools now. He says he'll help."

"Nice to meet you," said Matt.

Harry smiled at her and at everyone. "Nice to meet all of you. Amazing to be here," he said. "Lia doesn't talk much about where she came from, but once in a while she lets something slip. This is like meeting legends. There's a lot of strange energy around here. I feel like I'm in the middle of something big." He looked up at the ceiling. "House?"

"Boy?" said the house.

Harry shivered. "Honored to meet you," he said. He glanced at Nathan, who smiled.

"Well, we're glad you're here," Terry said. "Welcome to our war conference. First thing we should do is cast some more protection, don't you think, Nathan?"

"Couldn't hurt," Nathan said, "and it would give us a chance to see what we have to work with."

Deirdre got up and grabbed Suki's hand. "Let's go to the kitchen and make a bunch of tea or something."

"Don't you want to watch?" Suki asked, without rising.

"It'll just make me mad."

Matt came to them. "I'll help you," she told Deirdre.

"You can make the stove work?"

"Bet I could," said Matt.

"Let's go."

．　．　．　．　．

IN the kitchen, Deirdre sat by the butcher block table in a chair she had taken from the dining room. Matt filled the kettle and set it on the stove, asked for heat from the past and got it, grabbed a second chair from the dining room and sat down facing Deirdre.

They left the door to the dining room open. They could hear everyone else having a discussion in the living room beyond. Terry's voice predominated. The words weren't clear; every once in a while a phrase rose above the rest.

"What am I doing here?" Deirdre asked.

"Do you want to leave?"

Deirdre held out her hands. "Here I am, back in the middle of all this magic, and I'm still completely normal. Edmund runs off, finds you, whatever you are. Julio runs off, finds this Harry boy, some kind of witch. Suki doesn't even have to look, she just has to come home to Nathan. Twins run off. Well, I don't know what came of that, except Tasha has some boy she maybe could bring into this, and Terry has this Galen boy walking up to her in bars and tide pools and restaurants and vanishing in midair. I run off and go to college for years and years, learn a lot, get married, get divorced, graduate, do an internship, start my practice. I know everybody in town and they know me, and except for an occasional bar story about strange doings in the desert, everything I run into is normal. Is there some kind of secret handshake?"

Wind howled around the house. Someone in the living room yelled, "Okay, that's a touch too much, Tasha." Wind quieted.

"You know the handshake. Here you are."

Deirdre clapped her hands to her cheeks. "Okay. You're

right," she said, exasperated, "and either way, I whine about it, huh?"

Matt got up and rummaged through the cupboards. In one she found a box of Mystic Mint cookies, in another a chipped crockery plate to put them on. She brought the cookies to the table and set them near Deirdre, who sighed and took one.

"I woke up one day, and everything was different," Matt said.

"You haven't been doing whatever it is you do since birth, huh?"

"Nope. Seemed like it happened overnight. That was a while back. Ever since then . . ." Matt stared at distance, and smiled. "Everywhere I look, when I really look. Everything I talk to, long as it's shaped by people somehow. I can't talk to plants or most dirt, or the ocean or sand or mountains, all the stuff Edmund's good at. But most of the stuff I see every day—" She touched the table, ran her thumb along the edge of the plate. "It's all alive, Dee. Most of it's not very wide awake, but it's there."

"Like Jonny Box."

"Yeah."

"It started with talking?"

"Talking and seeing."

Deirdre ate her cookie and wiped her mouth on the sleeve of her sweatshirt. For a moment she was silent. Then she said, "Last week a coyote came right up to me out of the desert."

"Coyote," Matt repeated. Tasha had mentioned this twice.

"She had a wound on her front leg. I treated her, fed her, let her go. And then she spoke to me."

"Talking," said Matt, after a minute.

"Tasha said the coyote's still here."

"When Edmund did a seek spell to look for you, there was a coyote in it."

"What do you mean?"

"He does this spell thing where he says some words over special dust, then holds it up and lets spirit move it some direction or other, and that tells us where to go. We used it to find Suki, and you. The dust flew up off his hand and turned into an animal. I thought it was a wolf."

Deirdre looked back over her shoulder. The kitchen beyond her just looked like the kitchen.

Orange light flickered outside the kitchen window. Matt glanced toward it, wondered if the house were on fire. The air shimmered with sparks and darkened with smoke.

"Can you make it invisible?" someone said in the living room.

The net of orange sparks and smoke faded.

"Much better."

"You talk about seeing, but I don't know what you mean," Deirdre said. "Can you see my coyote?"

Matt opened dream-eyes.

Deirdre's mental landscape held a tall doll, in some kind of fancy pink-and-green Chinese outfit overlaid with gold net, edged with white fringe, heavily ornamented, and detailed in red and white. Its high headdress was studded with silver wires and pink-and-white pom-poms. It wore a scabbarded sword at its waist, and banners at its back displayed golden dragons. In one graceful hand, the doll held a silver-headed spear. It held the other hand twisted above its head in a movement that might have come from dance or from martial arts or both. It was not a doll Matt remembered seeing in Deirdre's collection. Matt wasn't sure what the doll meant to Deirdre. Maybe it was a guardian?

The doll lowered its spear and glanced down and to the side, and Matt followed the direction of its gaze.

The coyote sat beside Deirdre's chair, its tail curled around its front paws. It stared at Matt with glowing yellow eyes.

"Right there," she whispered to Deirdre.

Deirdre looked down beside her, then up at Matt, her eyes sad.

Matt gripped Deirdre's hand. —Look,—she thought. —See.— She stared at the coyote, who huffed a quick breath and studied Deirdre's face. Deirdre's eyes narrowed. She glanced down again.

—See,—Matt thought, then realized she had never been able to talk to another living human this way except Edmund. This was thing-speak. Edmund had a different form of thing-speak, but he and Matt could still communicate. Could Deirdre even hear Matt? Even if Deirdre heard, how could Matt get her to see something?

The only time Matt had been able to share her vision with anybody was when Nathan helped her, or borrowed magic did . . . or the house.

Deirdre shook her head. Frustration furrowed her brow.

Matt let go of Deirdre's hand. "Got another idea." —Hey. Coyote. Okay with you if the house and I let Deirdre see you?—

—Whuff.— The mental sound was more a huffing of breath than a bark. The coyote lowered its head twice, peered up under its brows at her, shifted sideways.

—The house can make things visible,—Matt said.

—Fff.—

Matt slid off her chair and sat on the floor. She put her palms against the wood. —House?—

—Yes? I'm kind of distracted now. Sorry about your tea water. The witches are doing all kinds of things to me that tickle.—

—Do you know there's a coyote here?—

—Yes. It followed Dee in, walked right through the wards. I hope it's a friendly spirit.—

—Can you make it visible to Dee?—

—What? Oh. Of course, if it consents. Give me your hand so I can use your eyes.—

Matt shoved her hand down into the floor.

"What are you doing?" Deirdre said, her gruff voice a little high. "What happened to your hand?"

Instead of sinking into the house, Matt felt the house rise in her. When she had done this before, Nathan had been inside her, translating between her vision and the house's ability to make things visible. This new method felt strange and familiar at once. She and the house had spent a lot of time entangled lately. She felt the presence of Other, but it didn't intrude so much as augment.

Together, Matt and the house looked at the coyote. It barked and took two steps back.

"I don't want to hurt you," Matt said. "I just want to let you be seen. Okay?"

—Ff.— It ducked its head twice, then sat.

House did something to the air the coyote occupied, and it stopped looking translucent, shifted from shadow to solid.

"Oh!" Deirdre cried.

The coyote cocked its head at her, rose, walked closer.

"You're here," whispered Deirdre. She held out her hand, and it sniffed along the bottom and the top.

—Whuff.—

"Thank you for coming."

The coyote shook its head as though it had a fly in its ear, then backed off.

—Is that enough?—the house asked.

—Can you let it decide?—

—It could do visible itself if it wanted. Sister, do you want us to remove our influence?—

—Whuff.—

The image of coyote thinned. Matt closed dream-eyes, and it was gone.

—Thanks,—Matt thought to the house.

—You're welcome.—

Matt slowly pulled her hand out of the floor. She felt her hand as it formed on the end of her wrist, a very strange sensation, warmth spinning into solid.

"So she's gone again?" Deirdre asked. She leaned forward and watched Matt pull away from the floor. "What are you doing? That is *so* weird."

"She's not gone, she's just not visible anymore. This?" Matt's fingertips rose from the floor, as though the floor were water; like water, the floor closed behind them, though without ripples. Matt frowned at the floor for a minute. "The things a person can get used to," she said. She stared at the tips of her fingers.

"Makes sense to me that Nathan can walk through walls," Deirdre said. "He's dead. You're not a ghost, are you, Matt?"

"No. I never walked through walls before I came here. This house isn't like other houses, though."

"I'll say."

"House forgot about our hot water. It says the things the witches are doing tickle it."

Suki came to the kitchen door. "We've set up as many protections as we can think of," she said. "Now the house is going to tell us what it wants."

Chapter Fourteen

. . . . .

MATT stood beside Nathan in front of the empty fireplace. Everyone was grouped in a loose circle around the room. The twins sat side by side on the fainting couch. Harry leaned on the wing chair that Lia sat in. Edmund, Suki, and Deirdre sat in chairs too, Suki directly across from the fireplace and the portrait of Nathan's mother.

"What is it?" Suki said at last. "How can we help you, House?"

"My children," said the house. It hesitated.

Matt glanced around the circle and thought, yes. In a way, they were all the house's children—except Harry, and it looked like he was going to marry into the family. They had each been changed and partially raised by the house.

"I am tired of being a house."

Everyone shifted in surprise, glanced at each other, then peered up at the ceiling.

Terry straightened and frowned. "You want us to change you into something else?"

"Yes."

"Into what?"

For a long time, the house kept silent. "A human," it said finally.

"Would that work?" asked Deirdre. "*How* would that work?"

"I don't know," said the house. "I don't even know if it is right for me to want this, or to ask for it. What I know is that I have been here in this place for a long, long time, locked in my half acre, clinging tight to my son, and I am weary of it. You have all Hedged beautifully. I want to follow you into the sky."

"What happens to Nathan if you leave, House?" asked Suki.

"I don't know."

"Do we change your actual physical structure into a human being?" Terry was still frowning. "There's way too much of you for a human body. And it's the wrong kind of stuff. If we just use some of it, which parts? How do we change it into what we need?"

"That's not right, Terry," Tasha said. "Transformations usually take place between two forms that aren't equal mass. When I turn you into a Pekingese, you don't get more dense. You get much smaller and lighter in weight. There's a matter bank in a neighboring dimension. You put what you're not using in, or take what you need out."

Terry scowled. "That's just your theory."

Tasha shrugged. "Come up with something better that matches the evidence. I don't care. All I'm saying is that we've observed that the transformation of objects is not about conservation of size or mass."

Terry thought for a minute. "So it might be simple, House, but we'd want to think it through so we can get it right. All the transformations I've performed have time limits on them, or triggers that release them in response to certain stimuli. Maybe we could change you into a human for a day, or a week. Would that be enough?"

Suki cried, "Wait a second. What kind of chains are laid on Nathan? If we change you into something that can leave, will he still be bound to you? Or will he—" Suki jumped to her feet and ran to Nathan, stood beside him, her hands tight fists; she couldn't touch him. "What if this kills him?"

"Then we shouldn't do it," said the house.

Nathan said, "Suki, I'm dead already."

"Not always," she whispered.

"If we can figure this out for the house," said Terry, "maybe we can figure it out for Nathan too."

"Aren't there a bunch of rules about this?" Harry asked.

"What do you mean?" said Tasha.

"I'm new to this, and I'm still learning basic lessons. I keep bumping into rules, and if I don't know them or don't follow them, I get into trouble. Why does a ghost happen? How does a house wake up the way this one has? Once these beings exist, what limits them?"

"We know some of the rules," Matt said. "Nathan's not allowed to leave the house, except if there's a séance or it's Halloween."

"When we first started coming here," said Deirdre to Nathan, "you told us all you could do was scare people."

"I used to believe that," Nathan said. "But I didn't confine myself to it. Maybe I've been breaking little rules all along. When we became friends, instead of scaring you, I welcomed you; I helped you when I could; but above all, I changed Edmund, Tasha, and Terry into witches, and I'm sure that was against the big rules."

"Who told you the rules?" Lia asked.

Nathan shook his head. "When I grew aware of my continuing posthumous existence, the rules seemed self-evident. I died in 1919, and didn't truly wake to an understanding of my condition for several years. I haunted the house before I woke, but it was as though I sleepwalked. A family moved in a year after I died, the Hawkinses. Two of the Hawkins children saw an image of me—" He frowned.

"Doing something," Deirdre said.

"Repeatedly. The same thing every night. They became accustomed."

"What did you do?" asked Deirdre.

He glanced at her, closed his eyes. "Hanged myself in my room."

After a brief silence, Deirdre said, in a hoarse voice, "They got used to that?"

He opened his eyes again. "Apparently. They were quite small when they were placed there. The family set my room up as a nursery. The children were one and three, and I manifested after the nurse had put them to bed for the night. I think the older one was six when she finally asked someone who I was and what I was doing that hurt so much."

"Jeeze," said Matt. "Then what happened?"

"I had to reconstruct this afterward with the house's help, because I wasn't aware at the time. There are different kinds of ghosts. Some are just the residue of an event with strong energy or emotion attached to it, a repeating image of something that sank into a place or an object and has not yet worn away, like an odor. I think I started out as that sort of ghost.

"I suspect one of the Hawkins parents or both of them listened to Genevieve, the little girl, and saw me. The family engaged a spiritualist. She tried to lay me to rest. In the process, she somehow woke me up, and I—" He frowned. "A ghost haunts. That seemed like the rule. It seemed to me I knew what to do: my job was to scare them. So I practiced scaring. I learned that I could do things that frightened them. Appear, disappear, make things float, walk through walls, make terrible sounds. Eventually, I drove them out of the house."

"Jeeze," Matt muttered.

Nathan glanced at her. "I was convinced that was what I had been brought back to do. Terrify. I spent decades doing that. The one night a year I was loose, I traveled the world to find other ghosts and learn more techniques from them. I wonder about that spiritualist. Obviously she had gifts: she pulled me back to myself. She certainly didn't talk me into a quiet grave, though."

Lia asked, "House, what were you doing while this was going on?"

"I had been awake and aware for forty years by the time Nathan died. His grandmother studied spiritualism, and had held séances in me before the turn of the century. Something she and her clients did opened—started—initiated—I can't explain it. But she woke me, and she gathered energy in me, and from her I learned to collect my own energy. I grew stronger through time, more awake, more able.

"When Nathan returned in spirit form, something bound us together, a power greater than ourselves, and unknown to us. We had these rules: he could not leave me. I was his captor. He could not physically harm anyone who came into me, but he was free to scare them into harming themselves."

"We hated each other," Nathan said suddenly.

"How can that be?" asked Edmund.

"We worked at cross-purposes," said the house. "I wanted a family to live in me. Part of my life force comes from having people inside. He wanted to scare everyone away."

"Dark years," said Nathan.

"Terrible battles."

"We were tied to each other. Neither of us could escape. All we could do was wound each other." Nathan sighed and scuffed the floor with an immaterial foot. "So the house weathered and wore down and got a reputation for being haunted, and no one would buy it. Without people in the house, both of us suffered. Without people to scare, I faded, lost consciousness. Then House found something else."

"I reached out and found a way to expand, to tap into other energies. I grew stronger. Then I called people to me."

"People moved in here in the sixties, squatters," said Nathan. "Their being here woke me up again, and the house convinced me not to scare them away. That's when House and I started working together and making the best of our situation. There were six of these people initially. Some left, and some new people came. They lived here five years before the sheriff kicked them out of town. They experimented with a lot of things, drugs, religion, ways of thinking. They had passionate discussions about everything, and brought newspapers and magazines into the house. We watched and learned and used them to nourish us."

"I began to tamper with them," said the house.

Nathan nodded. "They were interested in parapsychology, among other things."

The house said: "I helped them develop their psychic abilities, very slowly and gently. Sometimes I made mistakes, but none caused lasting harm."

"I wonder whatever happened to Russell and Linnet," Nathan muttered.

"You were practicing?" Lia asked the house. Her voice was strange and distant.

"Yes," answered the house.

"Building the people you needed to grant you your wish."

Matt glanced around. Tasha and Terry clasped hands on the couch. Both looked sober. Edmund sat up straight, his green eyes silvery. Lia had a faint orange halo around her, and Suki stared at her hands in her lap. Deirdre looked serious and a little mad, and Harry frowned in concentration.

"Yes," said the house after a moment.

Lia said, "Are we the people you need?" Her voice was cold.

"I don't know," said the house. "All I can ever do is give you feathers and hope you build wings. And you have, and now you've flown home. I can only ask for help. You don't have to give it."

Matt hunched her shoulders. "No matter why she did it, she always loved you, and she still does. Do any of you wish it never happened?"

They looked at each other. Matt was tempted to open dream-eyes, but she resisted.

"Not I," Edmund said. "It was my dream come true. Thank you, House."

"You are welcome."

"I wonder who we would have been if it hadn't happened," Terry said.

"I'm insanely happy," said Tasha. "I can't think of a better life than the one I lead."

"You give the word 'airhead' a whole new meaning," Terry told her twin.

Tasha socked Terry's arm. "If it hadn't happened, we'd be the same people, but we wouldn't have half the fun," she said. "Thanks, House."

"You always gave me refuge when I had the strength to seek you out, and refuge was what I needed most. Thanks, House," Suki murmured.

"You are welcome."

"What happened to me wasn't even your fault, and you helped me deal with it and protect myself from its consequences," Lia said. Harry touched her shoulder. She gave him a small smile, then spoke to the ceiling. "I'm sorry, House. I felt a chill when you talked about engineering people and I realized you had shaped us toward your ends. I don't think I could have found a better mentor or a better direction."

"Thank you," the house whispered.

"So how come you never did anything to me? Don't you know that drives me crazy?" Deirdre asked.

"Opportunity had to operate for me to act," said the house. "Each time I managed it, there was a collection of circumstances that let me . . . break a rule without severe penalties. I never found one for you, Dee, but I can keep trying."

"All right," she said. "I have the coyote. Do I still have the coyote, Matt?"

Matt peeked with dream-eyes and saw that the coyote sat beside Deirdre. "Yes."

"So that's something, anyway. Thanks, coyote."

The coyote touched its nose to Deirdre's hand. She started and looked down toward it.

"The first thing we should do is hold a séance," Edmund said. "If we free Nathan from the house, then we can try some transformations on the house itself; maybe they won't affect Nathan if he's free."

"Brilliant," said Terry.

Something hard rained down on the roof above them.

"House?" cried Lia. They all stared up.

"The demon-man has come," said the house.

Chapter Fifteen

· · · · ·

"WHAT about the wards?" asked Terry.

The house said, "He does not attack directly with magic. He uses stones, and the wards do not stop them." Another wave of sound, hard thunks and clattering, as stones rained down on the roof and then bounced off.

"We didn't make an earth ward," Terry said. "None of us is strong in earth." She had to shout to be heard over the sound of the rocks, which now hit the sides of the house. A window crashed somewhere upstairs, and then another in the dining room.

Lia rose to her feet and spread her arms, stretched her fingers wide. A tide of flame flowed from her fingertips, melted into the walls of the house, accompanied by a strange flow of music, soft but pervasive, building, racing violin triplets doubling back, syncopating.

Orange fire blazed outside the living-room windows, driving back the night.

The next stonefall was muted.

Then the hard rain stopped. The subsequent silence shimmered and dazzled.

Lia stopped sending out new flame, and gradually the cocoon of flame beyond the windows faded, and the night sky showed. She stood in the center of the living room, lowered her arms, and glanced around. "Tell me if it starts again, House," she said.

Matt went to the kitchen and got the plate of cookies, brought it to Lia, who blinked, focused, and took a cookie. Lia smiled. "It's okay, Matt. I've learned a lot since then. I've found places to draw from, ways to store energy for later. But thanks."

Matt set the plate on a nearby table and walked over to press her hands against a wall. —How hurt are you?—

—Two windows broke, some shingles fell; it is nothing, and puzzling. I am already rebuilding. Why would the attack come in that form?—

—Maybe he's testing the defenses. Is the guy standing around outside?—

—Yes. He and the younger man whom we saw in Julio's memories, and there are three strange beings behind them. They stand in the street, just past my edge, and stare toward us. Wait. He gestures again.—

Sirens sounded, drew nearer.

—Wait, he's stopped,—said the house. —Now they're gone.—

A fire truck raced up, sirens howling and spinning lights blazing.

"The attack guys are gone," Matt told everyone, "and the firemen are here. Guess the neighbors noticed, huh?"

Pounding sounded on the front door. Suki stood. "I'll get it," she said.

"Everyone else, let's hide. Maybe the furniture should too," Terry suggested. "Nathan, has Suki established residence here?"

"She's working on it."

Matt looked back over her shoulder at a living room empty except for Deirdre, standing now. Edmund's voice said, "Dee, let me take your hand." Deirdre held out her hand and disappeared.

Matt pushed into the wall and seeped into the house's system.

"Jeff?" Suki said. She stood on the threshold, facing someone.

"Susan? Is that you? Susan Backstrom?"

"It's me. I've changed my name to Suki. Hi, Jeff."

"Well, good grief, hi, Susan. The next-door neighbors called 911 and said this old place was on fire. We didn't know anybody lived here, and there was a couple minutes there where we thought we might as well let the place burn down, but who knows what it would have taken with it."

"Fire's out."

"What are you *doing* here?"

Suki poked her toe at the porch. "I live here," she said in a soft voice.

"Everything all right at the house?" yelled someone from farther away. "Chief, how'd you get through these damned blackberry bushes?"

Matt could feel how the big bushes, part of the house's network, had woven closed over the path, their canes like iron and thorns like knives, holding everyone else back from the house. Why had they let this one man through?

—We needed to let one see that there's nothing wrong,—the house explained.

Jeff walked to the edge of the porch, and yelled, "There's no fire here, Nils. I'll be back in a minute." He crossed to Suki. For a moment he was silent. "You live here?"

"I do. I've always loved this house. I don't know what the legal situation is, who owns it or how I could rent or buy it from them, but I needed a place to stay, and this was available. So I live here."

"When did you get back to town? Somebody said—but I thought they were kidding."

"I've been back about a month. I just got a job working for Dr. Weathers down on the bay. I'll take care of the house situation sometime soon. You know who's the owner of record?"

"I have to figure it's the bank. I've never heard of anybody living here. Are you okay out here all alone?"

"Yes. I'm fine. And I'm not exactly alone. Right now I have some visitors."

"Come to think of it, there is a bunch of cars out front." More silence. "This is a pretty strange situation. Isn't this place haunted?"

"Only in the best way," said Suki.

"I mean, we were terrified of this place when I was a kid."

"But we're grown-ups now, Jeff."

"Guess we are." His voice roughened a little, and he took a step closer to Suki.

"Suki?" Edmund emerged from his cloak spell just behind Suki in the front hall. "Tea's ready. Oh, hi, Jeff."

"What? You're back too?"

"Visiting," said Edmund.

"Old home week. Who else came back? Your other friends? The tomboy and the little guy? Four cars out front."

"Them, and a couple other people."

"Well, try not to set anything on fire, will you? We don't like false alarms."

"We'll be careful. Thanks for coming."

"Nice to see you again, Jeff. Please don't set the sheriff on me. I'll get this situation normalized as soon as I can. See you around town." Suki stepped back into the house and the front door closed gently.

The bushes moved aside, leaving the path clear for the fireman to leave. They closed behind him.

Matt stayed inside the house, senses wide. There were other people in the street besides the firemen. "Was everything all right?" someone asked. "It was burning like a bonfire ten minutes ago."

"Not a scorch mark on it," Jeff's voice said.

"How can that be?" asked the bewildered voice.

"How long have you lived next door to that eyesore?"

"Five years."

"What do you know about it? Haven't you heard the stories? It's haunted. Anything's possible at that old place. Hey, Nils, there's a bunch of people living in there. One of them is that bastard Backstrom's daughter."

"The ice princess?"

"Right. How long has it been since you last saw her? Fifteen, twenty years? Still gorgeous. All grown up."

"Wait a minute, sir," said the neighbor's voice. "You say there are people living there?"

"Haven't you noticed the increased traffic?"

A few minutes of silence. "Of course. I wondered about the cars. I was going to call the police if they stayed much longer, but most of them just arrived today."

"We better get back to the station and write up an incident report. Good night."

"Before the fire started, there were horrible pounding, thudding, crunching noises," said the neighbor.

"Nothing we can do about that, ma'am. Probably just ghosts."

"Ghosts! How can you talk about ghosts as though they exist?"

"Well, ma'am . . . I only know what I've seen. Excuse me now."

—Matt?— Edmund pressed his hand against her side.

She eased out of the house's sensory network and oozed slowly from the living-room wall, recollected herself beside Edmund. A glance down showed her she was still wearing what she had on before she had stepped into the wall, jeans and shirt, still too blue, and the leather boots from House. Her hair wasn't too long this time.

Everything in the living room was also back to normal, furniture solid again, people pretty much where they had been before the fireman came to the house.

"Jeeze Louise, Matt! How long have you been doing that?" Terry cried.

Matt yawned. "I don't know. A couple days, maybe longer."

"How did that happen? That's not like anything I've seen you do before."

"It's how the house is my mother," Matt said.

"You were wild and strange before you ever came here," said Terry. "You didn't need the house's help. Are you saying the house engineered you, too?"

Matt leaned against the wall and thought for a minute. "Yeah, House has changed me. For one thing, it gave me the power to break spells." She smiled.

"Oh-ho," said Terry. "I wondered where that came from."

"Excuse me," said Harry. "We were just attacked. Will it happen again? Will it take the same form? How should we prepare? What do we do next?"

"Good questions," Terry said. "Biggest question: what the heck does that guy want with us, anyway?"

"Thirty-five years ago, when I was building my first group, someone else attacked us," said the house. "It was skilled and subtle: we did not know we had been attacked until everything fell apart. It came in dreams. I didn't know enough about dreams then to stop it. It drove one of my women from the house, and made one of my men lose his faith. The others suffered, too. The group broke, even before the sheriff stepped in."

"Who attacked you, House?" Lia asked.

"We never knew. I think whoever it was accomplished his or her aim, because after my group dissolved, nothing else happened. Maybe we have been breaking too many rules. Maybe this is what happens when you get close to breaking a big one."

"But," said Suki, "when this demon-guy came last time, we weren't close to breaking a big rule at all, were we?"

"Not as close as we are now."

"I don't think the one who attacked us in the sixties and the master wizard are the same person," Nathan said. "The man who attacked Julio fifteen years ago was someone else. Completely different methods, and apparently different aims. He wanted to know more about us, not pull us apart."

"Yet we fell apart." The house sighed. "Maybe forces operate toward an end without understanding why. Smaller goals get swallowed up by larger ones. Now we are close to my dream, and someone comes to attack us again."

"That Galen boy said his master has new people he's made into slaves, and he'll use them to attack us," Matt said. "He had three other people besides Galen with him just now. They all disappeared when the fire truck showed up."

"The master is very good at disappearing," Terry muttered. "Himself, and other people. I wish I could do that as well as he does."

"We don't know what he wants," Edmund said. "We don't know much about how he fights. Last time he grabbed Julio, and that didn't work. Maybe it looked simple to him; maybe he didn't know we could resist it. He knows now. And he knows now that our wards can stop a physical attack. Terry, if you were this guy, what would your next move be?"

"Why are you asking me?"

"You're our best tactician."

She frowned. She shrugged. "If I were trying to attack the house . . . I might try some more feints, to spy out the house's strengths and abilities, test its limits, see if there was something easy I could do to win. Or, if I was confident that I had much more power than the house, I might mount an all-out attack. I don't think he knows our strengths or our weaknesses. I'd want to know that before I committed my forces. I'd test more if I were him."

"So we can expect more attacks, probably, and we don't know what kinds." Edmund frowned too. "This is outside my realm of recent experience. Anybody here play war games?"

Everyone shook their heads except Nathan, who raised his

hand. "I used to haunt, and I went all out. I don't know if that's the kind of war game you're talking about. The people I was haunting didn't have many defenses, so I didn't learn much about losing."

"Forget trying to do this the way other people would. We should do the things we're good at," Matt said. "Edmund, ask spirit if it has any directions for us."

Edmund's brows pinched together. "Would spirit—" He shook his head. "Why not? Somehow I feel like spirit wouldn't concern itself with battles, but spirit is everywhere. Why should this be outside its range?" He got out his devotions kit. "I need quiet for this. I'll go upstairs."

"Nathan and the house can keep watch in case those guys come back again, right? You guys don't need to sleep, do you?"

"We can tell when things step into our sphere," Nathan said, "but we don't know what happens out past our edges."

Matt looked at Terry. Terry shrugged. "How much farther out could we guard, anyway? What more do we need, if we all stay within the house's sphere?"

"Is there some witch thing you can do, some kind of spell that would tell us when anything that wanted to hurt us came close?"

"I'll see what I can do. I don't have anything like that yet."

Matt stepped away from the wall. "Me, I can talk to things. I wonder if those guys left any clues when they disappeared. I want to go out and talk to the street."

"I can ask air," Tasha said.

"I'll go with you too," said Lia. "I can look through the lens of fire and see if they left any traces."

"I'll work on that alert spell. I'll try to come up with defenses against things I might try if I were the master," Terry said.

"May I watch?" asked Harry. "I think your type of witchcraft is closer to what I'm learning than anyone else's here."

"Sure. I brought some spell supplies with me. Gotta go upstairs and get them. I think we should work in the kitchen. I need the stove for some of what I do. Suki, will you help me too?"

"Yes," said Suki.

Deirdre stood up. "Matt?" She looked unhappy again.

"Please come with us, Deirdre," Matt said.

"Okay."

Matt ran upstairs and got her army jacket.

The spring night was cold enough that they could watch their breaths rise. Stars glittered in the clear sky. Matt hunched deep in her army jacket. After a minute she pulled a knit cap and leather gloves out of a pocket and put them on, then glanced back at Deirdre. Lia and Tasha could control their atmospheres enough not to get cold, but Deirdre was shivering.

"I've got a heavy coat in the car," she said, edging around Matt and going on ahead.

"Wait, Dee," said Lia. She flew after Deirdre and caught up before Deirdre reached the fence. "We don't know what's out there. We should stick together. May I touch your clothes?"

"Another weird-ass question!"

"Just say yes." Lia's voice was laughing.

"Okay, okay. Sure. Touch me all you want. No tickling, that's all I ask. Hey, what—what? What did you do?"

"Made your clothes warmer."

"Wow. This is great! Like really portable electric blankets. Thanks."

"You're welcome. Matt?"

—Jacket?—Matt thought. —How would you feel if someone put fire in you?—

—Would it burn me?—

"Does it burn the clothes?" Matt asked Lia.

"No. It just excites the molecules. I set it so it only works when the air is cold and the jacket is on you. It will accelerate aging, but only in certain conditions."

"Sounds good," Matt said. —If you don't like this, I'll ask her to take it away again.—

—All right.—

Lia put her hands on Matt's shoulders for a moment, and then Matt's clothes warmed up just enough. Lia touched Matt's cap, too.

"Thank you," Matt said. —Okay?—

The jacket's reply whipped past too fast for her to make out. She got the sense it was positive, though.

They reached the fence. Matt gripped weather-silvered wind-warped pickets. For a moment they stood and stared at the road beyond.

"This is weird," said Tasha. "Suddenly the world feels dangerous. I go everywhere and never worry about a thing. Now I'm scared to go out the gate."

—House? Can you sense anything out there?—

—Only the cars and you.— The gate creaked open.

"But that's silly," Tasha added. "Air is everywhere." She floated through the gate, her feet six inches above the ground.

Matt followed, then passed Tasha and went to where the strangers had stood earlier, just beyond the edge of the house's influence in the street. Four cars were parked head-in along the curb: Edmund's Volvo station wagon, Deirdre's black Volkswagen Beetle, Terry's Miata, and the beat-up but venerable green Geo Metro Edmund and Matt had helped Suki shop for at a Guthrie used car lot. After Matt had finished tuning the engine and Edmund soothed the car's spirit, it worked great.

Matt got down on her knees and pressed her hands flat to the road. —Hello, road.—

—Hello! I know you! What are you?—

—I'm Matt,—thought Matt.

—But . . .— It sent her the impression of several layers of asphalt mixed with gravel, with compacted earth beneath, a history of things running across her—

—Oh! Yes, I was part of you,—she thought, remembering that the house was in the road, and she had been inside the house. —I'm Matt. Sometimes I'm part road.—

—One changes?—asked the road, and then,—Many strange things on me tonight.—

—That's what I was wondering about.—

—Big thing! Almost as heavy as the ones who built me.— Image of weight, surrounded by the much lighter weight of footfalls. A trail of footfalls, too, came from the neighbor's yard, wandered around, and went back to the neighbor's yard. The road could tell the difference from one foot to another. Mostly it was excited about the big thing, though.

—The fire engine,—Matt thought.

—Also, these things that are not like normal walkers.—

Matt absorbed the flavors of five pairs of feet, as sensed by the road. Each of them seemed strange: one swamp-violet, another chili-pepper-ice, the third sugar-garlic, the fourth blood-apple, and the last dust-peppermint. Something clicked in her mind: she knew the last one was the boy Galen, though she didn't know how she knew it.

—And now you and these others.—

—What do we taste like?—

Beef stew-ginger, pine-chocolate, chili-pepper-music, sage-brush-carrion, juniper-cinnamon, sugar-garlic.

For a moment Matt was lost in the pleasant puzzle of figuring out who tasted like what to the road. Chili-pepper-music had to be Lia, but which one of them tasted like dead meat? Which one was Matt?

Why were there six flavors, when there were only four of them? Had somebody else joined them? Carrion and sagebrush? Deirdre's coyote, maybe. But that still only added up to five.

She jumped up. Sugar-garlic! One of the attackers!

"Hey," she said. She whirled and hunted. She didn't see anyone else, even though the road knew they were there: Lia, Tasha, and Deirdre had all disappeared. Fear shuddered through Matt. Was she here alone with one of the bad people? She had been fending off ill-meaning humans for years, but she didn't trust her strength and skills against people who had magic—she had no practice. She didn't know how strong her house protection was.

Where were the others?

"Yip! Yow! Ruh ruh ruuur!" High-pitched cries came from behind Deirdre's black Volkswagen.

Matt ran around the car toward the sound. In the bushes beyond the road stood a tall glowing man, his pale face unearthly and beautiful, his long white hair unbound and wavy, lifting and weaving through the air around him, his clothes flowing and green, tied here and there with jeweled bands and cinched at the waist with golden mesh. He murmured a question, and Matt heard the persuaders and invitations in his voice.

Deirdre stood facing him, her back to Matt.

"Wait—" Matt cried.

The glowing man held out a long, graceful hand, and Deirdre put her own in it.

"Stop!" Matt yelled. Tasha and Lia formed out of the air beside Matt and all three of them ran toward Deirdre.

The coyote howled, but Deirdre didn't even turn around. She took a step toward the man, and then both of them vanished.

Chapter Sixteen

. . . . .

"THE coyote followed her," Matt said.

"I tried to grab the path, but it vanished." Lia sat, shoulders hunched and arms crossed over her chest, in a wing chair. She looked tired and discouraged.

"I tried to get air to close around them and hold them, but they slipped away. I couldn't stop them." Tasha was pale and disheveled.

Edmund sat with his silk devotions kit on his thigh. He fiddled with the zippers. Matt felt upset radiating from him.

"What if he casts Deirdre out of her body the way he did me?" Lia cried. "Why didn't I stay with her?"

"Maybe she'll be able to find her way home if that happens," Nathan said. "She knows you did it before. Did you discover anything before she disappeared?"

"The magic was clean and left almost no trace," Lia said, her voice flattened with despair.

"Air had some scents, but it didn't interpret them one way or the other." Tasha also sounded subdued.

"Sugar offered Deirdre her heart's desire," said Matt.

"Sugar?" Terry said. "Who's Sugar?"

"The road told me what they tasted like. That guy was sugar-garlic. The other ones, let me see. Chili-pepper-ice, blood-apple, dust-peppermint—that one's Galen, I think—and, what was it? Swamp-violet."

"Sugar offered Deirdre her heart's desire?" Suki said. Like the others, she was pale and upset.

"That's what he said. 'Come with me and I'll give you your heart's desire.' He held out his hand, and she took it. She wants magic," said Matt. It seemed strange to Matt that in all the time the house had known Deirdre, it had never managed to give her this satisfaction. The house hadn't hesitated to move into Matt's dreams, offer strange food, suck her into its walls. It didn't seem to suffer for doing those things. Why *had* it left Deirdre out, if it was engineering people right and left? Matt could understand Deirdre's frustration.

Edmund dug into a pocket and pulled out the fishing weight on a string he used to dowse for people. "We have to find her," he said.

"Wait a minute." Pink dust sparkled on Terry's forehead, and she had a streak of frost across one cheek. "I vote we go back to my first plan. Change the house before anything else happens, so they can't stop us, if that's what they're trying to do. *Then* find Deirdre. Maybe that will destroy their motivation for kidnapping her in the first place."

"But Terry—what if she's in terrible pain?" Flames glowed in Lia's eyes, flickered above her head.

"Why would he try the same thing again? It didn't exactly work in his favor last time."

"So what if he does something different, and it's even worse?"

"I'll be right back." Terry dashed out of the room.

"We can at least hold a séance and get Nathan loose of the house so he can travel with us if we find out where to go, and maybe stay safe if we transform the house," said Edmund. "Is that all right, Nathan?"

"Yes. Please."

"House?"

"Yes!"

Edmund rolled up his devotions kit and tucked it into his pocket, stowed the fishing weight in another pocket, then moved to the floor and held out his hands. Tasha dropped and took his right hand. Lia took his left. Suki took Tasha's right hand, and Harry took Lia's left.

"How does it work?" Matt asked.

"We form a circle. We summon Nathan to its center. Then someone lets go of someone else, and that person has freed Nathan from his bond to the house for a night and a day and is in his power."

Matt sat on the floor beside Suki and took her hand. Harry's hand was in reach. "Do we wait for Terry?" Matt asked.

"Yeah," said Edmund. He almost smiled. "If she shoots this idea down, though, I think we should do it anyway."

Terry rushed back into the room and set a small red-velvet bag on the floor. "Oh! Right. Let's do this part, then we can check the crystal ball, see if it'll show us Deirdre." She sat between Harry and Matt, gripped their hands.

"Close eyes, everyone, and take deep, slow breaths," Edmund said, his voice warm, musical, and persuasive. "In for the count of eight. Hold for the count of eight. Out for a count of eight. In . . ."

Matt listened to the soothing metronome of his voice. Her breathing steadied and synchronized with everyone else's. She sensed a strange calm descending on them.

"Spirits of east and earth, spirits of south and fire, spirits of west and water, spirits of north and air, spirit of place, spirit of now, spirit of before, spirit of future, hear our request. Please summon the shade of Nathaniel Blacksmith into our circle; release him from his normal bondage; maintain in him all the powers of the spirit and endow him with all the advantages of flesh, and put him into our power, if it is right for us to ask this at this time."

Terry's hand in Matt's squirmed a little. Matt squeezed Terry's hand.

"I am here," Nathan said. His voice sounded strange, somehow squashed. Matt opened one eye, then the other. Nathan stood right in front of her, looking more solid than usual. "What is it you wish?"

Suki's hand slipped from Matt's. "Hey," Suki said, holding up her hands and waving them.

Nathan smiled. "Hey." His voice had gone back to normal. He dropped to his knees in front of Suki and stared into her face, his smile widening into the goofy range.

"Spirit, we thank you for your gifts, we bless you, we release you," Edmund murmured. Matt felt something draining away.

"You can let go now," Terry said. "God, what a grip, Matt."

"Sorry." Matt let go of Terry's hand. "You shouldn't've gotten so squirmy right in the middle, though. What was that about?"

"I never heard a séance called like that one. Edmund's changed a *lot*."

Nathan leaned closer and closer to Suki, and finally kissed her. She put her arms around him and kissed him back.

"Hey! Take it upstairs!" Terry said.

Without interrupting the kiss, Nathan held out his hand and flicked his index finger at Terry. A spark leapt from his fingertip to her chest. She jumped. "Hey!"

"Leave 'em alone," Matt said. "She hasn't had enough magic to do solid in a while."

"What are you talking about?"

Oh, yeah, Terry hadn't known about wild gold magic, or any of its uses or powers. Way too long a story to try to tell now. "Never mind. Is the crystal ball in that bag?" Matt asked.

Terry glared at Matt with narrowed eyes.

"Can I see it?"

Terry scrambled across the floor and grabbed the small bag she had brought. She opened the drawstring mouth and pulled out three pieces of carved teak. Two deft gestures, and the pieces had puzzled together into a three-pronged stand, which she set on the floor. Then she pulled out something wrapped in white silk. She unrolled the silk carefully, revealing a crystal ball of beautiful clarity. She set it gently on top of the stand. "House, could you dim the lights a little?"

The lights obliged.

Matt, Lia, Harry, Tasha, and Edmund came to where Terry sat and gathered around the crystal ball. Terry reached into the velvet bag again and pulled out something small. "Air and clarity, give us vision," she murmured. "Water of worlds, grant us the dream roads. Fire of friendship, seek the spark in our friend. Earth in the working, ground us true. Show us. Show us. Show us." She wrote with the small thing in her hand over the surface of the crystal, tracing what looked like letters in an unknown alphabet.

The crystal's center turned dark for a moment, and everyone leaned closer.

A hand dropped on Matt's shoulder. She glanced up and saw Nathan, somehow different: older, taller, more solid, his face filled out and grown up. He sat down beside her and leaned forward to look into the crystal ball with everyone else. Suki joined him.

"Show us. Show us. Show us. Please."

Image of a tiny person, pale face, dark braid, dark sweatshirt and jeans, arms folded over her chest.

"Closer. Closer. Closer. Please."

The view swooped down on Deirdre, brought her face closer. She looked clear-eyed and unhurt, though unsmiling.

"Is this our true sister? Is she in her right mind?" Terry asked. She traced more symbols over the surface, and the image remained.

Deirdre frowned ferociously. Her mouth moved in speech. A glowing hand with unnaturally long fingers moved into the image, touched Deirdre's mouth. She stopped talking, but she still looked mad.

"Sugar," Matt said.

"Sugar," repeated Nathan. His voice had dropped an octave.

"Sugar-garlic, the man who stole Deirdre. That's his hand."

"Ah."

The image faded.

"Well, she doesn't look like she's in immediate danger." Terry traced some more symbols over the crystal ball, murmured thanks to it, and stowed it and its stand back in the bag. She peered up at everyone else. "If you agree that we should now try to transform the house, I think we should move all our stuff out."

Matt said, "Edmund, did you ask spirit about this?"

"Things didn't stay quiet long enough."

"You could ask now. What do you think?"

"I'm going up to pack," Terry said. She jumped up, hefted the velvet bag. "First I better get all the fixin's out of the kitchen, though." She vanished into the dining room.

"Matt," said Nathan. Matt turned to look at him, confused again because he sounded like a grown-up, and he looked like one too. "This is something you really want?"

"I don't know a lot about what's happening," Matt said, "but I trusted spirit before, even though I don't understand it, and it helped us find Suki and Deirdre. Before that, it gave Edmund permission to come back here. We wouldn't be here without it." She glanced around the circle, at Tasha, who smiled at her, at Lia and Harry, side by side, at Suki, gripping Nathan's hand. Finally, Matt turned to Edmund.

He looked tense. "It's something I've always done alone, except for the times when Matt was with me," he said. "I have no desire to persuade anyone else to think this way, but this is how I've lived since I left. It got lost in the noise of reunion." He smiled at them.

"Spirit is your guide," Nathan said, "still?"

"Yes."

"No matter what Terry thinks, that was the best summoning I've ever had," Nathan said. "Look. I got to grow up. Nobody gave me that option before. This craft you've come to works for me."

Terry breezed out of the kitchen carrying a gym bag. "Whatever you guys are planning, you better hurry. No guarantee the master will wait between attacks," she said, and stamped up the stairs.

"Go ahead, Edmund," Lia said. "What do we do?"

He pulled out his devotions kit, laid it on his thigh. "Breathe," he said softly. "In for the count of eight. Hold for the count of eight. Out on the count of eight. . . ."

This time Matt kept her eyes open. Edmund's voice talked them all into breathing together again. Tasha's eyes were bright. *Air,* thought Matt. *Maybe this is something she understands.*

Presently Edmund opened one of the pockets of his kit and took out a pinch of something, then took something out of another pocket, and mixed them on his palm. "Spirit be with us, spirit be in us, spirit surround us, spirit protect us, spirit please help us, spirit please guide us: do we go changeways? Do we grant wishes? Do we seek rescue? Do we do nothing?" He held his open hand up. For a moment nothing happened except the synchronized sounds of breathing. Then the dust rose from Edmund's palm and danced, spiral, counterspiral, a long thin silvery snake, fluid as fire. The snake rose in a dragon dance, and then suddenly the silver shredded and a brown bird with wide green wings and a long, lyre-shaped tail flew out of the remnants. It rose to the ceiling and dissolved into mist that melted into the plaster.

"Spirit we thank you, spirit we bless you, spirit release you," Edmund murmured after a moment. Again, Matt had the sense of something completed. People's breathing speeded up again and everybody looked at everybody else.

"Interpretation?" Nathan said.

"Change the house," said Matt.

"Let's go get our stuff." Edmund rolled his kit shut and tied it with a red silk cord, then rose. Everyone stood. Nathan was almost as tall as Edmund, now, and his shoulders were wider. His clothes had changed: he still wore a white shirt, but instead of short-leg pants, he had on long dark pants with creases down the front of the legs. The suspenders had disappeared, replaced by a slim black belt at the waist of the pants. He looked like a stranger.

"Harry and I don't have any luggage," said Lia. "Who wants help?"

"Can you pack Deirdre's room?" Nathan suggested. "Suki and I can probably handle Suki's things, though she's more moved in than anyone else. What are we going to do?" His voice emerged mournful and a little wavery at the end.

Matt realized that, like it or hate it, Nathan was going to lose the place he had been locked to for decades if the change worked, and Suki would lose the home she had just made. Culture shock, uncertain future, wild difference of life just ahead.

If Nathan ever wanted to know, Matt could teach him how to be homeless. She wondered if he would still be able to talk to buildings.

Would he still be around with the house changed?

"We'll be all right," Suki said, squeezing his hand. "Come on. I better unplug the laptop before something shocking happens to the electricity again."

Everyone went upstairs. On the landing, they split up.

Matt's and Edmund's packing took almost no time; Matt only took things out of her big garbage bag when she was going to wear them, and put them in the second, smaller bag when they were ready to be washed. Also she had a little bag of toiletries. She threw the smaller bags into the bigger bag, and she was finished.

Edmund actually had a cloth duffel bag, but he hadn't taken many things out either. He looked around the room. "House?"

"Boy."

"Do you know how this is going to work? Will everything just disappear?"

"I don't know," said the house.

"The furniture is really great."

"Take it if you like. Or don't take it."

Edmund stroked the carved headboard of one of the twin beds, glanced at Matt. She smiled and shrugged. "We'd have to have someplace else to put it," she said. "Next thing you know, we'd have storage, or an apartment, or something, and then—"

They smiled at each other. Edmund put his bag over his shoulder. Matt followed him out of the room.

The door to Suki's room stood half open. A strange, low, muffled cry came from inside. Matt and Edmund dropped their bags and rushed in.

The secret panel was open. Suki bent to look into the dark space. "What happened?" she asked.

"I thought I should get my skeleton out," Nathan said from the darkness. "But when I touched it, it—"

"It what?"

"It jumped into me."

Suki backed away from the secret passage and straightened. Nathan crawled out, his face and white shirt smudged with dust. He stood and patted his stomach, his chest, his head. "I put my hand on it, and it leapt at me and melted into me. God. It was creepy."

"How do you feel?" Edmund asked.

"Scared. A little unsettled." Nathan's grin made his face look wolfish. "Haven't felt either of those in ages." His brows drew together. He pressed his hand to his chest. "I feel odd now, truth to tell."

"Tell us if we can help you," said Edmund.

"I will."

Lia and Harry came in. "What happened?"

"Nothing. Nothing," said Nathan.

"This is all Deirdre brought." Harry held up a small soft-sided suitcase.

"Anything we can carry?" Lia asked.

Suki had plenty of things. After she had decided to move to Guthrie, she had called her aunt Caroline and had some of her belongings shipped up. Plus, the bedroom had a lot of furniture in it. "I'm going to go on living in Guthrie for now, if everything works out," she said, "and I'll need furniture, and some of the stuff in the kitchen."

Everyone took something of Suki's. In the hall, Matt and Edmund picked up their bags again. When they got downstairs, Terry and Tasha were already outside, their things beside them.

Everyone went back inside and helped pull furniture and kitchen things out for Suki. Lia snapped her fingers, produced fairy lights, small yellow globes that floated in air and lighted the house front and the pathway. The house had the blackberry bushes draw back, to form a clearing near the house where everyone put the furniture and utensils. They'd have to come back with a pickup or a trailer to get it later, unless . . .

If the spell-casting didn't work, the house would probably still be there.

"How's the perimeter?" Terry asked.

"No signs of disturbance," the house reported.

308 · Nina Kiriki Hoffman

"Let's load the cars and then get to it."

Tasha helped by having air carry the heaviest things to the cars. The light globes bobbed along beside them, above them, before them. Suki loaded clothes and personal belongings that didn't fit into her Geo in the back of Edmund's station wagon. Deirdre's stuff went into the station wagon too: she must have her car keys with her, because no one could find them in her purse. Matt figured she could probably talk Deirdre's car open, but nobody wanted to take the time. Terry placed wards on all the cars, and then they went back to the house.

They stood in a line in front of the house and stared up at it. By this time, it was nearly midnight. Light glowed from the living room windows, and stray street light dusted the weathered boards with orange. The fairy lights hovered, then lined up along the porch roof like Christmas lights.

"How are we going to do this?" asked Terry.

"Who's done the most transformations?" Edmund said.

"Tasha used to, all the time."

"I'm rusty," said Tasha. "Terry should direct."

"What about Harry?" asked Terry.

Harry shook his head. "I've practiced some easy things, like water into wine, but nothing big like this. Nothing alive."

"My element is transformation," Lia said. "Fire changes everything from one form to another."

"Do you want to direct?" Terry asked.

"I want Edmund to direct," said Lia.

"I do too," Nathan said. "Is that okay with the rest of you?"

"Ask the house," Matt said.

"Edmund," said the house.

Edmund looked surprised, but he didn't say no. "Let's sit on the porch."

They climbed the porch stairs and sat in a circle on the porch. Their breath misted up in the cold night air. Terry shivered once, then stopped.

"Those who connect with the house by touch, place your palms flat on the porch," Edmund said. Matt, Lia, Nathan, and Suki put their hands palms-down on the porch. Matt felt a warm touch against her palms.

Edmund talked them into breathing together again, and this time Matt felt the house breathe along with them. Calm settled over them; Matt dropped into some other kind of consciousness, not awake, not asleep, only waiting.

Finally, Edmund said, "Spirit be with us. Spirit be in us. Spirit surround us. Spirit protect us. Spirit please hear us. We offer our skills. We offer our powers. We offer our efforts in aid of this work. A being here wishes from one to another to change shape and stature. We ask that you shape her. We ask that you help her. We ask that you fill us and take what we offer, help us to shape her into what she wishes, and so let it happen by will and by wishing and for good of all. We ask that you enter, we ask that you gather, we ask that you heed her, we ask that you hear us. . . ." He kept speaking in a low, soothing voice.

Matt felt gathering power. It blew around the circle, a wind that teased something out of each of them. Strands of power. Matt opened dream-eyes and watched colors flow from them to form a spinning and braiding rope in the center of the circle: red and orange from Lia, forest green and gold from Edmund, pale blue from Tasha, yellow and ice-blue and red from Terry, lavender and sea-green from Harry, clear, rippling strands from Nathan, gold and gray from Suki, and from Matt's own chest a strange mix of asphalt black and sputtering all colors, butterfly-wing patterns. From the porch, a tide of turquoise flowed. Everything blended in the center of the circle, spinning and twisting and twining together, as beautiful in its strange cloud of colors as anything Matt had ever seen.

Sparkling rope rose up from them as Edmund murmured. The rope twisted through the air, traveled around the corner of the house. Matt heard drumbeats and the clang of finger cymbals as the rope danced away from them. Edmund's voice twined into the music; sitar joined it. The rope danced. The longer it grew, the weaker Matt felt, but she also felt happy and strange.

Eventually the rope had danced all the way around the house and came back to drop its beginning into the circle beside the place where it spun from. Each end kissed the other, wove together. Edmund murmured, with music, and the music rose and speeded. The rope floated up free of the circle and bound itself entirely around the house.

Then the Earth moved.

Tremendous wrenching and creaking sounds came from the house, and the porch shook beneath them.

"Hear us. Protect us. Hear us. Protect us. Hear us. Protect us."

The house shook and shivered. Shingles fell. Glass shattered. Boards buckled. The rope tightened around the house, and then, somehow, kept tightening. It plunged through the walls without breaking them and was gone from sight.

The house stopped shaking. Matt, exhausted, could not sit

upright anymore, and collapsed on her back on the buckled porch boards. Everyone else wilted too.

"Spirit, we thank you, we bless you, release you," Edmund whispered several times.

Matt rolled over and crawled to him. He lay on his back and stared sightlessly upward. Matt lifted a heavy, heavy arm, managed to touch his face, crept her fingers up across his cheek and touched his eyelids down over his eyes.

"What. Happened." Terry's voice came out in a hoarse wheeze. "That. Wasn't. Transformation. Nothing. Happened."

The house's front door creaked open, then cracked off its hinges and fell backward into the house.

A woman stepped out onto the porch. She was tall and broad, muscular and fat, and her skin was the color of acorns. Thick silver hair rippled from her head down around her shoulders. She wore a dark green full-length dress, and she carried a tray with a pitcher and some cups on it.

Matt lay with her head on Edmund's chest and watched from under half-open eyelids. The woman looked a lot like the house had in Matt's dreams.

The woman crossed the porch to where they sprawled and sat down beside Nathan. She set down the tray and said, "My son. My son." Her voice was deep and rich. She stroked her knuckles down Nathan's cheek. His eyes fluttered. She poured something from the pitcher into a cup, then lifted his head onto her thigh. "Drink," she said, and held the cup to his lips. He swallowed. She made him drink a whole cupful, then laid him down.

Next, she stroked Suki's face, lifted Suki's head and supported it on her thigh. "My daughter." The woman gently fed Suki, too.

The woman came to Matt, brought a cup. "Hey, Mattie. Hey, little one." She touched Matt's face, brushed a finger across Matt's lips. Her hand was warm and rough, and her eyes were turquoise. She lifted Matt's head. "Drink this."

The liquid was cool and tasted like milk and tropical fruits. It warmed Matt from the inside. "Wah," Matt said. The woman eased her down again, and Matt lay with her eyes closed, feeling how the warmth spread from her center all through her. The tired seeped away.

"Edmund? Honey, wake up and drink this." The woman went all around the circle, feeding each of them. Matt listened to her gentle murmurs, and the occasional sleepy protests from some of the others.

Presently Matt sat up. Nathan held Suki upright, muttered to her. Suki shifted her shoulders and wiggled her feet. Nathan gripped her elbows and helped Suki straighten.

Edmund sat up beside Matt. He rubbed his forehead. He glanced at the house, which still stood, though the front door was a gaping hole now, and everything looked more decrepit than before. "Guess Terry should've done it," he said.

"Why?"

"Everybody got tired, and nothing happened. If the master attacks us now—"

"Nothing happened?" The woman came to Edmund and felt his forehead. She poured him some more drink from the pitcher. "Drink this," she said.

"Okay." He drank.

She knocked on his head with her knuckles. "Now, wake up."

He blinked three times and looked at her.

She smiled a dazzling smile. "Hello, Boy."

"House." He scrambled to his feet. "House!"

Everyone else blinked and sat up and stared.

"House?" Terry said in a very small voice.

"Terry."

"It worked?"

"Most wonderfully." She held out her arms and whirled, her hair wild and her dress flaring. "Thank you, children. I am eternally grateful for your help."

They all stared at her. Edmund hugged her, and she hugged him back. "Beautifully done," she murmured.

"But the house—" Terry pointed.

They all looked. Shingles pattered down. Boards looked cracked, dry, brittle, twisted.

Matt pressed her hands to the porch. —House?—

Nothing answered. It shocked Matt. She was used to getting some response, even if only a snore, from everything shaped that she touched. This was the first time she had found no one home in something. It felt eerie and disturbing.

"My shell," said the woman. "My home no longer. Returned to nature. Don't go inside again, children. It's not safe. In fact, we should get off the porch."

Tasha and Lia, both as light as air, had less trouble rising than the others. They helped everyone else stand, steadied elbows as people stumbled down the porch steps. They went as far as the furniture Nathan and Suki had pulled from the house, and then they sat again, Tasha, Terry, Suki, and Nathan on the bed, Lia and Harry on the desk, and Edmund in a chair with Matt on his lap. She felt very silly. He was big and warm and comfortable to sit on, though, and he put his arms around her. Matt rested her head against his chest.

"House," Nathan murmured, and shook his head, smiling.

The woman refilled cups and handed them around again.

"What is this, House?" Terry asked.

"Restorative."

Matt drank again. This time the drink tasted different, like bittersweet hot chocolate. She held out her cup for more, and tasted mulled cider. She felt its strength flow into her and wake her up.

"Let's go after Dee now," said Lia.

"I'm so tired!" Terry said.

"Drink some more. We have to go after Dee now," Matt said. "And could you get that crystal ball again so we can check on her first?"

Terry grumbled and got up, then stomped off to the cars.

"Do you want us to keep calling you House?" Harry asked.

The woman placed her tray on a table and sat beside Lia and Harry on the desk. "That would be confusing in the outside world, wouldn't it? I suppose I shall need a name. What name should I choose?"

"What was your mom's name, Nathan?" Matt asked.

"Irene."

"No," said the house. "I don't want to use the name of someone I knew. And I would rather not have the name of someone alive whom I might run into. Though I suppose just because they're dead doesn't mean I won't run into them."

"My mom's name was Beth," Matt said. "Suki's mom's name was Gloria."

"Beth. I like Beth," murmured the house. "Would it be all right with you if I used Beth, Matt?"

Matt felt strange. If she didn't want House to use the name, why had she volunteered it? Because House had been like her mother some of the time. "Yeah, okay," Matt said, her voice gruff.

"Beth," muttered the house. "Beth what? Beth House. Beth Lee. Beth Guthrie. Beth Blacksmith."

"Beth Blacksmith," Nathan said.

"Beth Blacksmith," the house repeated. She smiled.

Terry returned with the red-velvet bag. She sat on the ground and set everything up the way she had before, only this time the fairy lights hovered above them all, dimming when Terry asked for it.

An image of Deirdre appeared in the crystal. She looked the same, still dressed in the clothes she had worn out of the house, her eyebrows fierce and angry, but she didn't look like anything had hurt her. Something flurried near her and her mouth moved in what looked like shouting.

"She looks okay," Lia said.

Matt leaned forward, watched Deirdre frown. "Can you ask that thing how to find her?"

Terry wrote symbols on the crystal ball with whatever she had hidden in her hand. She murmured some more. Deirdre faded to black, and then they saw an ornate house, its façade made of pale, ornamented stone. "Pull back," Terry said, and the view pulled back until they were staring at the house from a street. The house had a black iron fence around it, topped with sharp spikes. "Has anybody ever seen this place before?"

"No." "Nope." "Uh-uh." "Looks like something from the *Addams Family*."

Terry sighed. "Now please give us the nearest corner."

A signpost appeared: 34th and Blaine.

"Thanks. That's very helpful." Terry's tone was sarcastic.

The image wavered and vanished, replaced by something new.

A different street. Four cars, two black, two lighter, all differently shaped, lined up at a curb by a shaky, silvery picket fence, with dark bushes beyond. The orange glow of a streetlight. Deirdre stood in the street, surrounded by shadowy figures.

"Hey, you guys!" she yelled. "They're here!"

Nathan jumped up and looked toward the street.

"The dorks are here," Deirdre yelled again, both in the crystal ball and in the present.

Everyone jumped up and ran to the fence, where they lined up and stared at the street.

Deirdre stood a step behind the master, a tall man cloaked in black with a deeply lined somber face, pale eyes, and silver hair. Galen stood beside the master, one hand buried in his pocket, the other clutching a silver dagger. The glowing silver-and-green person Matt had seen before stood with his hand on Deirdre's shoulder, and behind Deirdre lurked a tall woman with cascades of heavy red hair, and layered scarves of black clothes. To the side stood an ink black figure the size of a child. A strange aura surrounded the little one.

"You see, child, they do not care about you," the master said to Deirdre, his voice rich and deep and persuasive. "I care about all my children. Don't you want to be one of mine?"

"We do too care!" Terry cried. "We were working on finding you! Thirty-fourth and Blaine! We were just going to go there, but you came here first!"

"What took you so long?" wailed Deirdre.

"We had to do a couple things first, but we checked on you and you looked okay," Terry said.

The master's cloak parted and he stretched out long, thin hands. He rubbed thumbs across his fingertips. His eyes narrowed. "What have you done? The whole power configuration has changed! What have you done?"

"Dee, are you all right?" Matt asked.

"Guess I am." Deirdre brushed the glowing hand off her shoulder and came toward them. "Nathan? What happened to you?"

The master grabbed her shoulder and jerked her back.

Deirdre karate-chopped backward, dislodging his hand. "Hey, buster, quit it."

His eyes widened and his nostrils flared. He murmured something and gestured toward Deirdre.

Lia screamed and leapt over the fence. She flew to the master and gripped his wrists. "Don't you dare," she cried, her voice sharp and bright, each word a slice. Her hands glowed red, then orange, then yellow, then white, sizzling into the master's skin. There was a smell of searing meat. "Dee, go back!"

Harry, Tasha, Terry, and Nathan jumped the fence too, with Edmund close behind.

The master shook his arms, worked them, tried to dislodge Lia. Her hair lifted and flared like a torch. She glowed golden except for the white heat in her hands. He spoke a string of words, and she only laughed, a hard, dark sound.

Deirdre broke and ran toward her friends. Edmund grabbed her and hustled her back behind the fence into home territory, thrust her toward Matt, who hovered, dancing, just behind the fence, wishing she could jump in and fight, afraid there was nothing she could do to help.

The master spoke three words. They thudded like an avalanche and knocked Lia loose, pounded her to the ground. She screamed. Harry and Nathan ran to her.

"Don't just stand there, my children," said the master to his team. "Deal with these creatures!" He gripped each wrist in the opposite hand and muttered some kind of spell.

Matt pulled Deirdre farther inside from the fence. "Are you all right?" Suki joined them, put her arms around Deirdre. Sounds of battle and chanting came from the street.

"I'm, I guess I'm all right, but I'm mad as hell. Those people! Well, that Cross guy, he's the one Galen calls the master, and a bigger asshole—"

"Did he hurt you?" Suki murmured.

"Some of it wasn't pleasant," Deirdre said in a gruff voice. She shuddered. "Nothing I couldn't handle."

"Did they give you your heart's desire?" asked Matt.

"My heart's desire?"

"Didn't you go with glow-guy because he told you he'd give you your heart's desire?"

Deirdre blinked. She glanced up at three fairy lights, which hovered above them. "What are those?"

"Lights," said Matt. "Listen, if you don't want to talk about it, it's okay. I got to go see if I can help." She left Deirdre with Suki and ran back to the fence.

So many things were happening in the street she couldn't see them all at once.

Nathan had retrieved Lia, pressed her into the house's arms. Harry, Tasha, and Edmund grappled with the master's minions. Terry dashed forward and pressed something against the small dark thing's head. It let go of Harry's legs, cried out, and turned into a small fat yippy dog. It ran around barking, dancing in and out among the other people. It looked happy.

Terry tried to spell the redheaded woman, but the woman slapped Terry's forehead with a piece of paper that stuck to it, and Terry changed into a statue.

Edmund faced the glowing white-haired, green-robed man who had stolen Deirdre. They held their hands up, palms out, facing each other. Occasionally one or the other stroked the air between them, but they didn't touch each other. It looked more like a silent conversation than a fight.

Cross still gripped his wrists and muttered. Nathan started toward him.

Matt couldn't figure out what to do.

Galen stepped in front of Cross and tried to stop Nathan. Tasha, airborne, reached down and grabbed Galen's arms, lifted him and brought him into the yard. "You don't really want to fight us, do you?" she asked.

Matt opened the gate and went out into the street. She knelt, put her palms down on it. —Road?—

—Matt! See what's happening on me? See? This is different! It tastes wild!—

—Yes. You want to be part of it?—

—How? How, more than I already am?—

—Grab their feet and suck them down.—

—What?— The road had never considered such a thing.

—Just the new guys, the ones you told me before. Swamp-violet, chili-pepper-ice, sugar-garlic, blood-apple. What do you think? Can you open and swallow their feet?—

—How?—

She told the road what it had been like when the house had

swallowed her, how other things she had known learned of their own plasticity, how the road might be able to do such things too.

The road got excited. —I'll try it!—

It thought very hard, and then, suddenly, the asphalt went warm and soupy under her palms. She sank into it up to her wrists, her knees and toes sinking in too.

—Okay, good,—she said. —Can you do the other guys now?—

—Yes! Yes! Yes!—

The calling, thunks, and chanting of the fight suddenly changed to startled yelps. Matt looked up, saw pavement close over Cross's feet, the redhead's feet, the glow-guy's feet. The Pekingese was dancing too fast to be caught.

—Great!—Matt said. —Okay if I escape now?—

—Oh, sure. Hey! I love this!— The pavement pushed her back up on top of it. —You want me to hold them?—

—If you can. They might get violent. They might hurt you.—

—Huge things roll around on my back all the time. What can hurt me?—asked the road.

—I don't know, but there might be something. Be careful. And thanks!— She stood up, brushed off her palms.

"Hey!" she yelled. "What's this all about, anyway?"

Everyone stopped and turned toward her.

"What kind of spell is this?" Cross asked in an ominous tone.

"My kind. What do you want, anyway? What's the big idea, coming after us?"

"I sensed a concentration of powers here. I always go after them; it is my lifelong quest to collect them. They are jewels; they can be family; I can train them and use them. There was such a beautiful gathering here, centering around something in an egg, something about to hatch. Everything has changed, though." He turned his head, searched his surroundings. "What has happened? It is all different, but still . . . delicious."

"I don't think we want to be in your family," Matt said. "You hurt your children." Look what he had done to Galen. Look what he had done to Julio. Who knew what he had done to the others?

"I must," Cross said. "It's a necessary part of discipline. It strengthens us all. You can all learn and grow stronger. Only come with us." He gestured and spoke some words. Silvery blue sparks fizzed in the air around him and his team. Chimes sounded. A moment passed, and the sparks faded, leaving everyone where they were.

"What is this spell!" Cross cried. He tried to lift his feet free of the pavement. "What is this power?"

Matt felt the road laugh under her feet.

Cross growled and spoke words and directed gestures at the pavement. The surface bubbled. Cross cried out and changed tactics, said a different chant that froze the road.

"How does it feel to be trapped?" asked the house. She carried Lia in her arms. She walked out the gate and went to stand before Cross.

Cross glared at her. "What are you?"

"I am what hatched." She turned to Harry and gently handed Lia to him. Lia groaned and clung to Harry's neck. "I stood for more than a century with my feet caught like yours. Now my chrysalis has opened, and I've taken my first steps past the edges of where I was. What I see of you is that for more than a century you have trapped others and kept them under glass. Maybe it is time you changed, too." She went to him, took his face in her hands, and kissed him on the mouth.

Chapter Seventeen

. . . . .

WHEN Beth released Cross, he stood silent and staring. She stepped back and studied him. All the struggles around them stopped.

"Master?" Galen whispered. He ran up and touched Cross's arm. Cross blinked but didn't look at him.

"What did you do?" Galen asked Beth in his monotone voice.

She touched her fingers to her lips. "I don't know. I kissed something out of him. It tasted sour and shadowy and smoky. There was a curse in it."

Galen tugged on Cross's sleeve. Cross glanced around, looked down at Galen and away. A faint frown puckered the skin between his brows.

Matt had other worries. "What did you do to Terry?" she asked the redheaded woman. The woman shrugged. Matt put her palms against Terry's back: solid, hard as stone. —Terry?—

—Matt! What's wrong with me? I can't move! I can't see! I can't feel! Where am I?—

—This woman put some kind of statue spell on you. She slapped a piece of paper on your forehead.—

—Take the paper off, will you?—

Matt went around Terry and tugged at the paper on her forehead. It had something written on it, Chinese or something. It wouldn't come off. "Lia?" Matt said.

Harry came to her, carrying Lia.

"Are you all right?" Matt asked her.

"No. Cracked a couple ribs or something, and I'm tasting blood. Whatever it is, it hurts. I should have gone to fireform. Nothing can slam that down on the pavement. Wait. Fireform. Oh yes. Go to fireform, re-form into a healthy self. Excuse me, love." Lia flashed into a dancing pillar of many-colored fire.

The redhead gasped, and so did the glowing white-haired man. "You consort with demons?" asked the redhead.

"Sure," said Matt.

Fire condensed back into human form. "Oh, good," Lia said. She felt her chest. "That worked! Wow! Matt, what did you want?"

"Can you burn this spell off Terry's forehead?"

Lia touched the paper. It charred and blew away. Terry sagged, stone no longer. "Whoa," she said, staggered, bumped into Nathan, who took her shoulders and helped her straighten up.

"Interesting taste," Lia said. She licked her fingers.

"Are we to stand here all night?" the redhead asked.

"I don't know," Matt said.

Edmund, beside the white-haired man, said, "Matt, this is Fern. I think he'll be all right if he's free of the master."

"Are we free?" asked the woman.

"Is that what you want?" Matt asked.

"Above anything," she said. She frowned. "Long ago he told me he'd be a father to me. For sure he cared more about me than my own ever did, and he taught me mastery of my craft, but he hurt me, too. He hurt us all."

Matt knelt on the road again and put her hands on it. —You did a great job,—she told the road. —Thank you so much.—

—I love this.—

—Are you ready to let go?—

—Of all of them?—

—Which one is this?— Matt patted the road that trapped the redhead's feet.

—Blood-apple–salt water.—

—Who is that?— She patted the road by the man Fern.

—Sugar-garlic-plum-cinnamon.—

—Could you release those two?—

—I can taste them better like this.—

—Well.— Matt sat back on her heels, at a loss.

—I have tasted enough.— The pavement parted, releasing Fern and the redhead.

"Am I truly free?" Blood-apple asked. She pressed her palms together, spoke something in another language, and vanished.

Fern walked forward, stooped, picked up the little dog. "What becomes of Pwca?" he asked.

Terry rubbed her eyes. "The spell will wear off in half an hour or so," she said.

"What becomes of Cross?" Fern asked in a lower voice.

Matt gave the road a final thanks as it smoothed itself, then followed the rest of them around to look at Cross. He stood quiet, blinking and confused. He stared at them without recognition.

Deirdre came to stand beside Fern.

"What happens to him now?" Matt asked the house, Beth.

Beth shook her head. "I don't know what I took from him, only that it tasted like fire and needed to come out. I don't know who he is now. Will the road release him?"

"Is that safe?"

"If it isn't, we'll deal with it."

"God, I'm tired," Terry said.

Matt knelt and asked the road to let its last captive loose. The road complied. Cross stood where he was. He shook his head, then nodded, then shook his head again.

"It's after three A.M. We're all tired. We need someplace to lie down. We could try to find a hotel," Suki said, "but I don't know if they'd answer the bell at this hour."

"I'll find us a place." Matt still had her hand on the road, and she sent out a call: was there a nearby house with lots of bedrooms and no people in it, one that was willing to have visitors?

In a moment she had five answers from nearby. Guthrie had its share of weekend houses for inland families who came to the coast only sometimes. "Okay," she said. "Grab what you need and let's go."

Beth took Cross's hand. No one got any of their things. They just followed Matt down the road. She led them for a block and a half, then turned in at a driveway that led to a giant three-story house. She put her hand on the door and said,—Hi. I'm Matt, and I have a lot of friends. May we come in and sleep for a while? We won't hurt anything, and we'll clean any messes we make.—

—Please do come in,—said the house. Its door unlocked and opened. Lights switched on in the hallway. Extravagant shag carpet in orange and yellow floored the hall, and badly executed oil paintings of seascapes hung on the walls. Matt heard a heater switch on and thought, *oh boy.*

—Thank you,—she thought, her heart in it.

—Who are you? Some of you are not people as I understand people.—

—It's a long story, house. I'm too tired to explain right now. Maybe in the morning?—

—Very well.—

The wall facing the sea was all windows. On the main floor, there was a big living room with four couches, coffee tables, some recliners; also a big bathroom, and a well-equipped kitchen. A loft above held three double beds, and down on a lower floor beneath the main floor there were four bedrooms and two baths.

Some staggered in and fell onto the couches and into sleep. Some of the others explored the house. Beth led Cross to a couch and gently pushed him down on it. He was like a large confused robot, obeying hand commands without understanding anything. Galen sat next to him, studying his face.

Beth took Matt's hand and led her through a door in the window wall out onto a broad balcony.

The night was cold and foggy, but when she looked straight up, Matt could see stars.

Beth sat on a dew-wet chaise longue, tugged Matt down, and hugged her. "Finally I can do this out in the world," Beth whispered.

The house's big warm presence enfolded her. Matt sat stiff in her arms.

Beth sighed and let go. "What's wrong?"

Matt shook her head. "I've been inside you, and you've been inside me. I know it. But I feel like I don't know you. I don't like people to touch me without asking."

Beth thought for a moment, then nodded. "May I hug you now?" she said.

"All right."

The house hugged her again, and this time Matt leaned into it. Beth smelled like cinnamon and warm milk and bread baking. She felt comfortable.

How long had Matt's mother been dead and gone? Matt couldn't remember the exact number of years, but it seemed like a long time. A year and a half before Matt left home, anyway.

The house's hugs in dreams had warmed her, and the house's acceptance of her had given her a home after years of wandering.

She could let this happen.

Matt pressed her ear to Beth's chest and heard Beth's heartbeat, slow and steady, muffled thunder, the ticking of the world.

Presently Matt stirred. "I am a grown-up, you know."

"I know." Beth lowered her arms, and Matt straightened, leaving the haven of her warmth. The night was colder than she had remembered. "People come in and go out. I know you'll leave again, and this time I won't have shelter to offer you when you come back. A human's connection to another human is different from a house's. I used to be able to keep people all their lives. With Nathan it went beyond even that. I know things will be different now. Sometimes my children left. I know how to let go."

"Can I—can I come back?"

"Oh, yes. Anytime you like."

"Now?"

Beth smiled and opened her arms.

MATT led Edmund up to the loft, picked the bed farthest from the staircase, shucked out of her top layer of clothes, and sat on the bed. Edmund sat down beside her, leaned back until he was lying across the bed on his back. She lay next to him.

"Hey," she whispered.

He smiled without opening his eyes.

"Awesome."

The edge of his mouth drew up, deepening his smile lines.

"You did great work today," she whispered.

"We all did." The words slipped voiceless from his mouth.

She patted his face.

For a while she lay, listening to everyone else find sleeping space—Lia and Harry, Suki and Nathan took the other double beds in the loft, and everyone else found bed space or couch space below.

Matt stirred, roused Edmund. They crept under the covers. Matt spooned with Edmund, pulled his arm over her. He tugged her close and tucked his chin down on top of her head. There were settling noises elsewhere in the house.

A whispered comment drifted from a nearby bed. "What if this is our last night together?"

But why? Before she could figure it out, Matt dropped into profound sleep.

· · · · ·

MATT woke to the smell of coffee.

She slipped from Edmund's embrace and went to stand in front of the windows. Day revealed the big balcony, an array of cement seagulls perched along the railing, and a beautiful view of a clear blue sky and an endless expanse of green-gray ocean. There was the chaise longue she had sat on last night with Beth. Other summer furniture was scattered over the concrete expanse.

Matt stretched, then went to pull on the jeans and shirt she had shed last night. Her clothes smelled like fire and asphalt, sweat and magic. Pew! She really wanted to do laundry. She had gotten out of the habit of smelling bad.

She went downstairs and found the bathroom, then tiptoed through the living room on her way to the kitchen. People sleeping on couches in the living room had blankets of shimmering colors wrapped around them. Matt wondered where those came from.

In the kitchen, Deirdre sat at a small table with a mug of coffee in her hands. Matt found a mug and poured herself some coffee. No milk in the fridge, but there was sugar on the table. She sat down beside Deirdre.

"Did you get your heart's desire?" Matt whispered.

"I did," Deirdre whispered back. She sipped coffee.

"How does it work?"

"How does what work?"

"Your magic."

"Oh, that. No. That's not what I asked for."

"Oh, man! What was your heart's desire?"

Deirdre looked away, smiled, glanced back. "I tell you what, Matt. After ten minutes with Cross, my heart's desire was to come home to all of you. So it worked out okay."

"He was really mean to Julio. Was he mean to you?"

Deirdre's shoulders hunched. "He tried a couple things. He wanted me to tell him all about us, who we were, what powers we had, what we were trying to do, but I wouldn't talk. He threatened me with transformations, and he did some awful spell thing that made my skin burn, but I stayed quiet. Then he did this other spell thing that made me want to talk—"

"Truthtell," said Matt. "Terry used that on me. I hate it."

"Huh? Tell me later. —But every time I opened my mouth to answer one of his questions, the coyote howled right over me. That coyote was so great!" She glanced around. "Uh—"

Matt opened dream-eyes and checked the kitchen for invisible beings. No coyote. "She's gone."

"Oh. Damn, I wanted to thank her. Guess I'll do it when I get home. And then Fern told Cross to leave me alone, and Cross did something that made Fern shrivel up, and I stomped Cross's toe. He yelled real good." Deirdre's smile was grim and fierce.

"What is Fern?"

"He's an explorer from someplace else. I mean, he's not from this world. He came here to check the place out, and Cross was one of the first people he met. Bad luck for Fern. Cross adopted him, and that involved some kind of trapping spells that bound Fern to him—that's what he did with all his people, but he couldn't get some of them to fight for him. I only met a few, but I know he has a bunch of people trapped in his house. His children." Deirdre shook her head and grimaced. "I don't know what that woman did to Cross last night, but I think it broke the trap spells on Fern, Elizabeth, and Pwca. Galen's trapped another way. Who was that woman?"

"The house."

"The house!" Deirdre gulped coffee, set her mug on the table, and went into the living room. Matt followed.

On the largest couch, Beth lay under a blanket that was many shades of turquoise. Her silver hair rayed out around her head, some flowing over the couch arm, some hanging over the edge all the way to the floor. Deirdre stared down at her broad, tranquil face.

In a moment, Beth drew in a large breath and opened her eyes. They gleamed bright turquoise. She gazed up at Deirdre and smiled.

"House?" Deirdre whispered.

"Deirdre."

"Wow, it worked! Wow!"

The house sat up, pushed back her blanket. "How strange. I have seen sleep, but I have never done it before. I'm not sure I approve."

She held out her hands to Deirdre, and Deirdre gripped them. "Come," said Beth, tugging gently. Deirdre sat down beside her, and Beth put her arms around Deirdre.

"Oh, House," Deirdre murmured.

"I've stepped outside my rules," said Beth. "Now I can give you what I always wanted to give you."

Deirdre pushed out of Beth's embrace. "Wait," she said.

Beth took Deirdre's hands.

"Did you see my coyote?"

"I sensed it. A magnificent creature."

"That coyote came to me. I was out there in the desert, and

the coyote came to me. Then she came with me. I guess I found my own magic. All I have to do now is go home to it."

Beth stared into Deirdre's eyes for the space of three deep breaths. "You're sure?"

Deirdre frowned. "Mostly."

"Find me if you change your mind."

"Okay. You sure you still have power to give? Maybe you're more different than you know."

"Hmm." Beth smiled. "We'll see." She put her hand on her belly. "What's this?"

Matt leaned closer, heard her stomach grumbling. "You're hungry," she said.

"Ah. I remember that, from dreams. Grilled cheese sandwiches."

"Dee, you got any money? I still don't," said Matt.

"I've got some," Deirdre said.

"So if we find anything to eat in the kitchen, we can replace it. And the coffee."

"Right. Or I could take you out to breakfast."

Matt shook her head. "That could get complicated. There's, like, fourteen people here, and I bet a lot of them left home without their wallets."

"There's always plastic. But . . ." Deirdre leaned close to Matt and whispered, "Most of them are still asleep. If we leave now . . ."

"Woof!" The Pekingese bounced up to them and sat on the floor, stared up with bulging dark eyes.

"Terry said that spell would wear off after half an hour," Matt muttered.

One of the other people lying on a couch sat up. The glowing man, Fern, but he wasn't glowing this morning; he just looked ice-pale, his wealth of hair the opaque white of ivory rather than blond, his skin as pale as milk. His eyes were yellow-orange as owl's eyes. "He likes that shape," he murmured. "I, too, am hungry."

"I'll go see what I can find." Matt went into the kitchen and consulted with the house. It told her that it had some supplies, but nothing perishable. A five-pound can of coffee in the fridge; sugar, spices, tea, hot chocolate in foil packets.

—My family always shops before they come to me. They haven't visited in months.—

—Oh, well. Thanks for helping, and thanks for the hospitality.—

—I like having people inside me.—

Matt went back to the living room. "Drinks is what we've got here," she told the others. She glanced over the couches. The only person still lying down was Cross. Fern had folded his own shimmering blanket, and the blanket on the couch where the Pwca probably slept, and Beth had wrapped hers around her shoulders. Deirdre sat beside Beth on the couch. "Guess we should either go shopping or go out for breakfast."

Beth rose and went to Cross. She leaned down and touched his shoulder. "Dominic?" she said gently.

Fern and the Pwca drew back.

Cross opened his eyes. Matt joined Beth and looked down at Cross. He blinked. "Who? Where?"

"Do you want to sleep some more?" Beth asked.

"Sleep," he said. He closed his eyes and turned on his side, his face away from them.

Beth straightened his blanket so it covered his shoulders, then stood. She turned to the others. "I guess he's not interested in breakfast yet. So did we all sleep in our clothes?"

Everyone looked down at themselves. "I got undressed," Deirdre said. "But I didn't have anything clean to change into."

"I can fix that." Tasha came into the room from the staircase to the lower floor. "Everybody, spread your feet apart, hold out your arms, close your eyes, and stand still for a minute."

"What the hell," said Deirdre, and followed instructions.

Matt did too. Warm wind wrapped around her, curling around her arms and legs. It smelled like spring. She heard wind moving through the room. —Edmund?—she thought.

—What?—

—Tasha's cleaning our clothes. We're going out for breakfast. Want to come?—

—Still too sleepy,—he thought.

—Okay.—

"Done," Tasha said. "You can open your eyes now."

Matt looked down at her clothes. All the creases, wrinkles, and dirt were gone. She lifted her arm and sniffed near her armpit. A fresh smell, like poplars leafing out. "Wow. Totally cool, Tasha. Thanks."

She glanced around. Fern and Beth both wore green dress-things that covered almost their entire bodies, and their thick, wild hair flowed free around their shoulders. Fern's kimono-like robe had jewelry banding the more flowing parts, and was belted at the waist with gold mesh; Beth's gown looked like a big comfortable muumuu patterned with different shapes and colors of leaves. She had draped the bright turquoise blanket around her shoulders like a shawl.

Tasha wore a yellow shirt that looked stylish enough to belong to Terry and probably did, black stirrup pants, and toe shoes. Dee had on her same sweatshirt and jeans, and Matt was wearing her everyday clothes, jeans and a flannel shirt over a long-underwear top and briefs. Oh, and riding boots. The Pwca wore fur. Nobody but Dee looked normal, but everybody looked clean.

Everybody else thanked Tasha.

"You're welcome. Can I come with you?"

"Of course," said Beth.

As they left the house, Deirdre helped Fern braid his hair. "It might be good if we could lower the weirdness quotient a couple notches," she muttered, "though, I dunno. There's no dress code on the coast. They'll just think you guys are from California. Where are we going?"

"Catch of the Day," said Matt. "They might not let Pwca in."

"Woof!"

"Right," said Deirdre. "We'll just say he's starving, and I'll hold him up, and they'll see how cute he is. I bet that'll work. Fern, you have a hair tie?" She had braided his hair into a single braid as thick as her arm that flowed down his back to his knees. She held the end up in front of him. He grasped it for a moment and let go; a ring of sapphires circled the end and kept it from unraveling.

"Fern, now that you're free, can you get home from here?" Matt asked.

"Home? I'm not ready to go home. I still have exploring to do." He smiled. "I just have to be more careful whom I talk to. For now, I want to go to the desert with Deirdre."

"What?" said Deirdre. "News to me."

Fern's braid flipped forward and wrapped around Deirdre's wrist. "Have you not been speaking to me, inviting me? Maybe this is a language problem," he said.

She stared down at the braid around her wrist, then frowned up at him. "You talk with your hair?"

"Sometimes." The braid unwound from her wrist, flowed up over her shoulder to wrap around her own braid, then let go. "What you just did is like a marriage proposal where I come from."

"Whoa, Buster, it totally means nothing around here!"

"I apologize. Do you want me not to follow you home?"

"I didn't say that."

Matt walked down the street with the sun on her back, smiling at the ocean.

AFTER breakfast, they went to a Circle K minimart. Deirdre bought two dozen assorted Danishes, two boxes of cereal, three quarts of milk, some prepackaged filters with coffee grounds in them, butter, two dozen eggs, two loaves of bread, some bananas, and a box of sugar.

At the house, everyone else was awake. They fell on the food and made most of it disappear.

After breakfast, Galen came to Terry. "Please," he said. "Will you help me now?"

"Let's give it a shot. Everybody who's interested, let's go out on the balcony," Terry said.

Edmund, Matt, and Tasha followed Terry and Galen outside.

Galen pulled the silk-wrapped crystal heart from his pocket. "After all, I found I was not comfortable without it," he said in his flat, considering voice. "When I left it with you, that was the first time since it was made that I let it out of my hands."

"Galen, is that guy Cross still your master?" Matt asked.

The boy glanced up at her. "Tasha says he isn't. I can't work it out, myself. I asked him for two things when I apprenticed myself to him: that the children would be taken care of and wouldn't feel hunger, cold, or shame, and that he wouldn't ask more from me than I could manage. In exchange I promised to bind myself to him, learn what he taught, give what he asked, and follow his instructions." Gently he unwrapped the silk around the heart, cradled the crystal in both hands. "Here they are, safe from hunger, cold, and shame. I have managed everything he asked. How can I break these bonds?"

"Hunger," Matt said. "Hunger? They just said safe and warm."

Galen leaned toward her. "They said?"

"I asked them how to get them out of there. They said, 'Where's Galen?' They said they were stuck inside this heart forever so they'd be safe and warm, and you gave your heart to make it happen. They didn't say anything about hunger."

"You can speak to them?"

"Yes. There's more than one kind of hunger," Matt said.

"That's it, Matt," Tasha said, her voice vibrant. "Ask the children if they're hungry."

"What are their names?"

"Basil and Lexa," Galen said.

—Basil? Lexa?—

—Galen! Galen? Who's talking to us?—

—My name is Matt. I need to know if you're hungry for anything.—

—We don't need food.—

—What about other things? Wind on your face? Stars in the sky? Road underfoot, someone to talk with, the taste of chocolate, crickets, fireflies?—

—Fireflies,—moaned the girl.

—Mother,—cried the boy.

—Sunsets.—

—Carousels. Cotton candy. Stone lions in front of the library. Steam coming up from the vents on the street when it's snowing.—

—Books.—

—School!—

—Someone to hold my hand.—

"They're hungry for all kinds of things," Matt said, and repeated what the children longed for.

"I told you the words were broken," Tasha said.

"Now I understand." Galen stood up straight, shook his shoulders. "My apprenticeship is over, and Dominic Cross is no longer my master. There were two bargains struck, though. The first was the one that made Cross my master, and that was between us. The second was the one I made with Monument. I gave him my heart so that the children would be safe forever."

"Does this Monument guy have anything to do with the fact that you change personalities when you touch statues?" Terry asked.

"Yes. He lets me feel my heart when I touch shaped stone. It's a strange sensation. I used to dislike it; it's much easier to live without that pain. But I keep going back to it."

Matt dug down into a pocket and unearthed the small stone monk she had taken from Tasha's room ten years before. She held it out to Galen.

He hesitated. Then he took the monk from her. His face lit up. "Yes," he said, his voice alive.

"We couldn't figure out how to open the heart," Terry said.

"My master built it. He built strong spells into it. Monument put the children inside." Galen sounded completely different. Emotion shaped his voice.

"Is Monument in this rock? Let's ask Monument how to get them out," Matt said. She touched the monk in Galen's hand.

—Monument?—

—Matt?—

She jerked her hand off the stone. How did Galen's god know her name?

Galen stared at her, eyebrows almost to his hairline. "What are you doing?"

"Talking, just talking." Matt edged her hand forward and touched the monk again.

—Monument? You're in my monk?—

—Matt, I am in all shaped stone. We have spoken many times.—

She jerked her hand away again, sucked breath in through her teeth. A third time she reached out to touch the stone monk. —But I always thought I was talking to the things. The stone bench, the street, the car. Are you in cars too? Have I always only been talking to you?—

—No. Of course, you are talking to beings. I am the spirit beyond the beings, and I found and adopted you long ago.—

"Matt, are you all right?" Edmund asked.

Her breathing deepened. She looked up, unseeing. She stared into the past, to the morning she woke up and heard what the park bench she had slept on said to her. That day her relationship with the world changed. She found caring friends everywhere: not human, but in many ways better than human. That day she also found her dream-eyes.

"Matt!" Edmund cupped her face in his hands. "Are you all right?"

She blinked and looked up at him, then smiled as wide as she could. "Oh yeah. I'm good. I think I can work this out now."

—Monument,—she thought.

—Matt.—

—Thank you for everything.—

—You are welcome in all ways.—

—You're the best parent I ever had.—

—You are a wonderful child.—

For a moment she stood and thought about that. Then she thought,—What about this Galen guy? What do you need with his heart?—

—I am keeping it safe for him. Does he want it back now?—

—He wants it back, and he wants the children out of the glass heart. Is that something we can do?—

—If I give him his heart back, our bargain is over.—

She thought about that for a little while too. "Galen, if Monument gives you back your heart, then I think the kids will come out of the crystal heart. Is that what you want?"

"Yes. Yes!"

"Okay. Let's do it." —Let's do it.—

Wind picked up on the deck. Something gathered beside them, gray particles swirling out of the air, collecting into a shape, coalescing slowly until something square and stone and huge stood beside them. The porch groaned under its weight. It smelled of earth and dust, and radiated age. Its face looked human. Its eyes were blank mother-of-pearl almonds. It had the tusks of a boar.

It reached out to Galen, put its fist against his chest, then pushed farther. Its hand vanished inside Galen. After a moment it pulled its hand out again, open now.

Wind rose again and weathered the statue away. Before it vanished completely, it touched Matt's cheek. Warmth streaked through her. She turned her head and kissed the last tatters of stone.

A crystal crack rang out. The heart in Galen's hand shattered. Twin streams of smoke rose from it, ghosted a little ways away, then spun above the porch. Two children formed from the smoke, dressed in beautiful antique clothes.

"Ooo, Galen, I'm going to kill you!" yelled the girl.

"How could you?" the boy cried. "Don't you ever do that to us again!" They rushed Galen, pummeling his stomach and his back, and he just gasped and laughed.

He dropped the little monk statue, and Matt caught it and pocketed it.

Then Galen was crying. He stooped and put his arms around the children. They punched him a couple times, then subsided, pressed their faces against his. "Now we can start over," he said, his voice thick and tight with tears.

LATER in the day, Nathan, Beth, Suki, Edmund, Deirdre, Lia, and Matt walked back up Lee Street to where the haunted house used to stand.

The yard felt dead. The blackberry bushes were static.

Suki's furniture was where they had left it, warded by Terry so that dew hadn't even touched it.

The house looked like a skeleton; its boards had contracted, withered, twisted. As they stood watching it, a breeze came up and rattled more shingles loose.

"I don't think it's going to come alive again," Beth said. "Now it's just a hazard."

"Shall I—shall I make it a pyre?" Lia asked.

"Maybe that would be best. It's just a shed skin. Not safe for children or anyone to go near."

Lia held her hands out, pointed fingers in the air, and spun herself a fiddle out of fire, then a bow.

"Wait," said Suki. "What happens when Nathan's twenty-four hours are up tonight? What if he has to come back here? How can he come back to a burned-out shell?"

"What's there to worry about?" Nathan said. "Weather won't bother me. Why should I care if I have a house or not?"

"When this house is gone, we can build another," said Beth. "When Nathan's twenty-four hours are gone, we can have another séance. We'll be all right, my daughter. Now, play me a grand dirge, child."

Matt ran back to the street, leaned against a telephone pole, asked the phone line not to let the neighbors call 911 just then.

Lia lifted her bow and struck a symphony full of the joyous cries of well-fed fire out of her violin. The house burned, and it burned well.